SHARON ASHWOOD

is a novelist, desk jockey and enthusiast for the weird and spooky. She has an English literature degree but works as a finance geek. Interests include growing her to-be-read pile and playing with the toy graveyard on her desk. Sharon is the winner of the 2011 RITA® Award for Paranormal Romance. She lives in the Pacific Northwest and is owned by the Demon Lord of Kitty Badness.

SHARON ASHWOOD

Possessed by a Warrior

and

Possessed by an Immortal

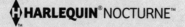

Recycling programs for this product may not exist in your area.

ISBN-13: 978-0-373-60636-8

POSSESSED BY A WARRIOR AND POSSESSED BY AN IMMORTAL

HARLEQUIN®
™ www.Harlequin.com

Printed in U.S.A.

CONTENTS

POSSESSED
BY A WARRIOR

For Mom, who taught me never to give up.

To love someone deeply gives you strength.
To be deeply loved gives you courage.

–Lao Tzu

Chapter 1

Sam Ralston shed his robe, tossing it to the floor. He'd done so a thousand times, in many contexts. Most involved women.

This time, however, he was staring at a wall of knives. They were eight inches in length, set about four inches apart, each point aimed straight out like the quills of an angry porcupine. In the half light, the blades gleamed softly, stainless steel polished to the understated efficiency of a showcase kitchen. The wall of blades blocked the room from end to end, leaving only a narrow gap near the ceiling.

Getting over the wall was his first challenge. Sam gave a derisive sound that wasn't quite a laugh. It echoed oddly in the otherwise bare room, adding nothing to the gray-on-gray atmosphere.

Trust *La Compagnie des Morts* to come up with an obstacle course designed to shred the runner right at the start. Everything that came after would be painful in the extreme, even for vampires.

But Sam was one of the Four Horsemen, *La Compagnie*'s crack unit named after the riders of the Apocalypse: Death, Plague, Famine and War. Units like theirs were called in after the CIA, the FBI, MI5 and all the rest of the international alphabet soup had failed to get results. Then they swept in and saved whatever needed saving.

As jobs went, the hours were bad but it was never boring.

Sam was War, and he was better than any trial the Company of the Dead could dream up. He'd proven it, mission after mission. Nevertheless, the Company put all their operatives to the test every so often, which was why he was standing in their Los Angeles facility, wearing nothing but running shorts, sneakers and fangs.

He flexed his knees and leaped. The gap was too narrow to land on top of the wall—that would have been far too easy. Instead, Sam caught the edge with his right hand, forcing himself to pause in a kind of one-armed pushup before he swung his feet onto the ledge. He felt the muscles in his shoulder and stomach bunch to hold his weight. The maneuver was almost perfect, but one blade kissed his left calf, leaving a trail of blood to snake down his leg and into his shoe. He cursed, mentally docking himself a point.

Without pausing at the top, he flung himself onto the mat on the other side. Wooden arrows hummed through the air, whispering against the back of his neck, skimming his chest right above the heart. He rolled, grabbing a SIG Sauer from the rack on the wall and taking out the two mechanical bowmen within seconds. He dropped the gun, knowing there were only two bullets inside. Miss once, and he'd be staked.

Dispassionately, Sam scanned the room for the next course on the menu. The room was lined in more stainless steel, and he could track his movements in a blurry reflection. Dark hair, gray eyes, a body coiled more like a beast than a man. No more emotion than a machine.

He heard a door open, and an enormous wolf bounded forward. A werewolf, actually. Famine, one of the other Horsemen—but the fact they worked together didn't mean Kenyon would give him an inch. For the first time, Sam felt his stomach tighten. Everything so far had been a test of strength or coordination. Kenyon, on the other hand, had a very crafty mind.

The wolf stopped a few paces away, crouching with a warning growl. Pale gold eyes raked over Sam, sending an electric prickle across his shoulders. He growled right back, feeling the low rumble in his chest. His fangs were down, adrenaline bringing out his own beast. His calf stung from the knife wound, and he could smell the blood, the coppery scent almost, but not quite, like a human's. From the gray wolf's twitching nose, he'd noticed it, too.

Kenyon sprang. Sam leaped to grab the wolf in midair, twisting so that they both fell hard to the floor. Kenyon writhed, jaws snapping, hind legs slashing. Sam straddled the beast, the coarse hair rough against his skin. At the same time, he had the wolf's head between his hands, trying to immobilize him. They were matched for strength. Sam's only hope was to keep him off balance.

It might have worked, except Kenyon chose that moment to shift. The burst of energy sent Sam sailing backward. His back had barely hit the floor when Kenyon was on top of him, huge hands around Sam's throat, shutting off all air.

"Sucker," Kenyon gloated. A manic grin lit his Nordic features.

Sam replied with a hard right jab.

"Ungh!" Kenyon fell sideways, releasing Sam's neck.

Sam got to his feet and glared down at the werewolf, putting one foot across his throat. "Vampires don't have to breathe, remember?"

Kenyon rubbed his face and swore.

"Time." The voice came from somewhere in the ceiling. "Two minutes, fifteen seconds."

Sam grunted. Not bad. Not his best speed, but close. He held out a hand to Kenyon, who took it and pulled himself up.

"You're not even sweating," the wolf complained.

"Cardio only applies if you have a pulse."

Kenyon gave him a scathing look. He'd heal quickly from Sam's punch, but he'd have a black eye first. "I should have had you."

"Dream on, dog breath."

The door opened again, and this time one of the human technicians came running in holding Sam's cell phone. Sam exchanged a look with the wolf, seeing his own question in Kenyon's eyes.

The tech waved Sam's iPhone, a harried look on his face. "For you. It's Death."

"Sam, I need you and the others at Oakwood pronto. Code...whatever. Code the whole damned spectrum. Just get your butts over here."

Jack Anderson, also known as Death, threw the phone onto the seat beside him, needing both hands on the wheel. He should have been using the hands-free option, but driving with undue care and attention wasn't Jack's issue.

It was the jackass trying to make a hood ornament out of his Porsche that was the problem. Not that anything could outrun his silver Porsche 911 GT2 RS—or at least not here, on the back roads of Wingman County, where soccer-mom SUVs and handyman trucks ruled the two-lane highways. Except the car behind him was a black Mercedes SLS complete with a sniper in the passenger seat.

Jack navigated a sharp turn, hugging the cliff and ignoring the sheer drop to his right. A bullet punched through the back windshield and tore through the leather seat. *Bloody barbarians!*

He could have sworn the bullet had glinted like silver. *They know I'm a vampire.* Jack stepped on the accelerator, taking advantage of a straight stretch of road to leap ahead. Then the downshift, left turn, and he was on the wooded road leading home.

The next bullet made a spiderweb of the windshield. *Who are these guys?* They were bad shots, or maybe just not up to Jack's standards. Sam would have taken out a tire and sent the car over the cliff. *That* was how you ended a car chase: one bullet, no fuss.

He'd picked up the yahoos on his tail about halfway home, just after he'd left the populated part of the coast. They'd started shooting as soon as he was on the treacherous cliff road and couldn't get away. Jack drove as fast as he could, but the twists and turns held him back. The fact that it was two in the morning and pitch-black didn't help, either. Vampire night vision only did so much.

Just like his so-called immortality had its limitations. He was hard to kill, but a silver bullet or a fiery crash could take him out. Whoever was behind this attack had done his or her homework.

What do they want? There were plenty of people who

wanted him dead. Okay, extra-dead. Re-dead. Whatever. Which ones were these?

Another turn, this time to the right. Now it would be safe to jump out of the car, vampire-quick, but he was almost home. He could do it. He could beat them.

He could see the massive iron gate of Oakwood, his mansion with its handpicked security staff. Oaks flanked the entrance, huge, gnarled sentries. *Thank God.* Jack's heart leaped with relief. *Safe.*

Then, finally, a bullet took out the rear tire. The Porsche bucked and slid. Jack swore, one curse running into the next. He'd been going too fast, and…

Chapter 2

"Is there a problem, Ms. Anderson?" said the attorney, who was visibly sweating in his penguin suit of funereal black.

Is there a problem? Chloe mused, tears threatening to seep through her defenses. *Let's see. My billionaire playboy uncle Jack wrapped his Porsche around the oak tree out front because he supposedly drank too much at the yacht club, and now our dysfunctional relations are circling like hungry raptors. And, oh, yeah, he named me executor. Fun times.*

The sarcasm couldn't shut down the pain squeezing her heart. She already missed her uncle like crazy—but right now it was her job to be cool, collected and businesslike.

"No, there's no problem," she said in a tight voice, memories choking her until her words were little more than a whisper.

Thankfully, she hadn't been the one to identify Jack—his butler had done that honor before she'd even arrived at Oakwood. The faithful old servant had quit after that. She didn't blame him one bit.

Chloe swallowed hard, feeling faint as she unfolded the scrap of notepaper with the combination to her uncle's private wall safe. It was slow going because her hands were clumsy and sweaty. The cause wasn't nerves, exactly. It was more like her body's attempt to melt away so she wouldn't have to deal with whatever was behind that steel door. Opening the safe was like admitting Jack was gone. She didn't want to believe it.

What happened, Jack? Did you really drive home drunk? For a moment, tears blurred the numbers on the notepaper. *It just doesn't make sense. None of it does.*

For one thing, Jack was never a drinker. Chloe had told that to the police. They'd given her a pitying look, as if she were a rosy-cheeked innocent. In the end, they hadn't listened to a word she'd said.

Her tears dried as she felt a pair of steel-gray eyes boring a hole between her shoulders. Irritation flooded her, momentarily washing out grief and the daunting sense of responsibility thrust on her as executor. *Is there a problem? Oh, yeah, there's a problem. The room is a thousand degrees, my feet hurt in these stupid shoes and that guy over there is giving me the screaming willies.*

The guy in question was named Sam Ralston. He'd shown up for the funeral along with two of Uncle Jack's other friends. They were big, handsome men, pleasant, mixed with the other richy-rich guests well enough, but there was something off about the lot of them. Something *other*.

Who was Ralston to Uncle Jack? It was hard to say. Although she referred to Jack as her uncle, he was actually a distant cousin, and she'd never quite worked out his place in the family tree. Even though Jack had been her guardian after her parents' death, he'd not been around a lot of the time. At fourteen, it wasn't as if she'd needed supervision 24/7—at least not once the initial shock had passed. So, there were chunks of Jack's life she knew nothing about, Sam Ralston among them.

Jack had named him as the other executor, which was why he was here with her and Mr. Littleton, the family lawyer. Whatever was in the safe Jack had installed in his palatial bedroom would have to be documented as part of the estate, even if it was meant for Chloe.

Too bad. When she'd found out Ralston would be her partner in settling the estate, Chloe had actually shivered, as if someone had opened a refrigerator door right behind her.

"Do you need help?" Ralston asked, his baritone voice threaded with impatience.

"No," Chloe returned.

"You know you need a key, too. The safe has a double lock."

"Got it." She turned and gave Ralston a look over her shoulder.

The view, at least, was no hardship. More than once, she'd found herself staring at him, her body clenching with an unexpected and unwelcome fever of desire. He was somewhere in his thirties, tall and hard-bodied, with thick dark hair combed back from a broad forehead. He had the kind of face advertisers of leather jackets and fast cars would have liked—strong bones, a few character lines, and a dark shadow of beard no razor could quite obliterate. His nose was blade straight, his lips full and sculpted above a slightly cleft chin. The set of his head and shoulders said he owned whatever room he was in, and the rest of the planet besides.

Yummy and forbidding at the same time.

At the moment, he was returning her glare with a face carefully scraped clean of expression—and yet every line of his body screamed "Hurry up!"

So what's the rush? she wondered. He'd been like this—barely repressed urgency—ever since he arrived.

A career as a wedding planner had honed Chloe's skills at reading people. Too many couples ordered an event based on what they thought was correct rather than what was in their hearts. Chloe was good at ferreting out the truth from a shared look, an inflection in the voice, a finger drawn down the picture of a fluffy white dress in a magazine.

Just like her gut said Ralston and his buddies might have fat wallets and Italian-cut suits, but they'd break heads just as easily as they tossed back their single-malt whiskey. Now he was standing a little to the side, just out of the splash of late afternoon sunlight pouring through the French doors—a shady guy staying in the shade.

Ralston shifted, making a noise like a stifled sigh.

"Cool your jets," Chloe said evenly. "Whatever's in here is what Uncle Jack left me."

"He already left you a nice bequest," Ralston pointed out.

"So?"

Chloe cursed the lawyer for staying tactfully silent. She turned back to the safe and away from Ralston.

"Whatever is in the safe is going to be the interesting part." He sounded amused, the first sign of warmth she'd seen in him. "He liked his secrets."

"How do you know?"

"I know—knew—Jack." Now he sounded sad. She liked him better for it.

"How did you come to know him?"

He gave the same nonanswer he'd given her once before. "We hung out in a few of the same places."

Chloe began spinning the dial on the safe, her mouth gluey with unease. What was in there? Gold bars? The deed to a private island in the Caribbean? A stack of bearer-bonds with tons of zeroes? Jack had possessed a Midas touch, turning every business venture into a wild success.

Poor Jack. People would remember his *GQ* style and his tragic death, but Chloe would remember him starting a game of hide-and-seek with her when she was six. He'd sent the care package of flowers and chocolate when her engagement had fallen apart. He'd always been there, a steady friend and the best of listeners in a world where people were too busy to slow down and truly care. Sure, he'd had money, but he'd always offered his heart, too. People—especially their family—had never stopped grabbing long enough to notice.

Chloe swallowed hard, her fingers fumbling with the dial. The safe lock clicked. She swallowed again, feeling as though she was gulping down the entire situation and it was stuck painfully in her throat. Blinking to keep her vision clear, she took the key to the second lock out of the pocket of her sleeveless, indigo sheath dress.

The key slid into the lock. Chloe turned it and then pushed down on the long handle. The safe opened on a silent glide of hinges. It was wide enough that she had to step back to accommodate the swing of the door.

The men were suddenly behind her, Ralston so close that she could feel his lapel brush her shoulder. The lawyer was a bit better about personal space, but she could sense him hovering. If curiosity had a frequency, theirs was vibrating high enough to shatter glass.

All three of them made a noise when they saw what was in the safe. There was nothing but a white box about eight inches tall and maybe four feet by three feet, with a note taped to the lid. Chloe reached in, pulling the note off. The clear tape made a ripping sound as it pulled a tiny patch of the box's white lid away with it. She unfolded the note and felt the men lean in as she read.

> *Chloe,*
> *If you're reading this, I'm gone. Keep this secret and safe. When the story comes out, you'll know what to do with it, and I know you'll do the right thing. Trust Sam. Be careful.*
> *Love you, kid,*
> *Jack*

Chloe reread the note. *Trust Sam.* Why? With what?

"What could it possibly be?" asked Littleton, a little breathlessly.

"Let's find out," said Ralston, lifting the large white box out of the otherwise empty safe.

Chloe took it out of his hands before he had taken one step away from the safe. "Uncle Jack left this for me, remember?"

His eyes flared with surprise, as if people rarely snatched loot out of his grasp. "I was just going to put it on the bed."

Chloe looked up into his steel-gray glare and smiled sweetly. "Thanks. I can manage."

Her heart kicked a little at Ralston's frown—part fear, part perverse enjoyment. He was a bit too pushy for his own good. *Trust Sam.*

She walked the few steps to Jack's orgy-sized bed. The whole room was in a black-and-white color scheme, making the scene look like a homage to liquorice all-sorts. When she set the large white box on the ebony silk counterpane, the mystery of the package seemed even more emphatic.

The room was utterly silent, the rasp of Littleton's rapid breathing the loudest sound in it. Chloe felt for the box's opening. There was no tape. The lid lifted off, revealing a nest of blue-white tissue paper, the type meant to keep cloth from turning dingy with age. Ralston was at her elbow, close enough that her skin tingled with the breeze of his movements. Even now, her body felt magnetized to his nearness.

He pulled back one piece of tissue at the same moment that Chloe picked up the other. Despite the fact that they were strangers, they shared a look. It was utter astonishment.

"A wedding dress?" Chloe asked aloud. She touched the beaded bodice with one finger. The glittering stones were cold. Definitely not plastic. She's seen a lot of dresses in her career, and she could tell the work was exquisite.

"What the hell?" Ralston looked utterly stunned. "Jack would never have married."

"When the story comes out," Chloe said, repeating the note Jack had left. "What story? What was Uncle Jack doing with a dress?"

Ralston's eyebrows shot up with sudden dark amusement. "Well, it's tiny. At least we know it wasn't for him."

Chloe smiled, but her mind was already racing ahead. There were only so many reasons Jack would lock something away for safekeeping, whether it was treasure or weapons or even a gorgeous dress: because it was valuable, because it was meant for someone important to Jack or because dangerous people wanted it for the wrong reasons.

She was willing to bet the confection of lace and satin was all three.

Chapter 3

Death. That had been Jack's code name.

So who killed Death? It was almost a joke.

Irony sucks. Sam finally left the bedroom, taking a last look at Chloe Anderson bent over the white froth of the wedding dress. The image of her, sad and beautiful, stroking the symbol of so many feminine hopes and wishes—it brought a rush of something that was neither lust nor hunger, but held a hint of both. Strangely unnerved, he had elected to retreat. He could tell she wanted to be alone with her memories of Jack, and Sam appreciated that. The soft-spoken beauty was the only one in the family who seemed to care the man was dead.

And someone had to do the weepy thing. Sam was better at revenge.

The thought made his fangs descend, prepared to rip and tear in savage retribution.

His mind went back to Jack's last phone call, wringing each word dry of meaning. Jack had been running from his killer. Ambushed. Not much made Death run.

Sam banged out of the side door of the house, grateful to be in the clear air. The sun had just dipped behind the trees, making the outdoors safe for the undead. He took a huge breath, smelling green trees and the sweet pungency of the sun-warmed dirt. This was what he liked: solitude and no walls to hem him in. The past few days at Oakwood had been pure torture.

The people were the worst, and not just because they were a banquet of veins he couldn't touch. They were nasty. He didn't mind good, honest greed, but he couldn't stand all the whispered speculation about who would score big-time in Jack's will. And Sam called himself a mercenary. He was a rank amateur compared to Jack's aunt Mavis and that litter of useless, grasping cousins.

No wonder Jack was so good at covert operations. He'd needed them to survive his relatives.

Jack *had been* good. There went that verb tense thing again. It was hard to think of Jack in the past.

Sam swore under his breath. What were the Horsemen going to do now? There were only three of them left: Sam, the werewolf Kenyon, and Dr. Mark Winspear, the vampire they called Plague. Jack was—had been—their team leader.

He started toward the gate, his shoes crunching on the white gravel drive. It was so clean, Sam could imagine the hired help dusting each tiny pebble every morning, working inch by inch across the broad sweep that led back to the road.

Sam walked through the gates, approaching the oak tree where the Porsche had crashed. The tree had survived better than the car, but not by much. It would have to be felled before there were any serious windstorms.

One heavy branch dangled from the trunk, hanging on by a thin layer of bark.

Plague was frowning at the ground around the roots of the oak. He was tall, olive-skinned, and dressed in chinos and a short-sleeved shirt. The doctor looked enviably casual.

In contrast, Sam felt hot and irritable in the black suit he'd put on for the paperwork-signing and safe-opening portion of the entertainment. "Find anything?"

Winspear looked up, his dark eyes serious. "About half a mile down the road. Shell casings. The local cops missed them. Kenyon is going over the woods again, sniffing for more. Maybe he'll find a bullet in a tree."

His voice still held a faint trace of an indefinable accent. Despite the English-sounding name, he'd once mentioned growing up in Italy. The last of the Horsemen to join, he was by far the most private. No one could actually say they knew Mark Winspear. Still, he was the best at what he did. He was not only an accomplished doctor, but was what the vampires called an "eraser"—someone who possessed a rare ability to manipulate human memory.

"Kenyon looked at the casings and believes the bullets were silver," the doctor added. "We'll know more once we've gone over the car."

"So it was assassination," Sam said, stating what was rapidly becoming the obvious.

The doctor was peering awkwardly under the dangling branch, examining the marks in the soil, and made a sound that held a world of resignation. "The car had to be going eighty, by the amount of damage. That raises questions. Jack loved his Porsche too much to risk it at that speed on these roads. And you know how slim the odds are of a vampire actually getting drunk, despite the headlines."

Playboy Dies Living Fast and Hard. Sam swore. "He might have been drugged. Can you do a tox screen?"

Winspear's mouth was a grim line. "The body was badly burned, but if it's possible, I'll get the information we need."

He looked stricken, and for a moment Sam felt sorry for him. It didn't seem right that he had to do an autopsy on a friend, but who else had the expertise to examine dead vampires? Not the city morgue.

Sam shifted impatiently. "You have any theories about all this yet?"

Winspear stood, folding his arms. "I don't like to speculate before I have all the facts."

"Jack had a lot of enemies. We all do. We need some way to narrow down the list."

Winspear shrugged. "What stands out? What was Jack up to during the last month?"

"I don't know." The Horsemen had been taking a short break from the job and from each other—a necessary thing when so much of their work was all about death and carnage.

"I can't answer that, either—I was out at my cabin. It was just by chance that I'd arrived back in town when you called."

Sam grunted in irritation. Patient deduction wasn't his forte. He liked the part where he got to hit things. "Jack seems to have been close to his niece. He might have mentioned something. Small details can provide clues."

"Maybe." Winspear looked away.

Sam understood his doubts. The Horsemen were the only ones who knew who and what Jack really was. The rest was all playacting, learning to fit in with the latest slang and electronic gadgets. Remembering to hide every second of every day.

An unexpected jolt of melancholy hit Sam. He swatted it away with an answering annoyance. "I'll ask some questions. A few odd things have come up in the estate."

Winspear raised a dark brow. "Such as?"

"He left his niece a wedding dress." The image of Chloe and the dress came back, along with that strange, restless feeling.

"A dress hardly seems alarming. Unless it was, as I have heard human girls exclaim, a dress to die for?"

Sam closed his eyes, fighting down a sarcastic retort. "Never mind. It's a puzzle piece I can't make fit."

"Then I would talk to the niece. Maybe there's a dressmaker or a delivery company that can provide a clue."

Sam gave a small, ironic salute. "Shall do."

Winspear looked dubious. "Can you talk to—what's her name? Chloe? Or do you want me to do that?"

"I think I can handle her." In fact, handling her sounded like a solid plan—he could spend hours executing that particular mission, if he left his scruples at the door.

A faint trace of a smile lurked in Winspear's face. "I'd be careful if I were you. She looks like the smart, quiet type. They're dangerous."

"I'm a vampire. She's just a wedding planner."

Winspear gave a rare, low laugh. "So was Cinderella's fairy godmother. Don't underestimate her."

Sam stuffed his hands in his pockets. "I'll steer clear of mice and pumpkins."

It took little time for Sam to track Chloe down. She had taken the dress from Jack's suite to the room where she was staying. The door was ajar, allowing Sam to pause a moment before he had to knock. He used the time to study the location, as he always did before mounting an assault. It was a large chamber, one window, sparse furniture. Definitely a feminine space, with flowery prints on the walls and bedspread.

Chloe was standing in the middle of the room with her back to the door, looking sleek and polished from her high-heeled shoes to the twist in her dark blond hair. She was staring at the dress. It was hooked to the front of a huge, mahogany wardrobe, the dark wood showing off the white foam of lace.

Sam knew nothing about gowns, but he was pretty sure this one was exceptional. There was something in the proportions and detailing that said this wasn't some off-the-rack number.

The same could be said for Chloe. The curve of her spine drew his eyes, his gaze lingering on her exposed neck. Ever since he'd arrived at Oakwood, she'd drawn him. Sam desired women and had them, well and often, but few provided more than a moment's interest. War was not prone to the softer emotions—they were anathema to everything he was.

This woman, though, brushed his senses like the scent of a delicate perfume. She was pretty, but it was a sense of poised energy that made her remarkable—like an arrow about to fly. He couldn't help watching, expectant for the moment, wondering what would happen if she finally sprang loose.

Sam imagined that release of energy, feeling it with his whole body. It would be exquisite. The thought made his fangs descend, and he quickly began thinking of dull paperwork instead. *She's not for you. Women like her die around creatures like you.*

She turned, her brows drawing together when she

saw him there. "Something I can help you with?" Her words were quiet and low, but her voice resonated right through him.

You have no idea. A sudden stab of hunger pushed to the fore, reminding him again of what he was: a weapon meant for blood sports. She looked soft and delicious, as if she would taste of summer. Once again, his body tightened in anticipation.

Sam swallowed hard, wrestling himself as he had Kenyon's wolf, holding back the snapping jaws of the beast. *Small talk. Make small talk.*

"I can't help wondering what Jack was doing with that." He nodded toward the dress.

She relaxed a bit. "Me, too."

"It's good quality, isn't it?"

"Yes." She folded her arms and walked toward it. Sam trailed after her, using the moment as an excuse to get closer. The room was redolent with her perfume—something that reminded him of sunshine and lemonade.

He realized he was stalking her, and forced himself to stand still. "Should it be out of the safe?" he asked.

"Maybe not, but I can't learn anything about it when it's locked away."

Sam nodded. She had a point. "That's right. You're the wedding expert. Any insights?"

With a professional air, Chloe eyed the dress. "There's no label, but I'm sure it's made to order. The beading is hand-done. It's probably unique."

"Expensive?"

"It's worth a fortune. That's Italian silk or I'm a duck."

Sam slanted a glance at her. She was definitely not a duck. "None of your relatives tried to make off with it yet?"

She gave a rueful smile. "They don't know about it.

Fortunately, the last of the happy horde is leaving in the morning."

"How long will you be here?" He wouldn't be leaving a moment sooner.

She looked up. Her eyes were dark blue. "Until the end of the week or so. After that the house will be going on the market."

"You don't waste time."

She gave a soft sigh that made his skin tingle. "It's not me. Everyone wants their piece of the estate."

Sam watched her eyes sparkle with tears. Forgetting himself, he brushed her wrist with his fingertips, the lightest gesture of sympathy. One he would never normally make. She blinked, folding her arms across her stomach. Sam dropped his hand, the feel of her skin clinging to the pads of his fingers. *Silky.*

He forced his mind to the task of asking questions, doing his best to shut off his senses. The woman was like a drug, scrambling his thoughts. "Was Jack close to any family but you?"

"Not really. My father, but he died when I was fourteen. Along with my mother." She looked away. "Long story."

Something told Sam now was not the moment to ask for details. "No one was close, but the rest still think they should get a piece of all this?" He made a gesture indicating the house.

"Of course." Chloe made a slight movement, almost a shudder, as if she was trying to shake off a distasteful memory. "Jack had a talent for making money."

He also had centuries of financial experience, but Chloe didn't know that.

"Who were Jack's friends?" he asked abruptly.

"I thought that was you."

Winspear was right. He sucked at interrogation. Frustration made him resort to his usual bluntness. "You're in the wedding business. You said the dress was unique. Is there any way to figure out who owned it?"

"What did you say you did for a living?" She narrowed her eyes.

Too blunt. *Oops.* "Trust fund baby," Sam said lightly. "I don't do anything." *But I want to know Jack's exact schedule for the last six weeks.*

The set of her mouth said she didn't believe him. "But obviously you like solving mysteries."

"Why not?"

"Well, here's one for you to chew on. I don't think Jack died the way the police say he did."

Sam nearly started. He kept his voice very neutral. "Oh?"

Chloe sat on the edge of the bed, looking suddenly tired and much younger than she had a moment ago. "Jack had a hidden side. I don't think most people even noticed, but if there was a loud noise, he'd reach for a gun even if he wasn't wearing one. I never knew what that was all about, but I'd bet good money you and your friends do."

A very, very smart girl.

"Did Jack have enemies?" she asked, her voice even.

"They're mostly dead." *Or undead.*

Her hand, so fine-boned and soft, made a fist. "I think you guys missed one."

"What are you talking about?"

She shot him a look. "You've got that whole brothers-in-arms vibe going on. I think you watch each other's backs pretty closely, and I don't mean around the boardroom table. Well, try this one on. I don't think Uncle Jack smashed up his car by accident."

Sam stayed mute.

Chloe pushed on, her jaw set in a stubborn line. "He never drank as much as he pretended to. The whole play-boy thing was a game, like a mask he wore when it suited him."

Her fierce tone was doing something to Sam's insides, a painful, hot, sweet feeling radiating from deep in his gut. He was getting turned on in a big way. *Oh, good timing, Ralston.*

"I don't know," he said casually. "Once in a very rare while, Jack could tie one on."

Chloe grimaced. "He wasn't stupid. Not where the Porsche was involved."

God, she did know her uncle. Jack loved that car. This whole conversation offended his sense of fair play. *She deserves to know she's not the only one who thinks Jack was killed.* But if he broke cover, it wasn't just his existence on the line. *Women like her die around creatures like you.* The thought repeated in his mind like a tolling bell. He knew that from bitter experience. Everything about who he was, what he did, invited danger.

"Leave it to the police," he said reasonably. "They know what they're looking for."

Her eyebrows shot up. "Which is why your two friends are all over the scene of the accident? They've been there since day one like a pair of designer-casual bloodhounds."

Sam stomped on a snort of laughter before it could get away. "You're imagining things."

"Lame." The heat in her eyes said she didn't like being dismissed.

"You're just upset because he died suddenly. It's understandable."

"Lame." A flush of pink was climbing her cheeks. "I'm not a clueless child, Mr. Ralston. Don't try to hide information from me."

Irritation flashed through him. "What do you think happened? One of your relatives hired a gunman to get Jack's estate?"

Her blue eyes didn't waver. "I bet you'd know how to find out if they did."

He gave up. "I can't help you."

"Then get out of my bedroom."

Her expression was hard. Unexpectedly, Sam felt it dent his ego. He wanted to reach across the gulf his job and his nature put between them. It was a rare impulse, and one he couldn't do a damned thing about.

Probably just as well.

His gaze wandered to the wedding dress, taking it in for a brief moment. Marriage was just one more human entanglement he'd left behind, but for a split second he wondered what it would be like to be that unguarded with somebody. It had been too long to remember.

Sam turned and walked out of the room, leaving Chloe alone on the bed.

For now.

Chapter 4

Chloe curled up under the covers, her eyes sandy from lack of sleep. The room should have felt restful, for this was where she'd slept most of her teenage years—but too much had dramatically, tragically changed.

Someone had murdered Jack, she was sure of it, but she had no proof. She'd tried talking to the police, but they couldn't—or wouldn't—help. They'd treated her like a kid too young for grown-up worries. It pushed every one of her buttons. Still, how could she blame the cops? All she had to go on was Jack's character and the suspicious behavior of his buddies.

In the dark quiet of the bedroom, she surrendered to pain and loss, letting the pillow muffle her sobs. She just couldn't grasp the fact that she wouldn't see Jack again. Ever. For as long as she drew breath. But it wasn't just grief she felt. Hot, frustrated anger sliced along her raw nerves. She wanted to act, to avenge, but she didn't know how.

Chloe sniffed and rolled over, the sheets sticking to her hot skin. Outside the window, wind hissed through the trees, making a lullaby of the restless breeze. Chloe's mind ticked on.

Suspicion just wouldn't stop clawing at her. She knew she was right to speak up, but other people reacted like she was a hysterical freak—even Sam Ralston. Once she'd asked him about Jack's accident, it had been like talking to a wall, his handsome face wiped of expression.

Oh, well. At least stone-faced was a change from broody or bossy, which seemed to be his other settings. Too bad he had a magnetism that turned her insides to pudding. *Yeah, right. A broody, bossy blank wall with gobs of animal magnetism. Every girl's dream.*

She had worked long enough in the marriage business to know what she wanted in a man: dependable, home-oriented, quiet and sensible. None of her family's nasty competitive streak. An independent business owner or middle-ranking executive would be perfect. Solid, but not flashy.

Chloe pulled the blanket under her chin. *Someone who likes gardening and country fairs.*

Not Sam Ralston.

She rolled over again and froze.

What was that? It wasn't a sound so much as the sense of the air being displaced. As if something had passed in absolute silence. Chloe held her breath, listening.

The wind soughed outside. Almost beyond her range of hearing, she could hear the clock on the grand sweep of stairs chime half past midnight, and then the house was still once more. Logic said she'd been imagining things. There was no one there.

And yet every nerve ending strained with apprehension. A bead of sweat trickled down the small of her back, making her shiver.

She heard a faint exhalation of breath.

Not her own.

Someone's in the room with me!

Without moving a muscle, she scanned the darkness. The bedroom curtains were partially open, admitting just enough moonlight to separate one blob of furniture from the next. Opposite the foot of the bed, the wedding dress hung on the wardrobe door like a filmy ghost. She wasn't about to leave the dress unattended, but having it near made her feel closer to Jack so she'd left it there for the night. She suddenly wondered if that had been a wise thing to do.

Beside the tall wardrobe lurked a darker shape, and it was slowly moving. Like a stain, it crept across the white cloud of the dress, making the garment shift. The moonlight caught the crystal beads, making the bodice glitter with shards of cold light. Chloe heard the soft rustle of silk, and then the dress seemed to bob in the air.

Someone was stealing it. Outrage sparked through her, followed by flat-out disbelief. She was right there, mere feet away! Why would anyone risk her catching them? *And who knows I've got it?*

Aunt Mavis? Her hand snaked out from beneath the comforter, finding the switch of her bedside lamp.

"Don't." The male voice was hard and cold and not one she recognized.

The sneering tone made her more defiant than smart. Chloe swore under her breath and flicked the switch anyway.

She felt the rush of air as the figure lunged across the room. The china lamp exploded as it hit the floor. Chloe yelped in surprise, instinctively rolling away to avoid the spray of shards. Rough hands grabbed her by the back of her nightgown, forcing her facedown on the mattress.

"Don't," the voice repeated, the sneer turning to something more sinister.

Chloe panted in fright, her face turned away from her attacker and pressed hard into the bed. He had her arms pinned behind her back at a painful angle.

Let go of me! she screamed in her head, but somehow the words couldn't find her tongue. She was paralyzed, the man's hot breath stroking her skin as he chuckled, long and low.

"Can I trust you not to move?" he said.

It was then she felt the cold kiss of a gun muzzle against her spine. She sucked in a stuttering gasp. She felt his lips brush her ear. "I'd rather not shoot. I'd rather leave without attracting attention. Get it?"

"Y-yes," she whispered, feeling a hot sting as tears filled her eyes. She squeezed her eyelids tight, stifling a sob. She wanted to scream so badly, but her voice had abandoned her. She'd taken self-defense classes, but the gun trumped any tricks she knew. She'd never been so terrified in her life.

She felt a sudden weight on her back as the thief straddled her, pinning her arms with his body and squeezing the air from her lungs. Her head was turned to the side, but it was still hard to breathe. Chloe struggled, gulping air that stank with her attacker's sweat.

She sensed him grabbing a pillow off the bed. A moment later, the cool cotton muffled her face, filling her nose and mouth. A gun might make too much noise, but suffocation was silent.

Desperate, Chloe tried to squirm away.

"Damn you!" he muttered, and she felt his grip tighten.

Fighting would only get her killed a different way, but Chloe couldn't stop. The will to survive was too strong. She bucked hard enough that the pillow slipped and she gasped in precious oxygen.

Wham!

Her eyes went wide as the bedroom door slammed against the wall. The pillow fell away and a flare of sudden light filled the room as someone turned on the overhead. The thief swore, pushing Chloe's face against the bed with his bare hand. Her mouth flooded with the metallic taste of fresh panic.

"Get away from her!" someone barked. Someone used to shouting orders. It sounded like Faran Kenyon.

"Now!" That one was Ralston!

Chloe felt her attacker's weight shift.

The deafening noise from his gun came from right above her, making her skull ring.

Oh, God!

A hot spray of blood spattered the pillow in front of Chloe. She recoiled, covering her head, and realized a beat later that she could move her arms. Her attacker had leaped off the bed.

Or been blown off. She scanned the sheets in front of her, crimson spreading across the white like bright drops of paint. Nausea lurched in her throat.

Ralston vaulted over the bed with an unholy snarl, leaping for her attacker. Chloe twisted around to catch a glimpse of a dark-clad man lunging toward the window. She covered her face as the window smashed, her own scream sounding muffled because she was still deaf from the gunshot.

Her attacker disappeared in a hail of glass. Ralston skidded to a stop as he reached the gaping mess where the window had been. Kenyon joined him a second later.

Both had their weapons up, standing to the side of the window frame and scanning the grass below.

Chloe could guess what they were thinking. Her room was on the second story, but a porch roof jutted out below. Someone could use that as a halfway point while jumping to the ground.

"Do you see him?" Ralston demanded. He was wearing nothing but worn jeans and sneakers, his torso bare. His big body was still ready to spring, coiled muscles drawn tight.

"Not from here," Kenyon replied.

"Go."

Kenyon turned, running for the door and thumbing on his cell phone as he went. By the time he reached the door, someone on the other end of the connection had answered. "Close the gates!"

Chloe could make out the words, but beyond that was nothing but the muffled ringing from the gunshot. For a moment, her emotions felt the same: numb, stunned, distant.

I nearly died.

"You okay?" Ralston stared out the window, still scanning the darkness.

She cleared her throat. "I think so." The words quavered.

"Good."

As her pulse slowed, Chloe studied his back, her gaze tracing the muscles and bones of his broad shoulders. Half naked, he looked far more at home than he had in a suit.

It was as if, stripped of clothes, the real man was visible. Sam Ralston moved with an animal grace that stirred something primitive in her. Her fear responded to his blatantly male presence, wanting all that size and strength on her side.

"Is he gone?" she asked, her voice shaking.

"Not for long," he replied, his head moving slowly as he scanned the grounds. "He's going to pay for this."

Finally, Ralston turned away from the window, a furrow between his dark brows. His gaze flicked over her face. "You're not okay. You're pale."

"So are you."

His gaze flicked around the room. "It's the smell of blood."

"I hate it, too." Chloe hiccupped, feeling a wave of nervous energy shudder through her. The numbness was fading. She wanted to scream. Or cry. *He held me at gunpoint. He tried to smother me.*

The very idea was surreal. For a moment, she doubted that it had happened at all.

"You're safe now." Ralston took a quick step toward her. The speed of it, the size of him made her flinch. He stopped, looking at her for a long moment. Chloe felt her pulse speeding again, pounding in her head.

Slowly now, he set his gun on the nightstand and put his hands on his hips, a gesture that showed his broad chest. His gray eyes were dark and angry. "Do you know what he wanted?"

Chloe felt slightly dizzy. Adrenaline aftermath and unexpected desire hit her like strong brandy. *Sam rescued me!* A wave of new emotions—ones she couldn't even name—lapped dangerously at the edges of her thoughts. "He was after the dress."

They both looked over at the gown, which pooled like a deflated cloud on the carpet. Sam crossed over to it, picking it up by the hanger and replacing it on the wardrobe door. The gesture was surprisingly careful.

Something about it—the crumpled dress or the way he handled it—made her start to cry in soft, gulping sobs. Chloe covered her face, horrified at the pathetic sounds coming from her throat, but the feel of the pillow against her face, the attacker's hands on her skin played over and over again in her mind.

The bed dipped as Sam's weight settled next to her. He pulled a blanket around her, his gestures efficient but gentle, as if he were holding himself firmly in check. "It's over. He's gone."

"Then why am I crying?" she snapped. She was weirdly angry, as if it were all Sam's fault.

"You're in shock," he said quietly.

"I don't cry."

"I know." He sounded apologetic.

She wanted to demand how he could possibly know what she did or didn't do, but it was clear he was just being kind. Biting her lip, she struggled to stop weeping. She craved Sam's protection but was furious that she needed it. *I've got to pull myself together.*

Frustrated, her mind lunged for specifics. Something besides the horrible feeling of being pushed and crushed and threatened that played over and over in her head, like a bad song that just wouldn't shut up. "How did he get in?"

"Probably the window. I don't know yet."

Yet? That meant the mysterious Mr. Ralston was going to investigate. She swallowed down a fresh batch of sobs. "How did you know I was in trouble?"

"I heard something break."

"Uh-huh." That sounded too pat. Chloe's mind grappled for some way to probe his answer, but she was still too overwhelmed. "Thank you for saving me."

He gave her a guarded look. "No problem. I was

hoping to hit the guy in the leg so we could catch and question him. Didn't quite work out that way. I overcompensated my aim. I didn't want to risk shooting you by mistake."

"I appreciate that."

"Yeah." Sam touched her arm gently. She would have expected him to crush her to his chest, do the manly-man protective thing, but he didn't. He was being careful about how he handled her. He knew enough to give her distance, as though he'd dealt with situations like this before.

Chloe realized she was thinking of him as Sam now, and not Ralston. Sam, her savior. Super Sam. Oh, what the heck, he'd earned some girlish gratitude. She was just glad her mind was starting to function again.

A babble of voices came from the hallway. Was her hearing just coming back or had they been out there all along? She slid off the bed, feeling a little unsteady.

"Where are you going?" Sam demanded.

She gestured helplessly at the door. "My aunt. My cousin. People. They're wondering what's going on."

Sam held up a hand. "Let me."

He pulled open the door, looking like the sexy tradesman from a bored housewife's daydream. From where she stood, all she could see was the curve of Sam's shoulder and his denim-hugged backside. That would set the family's collective imagination spinning. *Go me.*

While he stood in the hallway, Chloe changed into a pair of yoga pants and a T-shirt. She saw with disgust the nightgown she'd been wearing had splatters of blood on it. She balled up the garment and threw it in the garbage can. There was blood on the sheets, too, and glass on the floor, but suddenly she was too exhausted to deal with any of it. She perched on a corner of the bed far from the blood, wishing she could just lie down.

No, no lying down. Not here. She could still feel the echo of a hand crushing her face into the bed.

"How are you doing?" Sam asked as he came back into the room.

The question wasn't the vague politeness of a stranger. To her utter surprise, Sam crouched in front of her, studying her face. His expression was concerned, almost tender. He reached out, catching her hands gently in his. His skin was cool and wonderful, the gesture infinitely comforting. "Look at me," he said. "You're going to be okay. I'm here."

Chloe met his eyes. A subtle shift came over his features, a tightening of the lips, his pupils eating up the steel-gray irises. There was concern there, but something else now, too. Desire. Possession. He lifted her hand to his lips, brushing the lightest of kisses across the back of her fingers.

The gesture was courtly, barely qualifying as a true kiss, but a flood of tingling arousal swamped her skin from head to foot. No one had ever touched her so intimately with so little flesh.

She gasped lightly, and the skin around his eyes flinched, a predator narrowing his focus. Now it was her neck that prickled with the faintest frisson of fear.

It was too much. Chloe looked down, unable to hold his hypnotic gaze a moment longer. Heat flooded her face.

"Chloe?"

His voice was soft, intimate. It sucked her down further, so she fought it, clawing her way back to the present. She'd just been attacked. Sam had chased the bad guy away.

Memory slammed back, ripping the cobwebs away.

"I wanted to fight," she said. "I wanted to cry out."

He made a noise as close to a sigh as someone like Sam Ralston would make. "You did what you needed to. It's called surviving. That's how we're programmed."

She took a steadying breath. "You didn't freeze. Neither did your friend. How did you just happen to be there with guns?"

"I always carry." In a blink, his face was back to his blank-wall setting. Sam rose and put an appropriate distance between them.

Chloe folded her arms, feeling suddenly as if a fire had been doused, leaving her in the cold. What had just happened? Had she asked one question too many? Too bad, because every answer he gave prompted a dozen questions more.

There was a sharp rap on the door. Sam opened it, looking relieved. Kenyon pushed his way in, a grumpy look on his face. His blond hair looked mussed, as if he'd been pushing his hands through it. He stopped, giving Chloe a once-over. "You all right?"

"Sure," she replied.

"Anything?" Sam asked his friend.

"Nope. The security here means well, but what can you expect?"

Sam swore lustily. "How can that happen? I shot him in the shoulder. He was bleeding."

"They don't have our training. Trampled the trail. Messed it up."

Chloe caught the shut-up look Sam shot his friend. *What training?*

Kenyon either didn't notice the look or pretended not to care. "So what was that guy after?"

"The wedding dress," Sam replied, gesturing toward the place where it hung.

Kenyon gave it a curious look. "Seriously?"

Then something seemed to catch his eye. Suddenly alert, he crossed to the wardrobe. He pulled a small Maglite flashlight from the pocket of his cargo pants and shone it at the beading around the gown's low neckline.

Chloe got to her feet, still feeling shaky. "What do you see?"

"Interesting decoration. It's not all crystals."

Chloe had noticed that, too. There was elaborate embroidery all around the neckline, much of it gold wire couched with silk thread and dotted with seed pearls. Dozens and dozens of set stones had been added to the design, giving a shimmering fire to every movement of the dress. "The headpiece has similar decoration. I think the pearls might be real."

Kenyon looked up, an odd expression on his face. "So are the stones."

Chloe gulped. "What do you mean?"

He gave a wry smile to Sam. "You remember last March?"

"That can't be right," Sam said dully. "Tell me you're kidding."

"You know your guns, I know my luxury goods."

Sam cursed. "We should have known the moment this turned up in Jack's safe. Though how he ended up with them…"

"Were you looking for a wedding dress?"

"No." Sam suddenly looked offended. "What in the nine hells was Jack up to?"

"What are you talking about?" Chloe demanded, her voice going shrill.

Kenyon pulled out his light again and played it across the bodice of the dress, making the stones dance with white fire. "These are diamonds. Whatever bride belongs to this dress could have bought a small country with this dowry. In fact, if I'm right, one almost did. I think these are the lost diamonds of the Kingdom of Marcari."

Chapter 5

Chloe's gasp hit Sam hard. He whipped around, alert to whatever had startled her and ready to smash it. But nothing was there. Her shock had simply been at Kenyon's words.

Nothing like a fortune in lost diamonds to stop a conversation cold. *And what were they doing in Jack's safe?* Sam ground his teeth. He wasn't big on surprises, and this was a whopper.

He edged closer to Chloe anyhow. That kind of ice on the lam meant danger permeated the air like a fine mist. The scum who'd attacked her would have friends. *The first one who touches her will lose an arm.*

The ferocity of the thought rocked him. He felt far too much for this human woman, but she had been brave, coolheaded despite her obvious distress. He could respect that. And he couldn't deny that she was lovely, even the curve of her cheek showing nature's geometry to perfection. But those weren't good enough reasons to let the weakness of emotions compromise War.

Better to focus on the fact that she was Jack's niece, and alone. Her relatives could not be counted on to keep her safe. They'd be more likely to strip the valuables from her cooling corpse. Therefore, she needed his help. That was acceptable. Best of all, it was a good reason to be near Chloe. Totally legitimate, even for a bloodsucking fiend. From this second on, Sam was the ultimate guard dog, protecting the girl, the diamonds and the dress. He owed it to Jack.

And he owed it to the Princess Amelie, the bride who belonged in that dress. He kicked himself for not realizing it was her gown right away. But then again, he'd never seen it before. And also—even with a connection to the family, why would Jack have the dress of a foreign princess half a world away? That was odd, even for Jack.

Chloe was definitely struggling to stay in the loop. "Lost diamonds?" She scrunched her face in confusion. "What are you talking about?"

"These are the Jewels of Marcari," Kenyon replied.

"Need-to-know," Sam growled in warning. It wasn't the Horsemen's case, but the blanket order to all the Company's agents had been for absolute secrecy about the heist. "We're doing this by the book."

At least that's what Sam would do. Or Winspear. They followed orders. Instead, Kenyon gave him an eye roll.

Sam clenched his teeth harder, sensing chaos about to descend. *Werewolves. Too valuable to strangle. Not valuable enough to lock away for good.* It was the way they'd always worked. Kenyon would push just enough to drive Sam crazy, simply because it was fun.

"You heard about the royal wedding, right?" Kenyon

said, addressing Chloe but with a sly look at Sam. "The Prince of Vidon and the Princess of Marcari?"

"Kenyon!"

Chloe shot Sam a startled glance. The look made him feel like a bully.

"The wedding?" she asked tentatively. "Sure, I heard about it. It was in the media for months, especially when Prince Kyle of Vidon was caught with his hand in the wrong cookie jar."

Sam snorted. The cookie's stage name was Brandi Snap. The wedding was off, but Brandi had a lucrative book deal.

Chloe's eyes narrowed. "So what…?"

Sam folded his arms and interrupted. "It's a long story."

For an instant, Chloe looked hurt again, and then irritation filled her eyes. "Spill. If the diamonds are in my bedroom and bringing out the bad guys, I have a right to the details."

Her voice, normally so low and soft, held an edge. She'd reached the end of her rope.

Sam scowled, torn between duty and a desire to tell her everything because she looked so vulnerable. He opted for a middle ground. "The stones belong to the Royal House of Marcari or of Vidon, depending on which one you ask. The two countries have been at odds since the Crusades. Part of the fight is over these gems."

"The wedding would have resolved it," Kenyon added. "At least in theory. The stones were recut in honor of the occasion. The finest were to form Princess Amelie's dowry."

"I knew that much," Chloe said. "Once the wedding

took place, the gems would belong to both countries. End of argument."

Sam shrugged. "Until Prince Charming ended up in the tabloids. Now peace is further away than ever."

Looking pale and shaky, Chloe rose from the bed and crossed to the dress, fingering the elaborately worked bodice. "Then this is Princess Amelie's gown. No wonder the workmanship is so exquisite."

Sam watched her hands, so graceful and precise as they stroked the cloth. He imagined them cooking food, winding a bandage, holding a baby. Things that no longer had a part in his life.

Her voice was wistful. "Speaking as a wedding consultant, putting the diamonds on the dress was a stunning concept. She would have shimmered like star fire. A symbol of peace. Everything a royal bride is supposed to be. What a tragedy it didn't work out."

Chloe turned, her gaze flicking from Sam to Kenyon and back. "So, how did these get stolen? How did Jack get them?"

"Good questions," Sam replied. They were ones Jack would never answer.

"You seem to know a lot about the diamonds."

"Jewelry is a special interest of mine," Kenyon put in, the picture of utter innocence.

Sam wished there was such a thing as a werewolf muzzle. He considered Chloe's doubtful expression. He could literally see her figuring out far too much, the thoughts flying across her face. If this kept up, they would have to wipe her memory.

He hated the idea. Selfishly, he wanted her to remember him saving her. *Why? You can't have her.*

"When did the gems go missing?" she asked.

"Their absence was noted in March. The fact was kept from the media."

"How do you know that?"

"I have friends."

She gave him a dubious look. He held it, giving away nothing even though his hands itched to cup her body and pull her to him. Her anger smelled spicy. She knew he was hiding something. Despite circumstances, the determination in her eyes tantalized.

A contest between them would be interesting. His strength. Her wits. It would never happen. Their worlds would intersect for no more than a few days, and then he'd be gone.

Just as well. War was meant for killing, not affairs of the heart.

Sam insisted that Chloe move to a different bedroom. Still spooked, she agreed without a fuss. In her books, Sam had earned the title of security expert that night, and there was no way she was getting into that blood-soaked bed anyway. Once the dress was back in the safe, Sam escorted her to a room in the south wing, where there were no other guests to complicate his security plans. He lingered outside her door until she locked herself in.

Not that she was going to sleep, exhausted or not. Her thoughts were caught on a carnival wheel, reeling up, down and occasionally wrong side up. How did Uncle Jack get mixed up with foreign royalty and diamond thieves? Sure, he was a man of mystery and all that, but this was—well, it was pretty out there. But he'd been murdered, so she had to snap out of the shock and focus on the facts.

Sitting cross-legged on the sea-green counterpane of the guest room's bed, she switched on her laptop and

opened her spiral-bound journal to a fresh page. If Jack
was involved, it might help to reconstruct his movements
for the last few months of his life. A person didn't just
happen on a royal princess's wedding gown, especially
one coated in jewels. It had crossed his path someplace—
and not in this town. Lovely though it was, Wingman
County was hardly James Bond territory.

Chloe handled a few of Jack's private business af-
fairs, so she usually knew when he went out of town.
She clicked on her electronic calendar and paged back to
March, when the diamonds had apparently gone missing.
Nothing of interest. She paged back further.

On February 15, there was a note that Jack asked her
to attend a luncheon on his behalf. He had gone to the
south of France—an intriguing detail, since it was a short
train ride from the Côte d'Azur to Marcari. *Okay, but lots
of people go to warm places that time of year. What's to
say he wasn't just enjoying the weather?*

When did he come back? She paged forward, landing
in April. She'd met him in New York, at a show by the
designer Jessica Lark. She was a friend of Jack's, though
Chloe didn't know how good a friend. Jack definitely
kissed, but he'd seldom told.

Jotting down the dates and places, Chloe stared at the
designer's name, remembering her brief meeting with the
woman. She'd been about thirty, hauntingly beautiful and
a rare talent Chloe had felt privileged to meet. They'd
shaken hands, firm and businesslike. No fake little air
kisses from Lark.

Recalling that night gave her the shivers. She could
hear the clink of glasses, the wash of too many perfumes
in the hot room. Chloe remembered the brush of Lark's
silk dress against her bare arm, Jack laughing at something she'd said.

An ache in her throat made her shut down the memory. A month later, Jessica Lark had burned to death in a fire that had destroyed her studio. Nothing—and nobody—had survived.

Of the three people in that scene, Chloe was the only one who hadn't been murdered. Yet. *What's the connection?*

The answer was obvious. Jessica Lark was—

Something thumped against her door. Cold terror snaked up her arms, sending her scurrying off the bed. The journal flopped to the floor, making her jump again. She took a breath to cry out, but it died as a chill lump blocked her throat. Memories of the attack came slamming back, pumping adrenaline through her blood. Her hands trembled.

The door had a lock, but no dead bolt. She glanced around for a weapon. Pickings were slim. This wasn't one of the guest suites, just a spare bedroom with nice but functional furniture. No suits of armor with convenient battle-axes. No ancient rifles crisscrossed over the fireplace. Just a bed and a dresser.

She knew where Jack had kept his SIG Sauer, but that was on another floor. *So why didn't I bring that with me?*

Because she wasn't used to actually needing a loaded gun. As a rule, this sort of danger didn't find wedding planners.

Chloe held her frozen position, suffocating with fear, for an entire, eternal minute. She heard nothing but the pounding of her pulse.

Blast! She had to know what she'd heard or she'd stare at the door for the rest of the night, wondering. Guessing. Expecting the worst.

Willing herself to move, she picked up a china shepherdess from the night table and stalked toward the door, moving as quietly as a shadow. She gripped the figure with both hands, the china slick and cold against her palms. As a weapon, it wasn't as hopeless as it looked. Bo Peep and her lambs might be frilly, but they were plenty heavy.

Chloe pressed her ear to the door, holding her breath to listen. Silence. Tentatively, she reached for the knob, balancing Bo Peep in one hand and gripping the cool brass with the other. In one quick move, she popped the lock and pulled it open. With a quick step backward, she grabbed the statue in both hands and hoisted it into the air, ready to bludgeon an intruder.

Sam sat across the hall, his back to the wall, his long legs stretched out. He'd pulled on a plain white T-shirt. His gun rested beside him, or did in the first fraction of a second that she was opening the door. Then it was in his hand, and he was on his feet.

Her breath stuttered, relief colliding with fresh panic. He wasn't pointing the weapon, just very clearly on the alert, but no one should be able to move that fast.

She slowly lowered the statue. "It's you," she said lamely.

Sam eyed the lump of china. "Is that a sheep?"

"Yeah." She watched, mesmerized by the play of muscles as he relaxed.

"That gives new meaning to offensive weapon."

Chloe cradled it in her arms, feeling weirdly sorry for Bo and her lambs. "It was the best I had. I don't carry a gun."

"You've got me." He took a step closer.

"Yeah, and you wear a gun more often than you seem to wear a shirt, but the rest of us have to improvise once in a while." She wasn't usually this snappish, but the night was catching up with her. Finding anyone, even

Sam, lurking outside her door wasn't doing her nerves any good. Neither was the fact that she wanted to move toward him and retreat backward all at once.

"Like I said, you've got me. Until this is all over, I'm your bodyguard."

She was about to retort something about not needing that, but common sense stopped her. Or maybe it was the memory of his gentle hands barely an hour ago, comforting her. Maybe she did need him or maybe she just liked the idea of having someone there, strong and reliable.

Don't get spoiled. He might be Super Sam, but he's only here for a few days.

She stepped back from the doorway, beckoning him into the room. She set the shepherdess back on the nightstand. "I think I've figured out why Jack had the dress."

Sam stopped cold. "You can't be mixed up in this."

Chloe folded her arms, staring into his eyes so that she wasn't gawking at the T-shirt straining over his chest and arms. "Listen to me. We're talking a wedding here. I'm an expert. And I know Jack. You're not going to get past square one without my help."

Chapter 6

"What are you saying?" Sam braced his hands on his waist and glowered down at her.

Okay, maybe she was overstating her case, but she could definitely contribute. Chloe fought the urge to poke him in the stomach just to deflate the arrogant set of his strong body. "I know what I'm talking about."

His brow furrowed. "Oh?"

The single syllable made her vision go scarlet. The tone of it was polite, but beneath the buttering of good manners was doubt. After all, how could she possibly think of something he hadn't already discovered? *Yeah, right. Here comes the ego. The macho guys always have the ego. Next thing he'll pat me on the head...or the backside.* She'd break his arm if he did that, bodyguard or not.

He'd been nearly as bad when they'd talked earlier that day. Trust fund brat? No way. She wasn't an idiot.

He had lied. He was some kind of detective. *He thinks I'm an idiot.*

So he'd saved her life. That didn't mean he got to patronize her. "Listen to me, Ralston."

He folded his arms. "I'm listening."

Every angle of his face said he wasn't, not really, but she charged on anyway. "Last April I met Jack at a design show in New York. It was the launch of a new collection by his friend Jessica Lark."

"Mmm-hmm."

"Lark was a designer. One of the most sought-after by a younger segment of the superrich." Chloe sucked in a breath, frustrated. Sam was looking at her as if she was speaking Martian. "Princess Amelie was one of her best clients."

"So?"

Chloe paused. She had theories. Good ones. "This is the fashion world we're talking here."

"Which means what?"

The man was clueless. There was a good chance the princess would have used Lark for the wedding trousseau. Those designs would have set the tone for the fashion industry for seasons to come. A sneak peek at the sketches would have been worth a fortune—but everything had gone up in flames on *almost* the same date that the wedding had been called off. It was as if the whole Brandi Snap fiasco was a distraction from the truly important event—whatever it was that connected the fire, the diamonds and Jack's murder.

And then there was the dress. If Chloe was right, that was Lark's work. Jack had been in Europe at the right time to pick up the diamonds and then take them to New York to be sewn on to the centerpiece of the wedding collection.

Apprehension crowded in on Chloe. She'd meant to blurt all this out, to share her thoughts freely, but Sam had returned to brick wall status. And he was a bored brick wall. This wasn't her wedding business, where people knew she was the expert. In Sam's world, she was just a girl in need of rescue. That look in his eyes was enough to make her rethink.

Chloe clamped her mouth shut. He might be Action Man, but this went beyond physical rough and tumble. Without meaning to, her eyes went back to that muscular chest. *Rough and tumble, huh?*

He raised an eyebrow, still waiting for her response.

She shrugged. "I thought it was interesting that Jack knew someone in the fashion world who was connected with the princess."

His expression said it wasn't very interesting at all. "Jack knew a lot of skinny women with big bank accounts. They were kind of a hobby of his."

Chloe's hand itched to smack him, except that there was a grain of truth in his words. *Thanks, Jack.* "What about the dress? What if Jessica Lark was the one who designed it, diamonds and all?"

"Someone had to. It might have been her."

Do I have to hand this to you garnished with parsley? "She's dead now."

Sam's eyes flickered as if she'd finally said something worth hearing. Chloe felt a tingle of triumph, but it didn't last. His expression returned to neutral almost at once.

"You can't get mixed up in this," Sam said quietly. "I mean it. You don't understand the danger involved. Go to bed. It's going to be dawn soon enough."

Chloe glanced at the china Bo Peep, wondering if Bo's sheep were half as dense as Sam.

"It's not safe to poke around in a murdered man's affairs." Sam touched her arm lightly. "We haven't caught the intruder yet. We will, but in the meantime I don't want you taking any chances."

She could feel a flush of hot blood creeping up her cheeks. All her life she'd been on a need-to-know basis. Her parents had never talked about their work or the strange people who came and went from the house. Same with Uncle Jack. Now they were all dead, and Chloe was left to figure things out without enough information to go on. And Sam was doing the same thing. Already he was pushing her away, trying to keep her ignorant. "You've got to believe me. I can help you figure this out."

"You can't give anyone reason to think you're still involved." He leaned closer, bringing his lips within inches of her ear. "Think about it. How did the thieves know you had the dress?"

How indeed? Chloe shivered at the thought, but there was an expanse of tight white T-shirt a mere handspan away. It smelled of clean cotton and Sam, and she had a ridiculous urge to wilt against all those hard, warm muscles.

She took a step back, afraid of losing her perspective. They were having a disagreement. Falling into his arms would confuse things. So would admitting that he had a point.

He stepped with her, gracefully mirroring her movement. Chloe felt a finger of unease tickle down her spine. The movement was predatory, a little too smooth, almost catlike. She raised her hand, instinctively pressing her palm against his chest to keep her distance. *What is he doing?*

The distance narrowed without her meaning to let it happen. She looked up, meeting his eyes. In the dim light of the bedside lamp, the gray irises had darkened to black, the pupils disappearing into shadowy pools. He was handsome, the face roughly sculpted with square jaw and high cheekbones, but the mouth—that held a promise of sensuality that made Chloe's chest tighten.

But there was hunger in Sam's gaze that went beyond a man thinking a woman was pretty. Beyond lust or possession or control. It was as if he wanted to devour her.

Chloe's mouth grew thick with yearning mixed with the coppery taste of fear. Sweat prickled the small of her back. She tried to swallow, but her throat wasn't working. Not even her lungs were working right, only pulling in small, shallow gasps of air.

Her fingers began to close on his shirt, gathering up a handful of cotton, fingers sliding over the hard muscle beneath. Her mind flailed, scrambling to make sense of what exactly was going on. He was just standing there, one moment her rescuer, the next…he was something else. For the life of her, she couldn't explain what had changed. It was like he had pulled back a curtain and someone else was looking through his eyes. A man she wasn't sure she could handle. Scratch that. *A man I know is dangerous.*

"Sam," she whispered.

The moment stretched, apprehension chilling her limbs with a strange cocktail of desire and foreboding. Finally, he blinked. The movement, slight as it was, made her start. Sam drew in a breath that was almost a sigh, his chest heaving under her hand.

As quickly as it had come, the moment ended. The shadows seemed to recede to the corners of the room. That electric charge had come and gone without a word spoken, without either of them making a move.

Chloe hesitated, poised between drawing away and drawing near. It was he who stepped back, gently freeing his shirt and leaving her hand hanging in midair. Regret flitted over his face, followed by a flash of…what? Shame? She couldn't place it. Most would never have caught it, but she'd grown up around people with secrets. She knew how to catch these slivers of truth.

She looked away before he noticed her scrutiny.

He was backing toward the door. "Go to bed, Chloe."

"Good night, Sam," she replied, frustrated and relieved when she heard the rattle of the doorknob. Half of her wanted to grab his arm and beg him to stay. But that would be insane. He frightened her.

And yet, she wanted his lips on her, his hands all over her body. That *was* insane. They had the long-term prospects of an ice cream cone in Hades. She wasn't into relationships—however sticky and sweet—that melted away the minute things got hot.

He still hadn't answered. He just hovered in the doorway, his mouth set in a hard line. If she had to guess, she thought he was angry with himself. On some level, he'd slipped. Their eyes met. His were steady, but there were lingering traces of that fierce heat.

"Good night, Chloe." The words were clipped. He turned quickly and slipped out of the room.

She took in a long, shuddering breath. Instinctively, she knew she'd made a lucky escape. She jammed a chair under the knob.

What the hell had he been thinking?

Sam stared at Chloe's door. The corridor was dark, but his enhanced vision made out the grain of the oak. The thick slab of wood would make a racket if he punched his fist through it. Sam growled deep in his chest. Too bad vampires couldn't actually turn to smoke and slip through a keyhole. The base part of his nature wanted back in that bedroom. *Fool.*

He turned away, pacing down the hall and back again, trying to burn off the energy jumping along his nerves.

He'd nearly kissed her. Thank God for that last sliver of self-control. It had been all that kept his beast on a leash. He hadn't fed properly since arriving at Oakwood, relying on the suitcase of bagged blood that was an agent's portable kitchen. It just wasn't the same as the real, live thing. When confronted with Chloe, the combination of hunger and desire gave the world a fuzzy-edged glow, a bit like being drunk. And, like a drunk, he obviously wasn't thinking straight.

He snarled into the darkness. Biting Chloe was the last thing he wanted on his conscience. Heedless, his fangs descended, sharp against his tongue. He wished he'd caught the thief. He would have been enough of a snack to take the edge off.

That last thought burned in his already overheated brain. How by all the dark powers had that thief escaped? The Horsemen never let that happen.

And here Chloe was, digging into the case rather than staying safely away from it. She'd found an interesting connection to Jack's designer friend, but Sam couldn't risk encouraging Chloe in her research. As much as it galled him, the only safe thing to do was shut her down, and as firmly as possible.

He'd seen the hurt in her eyes and hated himself for it.

This ridiculous situation had to end, and that would only happen when the thief was caught. Kenyon might have lost the villain's trail, but Sam hadn't had his turn at playing bloodhound.

He pulled out his cell phone, quickly dialing Kenyon. The connection rang and rang.

"H'lo?" the werewolf grunted when he finally answered.

"Get over here. Guard her," Sam said in a low voice. He didn't bother to identify which "her" he meant. There was only one that mattered.

"Why? Aren't you already there?"

"I'm going outside. I need to know who the intruder was." *I need to put miles between me and her, before I slip from bodyguard to predator.*

"I'm already all over it."

"I need to get out." He couldn't put it any plainer than that. "You know what I mean."

There was a significant pause. "Okay. Get one of Jack's men to babysit."

"I don't trust them like I trust you."

Kenyon grunted with resignation. "I'll be there."

"Now." Sam thumbed off his phone, shoving it back in its belt holster. His shoulders ached from tension, making the movements awkward.

Barely a minute later, an enormous gray wolf came trotting around the corner, tail and ears held high. Kenyon plopped onto his haunches before Sam and lifted his front paws in a classic begging gesture.

Sam stared, huddled in his bad mood. It was hard to keep up in the face of a grinning timber wolf. "Smartass. What happens if someone wanders down the hall? I'm tired of bribing animal control officers."

Kenyon flopped down in front of the door, rolling on his back to expose a hairy belly.

"Whatever." Sam gave up and went outside. Annoying or not, Kenyon would keep Chloe safe.

He'd meant what he said about a leak. Someone in the household had tipped off the thieves about the dress. Finding out the traitor's identity was top of his to-do list.

But, right that minute, he needed a break. He was no more domesticated than Kenyon's wolf. There was a reason he steered clear of jobs that forced him to mix among humans. He was the knife in the dark, the menace lurking on a rooftop. A predator. The only reason he was here was out of respect for Jack.

But somehow, Chloe had touched him. She'd seen a glimpse of the beast tonight and hadn't known enough to run for it. He'd seen her face, his own darkness reflected back at him through the desire in her eyes. She wanted all of him, even if she didn't understand what that meant.

That alone meant he owed her protection. He couldn't articulate why; it was simply a fact. Long ago, when he had been a man, he'd had a wife. He'd adored Amy from childhood, and he kept her memory deep, deep inside where he hid the treasured memories of his human life. But whatever drew him to Chloe was different. It was as primal a response as his hunger for blood.

Sam stood a moment under the night sky, letting the crisp air cool his face. The night smelled of the nearby forest, the scent of pine sharp and clean. Jack's estate covered around two hundred acres, enough room for even a vampire to feel free for a moment.

He set out for the patch of ground beneath the broken window of Chloe's old bedroom, passing a rose garden and a patio set with table and chairs. His gaze swept the ground, hunting the shadows for any sign of the intruder.

He looked up, calculating the distance the intruder had jumped. There was a low roof a story above, then another dozen feet to Chloe's window. A two-part leap to safety—one a trained human could achieve without much trouble. Except this one was wounded. Sam had winged him.

He knelt and examined the grass. This part of the lawn

was well trampled. The security guards, once roused, had given enthusiastic chase. Footprints would be hard to track. Blood, however, would not.

Taking a quick look around, he checked to make sure none of the guards still roaming the grounds were in view. Then he crouched until his nose was mere inches from the lawn. A vampire's sense of smell wasn't as good as a werewolf's, but it was better than that of a werewolf stuck in human form. There had been too many people around during the chase for Kenyon to get hairy. Sam might have better luck picking up the trail. Hopefully it wasn't too late to matter.

There. He caught the scent of blood, memorizing its unique signature. Sam crept forward, following the trace in a diagonal line across the lawn. Now that he knew what he was looking for, the muted glow of lights from the house showed him a particular set of tracks—a medium-sized man wearing soft-soled shoes. Drops of blood dotted the path, keeping the scent strong.

The path led up to a garden wall. It was brick and a good fifteen feet tall. Scuffed dirt at the bottom made it obvious that the intruder had climbed it—no doubt a painful process for a man shot in the shoulder.

Sam took a running step and bounded lightly to the top. He squatted for a moment, scanning the view before dropping to the other side. The wall drew a line between the order of Jack's gardeners and the wild kingdom beyond. Sam landed in a clump of weeds beside a gravel road. Across the road was untamed forest.

He could see where the intruder had stood. Blood had pooled there, but no trail of drops led away. Sam swore. The intruder must have had enough of a head start on his pursuers to risk stopping to bind his wound. Then, he'd splashed whiskey on the ground, drowning what scent there was in a fog of alcohol. Alcohol mixed with something that made Sam's nose numb.

That made Sam's job much, much harder. Was the guy using the smelly substance for disinfectant, or was he expecting tracking dogs? Or did he know there were vampires?

He was willing to bet the latter. Jack's killers had used silver bullets.

Sam walked up and down the road in ever-widening loops, searching for clues. The gravel was hard packed and dry, giving away nothing. Now that he'd left the protected zone of the walled garden, a freshening breeze was sweeping away any lingering scent. Not that Sam could smell much of anything anymore, after encountering that scent bomb the thief had left.

No wonder Kenyon hadn't had any luck. Sam stopped, jamming his hands in his pockets. He was coming up empty, too. *Come on. Everyone makes mistakes. What clue did this guy leave for me to find?*

He had to have escaped somehow. *If I were a villain, which way would I run?* Outside of a few other estates, there was nothing but ocean to the west. Sam followed the road east.

He'd barely gone a quarter mile before he found what he was looking for. A car had been parked by the side of the road—a small compact, judging by the tire treads in the soft shoulder. They weren't deep, and human eyes had missed them. The shadows were dense here at the edge of the forest, so Sam pulled a compact flashlight from his pocket, filtering the bright beam with his fingers and using just enough light to see without wrecking his night vision.

There weren't any obvious clues—no lost buttons or

dropped wallets. Just a few spots of blood that probably fell when he climbed into the car.

Sam narrowed his eyes. If he was reading the tracks right, there were two sets of footprints in the soft dirt. It looked as though the intruder got in the passenger side. Had someone been waiting for him?

Instinct made Sam follow the road about a mile to the first bend. The wind was starting to smell damp with a rain that would wash away any remaining clues once it fell. He was running on pure intuition now, all hunter, the beast in him adding its predatory cunning to his human intelligence.

Just around the bend he found the car. It was nose-first into the ditch, the front bumper crunched against a tree. The passenger door was partially open but jammed into the ground, as if the accident had happened when the door was ajar. Had someone bailed out partway through the crash?

Sam wrinkled his nose. Despite his deadened senses, a new banquet of smells, both revolting and enticing, pulled him toward the scene. He approached cautiously.

The driver was slumped over the wheel, obviously dead. Air bags hung like deflated balloons. Sam felt a wave of cold nausea as he circled toward the windshield, peering through the glass to catch a glimpse of the man's face.

A good deal of the man's head was splattered over the side window glass. The bullet had come from the passenger seat. Sam mentally reconstructed the events. *Bang, pop the door, jump out just before the car swerves into the ditch and smashes the tree.*

Risky, shooting the driver. Then again, he would have been slowing the car for the turn. A cold, calculated chance. Not for beginners.

Sam looked long and hard at the ruined face, finally placing it. One of Jack's security guards. Here, perhaps, was an answer. Gossip traveled through household staff like wildfire. News of the dress, however hard they'd tried to keep it quiet, would have been a particularly juicy tidbit. If this guard was in league with Jack's killers, that would explain how he came to be in this car. It also would explain how the thief got into the house. The question was, who were his contacts?

Sam circled around to the open door, covering his nose and mouth with his sleeve to filter the stench of carnage. Blood was one thing, but there were plenty of substances inside a human body that should definitely stay inside.

Digging his feet into the soft dirt, he pushed the car upright enough to free the passenger door. It was a fruitless effort; the hinges were bent. Bracing the car with his shoulder, he gave the door a solid jerk. It came off in his hands. Sam tossed it into the ditch and let the car settle back into the mud.

Now that he could get inside, he looked for a bullet casing, but found none. Either the shooter had somehow retrieved it or it had flown out of the car during the crash. He searched the glove compartment only to discover the car came from a cheap rental place that specialized in older, practical runabouts. Perfect for getaway cars.

Sam would lay good money the name on the rental papers was fake. Whoever the intruder was, he was an ice-cold professional. He would call Winspear, have him send one of the Company's crime scene experts, but he didn't expect that they'd find much.

Whoever this guy was, he was good.

Sam pulled his head out of the car, sucking in clean, sweet air. His head snapped toward Oakwood, where the lights glinted through the trees. He had found what he could for now. Time to get back. Kenyon was guarding Chloe, but that wasn't enough to stop the tsunami of Sam's protective instincts.

Chloe.

Then, as if on cue, a scream tore the night.

Chapter 7

Vampires moved fast, but at the sound of the scream Sam moved demon-fast, feet barely grazing the ground as he sprinted. The cry had come from the house. No human would have heard it at that distance, but a vampire could—especially one tuned to that particular voice. Within minutes he pushed through the side door of Jack's house.

He skidded to a stop, swearing explosively. The door was unguarded. Sure, the larger part of the security staff was searching the grounds for the thief, but an appropriate number had been assigned to watch the house. Had all of them run off to find the source of the cry? It made no sense. That was a beginner's mistake, and Jack hired only experts. Why would he have idiots watching his back?

He hadn't. This was simple, pure betrayal. Sam growled, remembering the twisted wreck of Jack's car, the attacker in Chloe's bedroom. Who else might be creeping around Oakwood's halls? He cursed again, this time long and low.

Sam bounded up the stairs, feet silent despite his size. He reached the second floor of Jack's house, then the third. As he reached the landing, he froze, listening. *Chloe?* Was that her voice he'd heard? He ghosted forward, eyes searching the shadows for her door. It was shut, but where was Kenyon? *A curse on that flea-ridden mutt!*

After she'd locked Sam out of her bedroom, Chloe had tried to go to sleep. If she'd let herself analyze her thoughts, she would have realized she was too scared to sleep—but she couldn't go there.

If she did, she'd feel like a victim, and she'd felt that too many times before. When her parents died. When she'd been abandoned on what should have been the happiest day of her life—there was a special place in hell for grooms that backed out minutes before it was time to walk down the aisle. No, she wasn't adding this episode to that box of extra-special horrific memories. She flatly refused.

Instead, maybe she'd blame her insomnia on Sam for putting her hormones in overdrive. What girl could sleep after an eyeful of that white T-shirt and all the smoldering manly goodness underneath? And that sculpted mouth... The thought of Sam made her skin feel itchy in that so-good-it-hurt kind of way.

He was just outside, watching over her. He was scary, but he was on her side.

And he was panting. The sound was faint, muffled by the thick door, but in the absolute silence of the middle of the night she heard—something very weird.

What on earth? Chloe sprang off the bed and raced

to the door, pressing her ear to the heavy oak panel. She definitely heard heavy breathing, just outside. A chill crept over her skin as her imagination painted bizarre explanations for the sound. The more bizarre the better, because she was full up on real-life horror.

What on earth could make that noise? Sam gasping his last breath as he was strangled by a giant squid? Zombie Sam slavering at the keyhole, hungry for her brains? *Now I'm never going to sleep. Ever.*

Cautiously, she dragged the chair from under the knob and cracked the door open. She peered into the hallway, but it was too dark to make anything out. This was so weird. No one was watching her door. Irritation niggled around the edges of her fear. Now that she wanted Sam to be lurking outside, where the blazes was he?

"Hello?" she said tentatively, clutching the thick folds of her terry cloth robe around her.

She thought she heard a clicking sound and stared hard at the darkness. There was only one thing that made that sound—animal toenails. Panting plus clicking equaled dog, not squids or zombies. *Boring, but a relief.*

But what dog? Jack had owned many pets over the years, but there were none at Oakwood right now. He'd been gone too much these past few years to look after one. Did the dog belong to the security guys? If so, why hadn't she heard the footsteps of its handler?

Maybe a stray was wandering the halls. After the intruder incident, the security guards were extra-jumpy. If the dog wasn't theirs, they'd probably shoot it on sight. That thought wasn't bearable. She had to be sure the animal was okay.

Chloe quietly thumped her head on the edge of the door. This so wasn't her night.

Silently, not quite sure if she was being bold or stupid,

Chloe crept into the hallway and glided for the staircase landing. She flicked on the light switch, the glow from the row of overhead chandeliers banishing the shadows. She looked down the hall, lit by a pool of light every few yards all the way to the end of the corridor. No one— with two or four feet—was in sight.

In the cold, clear sixty-watt light, Chloe felt tired and a bit ridiculous. She had to be hearing things. Surely, after the attack earlier that night, security had been drawn too tight for a mouse to get through, let alone something big enough to pant like that.

But the guy who jumped you got in. She'd forced the event away from her imagination. Just a tiny bit. Just enough to function. But now the feel of her attacker's hands forcing her into the mattress flooded back to her, and she shuddered violently.

Suddenly, the noise she'd heard seemed far more sinister.

"Sam!" This time she said it with a lot more force. "Sam?"

Silence.

She took a few steps down the hall where she thought she'd heard the clicking toenails. Then she saw it: a gray tail disappearing around the corner. *So there is a dog!* Pulling her robe closer, she hurried after it. It was headed toward one of the big third-floor bathrooms. The good news was, if she managed to herd the dog in there, it should be easy to shut the door and call someone to deal with it.

The bad news was she had left the relative safety of her bedroom behind. Bad guys used animals to lure soft-hearted victims to their doom.

Shivering, she broke into a trot, wanting to get this over with. She was nearly to the spot where she'd seen the tail disappear. The long terry robe tangled around her ankles, making her stumble. Yelping, she caught herself.

An instant later, a huge, gray head poked out from around the corner. Chloe's brain froze for a microsecond, her face going slack with astonishment. *A wolf?*

But there it was, that creature staring at her with huge yellow eyes, red tongue lolling out from between sharp white teeth. Not a nice dog, but a gigantic, wild *thing*. She screamed for all she was worth. But there was hardly anyone left at Oakwood, and no one sleeping on her side of the building.

There was just her and the great yellow-eyed creature, stuck in a staring contest. The wolf looked more wary than ferocious, but she didn't dare take her eyes off it. The moment went on and on, a stalemate neither was willing to break. Finally, desperate to make the thing back off, she kicked off her mule slipper and slowly, slowly, bent down and picked it up. The wolf watched curiously, but didn't budge. Chloe threw it, but her aim was bad. It bounced off the wall, ricocheting in front of the wolf's nose.

That startled the creature into skittering backward, giving her time to dive for the safety of the first open door. It was the bathroom. She barely reached it before the wolf was already behind her, filling the door frame and blocking any hope of retreat.

Ironic, when her first thought was to trap the wandering dog in the very same room. Now the tables were turned. She scrabbled on the counter for something, anything to defend herself and came up with an aerosol can. She wheeled around, holding it in both hands. "Back off!" she warned. Her tone was clear, even if it wouldn't understand the words.

The wolf didn't come any closer, but it didn't budge.

She glanced at the can's label. It was that ghastly hair-spray Aunt Mavis used, the kind that could hold a hairdo through a category three hurricane. She'd heard of women using the stuff like Mace. She aimed the nozzle at the wolf.

"Don't come any closer, or I'll shoot."

It was hard to tell, but the beast looked confused. It tilted its head, ears swiveling in her direction.

"Back off!" she snapped again, waving the can in hopes the wolf would get the message.

By this point, her nerves were brittle enough to shatter. She'd nearly been killed once already tonight! Where were all the security guards who were supposed to rush in and save her? Her relatives? She heard conversation, doors shutting, but no one was storming to her rescue. Where was Sam? He'd promised to guard her, but the moment she'd needed him he had vanished.

The wolf sat down, effectively trapping her. Hot, sweaty panic welled up, leaving her sick and shaking. She was in trouble, but no one was here to help her. Claustrophobia squeezed her chest. She had to get out of this bathroom!

"Go away," she shouted.

The wolf barked, making her jump so hard her feet actually left the floor. Reflexively, she squeezed the nozzle of the can, releasing a hissing cloud of perfumed spray. The wolf staggered backward into the corridor with a ragged whine. The chemical reek of the spray clogged Chloe's throat. She covered her nose with her terry-towel sleeve and blinked hard, but for a blessed moment the doorway was clear.

Instinct kicked in. Chloe bolted for freedom, her bare feet hardly touching the floor.

Then she saw security guards ahead, running toward

her and raising their guns at the wolf. A few of the other guests were peering around corners, too frightened to come to her aid.

"Don't fire!" she yelped, afraid for herself, the bystanders and the wolf. She glanced behind her.

Like a shaggy nightmare, the creature bounded after her, claws scraping and red tongue lolling. Chloe scrambled, running into the door frame in her haste to retreat. Her feet slithered on the hardwood as she tried to turn and shut the door.

The wolf attempted to stop, all four legs going straight. Its nails skidded on the hardwood floor.

Unsuccessfully. Golden eyes going wide with alarm, it bashed into her, the full weight of it colliding with her legs. Her feet flew out from under her and they both went down in a tangle of fur and terry cloth.

The wolf made a pathetic whimper. Chloe sucked in a shallow breath, terrified that if she moved, if she attracted its attention, it would bite. The stink of hairspray pervaded the air, making her want to sneeze. She froze, fighting the fierce tickling in her nose and throat. A sneeze might startle it.

It was a heavy beast, especially draped over her legs. The thick, coarse fur tickled and was disgustingly sticky with spray. Gingerly, she lifted her head a degree, peering down at it. The thing drooped its ears, giving her a wounded look with its great yellow eyes. Its ruff stuck up at odd angles, as if it was going for a fauxhawk.

"Where did you come from, anyway?" she murmured, forgetting herself.

It whined again, resting its chin on her knee, and gave a tentative tail wag. Apparently, it wasn't going to eat her. Maybe it had eaten someone already. Maybe Aunt Mavis.

At that thought, Chloe experienced a moment of mixed emotions.

Now the security guys were crowding around. Sam burst through them, SIG Sauer drawn and searching out the enemy. When he saw Chloe, he lowered the gun, his gray eyes giving her a look that melted her where she lay. She immediately forgave him for being late.

"You cried out." His voice was thick with concern. With a jerk of his chin, he sent the other men away. Obviously used to his command, they went at once, herding the scatter of bystanders back to their rooms.

Magnificent. It was the only word to describe Sam.

"Are you all right?" he demanded.

But unobservant. "I think so?" she replied from underneath the wolf.

Sam snapped his fingers. The creature rose, shaking itself, and gave Sam a dirty look. Chloe felt tingling through her legs as circulation returned. She struggled to sit up. Sam glowered at the beast.

"Is he yours?" she asked.

"Sadly."

The wolf edged toward Chloe, its tail between its legs. Sam narrowed his eyes. Chloe started to rise, but the wolf leaned into her, burying its head against her shoulder.

"Hey." Startled, Chloe carefully scratched the wolf's ears. "You're a good boy, aren't you? Such a big, handsome boy. I'm sorry I sprayed you, but you scared me."

The wolf wagged its tail, and she started to use both hands.

"Heel," Sam growled.

The wolf gave a start at the sound of Sam's voice, raising its head from Chloe's embrace.

"Now."

The wolf slunk to Sam's side.

"Why haven't I seen him before?" Chloe asked.

Sam's eyes flicked to Chloe's, then away. "I've been keeping him in the garden. I don't know how he got into the house."

Chloe heard the lie, but couldn't make sense of any of it. Her brain was too fogged with fatigue. Too preoccupied with the fact that, if the wolf hadn't been tame, she might have ended up chow.

Why had Sam left her alone and why had he just lied to her about having a pet? Big, strong and protective was great, but reliable and honest counted for plenty.

He noticed her frown. "Chloe?"

She shrugged, suddenly feeling a lot less forgiving. "It's dangerous to let your furry friend roam. Something could happen to him."

The wolf licked his fur and made a gagging sound.

"He's a big boy. I've been thinking of sending him to obedience classes." Sam offered her his hand.

Chloe took it, letting him pull her to her feet. "That's all you're going to say?"

"What else is there?"

"I thought you were guarding my door."

"I was doing some investigating. I left someone to take my place, but he wandered off without authorization. We're going to have words. Many words." He glared at the wolf again.

The hallway was empty now except for the three of them. Sam held her by her upper arms, so close that her robe brushed against him. "Chloe, I'm sorry."

She could see the darkness in his eyes again, just as it had been during that strangely charged moment in her bedroom. His look was one of possession, fired now by the adrenaline of the moment. He had come to save her—

from where, she couldn't say. The damp scent of the night clung to him, enticing in its mystery.

At that moment she realized that she'd leaned into him. Something about the man drew her like a magnet. She tilted her face up, staring into his steel-gray eyes. The need she saw there made her pulse kick up a notch, beating hard and thick in her throat. Suddenly the terry cloth robe was too hot, suffocating instead of cozy. She had a mad urge to peel it off, and then the nightshirt she wore under it, too. It was a fleeting, silly notion but it still wound through her thoughts, tempting her to give in to the demand implicit in that possessive look. Chloe tightened her belt, fighting an aching need to respond. Blood flooded to her face, chased there by the boldness of her thoughts.

A quiver passed over Sam's lips, not humor but another more intense emotion she couldn't read. He brushed the back of his fingers over her cheek, letting them linger there, as if testing the heat of her blush. The touch was cool, yet so light it was no more than the kiss of a wing. The stroke continued, curling around her ear, brushing under her jaw to hover over the pulse beneath her ear. She shivered, nipples suddenly aching. She wanted his cool hands on them. She wanted his wet mouth on them. She wanted him inside her.

In a blink, her whole body was aching and slick with need. This was crazy. She barely knew the man. She scrabbled to pick up the threads of their conversation, to make these insane thoughts disappear beneath the surface of adult conversation. What had he been talking about? Oh, yes.

"Well, did your investigation go anywhere?" Her voice was rough and breathy. She cleared her throat.

He gave her a careful look. "Yes."

"What did you find out?"

Sam did his best impression of a blank wall. Chloe sighed.

"I'm protecting you," he said, voice dropping almost to the range of a growl. "Everything I do is to keep you safe."

"If the dress thief is any indication, ignorance is a lot more dangerous." She pulled the robe tighter around her throat.

"I'm not sure about that."

She shrugged, aching, frustrated and tired of playing games. "Oh, forget it. It doesn't matter."

She threw the statement down like a dare.

Sam watched the shrug do lovely things to the sliver of skin showing at the neck of the white robe. She was trying to hide it, but it still showed like an arrow pointing toward more intimate beauties. Her golden hair hung in glistening waves down her back, much longer than it looked pinned up. All that gold and white softness gave her an angelic air, spiced by the strong scent of her desire. Sam's body tightened, transfixed for a moment by her loveliness, by the promise of pleasure. It was so different from his world of missions and weapons and blood.

He ached with wanting her, a sweet, slow pain filled with yearning and regret. Only part of it was a need of the body. His spirit reached for her, too, somehow knowing that she was a woman who would offer solace and strength. Things War shouldn't need.

She was a good person, and that was exactly why he had to walk away. They had no business being in each other's lives.

Then his brain caught up with what she was saying: "It doesn't matter." The look in her eyes said clearly it did.

But what could he say? That he'd found a dead body? Chloe didn't need one more thing to keep her awake tonight, and knowing the security guards had been compromised wouldn't help one bit. That kind of news could wait until morning.

The moment dragged by like a physical ache. Sam struggled, his instinct to take her then and there warring with the knowledge that whatever might pass between them would end badly. Human women were so sadly vulnerable. He could protect, but he could never *have*.

Then the moment faded, falling in on itself when the moment of burgeoning desire was ignored. Chloe's face grew set, the corners of her mouth pulling down. Sam felt his neck prickle, instincts responding to her darkening mood.

"Where did your pet go?" she asked, a little too crisply. "What's his name, anyway?"

Pet? Scrambling for a reply, Sam looked over to where Kenyon had been sitting. There was nothing left but a few dog hairs.

Sam cleared his throat. "Fido's shy of people. Some wolf blood, you know."

Her expression said she didn't believe any of that. "He's a marshmallow. I can't believe you didn't mention him before this. Why keep him a secret?"

Sam grunted, knowing he was going to lose if he kept talking. He was the guy who hit things, not the one who provided plausible deniability for werewolves. And something about that fluffy robe was shredding his thought processes. "I've got to go catch him."

"Yeah, there are too many gun-happy guards around." She blinked, her eyes shadowed with fatigue.

"Are you going to get any sleep tonight?"

"I keep trying."

Sam would have liked to personally tuck her in. Maybe she'd stay put this time. Maybe he'd stay there to make sure she stayed put. Yeah, what was that saying about foxes and henhouses?

He had a wolf to catch. "Good night, Chloe."

Her lips curved in a tired smile. "Good night, Sam."

He opened his mouth to keep talking, but she turned away before he could think of anything else to say. *Just as well.* He wanted a few seconds more, but then it would be a few seconds after that, and so on until sunrise.

She turned back, her expression oddly naked. "Are you going to guard my door?"

"Absolutely. Personally."

Her head drooped, not quite a nod. "Thank you."

To his regret and relief, she closed the bedroom door, and the moment passed.

Sam slowly turned to see Kenyon's human shape lurking in the shadows. He'd pulled on sweatpants and a hoodie.

Sam stalked over to him. "What happened?"

Kenyon snorted with disgust. "I heard Chloe moving around and tried to get out of sight before she opened the door. But she saw me. Then she chased me."

Despite himself, Sam chuckled. "*She* chased *you?*"

Kenyon gave a lopsided smile. "What's the point of being a monster unless you can have fun with it?"

Good question. He wouldn't have minded a show of feminine gratitude. After all, the vampires on TV got the beautiful blondes. Not that Sam watched, of course. He yanked his mind back to business. "We've got to call Winspear."

Kenyon ran a hand through his hair, wincing as his fingers caught in clumps of hairspray. "He won't have done the autopsy yet."

Sam recoiled from the image of Jack lying on a cold metal table. That was just so wrong. "Then the doctor had better get busy because I have another customer. I found the thief's getaway car, plus the driver. He was one of the security guards, shot in the head."

Kenyon's eyes widened. "Where? I lost the trail at the edge of the garden."

"A mile up the east road, just around the bend."

"Huh." Kenyon leaned against the wall, his chin sunk on his chest. "I wonder where they were headed?"

"Somewhere to regroup. They didn't get what they wanted, so they'll be back."

"Oh, goody. I can't wait," Kenyon said dryly.

"We'll do some recon. They've got to be hiding out somewhere nearby." The words had no sooner left his mouth than he remembered Chloe. He'd promised to guard her door.

Kenyon caught his look. "You're needed here."

"But nothing will change until we catch the thieves."

For once, the werewolf grew serious. "We have to find them first, and it's getting close to dawn. I'm your daylight operative, and you know I'm the best when it comes to this kind of detail work. Let me do my job."

It was true. When he put his mind to it, Kenyon could be relentless and methodical. It was one of the things that had made him an excellent jewel thief. "Fine. Report back the moment you find something."

"And when I hit pay dirt?"

Sam gave a grim smile. "Then we'll unleash Armageddon."

"Now we're talking. I'll bring the beer." Kenyon turned as if to go, but then paused. "She likes you, you know."

"Who?"

"Chloe. The way she looks at you. The way she smells around you."

"She doesn't know me. I'm just a hired gun."

"Uh-huh." Kenyon folded his arms, smirking in that irritating way he had. "Just one thing."

"What?"

"I don't remember her writing you a check, so you're not a hired gun. You're here for other reasons. That changes the game."

With that, Kenyon strode down the hall, giving a cheeky backward wave.

Chapter 8

By noon the next day, coffee had moved from beverage to plasma status. Chloe set the delicately fluted china cup on its saucer and rested her head in her hand. She'd drawn the curtains in Uncle Jack's study so that it was still bright but not obscenely sunny. Green-tinted light filtered through the clematis vines circling the window, the shadows of the leaves fluttering on the pale carpet. Like all the rooms in Jack's house, the study was beautifully decorated, the ceiling high, the furnishings classic and tasteful. The orderly atmosphere was soothing as a balm.

She sat at the fruitwood desk, her laptop open in front of her. Across the room, a portrait of a young man in eighteenth-century military uniform stared back at her with a wistful expression, as if he wanted some of the coffee, too.

She'd arisen two more times last night, peeking outside the door to see if Sam was guarding her door as promised. Although she wanted to believe his word—one couldn't be a wedding planner without an essentially optimistic view of human nature—experience had taught her to be cautious.

Both times he'd been there and patiently sent her back to bed. Nevertheless, it had been growing light when her stomach had uncoiled enough for her to relax and fall asleep. She worked in a pressure-filled industry where a lot could go sideways at any moment, but on top of Jack's mysterious death, the past twenty-four hours had blown her limit for excitement.

It might have also blown her grip on reality. The gardeners had given her blank stares when she'd asked about the wolf Sam Ralston had kept tied up on the grounds. None of the staff had seen so much as a stray Pekinese. She had been sure Sam was lying about his pet, but now she didn't know where truth ended and fantasy began. *Did I make the whole thing up?*

It wasn't a good feeling. In fact, she was feeling very insecure about a long list of things, from the unlikely crash of the Porsche to the wolf to that blasted dress and a bunch of stuff in between—including Sam Ralston.

She opened the desk drawer at the top of the right-hand pedestal of the desk. She felt around, past a stamp box, a squiggly pile of rubber bands and a stapler. At the very back of the drawer was Jack's SIG Sauer. Chloe pulled it forward and lifted it out of the drawer, the cold metal heavy in her hand. Besides sending her to a dojo, Jack had made her learn to shoot. Despite her protests—she was interested in the drama club, not target practice—he was fanatical about making sure she could defend herself. He'd never really say why, any more than he'd say why he kept a gun in his desk drawer when he had full-time security in the house.

She'd assumed he kept the gun around because he

was afraid of robbery. Now that he was murdered, she wondered if that were true. After all, no one had tried to take anything but the dress. Something else had caught up with him.

That thought turned her stomach into a cold, hard knot. Carefully, she determined the gun was clean. She hated violence, hated guns, and hated the fact she knew how to use them. That didn't mean she wouldn't defend herself.

There was a box of ammunition, too. She set the gun at the front of the drawer, but left it unloaded and pushed the drawer shut. She wasn't prepared to go full-on paranoid just yet, but she felt better knowing the gun was there and ready for action.

Turning to her computer, she clicked on her calendar to see what the next few days held—thieves, murderers and midnight wolves notwithstanding.

With a sense of surreal horror, she saw an appointment for one o'clock that afternoon. The Fallon-Venuto wedding. She was supposed to meet her clients in the nearby town of Thurston. Chloe squeezed her eyes shut, hoping that would make the bright yellow square of responsibility disappear.

Blast it. She'd booked the appointment before Jack's tragedy and must have missed it when she was clearing her calendar to attend the funeral. She hadn't been able to focus right then.

If she had, she'd have remembered that the bride's beastly mother moved in the same elite social circle as Jack. If Momzilla had had her way, young Elaine Fallon would have been walking down the aisle to become Mrs. Jack and, more important, the new mistress of Oakwood Manor and all of Jack's lovely bank accounts.

Quiet Elaine had dug in her heels and become engaged

to her childhood sweetheart, Leo Venuto. Always on the lookout for a good business deal, Jack had charmed Mrs. Fallon into hiring Chloe to design the Fallon-Venuto wedding. It was happy endings galore until the woman had suggested gilding the hooves of the white palfrey Elaine would ride down the aisle.

Elaine had hated the idea. Her mother hadn't cared. Chloe had been caught in the middle—and this had set the pattern for everything that followed.

Mrs. Fallon was the last thing Chloe needed in the aftermath of Jack's death. True, the show had to go on, but it could go on later, like when no one was trying to kill her.

The only reasonable thing to do was to put the appointment off. After checking her notes, Chloe picked up the handset of the massive old rotary telephone on Jack's desk and dialed Elaine's office number. The woman was a mathematics professor at the university and spent a lot of time in the classroom. Luckily, this time she answered on the third ring.

"Hello, Elaine, this is Chloe Anderson. How are you?"

"Chloe!" The woman's soft voice filled with concern. "I was so sorry to hear about your uncle. How are you doing?"

"One day at a time," Chloe answered, concentrating on keeping her voice even. "It was quite a shock."

"I'm sure it was." Elaine fell silent for a long moment. "Um. Listen. I was going to leave this alone, but now that you've called, my mother was bugging me to email the guest list despite everything that's going on with, well, the funeral and everything. I'm really sorry about bothering you right now."

"Don't worry about it. I'm glad you did. It's nice to be talking about a happy event." Chloe quickly toggled to her in-box and quickly scanned her list of unread messages. Elaine's was there. It had arrived about the same time she'd been opening Jack's safe.

"I'm looking at it right now." She double-clicked the attachment. "Oh, wow, six hundred for the reception."

And what a list it was—a who's who of the private jet set. Chloe's lips parted in awe as she read. The bride's family were old money—the kind of folks who endowed everything from animal shelters to public television. Between them, they owned a chunk of every major city on the continent.

The idea that this slice of the social pie would be at a Chloe's Occasions event—it made her palms sweat with excitement and apprehension. If everything went right, her fledgling business could be picking up referrals for years to come. Her company would have arrived at the big time. Who cared if the bride's mother wanted a gold-hoofed horse?

She tuned back in on Elaine's voice. The young woman sounded even more apologetic. "It was about half of what Mom wanted, but we're trying to be realistic, given the timelines. Oh, I think I forgot to mention in the email that we've finally picked a date."

"That's great to hear. Is it next June?"

She could almost hear Elaine cringe. "In two months. September 15. I'm sorry, didn't your assistant tell you?"

"That's ridiculous." The words were out of her mouth before she could stop herself. *Oh, crumb.*

"Pardon me?"

"I'm sorry, Elaine, but a wedding like yours…" She stopped herself, letting the wave of panic slide through her stomach and out the other side. "I'm sorry if that sounded abrupt, but an event like yours takes a great deal of planning. Two months isn't much time. I haven't even sat down with you and Leo. I've just been dealing with Mrs. Fallon."

"I know. And I'm so grateful that you found a source for those rare orchids she wants for the centerpieces."

"That's just it. I know what she wants, but what do *you* want at your wedding?"

She laughed at that. "I'm the easy part. I just want Leo. He just wants the wedding to be over. But you and I are scheduled to meet, just the two of us. In a few hours, in fact. Or, um, that's what we were planning until things happened."

"But…" Chloe had been calling to put the meeting off. Clearly Elaine would understand if she cancelled.

"But?"

Two months. Now there wasn't time to put Elaine off, and keeping the meeting made sense when she was here, in Wingman County, right now. "I think we should get together anyway."

"Are you sure?"

"Absolutely." She always met privately with her brides, sometimes traveling around the globe to do it. That one-on-one time was the best way to learn a client's true desires. Chloe's Occasions always gave the bride what she really wanted—and they seldom revealed it over the phone.

"I really appreciate this. You see, it's my grandmother," Elaine said softly. "She hasn't got long and she wants to be at the wedding. It forced us to pick something sooner than we would have liked, but making sure Grandma has a front row seat trumps trying to invite everyone that my parents think ought to be included."

Chloe rubbed her forehead. "I understand. There's no problem. I'll arrange an office in town where we can sit down and have a good talk. I'll text you the address."

"Sounds great. Thanks so much, Chloe. See you then."

The call disconnected. Chloe slumped in the desk chair.

They didn't even have a hall booked. A headache clamped her skull. She didn't need this kind of stress. Not now, with wolves and diamonds and thieves in the night to worry about.

"Chloe."

Sam chose that moment to stride into the room, circling close to the bookcases until he reached the windows. He unhooked the heavy velvet curtain from the brass hook that held it in an artful drape. The fabric fell, blocking out every scrap of sun.

Annoyance did a dance with relief. The darkness was kinder to Chloe's aching head, but now she couldn't see properly. She cleared her throat and flicked on the desk lamp, angling the shade to the wall. "Allergic to sunlight?"

"I need more sleep." He looked pale, dark stubble gracing his jaw. The morning-after look suited him. Mind you, he could have dressed as one of Santa's elves and still looked good.

"Coffee?" Chloe waved at the silver service the housekeeper had brought in response to her request for a simple cup of java.

Sam shook his head. "Not unless it's decaf."

"Sorry, it's fully loaded. I needed the jolt after last night." She studied him, enjoying the view for a moment. "How's your wolf?"

"I sent him home."

And where is home? Chloe had a fleeting image of a wolf getting on a Greyhound bus, backpack clenched in its fangs, but let the subject drop. She had enough to worry about.

"I want you to go home, too," he said. "It would be safer."

"I can look after myself." After all, she'd found the gun. She could shoot.

"Against trained hit men?"

Maybe not. "I thought these were thieves."

"I doubt that's all they are."

Chloe crossed her legs and watched him watch her do it. There was definitely a spark of interest between them. She wondered what would happen if she blew on it oh so gently.

Surprised by the bold thought, she pulled the hem of her skirt down. "I'm staying until the guests are gone."

"Your guests have left."

That was true. Half had departed before breakfast, the rest around midmorning. "I guess your pet scared them off."

The corners of Sam's mouth twitched. "Perhaps."

"Wolves rock."

"So, if there are no guests, how come you're not packing?"

She'd felt lighter for a moment, but reality crashed back in. "I have to sell this place, remember? I still have the Realtor to deal with. He called this morning and we're booked for next week. I wanted something sooner, but it's hard to get someone capable of representing a property like this. This guy has contacts in the right circles."

Sam glanced around the room. "Too bad you can't keep Oakwood."

Chloe swallowed hard. "I lived here all through high school. But, even if I could afford the upkeep, I have to divide the estate."

He swore softly. "I wish there was some other way."

"Me, too."

"You shouldn't have to deal with this." His voice was gentle. "Why don't you go home? I'm co-executor. I can deal with the Realtor."

For a moment, she nearly agreed, but she knew better than to believe it when someone said they'd be there for her. That's how a girl got left at the altar. "I don't—"

He held up a silencing hand. "I need to stay here anyway to arrange for the dress to be returned to Marcari. It's too valuable to pop in a box and take down to the FedEx office."

"Wait a minute." Chloe uncrossed her legs, leaning forward across the desk. "You know who to call? You've got the head of the kingdom's security on your speed dial?"

"I have his number, yes."

"Well, I'd already figured out that you know more than your average royalty watcher, but wow." A smidgen of sarcasm crept into her words. "You might have mentioned this last night. Are you, say, on the trail of the diamonds? A special agent on crown-jewels detail?"

"No, not that." He looked down, not quite abashed but clearly caught wrong-footed. "Actually, Jack worked with me on some security issues. That's my line of work. I didn't know the diamonds were here any more than you did."

She heard the ring of truth. Maybe not the whole truth, but it was progress. Her gaze lingered on Sam's face, the hard angles and strong bones. He looked like an operative of some kind. Stern. Commanding. Bossy. That wasn't always easy to be around. Would Sam be any different?

She picked up a pen, turning it over and over in her fingers. "So, once you call, what then? Does the head of the royal guard show up with a garment bag?"

That shadow of a smile was more pronounced this

time. "More or less. Him and a small army of men in black."

"For one dress."

Sam's gray eyes met hers. She caught a glimpse of the predator she'd seen last night. Her skin prickled, as if she were a fraction too close to a fire.

"For the diamonds," he corrected her. "And it's not just jewel thieves they're worried about. There's more than money at stake. There are their old enemies, the Vidonese, to consider. If they're involved, the game is for blood and honor, as well."

Chloe leaned back in the leather desk chair, no longer tired. "So how come the two countries both think the diamonds belong to them?"

Sam paced to the window, staying in the shadows but gazing out through a chink in the curtains. The gesture reminded her of a dog pining to go outside. "It's a long story, and I don't know all of it."

"Then tell me what you do know."

"You're changing the subject."

"I love stories."

"This one doesn't have an end."

"The best ones don't."

He didn't reply, but kept looking out the window, his back to her.

Chloe watched the set of his shoulders. He was tense, maybe even angry, but she wasn't going to give in and go home like an obedient dog. Or wolf. "I suppose it starts something like 'A long time ago, in a galaxy far, far away…'"

She heard a low reluctant chuckle, and then he began. "A long, long time ago, just after the fall of Rome, the Kingdoms of Vidon and Marcari were one."

Chloe visualized the map of the Mediterranean. The

two tiny kingdoms sat next to each other on the north edge of the sea. "Okay."

"During the time of the Crusades, the land was divided equally between two warring brothers."

Sam turned from the window, blinking as if that tiny amount of sunlight had hurt his eyes. Chloe waited while he sank into the chair opposite the desk, stretching out his long legs. For a moment, he looked lost in thought, his big, strong body in perfect repose. "The eldest brother, Vidon, pursued dreams of wealth and military conquest. Marcari, the younger, followed the path of books and knowledge. Both were power-hungry and a fierce rivalry grew between them."

He sat forward, and Chloe was caught for a moment by his intense gray gaze. It was hypnotic, almost invasive. Her mouth went dry, a sweet ache starting low in her belly. His very presence made her feel as if she were dissolving into a puddle of need, and she couldn't begin to explain why. It wasn't any one thing he did. It was just…Sam. Gorgeous and utterly wrong for her.

He was looking at her as if she were the last chocolate brownie on the planet.

He leaned forward another degree. She struggled to take in what he was saying, and then struggled again to make sense of it. "Then their youngest brother returned from the Holy Land with a great fortune in gems, thinking to share it with his brothers, for his heart was more generous by far. Tempted by the beautiful stones, the kings of Vidon and Marcari each separately schemed to cheat his siblings of the glittering prize. Unexpectedly— or perhaps not—the youngest brother was assassinated as he slept. Though the true killer was never discovered, Vidon and Marcari quickly accused one another. At once a huge battle raged between them, and the kingdoms have been at war ever since. The Kingdoms of Vidon and Marcari have fought so long that some factions cannot accept the possibility of peace. Their pride forbids it. The Knights of Vidon have made it clear that they will not permit a union between the two kingdoms."

Forcing herself to look away, Chloe poured more coffee out of the pot. She didn't want it, but she had to break the spell he had over her. Her heart was beating fast, her hands slippery with perspiration. "You mean a marriage. The war would have ended with the wedding."

Sam smiled, just a faint curl of the lower lip. She would have bet good money he was aware of the effect he'd just had on her. "The wedding. Yes, peace was the plan. Finally, the wealth would have been shared as was the intention of the youngest brother, Armand Silverhand, almost a thousand years ago. Keep in mind the diamonds form only a small part of the treasure."

That made Chloe blink. "Really?"

"There are far more valuable pieces in the collection— which Marcari has in its treasury, by the way. They beat Vidon in that first terrible fight for possession of the jewels."

"More valuable than what's on that dress?"

"Absolutely. Emeralds, rubies, topazes, moonstones. All specimens of the first quality, all of exceptional size and beauty. I don't know what battles Silverhand fought during the Crusades, but I have a feeling he hit a treasury somewhere along the route."

"And people are still robbing to capture the same prize." For a second, she could feel her attacker's breath on her neck, and she shivered.

Sam saw it. "Which is why I'd rather you were miles away from that dress."

Chloe shook her head.

He frowned at that. "What's so important that you're willing to risk your safety?"

"I have a business to run, for starters. I'm not blowing off a client like this one."

Exasperation brought a hint of color to his cheekbones. "Fine."

"Right. And on top of that, this is my uncle Jack's estate, which I'm responsible—"

"Half-responsible."

"Okay, half-responsible for. Furthermore, your case is about a wedding, which is my professional area of interest. I could be of help. And, on top of all that, I was the one who was attacked last night. This is my inheritance they're after. I know you don't want me involved, but I already am."

She paused for breath, watching Sam's face. He'd gone into brick-wall mode. Irritation threw cold water on her hormones. She swore under her breath. If she didn't stand her ground, he would steamroll right over her. The next words came out in soft, precise syllables. "Being rescued is very much appreciated, believe me. I would have died last night but for you. However, I'm intelligent, not reckless. I don't need to go down the basement stairs to confront the monster. If kept informed, I can take reasonable precautions."

Sam's eyebrows lifted. His expression said he was letting her win. "Very well, but I have rules."

"Good for you. Your rules are not mine."

"They are now."

They locked gazes, neither giving an inch. Chloe could sense his impatience, but she wasn't backing down. If she did, she would disappear from view, another problem tagged, bagged and forgotten.

Perversely, as much as she wanted to prove she could

look after herself, she wanted very much to remain Sam Ralston's problem. Was that what was making her so stubborn?

"What?" she finally snapped. "What are your rules?"

"You don't go anywhere without a bodyguard. That's me, Winspear or Kenyon."

"You can't enforce that."

"I found one of the security guards shot dead last night."

Chloe felt her breath stick like a barb in her throat. "Who?"

"A guy named Will Tyler. Did you know him?"

Chloe shook her head. "Just the name and face. He was new."

"It looks like he was the getaway driver."

Not sure what to say, Chloe picked up her coffee, staring into the cup. It was bad enough that someone had attacked her. Now a man was *dead*. An awful numbness crept up her body. *Am I really so tough? Should I just leave?*

"Chloe?" Sam prompted.

She cleared her throat, fighting back a prick of tears. "I can't believe Jack's staff would turn against him. Or me. He treated them like family."

"The diamonds represent a lot of money. He could have been a plant, Chloe." He shrugged, just a slight lift of the shoulder. "Plus, there are all the political implications of the royal marriage. Not everyone wants peace."

She swallowed hard. "That's crazy."

"That's why you don't set foot out the door without one of us. I'm not joking. From now on, I'm your shadow."

Perhaps she'd hit her limit for dread, or maybe it was the lack of sleep, but his statement struck her as funny.

She gave a short laugh. "Is that why you always avoid the sun?"

He looked at her sharply. "What do you mean?"

"Aren't shadows made of darkness?"

His smile was wry, but there was something softer in it, too. "Darkness still needs light to define us."

Us? Chloe wondered, but her thoughts scattered as Sam put his hand over hers, his thumb caressing her wrist. The cool, steady touch swept logic aside and, along with that, all her defenses. She let herself ride the swell of feeling. *My shadow. The darkness that is always with me.* That would always be touching her, because that was the way nature had made it.

Then he lifted her hand, as he had done last night, and brushed his lips against her fingers. Chloe's heart stuttered, a flame in a new and unfamiliar breeze.

He hadn't simply told her a fairy tale of gems and kings of old. He'd walked straight out of one.

Chapter 9

Later that afternoon, Chloe's fairy tale mood crumbled to despair.

I'll never sell happily ever after. Not here. Not unless someone is marrying their gun.

She'd never been to Jack's offices in town. They didn't resemble his house in the least. The sign on the door of the top floor suite said Gravesend Security. The decor was all hard steel edges and industrial grays. The pictures on the waiting room walls were hung with artful portraits of motorized vehicles designed to vaporize small towns. If Chloe's business represented Venus, this was definitely Mars's clubhouse.

Chloe knew where she could rent a perfectly nice meeting room just blocks away, but the large windows and street level entrance hadn't met Sam's security requirements. Instead, he'd insisted they come here, where the offices occupied the top floor. It made sense, he'd said, because the admin offices of Gravesend would be empty on the weekend and he had to pick up some files there anyway. He could combine business with the infinite pleasure of being her bodyguard. After a brief protest, and possibly because of that kiss to her fingertips, she'd given in.

To find herself in the least romantic office space on the planet. Just to make matters worse, Sam had dressed in head-to-toe black Grim Reaper chic. With pitch-black sunglasses. Indoors. *He looks like a GQ undertaker.* Handsome as sin, but he didn't fit with the happy, friendly Chloe's Occasions image.

As soon as they'd reached the suite of offices, Sam had prowled from room to room, checking for intruders. Any that did venture into Gravesend would have had to be brave with so much testosterone oozing from the walls.

"It's clear," Sam announced, relaxing an infinitesimal degree.

"Great," Chloe replied, taking her armload of bridal magazines to the small conference room and dumping them on the table. Sam followed with her briefcase, setting it down while she sighed at the bland walls. "I wish I'd thought to bring some flowers."

Sam whipped out his cell, hitting a speed-dial number.

"Who are you calling?"

Sam gave a brisk smile. "This whole building is Gravesend Security. There are people in the operations center monitoring surveillance equipment. There's always a gofer for coffee runs, things like that."

His focus shifted to a voice on the phone. "Hello, Ralston here. We need flowers on twelve." He looked up from his call. "Type and quantity?"

Chloe waved her hands in the air. "Mix bouquet about so big? In a vase?"

"Mixed bouquet. Container. Floral estimate forty-five centimeters across. Stat. Clients are incoming at fifteen hundred hours." He thumbed off the phone, looking pleased with himself.

"Thank you," she replied, struggling to wrap her mind around the conversation. Who said "stat" when ordering a bouquet?

She fanned the magazines on the table, made coffee and tried to soften the look of the place as best she could. There weren't any knickknacks around and, while opening the blinds would have made the place brighter, Sam probably wouldn't have liked it. For all her efforts, the place still had as much personality as the inside of a metal filing cabinet.

Elaine Fallon arrived ten minutes early. Despite her monied background, she was simply dressed in slacks and a sweater, her soft brown hair pulled back in a messy ponytail. She looked every inch the overworked professor, down to the courier bag stuffed with what looked like exam booklets waiting to be marked.

"Do you mind?" Elaine asked, pulling out a plastic container of salad and a fork. "It's the only chance I'm going to get for lunch."

"Not at all." Chloe had the feeling the woman was so busy she lived by a rigorously planned schedule.

"Thanks. So where do you want to start?"

"Have you decided on where you're going for your honeymoon? Last time we talked, that was still up in the air." That choice often gave Chloe a good clue to what they considered fun. That was an excellent building block of information to work from.

"Cancún," she replied between bites of spinach. "There's a Fibonacci Group conference on integers right around that time. I'm presenting the keynote."

A math conference? On her honeymoon? "And Leo?"

"He likes the beach." Elaine smiled, and there was a hint of mischief there. "We'll lie in the sun and pretend we're not going home ever again. After so many years in school and then working toward a tenured position, I'm not sure I remember what sun looks like."

Chloe heard Sam stir and realized he was standing by the door. "Lying on the beach sounds fabulous."

"I'm overdue. Leo is, too. He's put in a lot of eighty-hour weeks lately." Elaine looked around at the putty-colored walls. "So this place is some kind of military thing?"

"No, it was my uncle's private security firm." Chloe smiled apologetically. "I borrowed the space for today. The atmosphere is a bit more severe than my own offices."

Elaine's eyes softened at the mention of Jack. "It really was good of you to meet with me today given everything going on in your life."

"Thank you, but it's okay. As I said, weddings are something to look forward to. This will cheer me up."

"As long as you're sure." Elaine murmured, her gaze lingering apprehensively on Sam. He was standing with his arms folded, a perfectly neutral expression around the black lenses of his shades. He looked like a man in need of a martini—shaken, not stirred—or a kneecap to break. "Does he come with the place?"

"Sam, uh, provides advice on security arrangements for my wedding guests," Chloe improvised. "You know, when there are celebrities."

"Really?" Elaine raised an eyebrow. "Pity the paparazzi."

"Never," Sam said in a voice like the slamming of a tomb door.

It was only one word, but it left a chill on Chloe's skin. Elaine paled and set down her salad, still half uneaten.

Chloe seized the moment and began fanning out brochures. "Now, we have your guest list, which is great. Then, whether we're talking indoor or outdoor venues…"

They spent the next fifteen minutes going through the pros and cons of half a dozen sites. She'd found the places with an opening on the right date and put the trendiest sites at the top of the pile.

"I love the look of Philip's," Elaine said, folding out the brochure for the oceanfront dance club. More bohemian than most of the places Chloe had queried, it had an "it" factor that put it in very high demand. "Can't you see the reception here? There's a huge dance floor, and look at the views."

Chloe heard a note of longing that said Elaine was far gone in her fantasy, even before they'd visited the place. "It has a more relaxed atmosphere than many venues of its size."

"I know. I'm sure my mom will hate it."

"She has more traditional tastes."

"I know." Elaine made a face. "It's all white linen and tiaras. No way she'd go for, say, a theme park or waterslides."

Chloe caught the remark. *Waterslides.* This was the sort of information she'd been waiting for. As usual, it was hiding in an offhand remark. "Do you like water sports?"

Elaine smiled ruefully. "I want to have fun. I don't mind the whole princess bridal fantasy thing Mom's after, but I wish we could have foam rubber swords and a toy dragon to go with it. Maybe soaker guns. I think hard enough at work. A wedding should be a party."

"Why not go for it?" Chloe said.

Elaine shrugged. "There's my mom and six hundred of her nearest and dearest to consider."

She picked up a brochure for the golf club. "If I'm honest with myself, this is way more boring but much more appropriate. It's bigger and the parking would be better. And look, there are luxury guest suites right on-site."

Chloe could see the struggle between "want" and "should" in Elaine's eyes. It was her job to find a way her bride could have the best of both. "But…"

"Both Philip's and the club are outdoor venues. I would advise an indoor function," Sam put in, his voice still the monotone he seemed to use when in his bodyguard persona. "But, if you must be outside, the golf club is superior."

Chloe was startled. *Since when are you the wedding expert?* "What makes you say that?"

Sam turned in Elaine's direction, inscrutable behind his sunglasses. "I assume most of those on the guest list could be considered affluent?"

"Yes." Elaine's brow furrowed. "Some are highly placed executives with international corporations. Mom thought the club would be good because many of them play golf."

"It is also less exposed to the public. Philip's wine bar reception area backs onto the esplanade. Although the event would be roped off, it is hard to limit access to the public and, with them, pickpockets, unauthorized photographers and drive-by gunmen."

"Drive-by gunmen!" Elaine exclaimed, her eyes round and huge. "What are you talking about?"

Chloe sensed her client growing increasingly tense. She touched Elaine's arm gently. "It's just a worst-case scenario."

"I don't do worst-case," Elaine said sharply. "I do

mathematics, the more abstract the better. Nobody is going to shoot anybody at my wedding, okay?"

"Of course not." Chloe couldn't resist aiming a furious look at her soon-to-be-ex bodyguard. "Why don't we talk about the church for a while? There are *no security risks* in the church."

Sam opened his mouth, but must have caught her eye. He closed it again.

"My grandmother is going to be there, you know." Elaine was staring at Sam again with the look of a cornered rabbit. Chloe could almost see her nose twitching with anxiety. *This is a freaking disaster.*

"We'll take every precaution," Sam said helpfully.

Great. Now even Chloe was imagining mobster-movie massacres.

The door flew open, making everyone except Sam jump.

A man in a security uniform thrust a vase of flowers at Sam. The man gave a smart salute, wheeled and made his exit, pulling the door shut as he left.

An awkward silence hung in the room. Sam neatly positioned the vase on the conference table and retreated to his patch of wall. For a moment it was so quiet that Chloe could almost hear the dust settling on the industrial gray carpet.

Chloe studied the flowers, trying to understand exactly why no one was talking. The lovely bouquet of roses and baby's breath looked utterly out of place. It underscored how completely she'd wandered into the wrong world—Sam's world, where putty-gray walls were normal and of course you considered whether people could drive by and murder your guests. You'd be an inconsiderate host if you skipped that little detail.

No, this wasn't the safe, sunny fairyland Chloe conjured for her brides. She wasn't mistress of this realm. Her wedding fantasy magic wasn't effective here at all, and her client could feel it. Elaine looked, well, appalled. *Bridal fail.*

She cleared her throat and looked at her watch. "Uh, Chloe, I'm afraid I've got a class to teach. I have to go."

She heard the lie in Elaine's voice and couldn't even blame her. "I completely understand. Why don't I call you later to go over a few details? We are very, very short of time."

The woman nodded quickly, gathered her things and nearly bolted from the room. Sam let her out, locking the door after she left. Finally, in the windowless waiting room, he pulled off his shades. Chloe watched him, catching what might have been a disappointed sigh.

"She's not coming back, is she?"

"I don't know," she said bluntly, giving vent to a tiny burst of anger. It was a mere puff of smoke from the volcano she could feel brewing underneath. "I always address security issues, but I'm very careful how I handle it. Brides are typically stressed, always imagining the worst things are going to happen. In fact, they're usually a little bit crazy. I have to make them relax and believe their day will be happy and perfect."

His face tightened. "I shouldn't have said anything."

You should have listened to me. You should have let me use the nice offices. But…what could she do now? Water under the bridge.

A raging torrent sweeping my career under the waves and about to knock over said bridge. Chloe took a long breath, fighting for her poise. *Surely I can fix this. They've only got two months. They need me.*

Or I could just grab one of these weapons out of

Uncle Jack's display cases and thump Sam over the head with it!

The slight slump of Sam's shoulders said more about his distress than a litany of excuses. He rubbed his forehead. "I'm very sorry. I'm not good with the hearts and flowers. It's just not in me. To be honest, I'm a monster."

Chloe caught her breath, recognizing the raw honesty beneath the words. *Wow. That's how he sees himself. A monster.* "No, you're not."

Most people passed her over without ever sharing that much truth. Few guys had the honesty to face their own shortcomings. Maybe there was more to him than she had assumed.

He quirked a quizzical eyebrow. "You're going to argue about this?"

For a moment, she actually felt sorry for him. "Monsters don't care. You got the flowers. You found a safe place. You listened to what Elaine was planning and gave her the benefit of your experience. I can tell that you care."

Regret flickered through his eyes, followed by a deeper sadness. There was more here than Elaine and an ugly office. The whole monster comment resonated far beyond today's problems. Something had happened that had made him doubt himself, and she knew with every instinct that would be unbearable for a man like Sam Ralston. What on earth had happened? But he spoke again before she could chase that thought any further.

"I am sorry," he said. "If I'd found a better place…"

She sliced a hand through the air, on the edge of too much emotion. "It's not up to you to anticipate absolutely everything. Sure, I know you're the guy with the gun who's going to save the planet, but you don't know my business like I do."

He opened his mouth and then closed it, head tilting as his eyes searched her face. He was looking at her, really looking at her, as if she were the newest wonder of the world.

She couldn't wipe away the smile tugging at her lips. "Thanks for being more than just a suit with a sidearm. Maybe next time you'll listen to me about the kind of office I need for my clients?"

He nodded. "You know your business. Got it."

"Fair enough." Chloe raised up on her toes and kissed him on the cheek. His skin was cool but already roughening with the shadow of his beard.

"Don't." The word cut through the air.

Faster than she could follow, he turned to her, grasping both her arms with his large, square hands. He wasn't hurting her, but there was no way she was going anywhere. Faint color rose to his face, his steel-gray eyes wide and intense.

She grabbed a surprised breath. If she'd wanted honesty, it was there in his gaze. He wanted her, no question. The idea of it hit her bloodstream like strong liquor. "Don't?"

"Kissing me might be a door you don't want to open."

And yet, he'd kissed her. Or her hand. Twice. And perhaps she did want to open that door. If he could be vulnerable, maybe it was worth getting to know him after all. "Oh?"

The single syllable seemed to rob him of his will. "Chloe, be careful what you start. I'm the one in the shadows, remember?"

"No, you're *my* shadow. There's a difference." Chloe raised her hands, breaking his hold. He didn't resist, or try to stop her when she rested her hands on his shoulders. Automatically, he reached for her waist, almost as if they meant to dance.

Perhaps they did. As if by unspoken consent, he bent down and she reached up, their lips meeting at a perfect midpoint.

His lips were softer than she expected, as if every part of Sam Ralston capable of tenderness had been distilled for the purpose of kissing. An electric current seemed to rise from beneath the soles of Chloe's feet and rush to her head, leaving her dizzy but connected with some primal, earthy power. She leaned into him, relishing the hardness of his muscles beneath the crisp white shirt. He smelled of soap and man and something darkly spicy she couldn't place. Not cologne, but some element of him that was unique.

Her heart sped as Sam pulled her closer, his strong grip against her back. She ran her fingers around the back of his neck, burrowing through his thick, dark hair. It was like silk. Another softness she hadn't expected.

She opened her mouth to him, tasting as they explored each other. His mouth trailed down her jaw to her collarbone, his breath coming soft in a sigh that was all lust. She nearly crumbled where she stood, burned to ash by the searing heat of sensation.

"Sam," she whispered. She had no idea what she'd say next. She was lost in the moment and loving it.

But he pulled away. She looked up into his face and saw her own desires reflected in the drowning darkness of his eyes. And then, slowly, his fascination sank into regret.

"This isn't the time or place," he murmured, pushing a strand of hair out of her eyes. "Before you ask why not, there are surveillance cameras everywhere in here."

Chloe froze. Slowly, her fingers rose to check her buttons. Mercifully, he'd left them all in place. She fell back a step, putting air between them. She didn't know what to say.

When would be the right time and place? Her whole body ached to ask the question, but who was listening? A building full of her uncle's security guys?

Chloe raised her chin, not sure if she wanted to kiss Sam again or kick him in the shins for leaving her all revved up with no way to follow through. "You should have warned me."

"Back at you." Sam's smile was slight but full of mischief. "We should go."

"Fine," she grumped.

"Don't forget your roses." He returned to the conference room and came back a moment later with the bouquet.

"They really are lovely," she said, taking them from him.

He gave a slight bow. "Probably the prettiest things to see the inside of Jack's offices, present company excepted."

"How very gallant."

"Kind of you to say so. I'm sadly out of practice."

Because something made you think you're a monster, and you gave up on important parts of yourself. Chloe wanted to say it but didn't dare. She knew she didn't have the whole picture. "You should practice more."

He slipped his sunglasses back on, but she could still read his expression. He actually looked happy. "We shadows need light to give us purpose, Miss Chloe. Shine on."

Chapter 10

"How can I make this up to you?" Sam asked.

"Don't worry about it."

They were back in the car, which now smelled like the roses in the backseat. Chloe was staring out the window at the summer afternoon. Even through the heavily tinted glass of Sam's car, she could tell the sky was a brilliant blue, wild poppies a riot of orange in the grass.

The car was a bright red gull-wing Mercedes-Benz SLS AMG. What was it with the men in Jack's crowd and their cars? Every time she took a ride with one of them she half expected to find herself in an aftershave commercial.

Sam was silent. Telephone poles whizzed by. Chloe felt the weight of his regret, although none of it showed on his face. He needn't have worried about the unfortunate encounter with Elaine. She had let him off the hook, mostly. That kiss had bought a lot of forgiveness.

She summoned her no-problem voice. "I'll figure out a way to bring Elaine around. The Fallons are on a tight timeline, so they're not going to want to start over with someone else. Besides, Mrs. F. has decided she wants Jack Anderson's niece at her beck and call. Iris Fallon doesn't change her mind easily." *And, since she is the biggest client I've ever had, all that had better be true.*

Turning away from the hypnotic view of the roadside, she smiled sweetly. She felt, rather than saw, Sam relax a degree.

"I could take you to a late lunch," he suggested.

A pleasant twinge of surprise made Chloe smile for real. "I could accept. Unfortunately, there isn't a lot around here, unless you count roadside vegetable stands."

"I know a place."

"Where? I grew up here. If there was a place, I'd know."

"I have my ways."

"Oh, that's right. You're an international man of mystery. You have ways."

Sam made a most un-Samlike snort, and signaled to change lanes. "Jack and I went for dinner a few months ago. He wanted to show me one of his new business ventures. This place hasn't been open very long."

He took an exit that forked away from the main highway and wound toward the coast. The land was uneven, cloaks of grass and wildflowers thrown over jagged slabs of rock. Chloe could see swatches of ocean between the jutting boulders.

"Jack did like to play angel."

Sam gave her a sideways look. Sunglasses hid his eyes, but she could see the amusement at the corners of his mouth. "You mean financially?"

Chloe laughed, but it twisted inside her. "Yes, in the

angel investor sense. I'm not sure he would have volunteered for wings and a harp. Sitting on a cloud all day
wasn't his style."

"No." The amusement was suddenly gone, replaced by
the tight grief Jack's friends had worn ever since they'd
arrived.

Chloe looked out her window, fighting back a sudden
wave of loneliness. She had friends, but Jack had been
the only family left who'd really cared for her. His death
had left her disconnected, an oddment like a stray button that got pushed to the back of the drawer because it
went with nothing else.

Sam reached over, putting his hand over hers for a
moment. Chloe barely had time to form a thought before
his hand was back on the steering wheel. She blinked
quickly, banishing the tears the unexpected gesture had
summoned.

Neither of them spoke. Sam turned onto a steep incline
that crawled up a winding lane between tall stands of pine
and cedar. It was like plunging into a primeval forest.

She cleared her throat. "How does anyone find this
place?"

"It's meant for a select clientele. There's a helicopter
pad for those who don't care for the drive."

She could see the appeal for Jack. He worked every
hour of every day, but he liked his luxuries. "Who owns
this? It wasn't listed anywhere in his estate."

"The Hope family. The place is called Hope's Reach.
And I don't think he ever made a formal agreement. He
took risks once in a while, but people always paid him
back eventually. These folks did."

Chloe could see the Reach's sign now, arching over
the narrow roadway. As they drove beneath it the trees
opened up into a wide clearing at the top of the hill.

Ahead stretched an unobstructed vista of ocean, only a pair of eagles interrupting the view. *Breathtaking.*

The drive circled around a broad lawn set with a stone fountain. The main building was four stories and curved around the north side of the grass. Smaller structures that might have been private cabins were scattered farther away beneath the trees.

Sam pulled up in front of the main entrance, the Mercedes humming to a final cadence. The butterfly doors lifted gracefully. By the time Chloe picked up her handbag, Sam was at her side of the car to offer her his hand.

"A man of mystery *and* style," she said.

"There's no point to a poor effort."

The only sign of tension was a crease between his brows, and she realized this was perhaps the first time she'd seen him standing in full sun. The contrast between his dark hair and pale skin was striking enough that she had to force herself not to stare. It took him beyond handsome to something exotic.

The moment didn't last long. Valets ran forward, vying for the privilege of parking Sam's car. He tossed the keys to the fastest, and quickly escorted Chloe beneath the glass-and-fieldstone facade of the main building.

Inside it was dim and cool, all the light coming from floor-to-ceiling glass windows that were shaded by the dogwood and arbutus trees outside. With the rough rock walls carried through to the interior, it felt a bit like walking through an upscale cave.

"The dining room is this way." Sam led her up a short flight of steps that opened to a shady patio.

The hostess was a pretty brunette. "Welcome back, Mr. Ralston."

"Fay," he said cordially. "How are you?"

The woman dimpled in a way that made Chloe itch.

How well did these two know each other, anyway? *Don't be ridiculous. He's being polite.*

But Fay brightened under his pleasantry. "I'm very well, thank you. The corner table is free, if you would like that."

"Please."

She led them to a space that was sheltered from the ocean breeze, but still had a view. From this side of the hill, a steep cliff descended to the beach. Chloe could see a boardwalk and pier far below. The scene was utterly peaceful. Sailboats, some with white sails, some with brilliant reds and blues, floated on a silver sea. Sam held her chair, and then took the seat in the deepest shadow.

Chloe couldn't help herself. "You must come here often, if you know the staff's names."

"Fay is one of the owners. As I said, I came here with Jack when they first opened." He gave her a slight smile, just a twitch of the lips. "There are three Hope daughters, all young, beautiful and unmarried."

"No wonder my uncle invested."

"I didn't inquire about Jack's methods for testing the assets."

Chloe closed her eyes. "I'm not touching that statement with a ten-foot pole."

"Good. Just so we're clear, I came here for the wine list." He glanced over the top of his sunglasses. "Though I hear the spa offers an amazing hot rock treatment."

"Thanks for the tip, but I'm very selective about hot rocks and who is offering them."

"I'm relieved to hear it."

Fay returned. Chloe ordered seafood salad; he asked for the bisque.

"I've never seen you eat much," she said. "If you don't mind my mentioning it."

He answered with the air of someone used to the question. "My job requires rigorous physical training. That means following a very restricted dietary plan."

"And yet you drink."

"It's a failing. I'm not a saint."

"Fair enough." The wine Sam ordered came and Chloe sipped it. A Mondeuse blanche. Her tastebuds tingled at the citrus taste. "Not an everyday choice. I appreciate someone who knows their vintages."

"You apparently do, as well."

She shrugged. "I have to for my business. I have a lot of food and wine experts on speed dial. You never know what someone is going to ask for."

"What made you choose to spend your time arranging other people's weddings?"

She felt a twinge, like an old injury. "My own."

Sam frowned. "You are—or were—married?" He sounded shocked.

"Almost." She took another mouthful of wine. The memory of Neil was enough to drive her to drink. "My college sweetheart. It never happened."

"Why not?"

Chloe hesitated. "It's a long story."

Sam played with the spoon resting on his napkin, seemed to catch himself, and put it down. "Something must have made you decide against it." He was clearly curious.

She smiled, a bit wryly. "Actually, it was the other way around. He backed out the morning I was to walk down the aisle. Another hour and I would have literally been left at the altar."

Sam pulled off his sunglasses. "That's not possible." He said it quietly.

"I beg to differ. I was there." *And people wonder why I have abandonment issues.*

"What reason could he have?"

"There was another female in the picture. He wasn't up to sharing that tidbit of information until the last possible moment. Either I was blind or he hid it very well." She remembered the world dropping out from beneath her, the rage born of fear. Fear that she couldn't navigate a world where the one person she loved best could make such a fool of her. Fear that she couldn't trust anyone ever again.

Sam was studying her face, as if he could see her memories there. "He is fortunate I don't know his name."

"Jack made his feelings clear. Neil left the state after that."

Sam gave an unpleasant smile. It was enough to make a girl adore him.

Chloe gave a short laugh. "I guess when it comes to lovers, what you don't know can actually hurt you."

Sam had been reaching across the table to touch her but withdrew his hand. She pretended not to notice.

Time to change the subject. "The good part of it all was that I found out how much I liked weddings—the pageantry and celebration, the decorations, everything. I'd organized my own event pretty much by myself and had a blast doing it. So I thought, why not plan weddings for a living? I had just finished a fine arts degree in set design. There weren't too many jobs around in literal theaters, but with weddings the stage is wherever the bride and groom want it to be. It's one of the few moments in life where everyday people are the stars. I'm there to make it a hit production just for them, and it feels wonderful."

Sam nodded, his slow smile igniting something deep

in her belly. "Good for you. Good for turning the situation around."

"I consider my own experience a fortunate escape. That doesn't mean I think a happy ever after is impossible."

He raised his glass. "To an eternity of happiness, Chloe Anderson. May you be your own most successful client."

The food came, and there were many pleasant things to contemplate. Sam sipping his wine. The delicious food. The glorious day. Sam offering her a taste of his soup, then stealing a pecan from her salad. She'd never been tempted to gaze at a man for hours on end, but he was handsome enough. And interesting. Without showing off, Sam seemed to know something about every subject under the sun.

They talked lazily, drifting in and out of subjects the way the eagles overhead banked from one air current to the next. There was still the underlying tension of newness between them, like glue that hadn't yet set. A slip could still make everything come unstuck. And yet there was also an instant comfort, as if they'd known each other long before.

Sam had a confidence she normally saw in someone far more mature. It wasn't cockiness. To her it felt more like the ease of experience. He didn't have to impress. He just knew who he was. His sureness made her relax.

"Are you sure you won't try dessert?" he asked. "I understand their pastry chef is extraordinary."

"I wish I could, but that was a huge salad, and it was so good that I ate every bite."

"Coward." He smiled, and this time it was wide enough that she could see his strong, white teeth. Not that he'd used them much at this meal. He had only eaten about half his soup. How could anyone survive on so little food? She wondered if she looked in the backseat if she'd find a secret stash of fast-food wrappers.

"So tell me something about your work. What kind of security jobs did you do for Uncle Jack? Was it just bodyguard work?"

She regretted her words as soon as she spoke. He sat back, pushing the sunglasses back on. It was obviously not a welcome question.

"There's more to it than being a bodyguard, though that's mostly what I do."

"I see."

She had time to pour cream into her coffee before he spoke again. When he did, he looked away, as though he was talking more to himself than to her. "Being a bodyguard isn't as easy as it sounds. Sometimes things go wrong and innocent people die. Then you wonder if you were to blame."

The way he said it resonated with memory. Whatever had happened still stung, but he said nothing more. He was apparently done sharing for the day.

Was this the source of the "monster" comment? What was so awful that he couldn't tell her?

Chloe tasted the coffee, but the pleasure of it didn't reach beyond her tongue. Neil had kept secrets, but they were the simple kind. Another woman. A fickle heart. Unkind, but hardly lethal. She'd survived him. But Sam?

She watched him cautiously. There was nothing fickle about the set of his jaw or the square strength of his shoulders. And yet, she was willing to bet his secrets were far, far bigger than a second girlfriend. Even more disturbing, if she let herself fall for him, she wouldn't get over it so easily. Their kiss had told her that much. He would be the lover that destroyed her for anyone else.

The warm summer afternoon lost its charm. She set down the coffee cup, no longer thirsty.

Sam's dark black sunglasses were aimed her way, but they gave away nothing. The perfectly sculptured mouth—the one that had kissed her so beautifully—clamped into a hard line. "My work isn't as pretty as setting the stage for a wedding."

"No." What was she supposed to say?

"Does that frighten you?"

"What I don't know about you frightens me more."

He folded his napkin, setting it on the table. "Good call."

Chapter 11

Sam drove down the dark highway, wishing he could just keep going and leave Oakwood in his taillights for good.

There is a reason that vampires don't date, Sam told himself. It was confusing. Chloe wanted him, and that was natural. Vampires seduced; it was part of their hunting behavior. Their legendary attractiveness was no more than survival skills with a few pheromones thrown in. After all, what was courtship but a mild version of the predator's dance with its prey? That much Sam understood.

But there was more between them than that. Chloe had looked at him as if she actually saw who he was. Not the monster, but the man. The Sam he'd been long ago. And, more than anything, he'd wanted to believe what she saw was true.

But that was impossible. He'd barely caught himself

before he surrendered to the lie. He was a vampire. As War, he battled with murderers, thieves and abominations worse than himself. By nature, he was a killer surrounded by death. *Women like her die around creatures like you.*

Moreover, any kind of a relationship could get truly awkward. It would be impossible to explain who he was. There was no good way to raise the topic of sucking blood.

No, it was far less complicated to be the superhero in the background, protecting the golden-haired maid from the dark forces of villainy. That, at least, had dignity.

"What are you brooding about?" Kenyon asked from the passenger seat.

"I'm not brooding."

"Yes, you are. Your eyebrows get all wrinkly."

He cursed. "I'm planning how we're going to find the dress thief in this dive."

"If they're still around," said Kenyon darkly. "This neck of the woods is big on hunting and fishing. There've been a surprising number of guests in and out in the last couple of days, and it's not like we had a good description to go on. Just another bunch of guys with knapsacks and equipment."

"They'll be there. They didn't get what they wanted. They're too professional to give up just like that." At least that's what Sam was counting on. Kenyon had spent the entire day roaming the area in search of a lead.

And, although he'd said nothing to Chloe, the files Sam had searched out at Gravesend Security had been Jack's detailed notes on local tourist businesses. It seemed the Salmon Tail Hotel and Saloon had a reputation for renting rooms to scum.

Sam slowed as the sign for the Salmon Tail—missing a few of the old neon letters—came into view. He took a right into the gravel parking lot, parking the Ford Super Duty right in front of the saloon-door entrance. He'd borrowed the truck from Jack's garage. His own ride would have stuck out like a Thoroughbred among a herd of goats.

"Like I said, there's no other hotels or motels close by," Kenyon said. "It's a reasonable theory."

Sam grunted agreement. The Salmon Tail occupied a gray area between functional drinking establishment and dump. Sam noticed a dent in the siding where someone with a skinful had driven right into the west corner of the building. Another, smaller neon sign hung over the front window, representing a heifer doing a jerky cancan and holding a tray of burgers.

They got out of the truck, Sam's muscles grateful for the chance to stretch. He looked around. The town was tiny, no streetlights bleaching the velvety black night. Frogs chirped a counterpoint to the country music spilling from the bar.

Kenyon folded his arms, scowling at the ramshackle building. Sam ignored him, instead giving the parking lot a critical review. No vehicles he recognized. Not that he had really expected any. Kenyon took a step toward the door. Sam caught his arm. "Be careful."

"I'm new. I'm not brain damaged."

Sam dropped his voice to a murmur. "The thief who attacked Chloe was a professional, and that means subtle. We don't know who we're looking for."

"I thought you said it was the Knights of Vidon."

"That's my theory. They would be more likely than most to know about the gems. They're human, but they use silver bullets. And they hate the idea of an alliance between Vidon and Marcari. Covert ops is their specialty. Plus, they were always after Jack and had the guts to take him on."

"So they fit the profile. That's good, right? We've fought them and won before."

"Not like this. The Knights are at their deadliest when they're operating in secret."

Kenyon drew his eyebrows together, his expression a mix of sympathy and irritation. "Like I say, I may be fuzzy, but I'm not fuzzy-headed."

All the members of the Company had experienced a run-in with the slayers, but in the time-honored code of men they never openly spoke of it.

"I'll mind my manners," Kenyon said quietly. "But you know I could bend, fold and spindle any of them."

"Maybe one at a time. No one can take them all."

Kenyon gave Sam a toothy smile. "I wouldn't want to be greedy."

"I wouldn't let you." Sam jerked his head toward the door. "Let's go find Winspear."

Jack's autopsy would be done by now. Not that they wanted to think about that. Sam pushed through the double doors without another word. Kenyon followed a pace behind.

A sour fog of noise and slopped beer engulfed Sam the moment his boots hit the bar's wooden floor. The place was stereotypical enough for a movie set: dark, down-at-heel, complete with pool tables, rickety stools and strings of lights shaped like tiny chili peppers.

The atmosphere itself didn't bother Sam, whose first alcoholic experiments had taken place in a shack in the woods. One of his father's tenants had come by a recipe for home brew and, well, it had been a wonder any of them still had internal organs. Compared to that, this place was upmarket.

What bothered him was not knowing which of the blue-jeaned, flannel-shirted patrons were slayers in disguise. Sam let his gaze touch each person, assessing body language, posture, scent. No one stood out. Then again, they never did.

Eventually, his scrutiny fell on a lone dark-haired figure at a corner table, long legs stretched out and crossed at the ankles. Winspear. Sam and Kenyon navigated the room, skirting the pool table and a cluster of barely legals playing darts. Winspear straightened to a sitting position as they grabbed chairs.

Kenyon picked up the beer bottle sitting in front of the doctor. His eyebrows lowered. "Since when do you guys drink plain old pilsner? I thought you were all, like, Chateau Frou-frou Chardonnay types."

Winspear raised an eyebrow. "After a day in the morgue, my only criterion is that it's not formaldehyde."

"Another myth shattered." Kenyon set the bottle down.

While vampires had little appetite for food and drink, at times the ritual was comforting—but empty. Scratch the surface and the blood hunger bubbled up, poisoning everything.

Sam rubbed his eyes, suddenly exhausted in spirit if not in body. *Why did I let Chloe kiss me?* Actually, there hadn't been much "let" involved. She was hard to stop once she focused on something.

He'd nearly drowned in her eyes back there in Jack's old office. She'd had that hopeful look, the one that said you might be worth a woman's time and energy.

He wasn't. He was a monster. He'd flat-out told her so. And for someone who claimed no one ever told her anything, she was very good at ignoring his warnings. *Impossible woman.* Chloe Anderson was everything he didn't deserve, could not have and absolutely craved.

Worse, he was on the brink of giving in to his desire for her and didn't know if he could stop himself. If he wanted to. *Monster.*

The beer came and Sam grabbed his bottle as if it was a comfort object. The cold, sweaty glass felt good against his palm.

Nine hells, what was he thinking? He was a vampire! It would end up in some B-movie moment with Chloe in a white nightgown on a parapet and him with his fangs sticking out—hoping to get them stuck in her.

Sam frowned. That image was so wrong in so many ways. Did Jack's house even have a parapet?

"Something bothering you?" Winspear asked.

Sam snapped back to the present, irritated at losing his focus. "No."

There was no point in even apologizing for how phony his answer sounded.

"Then maybe we can get down to business."

Sam caught Winspear's impatient tone and lifted his gaze from the tabletop. The doctor's dark eyes were filled with a cold anger.

"What?" Sam demanded.

Winspear lowered his voice so that his words wouldn't be overheard. "You wanted an autopsy report. Here it is: The only thing I can say for sure about the body we pulled from the Jag is that it belonged to a vampire. I can't tell you anything else."

Kenyon looked sick. "Seriously? It was that messed up?"

Winspear leaned forward, lowering his voice yet further. "Vampires burn extremely well, and the fire from the crash was fierce. I'd hoped to get some viable samples for testing, but almost everything useful was consumed."

"I thought one of the servants identified…him." Sam couldn't bring himself to say Jack's name.

"There were personal effects. A watch, some jewelry. The physical build was right."

"Dental records?" Kenyon asked.

"We don't get cavities," Sam put in. "All vampires have perfect teeth."

"We do, however, have full body X-rays on file with the Company," Winspear continued. "Bone formation, skull shape, healed fractures and so on provide enough individual differences to identify a vampire. I took a set of films and sent them in for comparison. That should at least give us a positive ID."

Kenyon looked confused. "There's doubt that it was Jack in the car?"

The corners of Winspear's mouth twitched downward. "I'm a scientist. I require objective proof before I commit one way or the other."

Sam's stomach squeezed painfully. Given what little Sam knew of the doctor's history, Winspear didn't like or trust many people—okay, anybody—but he had respected Jack. He would feel his loss keenly. "Jack's gone, Mark."

A savage look flashed through the doctor's eyes. "I don't have to believe that yet. When the Company phones and tells me it's a match, then I shall mourn for him."

Sam looked away, trying not to react to Winspear's vehemence. Some vampires went feral as they aged, ran for the wild and ended their days like savage beasts. There had been whispers that Plague was headed that way. He was certainly centuries older than Sam. How many horrors had Winspear seen in all those years?

Sam shoved the beer bottle aside.

"So the autopsy is a dead end for now." He winced at the unintended pun. "What else have we got?"

"I checked the guest register," Kenyon volunteered. "I didn't recognize any names, but that's no real surprise."

"What about the bed-and-breakfasts in the area?"

"Nada," Kenyon said with exaggerated patience. "I also checked the trailer park, campgrounds, and looked through the community paper for short-term rentals. This is our best bet. If our visitors are still around, they're here somewhere, hiding in plain sight."

Sam took a quick glance around the room, wondering if Chloe's thief was in the crowd. Was it one of the college students? One of the men leaning on the bar? He considered each figure, assigning a level of probable threat to each. The Horsemen could have met somewhere else, somewhere more secure, but this felt right. War didn't hide.

Plus, Sam wanted this confrontation over with. It was so much faster when the battle came to you. Never mind what he said to Kenyon, he wanted to see just how many of the enemy he could take down. Those were the moments when it was good to be a monster.

"I'm happy to know you spent your day in constructive endeavors," Winspear observed.

Kenyon folded his arms. "Glad somebody noticed. All that legwork makes me want another beer."

"Fill your boots," Winspear muttered, pulling out his phone to check it. "Be your friendly self and soon the locals will tell you their every secret."

"Thanks, old-timer." Kenyon rose and sauntered straight toward the auburn-haired bombshell tending bar. He always went for the redheads.

Turning to watch the werewolf go, Sam watched with amused disgust. Then he stiffened. He knew the figure staring at him from the shadows of the doorway. The man was dressed as one of the locals, drawing no attention.

Sam stared at the vampire who had made him. The wave of recognition brought a complicated tangle of affection and resentment, but then it always did. More important, why had his sire come unannounced?

Dismay fingered the back of Sam's neck as his maker gestured for silence, and then vanished from sight.

Chapter 12

Chloe sat on her bed, too wound up to go to sleep.

She'd spent an hour on the phone with Elaine smoothing everything over after the disastrous appointment that afternoon. Okay, disastrous from a business perspective. She wasn't going to regret anything about that kiss with Sam. It had been far, far too long since she'd had that kind of a tingle in all the right places.

Not since Neil, and that was a pale shadow compared to what Sam inspired.

Odd that she'd thought about her ex-fiancé twice in one day. She'd blocked him out of her mind as much as was humanly possible. As Uncle Jack had put it, unfortunately some water under the bridge came straight from the sewers.

When bad memories bubbled up, good friends and chocolate were the only answers. She'd already eaten half a bar of dark Belgian supreme.

With a glance at her bedside clock, Chloe picked up her cell phone and thumbed in a number. It was eleven o'clock. That meant it would be eight in the morning in Vienna, which was early for Lexie but not indecent. After a long pause, she heard a ring.

"Alexis Haven."

The sound of her best friend's voice gave her a surge of comfort. "It's Chloe."

"Hey!" Her friend's husky voice suddenly brightened. "Are you back at work? Are you through sorting out the estate? What's going on?"

The warmth in Lexie's tone made her smile. "I'm back at work, more or less. In fact, I need you to photograph a couple of weddings, but that's not why I'm calling."

"What's up?"

Chloe paused a moment, not sure where to begin. "Some odd things have happened over this estate. I just sent a picture to your email. Don't laugh. I'm not a photographer like you."

"Hang on." She heard the distinctive sound of a Mac computer coming out of sleep mode, then a keyboard clicking. "Okay, got it. What is it?"

"I think it's a designer's signature." Chloe had taken the wedding dress out of the safe just long enough to search the garment for anything like a maker's mark. She'd found a tiny patch of embroidery along the hem, stitched in thread that matched the cloth.

"It looks like a bird."

"It might be. I have a dress on my hands and I want to know who designed it. You're working for that woman who organizes all the big shows, right?"

"Anastasia?" Of course she would be on a first-name basis with one of Europe's fashion queens. Although modest among friends, Lexie was an up-and-coming runway photographer just on the edge of being outright famous. It was a mark of their friendship that Lexie still made herself available to Chloe's Occasions.

And, at the moment, Lexie was Chloe's source for the info she needed. "Do you think she would know whose label this is?"

"Maybe. Do you have a theory?"

"I think it's Jessica Lark's, but I can't find anything online."

"Cool. I'll ask."

"Thanks."

"Where did you get the dress? Lark originals are hard to get."

"It was part of Uncle Jack's estate." Which was true, just not the whole truth. She'd tell her the rest later, when they could talk face-to-face.

"Huh. Interesting. I'll get Anastasia to email you directly." Chloe heard typing. Lexie was probably forwarding the JPEG as they spoke. "So you said something odd was going on. There's got to be more than just that, right?"

"Yeah, well, it's Uncle Jack's friends. You know he was in the security business, right? Among other things?"

"Sure."

"A handful of these G-man types showed up at the funeral. The one who's the other executor, Sam, is—I don't know how to describe him."

Lexie chuckled. "In a good way or a bad way?"

"More good than bad."

"You mean he's hot? Available? Tall, dark and handsome?"

"Sure, but—that's not it."

A dramatic sigh gusted halfway around the world. "How can that not be it? That's everything."

"He's different."

"Like how? Eats with a fork? Speaks in complete sentences? Chloe, you've had a dry spell the size of the Sahara. Count your blessings."

"He's a bit like a Swiss Army knife."

"Oh, baby!"

"Not like that."

"I like the corkscrew best."

"No, really. He's been with me through some real emergencies. Big ones. But you know how this always ends for me, Lexie."

Lexie caught the tone of her voice and sobered. "I know your history, and I get why you would worry about ending up with another Neil."

"Maybe I'm not being fair. Sam's been the only bright light in this whole mess."

"How serious a mess, Chlo? What exactly has been happening?"

"What would you say if I said I'd been attacked in my own bed by thieves, suddenly acquired a pair of bodyguards and found a wolf running up and down the hallways in the dead of night?"

She heard Lexie's intake of breath. "A wolf?"

"The attack part was worse. The wolf was kind of a sweetie."

For a moment, all Chloe heard was the crackle on the line.

"Chlo, what in blazes is going on?"

She gripped the phone, as if it could bring her physically closer to her friend. "I don't know, Lexie. And if I'm totally honest with myself, I'm a little bit scared."

Suddenly the shadows in the room seemed darker. Chloe pulled an afghan around her shoulders, burrowing into the crocheted softness.

"Who did you say this Sam guy is again?" Lexie asked.

"One of Uncle Jack's friends. There were three who showed up for the funeral. One left but the other two are still staying here. Sam and his friend, Faran Kenyon."

Chloe felt her friend's shock, even though there wasn't a sound on the line.

"Faran?" Lexie's voice smoked with ire. "You're not serious?"

Whoa! That was full-on Lexie temper. "You know him?"

"Only the most arrogant, pigheaded…"

Chloe suddenly smiled. "Is he that ex you always go on about?"

She remembered there had been an unnamed boyfriend when Lexie was in Cannes—an affair as passionate as it had been brief.

Lexie made a sound that would have done the wolf credit. "That's only half of it, Chloe."

Chloe sat up. "What do you mean?"

"How much do you know about these guys?"

She felt a niggle of alarm. "Sam saved my life. These are good people."

"*People* being a subjective term," Lexie muttered.

"What do you mean by that?"

Lexie sighed, her breath loud in Chloe's ear. "I can't explain. At least, not on the phone. Listen, I'm done here in Austria. I'm catching the first plane I can. It sounds like you need a friend. In the meantime, I wouldn't be going on any moonlit walks with your Swiss Army knife."

"How serious are you about that?"

"More than I like. I would be supercareful. Think about it. I don't do careful."

* * *

Sam was staring at the spot where his maker had been a second before. His vanishing act had been too fast for human eyes, but Sam saw the blur streaking out the door. Only ancient vampires could move quite that quickly. *What in the nine hells is going on?*

A moment later, Sam's pocket vibrated. He pulled out his phone. A text message was up on the screen. All it said was Parking lot. Code Gray.

Gray meant official business in Company-speak. Official as in need-to-know, supersecret, grab your decoder ring and eat this message if it doesn't self-destruct first. Combined with his maker's mysterious behavior, this could not be good news.

According to protocol, Code Gray meant he should go alone, mentioning the message to no one. Sam looked up. *That ship has sailed.* The werewolf had returned with his fresh brew and both Winspear and Kenyon were watching him stare at his phone, curiosity rampant on their faces.

Sam looked from one to the other. These were his brothers-in-arms. They might lack a lot of things, like a regular heartbeat, but they were loyal. *And there is something amiss.* He had a profound sense he was going to need his friends.

He rose, the legs of his chair scraping on the wood floor. "I have to take a walk."

Winspear gave a cool nod, checking his watch. "You're sure?"

"I promise to look both ways before crossing the street."

The doctor shrugged, eyeing Sam's cell phone. "Then go. I'll finish my beer just in time to come save your backside. You're not ending up on my examination table."

"What he said." The werewolf was peering down the

neck of the beer bottle as if expecting to see a tiny Moby Dick breaching the suds.

The tension in Sam's chest eased. There was no question they'd be watching him every step of the way. Protocol meant he couldn't tell them anything, but there was more than one way to ask for backup. Jack had done the same thing plenty of times. A Horseman was brave, but he wasn't stupid.

Pushing through the steadily growing crowd at the bar, Sam shouldered his way to the door. For a dive in the middle of no place, it was hopping. Outside, the summer night was deliciously cool.

He paused, waiting for the latest arrivals to head inside the Salmon Tail. Then he circled the parking lot, the soles of his boots silent on the gravel. Wind ruffled the trees, drowning out the constant chirruping of frogs.

Finally, he sensed his maker. When he spoke, his voice was conversational. "Hello, Carter. What's going on?"

A match flared from the darkness of the woods, stinking of sulphur. It was an old-fashioned lucifer, struck against the bark of a tree. The scent of old Virginia tobacco followed, and Sam wondered where Carter got it. Most modern cigars didn't smell like they had in the old days. Too many pesticides, he supposed.

The scent triggered a flood of memory. The first time he'd encountered that blend of tobacco was a century and a half ago. Then the sweet smoke had been mixed with the stink of his blood and bile. December 1862, near the Rappahannock River. Reflexively, Sam put a hand to his stomach, where he'd been gutshot. A wound to the belly is a long, painful way to die. Carter had saved him from the agony.

Sam turned to see his maker a few yards away, leaning against one of the Douglas firs that ringed the parking lot. Carter wasn't an especially tall man, but he was solidly built with a mane of gray-streaked hair and ice-blue eyes. He'd been in his middle years when he'd become a vampire, but he moved with the quick energy of a young man.

Sam's shoulders tightened, memories coming too thick and fast for comfort. He'd begged for a quick death. He'd been an officer in the Army of the Potomac, proud of his command, prouder still of his honor. He hadn't asked to live.

But instead of granting him peace, Carter had made him War.

"My boy." His maker took a puff on the cigar. The end glowed like a blazing firefly in the darkness.

"What are you doing here?" Sam kept his voice neutral.

"I thought you would be glad to see me." Carter's smile was half a challenge.

"I am." It was true, and not. However mixed his feelings, Sam knew Carter was the Company's best agent. "I just didn't expect to see the director of the Company in the parking lot of a backwater bar."

Carter flicked his ash. "A good man's dead, Sam. One of the best. It was time for me to stir my old bones."

"I'm not going to refuse help. Jack was murdered. We don't have a lot to go on."

"I know."

Sam closed the distance between them, feeling the years fall away with every step. There was no denying the pull of nostalgia. They'd fought together, watched nations rise and fall. Time and shared enemies formed a bond. He respected the man and regarded him as a second father, almost. If only he could forgive Carter for making him what he was, they might have been friends.

Families, especially vampire families, were ever complicated.

A little unwillingly, Sam dragged himself back to the present. "The Knights of Vidon are involved. I'm sure of it."

Carter's bushy eyebrows shot up. "What makes you say that?"

"You wouldn't be here if you hadn't read my report. They're after the diamonds."

"Are you so sure it's the Knights?" Carter gave him that familiar smile of his—half teasing, half fatherly. "There are plenty of thieves in the world."

"Who else would know the dress was in Jack's safe?"

"Whom did Jack trust?"

It was a good question. "The Company, of course."

"Not all the Company."

Sam frowned. Whom would Jack have distrusted? "Is that why you used Code Gray?"

"Did he trust the Horsemen?"

"Certainly, but we didn't know what was in the safe."

Carter's look was significant. "All we know for sure is that you didn't."

"But…" His words ground to a halt. "Are you saying Kenyon and Winspear knew Jack had the diamonds?"

He spoke the last in a low voice, suddenly aware that the other Horsemen were no doubt watching his every gesture. He'd broken protocol because he trusted them.

Carter nodded. "Keep an open mind. Someone had to get the stones from the castle vault to the dressmaker. The dressmaker had to give the gown to Jack. There were a lot of steps involving a lot of people. A jewel thief could have taken interest at any point along the way."

Sam remembered what Chloe had said. Jessica Lark was dead. Jack knew her. He'd never mentioned her murder, or the dress, or the diamonds. Sam suddenly felt a gulf between himself and the Horsemen's dead leader. "But why would Jack confide in Winspear and Kenyon and not me?"

A gust of wind stirred the trees while Carter framed an answer. "Walk with me awhile."

Sam fell into step beside his maker. They moved slowly, ambling like men out to enjoy the air. Nonetheless, Sam felt the creep up his spine that said they were being watched.

Now he wondered if he should have been more secretive. *But they're my comrades. Jack trusted them and so do I.*

Carter puffed his cigar for a moment. "You're a straight arrow, Sam, and everyone respects that. Jack, on the other hand, was coloring a long way outside of the lines."

"Why do you say that?"

The older vampire ran a hand over his face. "The king never authorized the removal of the diamonds. They're stolen goods."

Sam looked at him sharply. He knew that already, so there must be more to Carter's point. "Are you saying that Jack stole them?"

"If he hadn't, wouldn't he have simply handed them back once they came into his possession?"

"Could it be that he was curious to see who turned up looking for the diamonds?"

Carter raised his eyebrows. "You mean Jack set a trap?"

Sam shrugged. "Just a theory. It would be like him to wait and see what fish would show up to take the bait."

"That makes good sense. More than you know." Carter

kicked a rock from his path, sending it bouncing into the roadside scrub. "I need your help."

"What do you want me to do?"

"Three things. First, you need to assume command of the Horsemen."

"Pardon me?" He stopped in his tracks.

"Jack formed the unit because the Company needed a crack team. We still do. You were his second-in-command and, truth be told, the best soldier. You're War."

Pride shot through Sam, but not happiness. A promotion was good, but having Jack back would be better. "It was his team. He handpicked us."

"Now it's yours." Carter gripped his shoulder. "You were an officer. You enjoyed command, as I recall. The Company can't have a leaderless unit."

That made sense. It was only a matter of time before someone was appointed. It might as well be him. *But it makes Jack's death too real.*

Carter started walking again, Sam falling into place beside him.

"What's the second thing you need from me?"

"Turn the dress over to me. Quietly."

"You?"

"I'll take it back to Marcari while attracting as little attention as possible. That should throw the thieves off its scent until the diamonds are safely back in the palace vault. If we can pull this off, the king has agreed to keep Jack's theft out of the official record. No stain on his name."

Sam nodded. That appealed to him. "Do you need an escort?"

"No. Fewer people, less attention."

That made Sam curious. In his view, it was an unnecessary risk, one Carter would not usually take. "And third?"

"Watch your men closely. Like I said, Jack trusted them, and now he's dead."

Sam's jaw tightened, but he kept his voice calm. "What do you mean by that?"

Carter clasped his hands behind his back, head bowed. "Now, I just stated two demonstrable facts. It's the connection between the two that you're refusing to see."

"With good reason. I trust the Horsemen with my life."

"With your existence. Your life was over when I found you praying for death because your guts were spilling on the ground."

Sam didn't reply. Even now, the memory was still too vivid for comfort.

Carter gave him a searching look. "Sam, listen to me. Winspear's as socialized as a jaguar. He's got his own rules. He's a doctor now, but don't forget he spent the first few hundred years of his life as an assassin. Kenyon is a werewolf. He's not even one of us. And what else? Oh, right, Jack might have taken the boy in hand once he was all but grown, but Kenyon spent his adolescence crawling through windows for a team of international jewel thieves."

Sam stopped again. Like a kaleidoscope, all the pieces of his world were shifting into a new and uncomfortable pattern. "They are proven men."

Carter waved an impatient hand. "And you're a good friend. How nice."

Anger flared, and now Sam didn't care if Carter saw it. "The Horsemen are a team."

His maker's face sagged into regretful lines. "I'm not saying this lightly. Follow the facts. What two crimes do we know for sure happened? A jewel theft and an assassination. Who are your teammates? A jewel thief and an assassin. Give me a straight edge and a pencil, and I'll connect the dots for you."

Stunned, Sam was silent.

"I'm sorry." Carter put a hand on his shoulder. "We're vampires. You know all too well what that means. We may believe in loyalty and render great service to our king, but that impulse for good is a shaky thing. I've faced my true nature, mastered my base instincts. I've been the iron hand of the Company that keeps the vampires in check. Scratch the surface of any of us, and the pus of pure evil will come bubbling out. It's a fact of nature, as surely as the cock crows at sunrise."

Speechless, Sam could only stare. It didn't help that he'd been thinking the same thing only minutes before Carter had appeared.

Carter went on. "But none of this is news to you."

"No," he finally replied.

Chapter 13

If I survive this, I deserve my own reality show.

Chloe spent the morning in Uncle Jack's study pulling miracles out of her hat. Or, to make the metaphor more appropriate, her bridal veil. She'd booked the golf club. She'd found an orchestra and a DJ. She'd nailed the church. She'd got her staff started on finding limousines.

Oddly, working was doing her good. She was in a fairly good mood by the time Sam made his daily invasion into her territory. Today he looked more serious. Lines of fatigue etched deep into his face, as if he'd spent the night worrying. With everything going on, she'd be surprised if he hadn't. Still, she tried to ignore just how good he looked in his perfectly tailored suit. If she got sidetracked, she'd fall even further behind.

"What are you doing?" he asked when he saw her typing madly on her laptop.

"Working on Elaine and Leo's wedding."

Surprise flickered over his features. "I thought…"

"Yesterday was just a temporary setback. After all, there aren't that many wedding planners available and willing to work this quickly. At least, not with my contacts." Chloe let a note of defiant pride into her voice. "This is what I'm good at. And this is the agreement with the catering company."

She hit Send and barely resisted the urge to pump her fist in the air. Okay, she was overtired.

"Are you meeting Elaine in Thurston again?"

"Yes, at the nice offices I wanted to rent last time. From now on, I'm doing this my way."

Sam scowled.

Chloe scowled back but couldn't keep it up. "Bodyguards and bridal bouquets don't mix. I'll figure out some way to manage things sensibly. I have a friend coming back from Europe. I know she won't mind going with me to these appointments, just so that I'm not alone."

"Is she a weapons expert?"

"She's a photographer. I'm asking her to do the wedding shoot."

"A camera's not going to help if someone jumps you."

"I dunno. My friend's a redhead. I wouldn't try it."

"I'm serious."

"So am I." Chloe closed her laptop. She wanted Sam to feel appreciated, but this was her livelihood. "Everything has to go right this time. I appreciate your concern, but I can't afford to alienate my clients. They want sunshine and puppies, not a private army."

Sam folded his arms. "Kenyon and I are going with you."

"Sorry, I can't have you guys standing around brooding like angels of doom."

He winced. "I'll stay in the background. Everyone likes Kenyon. He can be the good cop."

Remembering Lexie's odd reaction when Faran Kenyon's name came up, Chloe balked. She still didn't know what to make of that conversation, but Lexie would be in town soon enough and could explain. In the meantime, she wasn't risking another disaster with Elaine. "No. I'll go by myself. Bridal talk is a girly thing. You're not girls."

"Chloe," he said, his voice close to a warning growl.

"Don't 'Chloe' me. I appreciate everything you've done, but I'm in charge of my own business appointments."

She felt his displeasure like a physical wall. Too bad. He was pushing her in a way that set her alarm bells ringing. And it set her imagination racing, taking that moment and painting it large. If she gave in now, what would happen down the road?

It was easy to guess. If she didn't stand up to him, he would take over everything, an inch at a time. And, sooner or later, he would leave—maybe not as dramatically as Neil, but men like Sam didn't do the domestic scene. Then she would have to pick up whatever pieces he dropped—even if that included pieces of her heart. Better to stand her ground now.

She took a deep breath, trying to sort fact from fear. This would be so much easier if she was more willing to trust. *And what if I am taking a stupid risk? He knows more about this security stuff than I do.*

She rose, drifting around the desk and crossing the thick Oriental carpet to the window. Sam had left the drapes alone this time, so she could look out at the garden. Not that she cared what was outside, but it gave her a moment to gather her wits.

It was gray out, raining lightly. She was wearing nothing but slacks and a sleeveless blouse, and the air near the French doors was cool. She rubbed her bare arms.

He finally spoke. "Chloe, with luck, this will all be over soon."

"What do you mean?"

"Things will go back to normal. The dress will go back to the princess. You'll go back to your home."

"And you'll go back to *your* home, wherever that is." She said it flatly. The implication that they'd soon be out of each other's lives was all too clear.

"Wherever. I have several addresses."

He said it inconsequentially, but the statement made her turn around. "That sounds—" She started, then stopped. "That sounds like a logistical nightmare, actually. I can barely keep track of my cable bill as it is."

He chuckled, a surprisingly warm sound for a man who didn't seem to get much practice. "You never say what I expect you to."

Chloe took a step toward him, feeling the cold from the window on her back. "It's a flaw of mine. I think I'm checking to see if anyone is paying attention."

"Who wouldn't?" His smile was filled with male appreciation. Unexpectedly, everything seemed to shift, the mood in the room lightening.

"Why do you have addresses and not a home?"

He shrugged. "I work here and there. I'm never in one place very long."

"Does that bother you?"

He touched her arm, just a light brush of the fingertips. "Honestly, yes. Sometimes I long for a real place, just so I know where I'm going to come back to."

Both his touch and his words made her shiver. Neither was an overt come-on, but she suddenly wondered if there was a possibility for something between them. It was an odd thought—a complete reversal—given their tense conversation a moment ago, but it wasn't completely unthinkable, either. She could feel his interest like an electrical field, invisible but still crackling along her skin. *I'd like to come back to you,* it seemed to say.

Get real. He has one foot out the door. He's just said as much. But maybe he wouldn't go if there was a reason to stay.

Her heart sped for a moment. Sam raised his head as if he could hear it. *Trust Sam,* Jack had said. On the other hand, Lexie had told her to run for the hills. The choice was wide-open.

"Now let me ask you something," he said. "Why are you so determined to put yourself in danger by going to Thurston by yourself? I promise Kenyon and I will be very, very good."

She stiffened. "You know why."

"You think we'll be in the way."

"Yes. Maybe. You scared Elaine half to death. And I have to look after myself. We all do."

"When it makes sense." Sam's hand traveled to his gun. "When it doesn't, I'm there."

Until you're not. Chloe dreaded having this conversation with anyone. It always sounded crazy. "I can't leave it up to you."

"Why not? Why not let me take care of you? It's what I'm good at."

"I'll try to explain."

"Good." His gaze held hers, but this time the gray wasn't like steel. It was like a far-off storm, dark and heavy with power.

"It's an old thing with me. My parents were scientists working on something supersecret."

"You said they died."

"When I was a teenager they were murdered in a home invasion. All I ever found out was that it had to do with their work. I still don't know what that work involved."

Sam didn't say anything for a moment, just frowned. "You were very young."

She folded her arms protectively across her chest. The atmosphere in the room was softened by the clouds outside, the jewel tones of the carpet and drapes washed with gray. "The worst part of their death has always been never knowing why it happened. Was there something I could have done to take precautions? Sure, I was only fourteen, but I still wonder. Had I said the wrong thing to a random stranger? Did I leave a door unlocked? Give away our phone number when I shouldn't have? Will whoever killed them ever come looking for me?"

Sam shifted, moving a fraction closer. "Unlikely. That was a long time ago."

"But I don't know because I have no idea what any of it was about. It's left me with doubts for the rest of my life."

Sam leaned against the bookcase, a boneless motion that reminded her of a big cat. It put his face only inches from hers. "And the point of this is that you see lack of information as a threat."

"Yes, that's part of it." Chloe exhaled. So few people understood, but Sam was keeping up.

He studied her, his expression intent. "Your uncle was full of secrets, too."

"He was."

"How did you feel about that?"

Gently, he traced a finger down her cheek. She shivered slightly, but was too mesmerized to pull away.

"Not great. And now look where that's got us. I adored Uncle Jack, but a safe full of hot diamonds? Not a great goodbye present. And yet, without telling me anything about what's going on, he leaves me a note asking me to do the right thing. How should I know what that is?"

"You think he abandoned you with a mess. That you'd learned to count on him and then suddenly he wasn't there."

"Yes."

His finger came to rest on her lips and hovered there, light as a bee, before pulling away. "Just like your fiancé and your parents."

Chloe nodded, a little amazed. No one had ever grasped what she felt that quickly. "It's not completely fair to them, is it? People don't mean to die."

He gave a lopsided smile. "Feelings and logic don't always go together."

"Nonetheless, I don't like counting on people. It makes me feel safer to stand on my own two feet."

"There's nothing wrong with being independent." Sam put a hand on her waist, stroking her ribs lightly with his thumb. "But don't think your parents didn't want to be there for you. And I don't know if Jack could have done anything different. He was my friend and we worked closely together, but there are a lot of things about him that I'm just finding out."

"Are you trying to say Jack's secrecy was nothing personal?" The feel of his hand made her want to curl into him. Her thoughts struggled to stay with the conversation.

"I'm sure of it in your case. I'm still trying to decide that in mine." Disappointment colored his expression. "He trusted you to do the right thing. Hang on to that."

"He trusted you, too."

He gave her an odd look. "I hope so."

"Have you found anything out about the thief? Or his murder?"

For once, he didn't shy away from answering. "I can tell you that there are no guests registered in the area who are likely suspects. Kenyon and I have been going through the names."

"Is that all?"

"So far."

"I don't want to be shut out."

"I get that." His hand slid to the small of her back. "I'm on your side, remember?"

She swayed into him and he reciprocated, letting the hard length of him brush against her hip. Suddenly everything felt so right. *Trust Sam.*

She ran her hands over his shoulders, enjoying their massive strength beneath the fine wool of his jacket. He was giving her his signature smile, the barest hint of amusement curling the corners of his mouth. His gaze roved over her in a way that brought heat to her skin, setting every nerve tingling.

Her touch strayed from his shoulders, trailing down his arms. They were thick with muscle, strong in a way that appealed to the most primitive part of her brain. The fact that she was holding him like this, her fingers spanning this much pure male power, sent a ripple of need low in her body. If he had taken her then and there, she would have been ready.

His eyes darkened, as if he sensed the change in her.

Impulsively, she put one hand on either side of his face, caressing the hard, strong bones of his cheek and jaw. His cheeks felt rough with beard against her palms. She pulled his head down to press her lips against his. Firm and swift, she caught him before he could resist.

And gave a cry when something sharp poked her lip. She broke the kiss. "Ow!"

A salty, metallic taste teased her tongue. *Blood.*

Instantly, Sam turned away.

Ugh. Embarrassing. "I'm sorry, honestly. Too much enthusiasm."

Much more slowly, Sam turned back to her, his color high. He had one hand to his mouth, as though she'd bruised him. "It's okay."

The words came out in a mumble. His eyes were nearly black, as if the pupil had expanded to fill the steel-gray irises. The room was dim, but she could see hunger in those black depths. Chloe shivered, falling back a step. There was a look men got when they wanted a woman. This was it to the umpteenth power.

"Okay, then," she breathed, her stomach going cold with unease and then melty with the need to answer that look.

Then, quick as if he'd flipped a switch, the look was gone, the emotion behind it locked away behind the wall of his self-control. Chloe blinked, wondering if she had seen it at all.

Tentatively, she reached out. She had to apologize to know what he was thinking.

It wasn't to be. He flinched away as if her fingers burned white-hot. Without another word, Sam walked out of the room, his shoulders hunched and his hand still over his mouth.

Embarrassment twisted through her, sending heat flaring up her cheeks. She could run after him, or she could stay frozen in abject humiliation. But what would she say when she caught up to him? *Sorry I knocked out a tooth, but it means I like you?*

Feeling twelve, she stayed put, as if her feet were nailed to the carpet. What *was* that look? Had it really been there? Had she ruined everything?

Chloe fell onto the library's leather couch and breathed

a curse to the rain outside. She touched her lip. It felt hot and sore, but there was no more blood. It had barely been a scratch, but obviously Sam was hurt.

How humiliating. She should have agreed to go home when this whole mess had first started. She buried her face in her hands.

Now she'd be known by all the Men in Black as the little wedding planner who kissed like a battering ram.

Chapter 14

It wasn't exactly news that he was a slavering beast. Sam just considered it a private matter. One didn't let *those* hang out in public.

Humiliating. Sam stomped down the basement stairs of Jack's mansion, feeling like Dracula returning to his lair. Cue the spooky organ music.

The problem with pretty girls was that, in their warm, soft way, they brought out a vampire's fangs. As if men didn't have enough involuntary physical reactions to deal with. Usually Sam's control was much, much better, but Chloe was in a league of temptation all her own.

As if things weren't already complicated enough. Sam slammed the door to Jack's office. His real office, not the study Chloe was using. This room wasn't all fine furniture and frilly china. This had a plain desk, several computers and not much else. All business. The door, hidden in the mansion's vault of a basement, was coded to chip cards only Jack and Sam possessed.

He flung himself into the squeaky desk chair. He wanted to break something. Assert his will. Prove that he had force and power. He was War. He wasn't a teenaged boy awkwardly asking for his first dance.

Cursing, he poked the desktop monitor to life. A login box popped up. While Sam typed in his Company email ID and password, his thoughts returned to Chloe. They'd done that every five seconds or so since the first moment he'd met her.

He had to make a decision. Not that there were any real options, of course, but just *pretending* that it would be okay to have an affair with a human woman—and Jack's niece to boot… Even wanting it seemed like folly.

Pre-vampire Sam had carried on functional relationships. Post-vampire War had lovers, but not women he loved. He'd learned the hard way to steer clear of such weakness. Until Chloe. For her, he could see staying in one place, going to bed with her every day, guarding her through the journey of her life.

Clearly he was losing his mind. If he took one of those magazine tests to find out who his ideal mate might be, Sam Ralston should be sending flowers to a wolverine. He was a predator with healthy self-esteem and a triple-A-plus alpha rating.

Which was all true, except when it wasn't. Part of him was still just Sam, terrified of what he'd become and afraid he was going to hurt someone he loved.

Disgusted with himself, he two-finger typed his way to his email. There was a message from Winspear. It was typically brief. "Death's medical file predates skeletal identification program. No comparison films on record."

So, Jack never got around to doing the full-body

X-rays. Sam shut the email with a curse. *It was just an X-ray, Jack. Couldn't you have done that much for us?* But no, that would have been too much like paperwork. Not Jack's thing. Neither, apparently, was turning in the crown jewels when they found their way into his personal safe.

Was Sam the only one who ever followed the rules? Who did his job because he'd taken an oath to say that he would?

A memory surged up of a crowded dance floor. Girls in scraps of dresses, Sam assigned to watch over them. It hadn't been his comfort zone. Parachute him into a jungle, give him a mountain to climb, and he was in heaven. But this time the jungle cats wore human faces. He was trained to spot the enemy, but it was harder when they looked exactly the same as the victims—kids on a dance floor, having fun.

He had been Princess Amelie's bodyguard. The shooter who had tried to kill her—and ended up killing the princess's friend instead—had been little more than a boy.

The kid had looked utterly blank, as if he'd just happened to be holding the gun at the time. Sam hadn't hesitated to bring him down, but he'd still been too late. Despite metal detectors and pat-downs, the guards had somehow let the boy into the club with a weapon.

Sam had been uneasy that night and had wanted to put his own men on the doors. But he hadn't because Carter had specifically told him to leave the usual security in place. War followed orders, especially Carter's orders. He was the weapon, not the hand that wielded it. *And didn't that work out well?* he mused bitterly. The guards had turned out to be traitors. The boy had claimed he had no recollection of the incident—almost like he'd been the victim of vampire mind control.

Impossible, of course. Why would any of the vampires hurt the princess?

That was just one more good question to tighten the knot in Sam's stomach. The incident had shaken his faith in those around him. Sam had started thinking a little harder about his orders since that night, an unease that had haunted him since.

He was thinking about his orders now.

So what was Carter's point about the other Horsemen? Kenyon and Winspear made good suspects. As well as having the right skills, they were close to the victim and involved in the investigation. Absolutely true. But Carter had no proof. *Why sow distrust without something to back up those accusations?*

He turned the question around. Why would Carter, iron hand of the Company's vampires, want Sam to believe his friends were traitors? Good question. Carter considered himself a one-person crusade against vampire-kind's vile instincts. Fierce discipline alone made these mad dogs into obedient warriors for good. Sam had always believed him.

Yet Chloe insisted that Sam wasn't a monster. She contradicted Carter's pus-and-evil assessment of true vampire nature. She had no idea he was the walking dead, but otherwise she was pretty perceptive. Sam didn't want to dismiss her opinion out of hand.

Then again, Carter should know how bloodsuckers thought. He'd been undead longer than any of them, except maybe Winspear. Had one of the Company's vampires suddenly lost their scruples and decided to steal the diamonds?

"No," Sam said out loud. "I don't buy it." If it had

been outright theft, why sew them onto a dress? That made no sense.

This is what Chloe meant when she said lack of information makes her nervous. Sam felt a surge of sympathy for her. Unfortunately, she had to be kept in the dark. Everything about this case—about Sam—was a secret. If she found out what he was, he would have to make sure her memories were erased. If it ever got out that Sam had revealed what he was and let her walk away, it could mean death for them both. Carter's rules.

A sick feeling invaded Sam's gut, as if something noxious was seeping upward from the floor. He had to let Chloe go. Anything else was unfair to both of them—but he couldn't walk away until she was safe. That meant getting the dress back to the palace as soon as possible.

Carter was waiting in the wings to do just that. But, good Company soldier or not, Sam wasn't ready to hand it over. With Chloe involved, he wasn't taking any chances until he was absolutely sure of what was going on. He'd made the mistake of going against his gut instincts that night in the dance club, and right now there were far too many unanswered questions.

Speaking of which...

He logged in to a restricted part of the Company's security system, then another, passing through firewall after firewall to access the database that listed agents. Sam had higher clearance than most.

He typed in the name "Jessica Lark" and then hit Search.

The database returned a terse message: Deceased. Special division.

So she was an agent! It had been a wild guess, but he'd been right. A tingle of satisfaction passed through him. He was finally getting somewhere.

There was a picture. It wasn't a portrait, but a candid shot taken in front of the Algonquin Hotel in New York City. Jessica Lark had been a beautiful woman. *I should have listened to Chloe. She hit on the truth when she couldn't even understand what it meant.* The woman's instincts were downright scary.

He stared at the monitor, his world doing that kaleidoscope shift all over again. Lark wasn't the only person in the picture. Between one cursor blink and the next, he thought he understood what was going on. Horror turned him cold, and for a brief instant he prayed he had it all wrong.

Chapter 15

Not long after, Sam tracked Chloe to the garden. He had two purposes in mind. The first was to listen again to what she knew about Jessica Lark. The second was to persuade her to accept a security detail for her afternoon appointment. Simply announcing that it was going to happen had brought out her difficult side, blast it. He had to regroup and try a gentler tone. That was going to take some imagination on his part. War wasn't used to saying "please."

She was walking slowly under the twisting branches of the Garry oaks, her head bent in thought. He studied her, squinting against the sun despite his sunglasses and the overcast sky. The sun hurt him, a hot pressure against his skin, sharp knives to his sensitive eyes. Still, if the outdoors was where Chloe was to be found, that was where he would go.

She'd slipped a loose sweater over her blouse and wore

low-heeled canvas shoes with a pattern of pink and green flowers. Sam thought he could see glimpses of the girl she had been when Jack had brought her, an orphan, into his house.

He cursed whoever had killed her parents. When he was done with this case, he would look at their file. He couldn't bring them back, but perhaps he could offer Chloe some justice.

He liked that idea. A lot. "Chloe."

She looked up, surprise lighting her face. "I'm sorry. I hope your tooth is okay."

Sam's step hitched. For a blessed moment, he'd forgotten about the dental incident. "I'll survive."

Her cheeks flushed a delicate pink. In the hazy gray of the overcast afternoon, her skin was a shade of tawny pearl, lightly freckled where the sun had touched it. Sam's fingers yearned to tame the wisps of hair blowing across her cheeks. He dared not risk it. He wanted her so badly that touching her invited his beast. He could at least begin the conversation minus the slavering fangs.

"I don't usually kiss like it's a contact sport," she grumbled.

"The idea has interesting possibilities. I'm curious about penalty shots."

That earned him a dark look. "Really, I'm better than that."

"I know."

He could feel his resolve crumbling. Her essence was more powerful than all of War's arsenal of strength and speed. The most he could do was try to stick to business.

He had to. What he'd realized when he'd opened Lark's file—or as much of it as his clearance allowed—had him worried. It confirmed his decision to keep the dress until he absolutely understood what was going on.

"Tell me again about Jessica Lark," he said, moving to the shadier side of the path.

"I don't know much more than what I already told you. One thing, though. I found her signature on the wedding gown." Chloe folded her arms, hugging herself. "I emailed a picture to someone who knows the designers. She wrote back this morning and confirmed it was Lark's. That means, even without the jewels, that dress is worth a small fortune."

Sam digested that. "How did Jack say he knew Lark?"

Chloe shrugged. "He knew all kinds of people."

The walk curved around a pond bordered by trailing willows. Ducks paddled across the surface, chuckling softly amongst themselves. Chloe stopped, pulling off one of her flats to empty out a stone. Her toenails were painted a pale pink.

Sam watched the play of bones and tendons in her slender foot. He had been born in a time when women hid their ankles. He suddenly understood why. They could be incredibly erotic. His blood stirred in an extremely unhelpful way. "Maybe one of Jack's girlfriends knew Lark? Bought from her collection?"

"No. I remember now." Her voice gained energy as she spoke. "It had something to do with old books. Jack was a collector. So was she. They met at an auction."

She smiled up at him, obviously pleased to be helpful. It was adorable.

It was also useful information. If Lark was an undercover agent, she would have needed a reason to publicly associate with Jack. That, in turn, might give a clue as to what she was involved with. "Any particular area of interest?"

Chloe pulled her shoe back on, wriggling her heel into

place. "Occult stuff. Jack has some odd manuscripts. He let me look at them whenever I liked."

Sam looked at her sharply. "Really?"

"He had a thing about vampires."

Shock slammed into him, his chest squeezing with alarm. "What?" *Had Jack lost his mind?* Vampires never showed an open interest in the occult, in case it raised questions.

Chloe turned, walking backward a few steps while she studied his face. She'd seen that moment of astonishment. "Yeah. He was an avid collector. Everything from Renaissance books of magic down to plastic teeth. It was his main hobby."

Sam took a deep breath, trying to still his churning stomach. "Why do you think he was so interested?"

"Maybe it was because he lived like a creature of the night. Up all hours. Bad diet. Coming and going without warning. Went through women like snack food. He was a great uncle, but he had his quirks."

The way she said it, so offhand, softened Sam's sense of alarm. "Did you talk about it much?"

"Some. He loved sharing his collection with a few people he liked. He didn't talk about it much otherwise."

In a roundabout way, Jack had been letting Chloe know who he was, telling her without telling her. If any of the Company—like Sam—had known, they would have panicked. But, as always, Jack had gone his own way. Sadness flooded Sam for his friend, and for all the secrets they had to keep.

As if sensing his melancholy, Chloe took his hand. "The books are still here, if you want to see them."

Her slender fingers were lost in his. All of her seemed fragile compared to the masculine world of his existence.

Irrationally, he felt afraid to close his own fingers lest he crush her bones.

Sam swallowed hard. "No, that's okay. I just keep trying to figure out Jack's connection to Lark and the dress."

They walked a few paces, Sam tucking her hand into the crook of his elbow. Leaves rustled on a thyme-scented breeze. It was hard to believe this was the same route Sam had followed, chasing the blood trail of Chloe's attacker. In the gentle afternoon light, the garden was a haven.

Chloe pushed a strand of hair behind her ear. "My guess is Lark trusted him enough to give him the dress for safekeeping. Maybe she knew something was up. And if a friend asked Jack to do something, he'd do it." She gave Sam a shrewd look. "Maybe Jack was just holding it for her, and then she was killed."

"Maybe. It's a good explanation, especially if his intention was to eventually return the dress to Marcari."

Chloe's blue gaze was steady. "Jack wasn't a thief."

"No, he wasn't." Sam felt the truth of her words, sharp and clean as a sword. She could see to the heart of people, and it made far more sense than Carter's dark view of the vampires.

Chloe's fingers squeezed his arm as they walked, the heat of her like life itself. Her lips quirked. "So now you know Jack's deep, dark secret."

"That he collected Count Chocula bobblehead dolls?"

She laughed softly. "I'm not sure there is such a thing."

"We all have something we'd rather not share."

"How about you?"

"Pardon?"

"Don't shy away now. Fair is fair. We shouldn't get to pick on Jack unless we confess our own peculiarities."

"I have Fido."

"He's just a pet."

You have no idea. "What are yours?"

"Isn't spending my life playing with balloons and confetti enough?"

"That's just a job."

Chloe ducked her head, obviously thinking of something but too embarrassed to say it. Sam grinned. "Okay, I'll go first."

She looked up. "What?"

"I'm a Civil War fanatic."

"What, with little armies covering the dining room table, or are you one of those guys who goes out to fight Gettysburg once a year?"

"I did Fredericksburg. Never made it to Gettysburg."

"Still, that's pretty hard-core."

"Now it's your turn."

She turned that rosy pink again. "I never threw out my collection of stuffed ponies. I still have them all in my bedroom."

He smiled. He couldn't help it. He had a ridiculous mental image of the Four Horsemen done in pastel plush. "Is this part of the same fantasy that requires a gold-hoofed palfrey for Elaine to ride down the aisle?"

"That's not my idea, Elaine's mom came up with that. But, yeah, I understand the fantasy appeal."

They'd reached the end of the path. Behind Chloe, delphiniums fountained in blue spires, matching the color of her eyes.

Without even knowing what he was going to do, Sam kissed her. It happened too quickly for second thoughts. She was suddenly in his arms, his fingers folded in the soft fabric of her sweater.

There was no straight line of reason in Sam's mind, just a burning need to do this right. Just once, he needed to approach Chloe as a man. A man who wanted her more than anything.

He began kissing her slowly, first the top lip, then the bottom, teasing until her body began melting into his, her weight sinking against his chest. Her fair hair tumbled over his dark jacket, reminding him of gold turning to molten liquid in a crucible. Gold, the one element that was incorruptible.

He was a creature of darkness, but she drew him into the light. The part of him that was still a man, the lost part, the lonely part, craved it the way a man abandoned in the desert for years craved cool, clear water.

Sam stroked her arm, the feel of the soft, plush sweater against his palm strangely arousing. Her fingers touched his neck, featherlight brushes. As her breath exhaled against his lips, his ears, he could feel her pulling him down to her, yearning to be closer. He drank in the warmth of her skin through his lips. She smelled golden, like the sun shining through a kitchen window. She tasted like everything he missed.

Sam ached through his whole being. Like an endless wellspring, there was ever more begging for his touch, no matter how much of her loveliness he claimed with mouth and hands.

His hand traveled up her spine, from the sway of her back and along the arc of her ribs. He found the warm fullness of her breasts, surprising in a woman so slender. She shivered under the pressure of his fingers, but it was in anticipation. He kneaded her gently, feeling her nipples grow hard and ready for pleasure.

The thought intoxicated him, drew him further into

the moment. Chloe broke away, her lips lingering near his before they returned, soft and warm, to kiss him back.

And this time he kept his fangs to himself. Everything was perfect.

Chapter 16

It was no great mystery how Sam eventually talked her into accepting his protection that afternoon. When she thought about it, Chloe felt sheepish. As much as she had tried, she was no match for his masculine wiles.

Happily, Faran readily agreed to go, as well. Cheerful and client-friendly, he would cover the interior of the small, pretty business center in the Eldon Hotel. Sam would watch the exterior. Two bodyguards seemed absolute overkill to Chloe, but she wasn't going to argue anymore. Maybe she was being naive. After all, she had limited experience with crazed jewel thieves, and Sam seemed to feel his presence was a necessary precaution. As long as he didn't talk to the clients, Chloe was okay with that. And he did kiss so very, very well.

However, she remembered Lexie's warning about falling for her Swiss Army knife the moment she got to the meeting room and pulled out her phone. There was a voice message from her friend. Chloe waited to play it until Faran had deposited her binders of photos and samples and went to park the car. Sam, of course, assumed his guard dog post outside the door.

Lexie had booked her flight from Austria for that day. She'd also booked into the Eldon, adamant that she would not stay in the same house as her former boyfriend. A quarter hour later, Elaine arrived along with Iris Fallon, the mother of the bride. Chloe summoned her brightest smile. "Lovely to see you again, Mrs. Fallon."

The straight-backed, trim woman had a firm handshake and a brisk, no-nonsense snap to her words. "I came along to make sure things don't run off the rails."

"Of course," Chloe replied, doing her best not to be offended.

It probably would have made no difference if she were. Iris didn't look the sensitive type. One might have broken china against that no-hair-out-of-place helmet of iron-gray waves.

"Please don't take this personally, but I don't trust anyone who doesn't come from within our circle to strike just the right chord." She gave Chloe an assessing look, as if deciding whether or not Jack Anderson's niece counted. "Speaking of which, I insist upon a harpist for the reception."

"I'm sure we'll all appreciate your insights," Chloe replied.

"I should say so, since I'm paying your bill."

They settled into chairs.

Chloe offered her sweetest smile, glad she'd decided to start with something easy. "I thought perhaps we could look at some cake designs, just to get a sense of what appeals. Then we can think about doing some tasting.

I have an excellent dessert chef who will deliver anywhere we like."

"Did somebody say cake?" Faran entered the room carrying a tray laden with coffee and cookies.

Chloe mentally crossed her fingers, hoping Bodyguard 2.0 would hit the right chord with Elaine. "This is Faran Kenyon, who will be assisting me today."

She needn't have worried. Faran gave a sunny smile and waved a hand at the tray. "The coffee shop had vanilla-hazelnut blend. It smelled so good, I couldn't resist. How do you take your coffee? Cream? Sugar?"

Elaine gave him a huge smile. "Cream and sugar, please."

Perfect. Chloe could see shoulders relaxing, spines curving into the soft and welcoming furniture. Within seconds, she saw Faran knew how to work a crowd.

Only Iris seemed reluctant to thaw. With a chilly smile, she flipped the pages of the photo album with an audible snap.

"So what kind of cakes are these?" Iris sniffed. "They're not that cardboard flummery you put out for show? I want the real thing under the icing."

"I assure you, those are real cakes." Chloe watched them speed by under the woman's rough fingers. There were the traditional tiered cakes, but also castles and ships, a huge sheet cake decorated like a football field. She'd been proud of every one.

"If I may." Faran pulled up an armchair and sat down. "What kind of cake batter you use is sometimes dependent on the style of the cake. It has to be firm enough to support the design."

Iris gave him a sharp look. "How would a young man like yourself know about that?"

Chloe wondered, too. Last thing she'd heard, he was

a spy with an unsettling interest in other people's jewelry. And she didn't need another Man in Black ruining her appointments.

But Faran just gave a pleasant smile. "I have my chef's papers, ma'am. Desserts aren't my specialty, but I know one or two things about cake design."

Elaine spoke up. "Chloe, you know some very interesting people."

"Elaine," Iris snapped, using her daughter's name like a reproach. "You can't believe every bit of nonsense a pretty boy tells you, and you'd be better off if you'd paid attention to that fact long before this circus came to town."

Chloe narrowed her eyes. She'd had enough. Weddings belonged to the bride and groom, and Elaine wasn't being heard. "Excuse me, Mrs. Fallon. I completely understand how you want everything to be perfect. That's why I'm here to help you." Gently, Chloe pulled the book of photographs from Iris's hands and set it on the table. "As you know, we settled on the medieval theme as a compromise between elegance and a sense of fairy tale wonder."

"Yes." Elaine said. "It was the one theme we all could live with."

"All right." Step one, get everyone back to a place of consensus. Step two, work out from there. "So our cake has to be in keeping with the medieval theme. What would be perfect for our fairy tale kingdom?"

"A castle," Elaine said, suddenly enthused. "We could have a cake that looked like a castle."

"A white castle with shining turrets," Iris added. "With pennants fluttering from the towers."

Chloe smiled warmly. "What an excellent idea."

Never mind she'd already thought of it. The castle itself could be fruitcake, the surrounding forest, moat and drawbridge could be spun sugar on a softer cake base. That way both bride and mom could have something they wanted. She didn't know the exact engineering required—her culinary experience barely stretched to scrambled eggs—but her dessert chef was a genius at these things.

Unfortunately, Elaine was looking a little glum again. Shining turrets were good, but not perfect. *Needs to be more playful.* "What does everyone think of adding a dragon?" Chloe asked.

"Oh, yes!" Elaine brightened at once. "A castle has to have a dragon."

Iris looked less convinced. "Maybe a small one."

"I'll see what the chef can do." She gave Elaine a wink. The woman smiled, ducking her head. "I'll have some samples sent for our next appointment. Maybe Leo would like to come to the tasting?"

Faran had moved to stand by the credenza where he'd left the coffee tray, out of everyone's line of sight but Chloe's. He made a thumbs-up gesture. Chloe tried not to watch him, keeping her face serious.

"He must send samples within twenty-four hours," Iris demanded. "Since the wedding will be next week."

"Next week?" Chloe squeaked. "You said it was in two months!"

Elaine looked abashed. "I'm so sorry, but that was before Grandma Fallon's last appointment. She's not going to last until late summer."

"You neglected to mention the new timeline?" Iris asked her daughter in freezing tones. But Chloe had noticed the flinch when Grandma Fallon was mentioned. Iris was covering up a lot of sadness.

Elaine closed her eyes. "I forgot. I think I remembered to forget. This is too fast. We can't ask Chloe to do it."

"Next week." Chloe's voice sounded weak in her own ears. Her head felt inflated, as it might float off her shoulders at any moment. "I can try, but I have no idea what to do about a reception hall on such short notice. They're booked months in advance, sometimes years."

Iris's thinly plucked brows drew together. "Well, this isn't the kind of service I expected. What kind of a wedding planner can't provide a reception hall?"

One with insane clients! Chloe longed to scream it as she lunged across the coffee table to throttle the woman, but no one hired a planner with a record of strangling her customers.

"I have an idea," Faran broke in.

Everyone turned to look at him.

"What about Jack's place? It's big enough for two weddings this size."

Chloe sat back, feeling dizzy with relief and dread. Faran was right. It had everything that she needed: parking, gardens, reception rooms, guest accommodations, kitchens and staff.

And thieves. If Sam was right, assassins.

"That's Oakwood Manor, isn't it?" Iris purred. "What a splendid idea."

Be careful, Chloe thought. *You might get the wedding you deserve.*

Chapter 17

The humans and Kenyon were eating their dinner downstairs. Sam was upstairs, pacing the hallway. He wasn't in the mood to pretend. He'd heard the whole wedding-at-Oakwood discussion through the meeting room door. Part of him wanted to say it was a terrible idea—a security nightmare—that should be squashed immediately. On the other hand, that amount of chaos would surely tempt his adversaries to make their move. In a perverse way, the Fallon–Venuto wedding would give Sam the opportunity to choose his battleground and he knew Oakwood inside out.

Sam wandered into one of the empty bedrooms on the third floor. It had the feel of an abandoned place, a little too cold, a tiny bit dusty. Still, it was a perfectly good place to make a private phone call. He pushed the door shut.

Sam was ready to deal with villains popping out of the

woodwork, but there were three other things to consider before he invited them to come get the diamonds. First was the shooting in the nightclub. The second was what he had learned about Jessica Lark. Last, there was Carter.

The shooter in the nightclub had always bothered him. Although an assassination would have furthered the agenda of fanatical elements invested in conflict between Marcari and Vidon—such as the Knights of Vidon—the shooter had no known political affiliations. In fact, the boy had seemed in a trance, almost as if he had no idea what he was doing. *Mind control.* Some vampires had the ability. Sam wasn't one of them, but both Carter and Winspear were. Both had been there that night. Both were here now. So were the Knights. Coincidence or connection? It was hard to tell.

And then there was Jessica Lark. From what he could tell from her records, Lark was not a vampire, but she wasn't human, either. Sam's guess was that the designer had fey blood. As a rule, the fey had their own agenda and weren't to be trusted, but the Company dealt with a few in a limited capacity. Only those agents with the very highest clearance went near the seductive, unpredictable creatures. The fact that Jack had been her contact made sense. He was an old and trusted agent of the Company. But why was Mark Winspear, a newcomer, the one in the photo with Jessica Lark?

And why was Carter really here? The Company's director didn't make pickup runs, no matter how important the cargo. Was he here only because he suspected Winspear and Kenyon to be traitors? He'd said as much, but Sam didn't buy it—no matter how sound Carter's reasoning. There had to be more to it.

He sat on the edge of the bed and pulled out his cell phone. *Do I really want to do this?* Once he dialed, once

he set things in motion, he would have to accept the results, whatever those turned out to be. Even if his friends
were in fact revealed as thieves and murderers.

But was that really a possibility? Kenyon had been
devoted to Jack, who had pulled him out of the gutter
and turned his life around. Kenyon wasn't an innocent,
but he had his own code. A heist for old time's sake?
Maybe. Anything more than that? Sam's gut said not—
to the point where he hadn't hesitated to ask him along
as Chloe's bodyguard. Sam didn't think Winspear would
kill Jack, either, and he'd sooner pull out his own fangs
than work with the Knights of Vidon. So what was his
involvement?

This was all wrong. Sam had always trusted his maker
completely, but the Horsemen were closer than brothers.
That changed everything.

He dialed Carter's number on his cell. Much would
depend on how his maker responded to Sam's plan.

"Sam, my boy," said the familiar gruff voice.

"Carter." Sam got up from the bed and began pacing
to the window and back. "The only way to end this is to
take the bull by the horns. Why don't we flush out whoever it is who wants this dress?"

Carter hesitated for a long, long moment. "Very well,"
he said at last. "That could put a lot of doubts to rest. I
know all this suspicion must be killing a straight arrow
like you."

Relief surged through Sam's tight muscles. Carter was
absolutely right. Certainty was the first thing he wanted.
The rest would follow.

The only real remedy for Chloe's headache would be
to lock Mrs. Fallon away for a week or two. Once Leo

and Elaine were safely out of the country, she could release the mother of the bride and present her with a bill.

She'd barely tasted dinner. After thanking Faran for
his help one more time—somehow he'd been roped into
helping with the reception menu—she retreated to her
bedroom and kicked off her shoes. She could almost feel
the blood rushing back into her toes. She wanted an aspi-
rin, a hot bath and fleecy pj's. It was all of eight o'clock.
The meeting had lasted hours. It had felt like days.

What Mrs. Fallon wanted, besides Jack's house and the
blasted gold-hoofed horse, included real cannons, flocks
of doves, and coffee beans that had been ingested and
then pooped out by an Indonesian civet cat. Kopi Luwak
was the most expensive coffee in the world and thankfully Faran thought he knew where he could get some.

This is insane. Chloe lay on her bed, fully clothed,
too tired to change. The only thing that made the stress
worthwhile was that pulling off this impossible wedding
would make her career. People who mattered would know
Chloe's Occasions.

According to Iris, between three and four hundred
guests would rearrange their schedules in order to attend. It was going to be a security nightmare. *Poor Sam.*

Chloe sat up, feeling bad. He really was being a sport
about moving the wedding to Oakwood. She wondered
whether he was really okay with the extra workload.

The only way to ease her conscience was to talk to
him. She got up and located kinder shoes.

Walking down the hall, she thought she heard his
voice. It was coming from one of the empty guest bedrooms, but that door was closed. Not so empty, then. She
stepped closer, listening to see if she was right.

Yes, it was Sam. The conversation sounded one-sided,
like he was on the phone, and he sounded tense. To inter-

rupt or not? She was just tired enough to be rude. Softly, she knocked.

Sam's words stopped abruptly, and then he said, "I'll call you back."

A moment later the door opened. He lifted one eyebrow. "I was wondering how long you were going to hover out there."

The man had to have the ears of a bat. She folded her arms. "The wedding's going to be here next week."

Sam stared at her blankly. "Yes, I know."

Nerves skittered through her stomach. She hadn't realized how worried she was about his goodwill until now. "I really, really hope you're okay with me having it here."

He stood with one hand on the doorknob, his big body blocking the doorway. "Is that what you came here to ask?"

This wasn't how she wanted the conversation to go. She wanted him to tell her everything was okay, and then they'd kiss again like they had in the garden that afternoon. He didn't appear to be in a comforting mood, though. She was going to have to help this along.

"Yes, well, I know there are a million reasons not to have it here." She pushed past him into the bedroom. "Not the least of which is that we won't get a break from wedding madness for days."

The muscles in his jaw flickered, as if he were clenching his teeth. His reply came out with a light dusting of sarcasm. "There are a few other reasons. Thieves. A man tried to kill you. Don't forget two people are already dead."

"I know, but maybe having more people around will actually make it safer."

His face said he didn't think much of that. "What are the reasons in favor of having it here?"

Chloe faced him, barely a foot of carpet between their toes. She could tell he was preoccupied with something that wasn't making him happy. His posture was stiff as steel. There was a perfectly good bed right next to them, and a closed door, but the timing just wasn't right for what should have been obvious next steps. The tension just made her more nervous.

She put a hand on his arm and tried to pull the frantic jitters from her own voice. "I can pull it off. If I'm on location 24/7 between now and the I-dos, I think I can make this work. It's very important to me, Sam. I need to make it happen for my career and, well, if I have to sell Jack's house, isn't a huge party the perfect way to bid it farewell?"

Something flickered behind his cool gray eyes. The line of his mouth softened. "Then we'll do it."

She wanted to give him a hug, but right now the line of his body wasn't inviting that. The shield he kept around his emotions was snapped shut.

"Thank you," she said, squeezing his arm. "And if it's important to me, just think how Leo and Elaine feel."

A smile flickered at the corners of his mouth. "No doubt like the center act in a three-ring circus."

"I'll have you know I run a very good circus." Chloe took a step back, remembering he had been in the middle of a phone call. Was that what his bad mood was all about?

He narrowed his eyes. "How many times have you planned this wedding?"

"First it was going to be next summer. Then in two months. Now it's Saturday."

"I thought so. If they get any closer, we can do it over breakfast." Sam smiled, but it didn't reach his eyes. "Doing everything this quickly is pretty unusual, isn't it?"

"I think it's safe to say it's unheard of."

"Don't worry. It'll all work out."

She prayed he was right. "One other thing."

"What?"

She rose on her toes and kissed him lightly on the cheek. Nothing intrusive. Just a reminder that he was more than just her security guy. Sam replied by kissing her lightly on the mouth, but that was it.

Chloe made her goodbyes and left the bedroom, closing the door behind her. She stood for a moment, her hand still on the door. What was wrong with him? Had something happened? *It had to do with that phone call. Is he going to call whoever it was back?*

Curiosity prodded her, but it was none of her business. *Yes, it is. I distinctly heard him say something about the dress. Whoever wants the dress.* She'd totally skipped over that in her anxiety about moving the wedding.

She had to know what the conversation was about. Unfortunately, Sam had that irritating talent Uncle Jack had possessed. He seemed to be able to see through doors. So, she walked away, making sure her footfalls were loud enough to hear.

And then crept back in stocking feet, holding her breath. It had worked with her uncle, sometimes. Tonight, it worked with Sam. She hovered near the door, careful not to bump against the wall.

"I'll have the dress. Can you come tonight?"

Chloe felt her cheeks grow hot. Sam had no right to give the gown to anybody without talking to her first.

"That's right," Sam said after a pause. "It'll be like throwing down raw meat. Let's see what animals show up to take a bite."

There was another long pause.

"In the garden, where Jack had that card party. Nine is too early. Make it eleven. That gives enough time to be sure the grapevine knows the details. I'll call a guy who'll tell his friends. We'll see who shows up."

Who was he talking to? The Men in Black with a garment bag? Chloe's temper was stirring. *Raw meat? Take a bite?*

It didn't sound as if he was returning a precious object to its rightful home. This sounded like a secret meeting after dark. Chloe leaned closer to the door, straining for every word.

"I haven't said anything," Sam went on. "Getting it will be easy. Knowing who's after it will be worth the risk."

Chloe's pulse pounded in her throat. Sam was doing the one thing she couldn't stand. He was leaving her out of the loop. *And he's using the dress Jack left in my care for bait!*

Chapter 18

How dare he!

Chloe silently slipped down the hall, eager to put distance between her and Sam. She really, really hadn't seen this coming. Sam was one of the good guys, or so she'd thought. It was bad enough that he was treating the dress as if he had a right to it—Uncle Jack had entrusted it to *her,* thank you very much—but Sam was keeping her utterly in the dark.

What was he about to do that he couldn't share with her? Nothing that would make her happy. Otherwise, why the secrets?

She was skilled at reading people, but never the men she liked. As usual, she'd totally misjudged the one person who counted the most. Chloe descended the stairs, only half aware of where she was going. For once, she was grateful Jack's house was so huge.

She couldn't let Sam shut her out. She had a huge stake

in all this, too. She might not have the skills to take down the bad guys herself, but she had a right to know what Sam was planning.

Chloe slipped back into her old bedroom. Flicking on the overhead, she paused by the door. The bloody bedcovers had been stripped from her mattress, leaving it looking oddly naked. Reluctantly, Chloe closed the door behind her, shutting herself in with the memories of being forced to the bed. *All the more reason to hurry.* The faster she moved, the shorter time she had to stay there.

Quickly, she crossed the room. She pulled open the drawers of the tall dresser, relieved to see her old clothes from college were still neatly folded inside. Emotion made her fingers tremble, but she cut herself no slack. A quick rummage produced an old black T-shirt, running shoes and a thick fleece jacket. She'd packed jeans when she came but didn't have anything else casual enough for what she wanted to do.

In the back of the bottom drawer she found an ankle sheath and knife Jack had given her. If she'd insisted on jogging on campus, he'd insisted she know how to keep herself safe. She'd hated the idea, but now she was glad she'd let him teach her a few things. Finally, she found her old camera. Lexie had given it to her years ago when they'd both been in a nature photography club, and it was far better for taking pictures in the dark than the point-and-shoot she carried now. She stuffed it in her pocket, just in case.

Chloe took everything back to her room and changed. Strapping on Jack's SIG Sauer, she did what she could to adjust his shoulder holster. It had definitely not been made for a girl. She finally got it into an acceptable position and then slid the fleece jacket over top. It felt bulky, but then again guns always felt too large to her. Thanks to Jack, she knew how to use them and wasn't afraid to shoot if she had to. She just prayed it wouldn't come to that. She was gathering information, nothing more.

Keeping out of sight, she crept down the stairs, stopping in the room where the security guys kept their stuff and scrounged a pair of night vision goggles. Then she went in search of Sam. He had to be around somewhere. He wasn't meeting whoever-it-was until eleven.

A search of the house took her downstairs and eventually outdoors. The night was clean, washed by a drizzle that had quieted to a hazy, starless night. Chloe made a circuit of the house, looking in the windows for signs of Sam.

It wasn't until she reached the side yard that she spotted him through the laundry room window. He stood next to a rack of clothes that had been returned from the dry cleaners. To her utter mystification, Sam tore the plastic off a pale dinner gown forgotten by someone who had come to stay for one of Jack's dinner parties. Normally, the staff would ship it on to the owner, but Sam apparently had other ideas. He was stuffing it into a gym bag, mashing the yards and yards of expensive antique white silk into its bulging maw and struggling with the zipper. *What the...?* And then it twigged with an electric tingle of amazement.

The dress was nearly the same shade of antique-white as the wedding gown. Sam wasn't taking the real wedding dress. Relief made her legs rubbery.

As soon as she recovered her wits, she ghosted away from the window. Sam was a professional security guy and, like Jack, seemed to have amazing senses. She didn't think Sam would find her snooping around endearing. He'd be more likely to lock her in with the dryer sheets and scrub brushes.

Sam emerged through the mudroom door, barely making a sound as he moved. Chloe squished herself into the deep shadows of the wall, holding her breath so that he couldn't even hear her intake of air. She needn't have worried. He barely paused to pull the door shut before he was walking through the garden at a brisk clip, the gym bag in one hand.

Chloe hesitated, counting the reasons to go back to her room. She was inexperienced and Sam seemed to hear everything. One mistake and he'd know she was there. And now she knew at least he wasn't stealing the dress.

But none of that changed her purpose. She needed to see who showed up every bit as much as Sam. From what she'd heard, whoever it was on the phone didn't know it was a substitute gown. Sam was playing an interesting game. And whoever fell for his bait was probably connected to Uncle Jack's murder.

A wave of pain and anger welled up inside her. She needed to know who had robbed her of her only real family. That was non-negotiable.

Moving as quietly as she could, she detached herself from the wall and crept to the head of the path Sam had used to disappear into the still darkness. If she squinted, she could just make out his form, a dim patch of black moving ahead. *He's headed toward the gazebo.* That made sense, given what Sam had said to the person on the phone. Jack had held plenty of card parties there.

With a rush of hard, cold satisfaction, Chloe set out along a separate path, planning to loop around and observe Sam's rendezvous from an entirely different vantage point, well away from any action. From there she would see everything, but not be seen. *It's okay. Uncle Jack taught you enough to handle this much.*

And Sam wouldn't have anything to complain about if he never knew she was there.

Set flush with the rock face of a small hill, the gazebo was one of the property's main features. Covered with wisteria, it was a large wood-and-wrought-iron structure big enough to house a table for eight.

Sam stood with his back to the structure, listening hard. At first there was nothing—no footsteps, not even a rustle of wind. The rain had stopped, leaving the air not only clean and cool but also washed of scent. He remained perfectly still, needing to hear whoever approached. He had told the regular security to vacate the gardens that night. He didn't want any unexpected incidents. Still, there were a few people scattered through the grounds.

The lights from the mansion glowed to his left, giving just enough illumination to see the figure silhouetted under the trees. The shadowy form crept closer, darting between the concealing bulk of the bushes and trees. He—for the figure moved like a man—was of medium height and build, and definitely human. Sam waited until the man was almost to the steps, and then stepped forward to grab his arm.

The figure made a surprised cry as Sam wrenched him around and slammed him against the gazebo's wooden porch. As he moved, Sam dropped the bag with the fake dress to the grass.

Like a striking hawk, another man swooped from the darkness to snatch it up, vampire-fast. Startled, Sam nearly let his prisoner slip from his grasp. *Didn't see that one coming.*

With a curse, Sam slammed the human to the ground, pinning him. The man whimpered, but Sam doubted he was doing any real damage. Then he saw the bandage above the man's collar, and recognized him as Chloe's attacker.

"Now I've got you," he snarled.

"Not before my friend gets you," the human replied.

Sam glanced up at the vampire, who was lingering a few yards away. The vampire's face was hidden beneath a hood, but Sam could see his Smith & Wesson clearly enough. "What are you hanging around for?" Sam snarled at Hood Guy. "You've got what you came for."

The only reply came when the vampire jacked a bullet into the chamber of his weapon. At the same moment, Sam became aware of someone moving along the rocky hill behind the gazebo. He caught the scent of lemon perfume.

Nine hells! Chloe! His gut seemed to make a corkscrew move, twisting until he thought he'd be sick. *What the blazes is she doing here?* Anger warred with panic. He absolutely couldn't let her be hurt. There were too many guns, too many possibilities for a stray bullet. He had to end this fast.

He didn't want to let his captive go, but he needed his hands free. Sam jumped to his feet, raising his gun in answer to the vampire's Smith & Wesson. The human scrambled upright and bolted, as Sam knew he would— but guarding Chloe came first.

"Your friend's free, now what do you want?" Sam snarled. "Get out of here."

The S&W fired, sending a bullet inches from Sam's cheek. A warning shot, but it was enough to make Sam flinch. A split second later, a muzzle flash flared from above the gazebo, and the vampire spun to his right, cursing with pain. Regular bullets couldn't kill, but they sure hurt.

"Chloe, duck!" Sam cried, dropping to one knee and sending three neatly clustered rounds Hood Guy's way.

The vampire dodged, but still managed to send a shot toward Chloe's hiding place. Chips flew from the wood and the bullet ricocheted from the wrought iron frame, rattling into the bushes.

Sam swore, emptying his clip. But when his sight cleared from the flare of the gunfire, his opponent had dissolved into the night.

Sam clamped down on his emotions, forcing his head to stay clear, and slammed another clip into his gun. "Chloe, are you all right?"

"Yes." Chloe's voice sounded small, but he smelled no human blood.

The moment she spoke, another shot spurted from the dark, aiming for the gazebo roof. Forgetting to play human for Chloe's benefit, Sam launched himself after the enemy, letting his feet fly over the rain-dampened grass. Wind rushed in his ears and stung his eyes, robbing every sense but that of smell. The vampire had come this way.

And then he realized he recognized the scent. The height and build were right, too, but he still didn't want to believe it.

Mark Winspear! Against all Sam's instincts, Carter had been correct. *But why is he doing this?*

Chapter 19

Chloe clung to the rock, fingers cold and stiff. It had been easy enough to get to this vantage point. She'd figured out how to get up here during her teens, when she needed a place to get away from adult supervision. Then, she'd been looking for trouble. Now, she'd found it.

She lowered the night vision goggles, letting them dangle around her neck. Their greenish glow was making her feel slightly sick, and she felt plenty nauseous already.

She'd shot someone. It had barely snagged his attention, but still. *She'd shot someone.* Hot tears spilled down her cheeks, her stomach roiling every time her mind replayed the moment.

A cold, practical part of her brain had taken charge and done the necessary thing. No hesitation. But all the training in the world couldn't prepare a person for the reality of that moment. It terrified her. She terrified herself.

And now Sam was charging through the darkness

after the two men, faster than she'd believed it possible to move. Would he stay safe? If she could pull a trigger, so could anyone else.

Her heart sped, racing on adrenaline until her head felt too light. *Please, please be okay.*

Night sounds seemed strange and muffled—her ears were still ringing from the sound of the gun. Chloe shivered, tightening her grip as she slid from the rock to the cedar shingles covering the gazebo roof. She'd picked this vantage point to take photos. She'd snapped just one before she'd drawn her gun instead. Now no one was around to shoot, in any sense of the word.

Time to get down. She inched over the shingles, hearing one crack as she wriggled to one of the corner posts. The gazebo had an ornamental facade that jutted above the roofline by just enough to give her a footrest. From there, she swung her legs over and crawled down its trellised side.

A body slammed into her the moment her feet touched the ground. She fell hard, her elbow landing on the edge of the gazebo's concrete foundation. Chloe yelped, her gun arm dissolving into tingling pain, utterly useless. Her weapon fell to the ground with a thud.

Hands grabbed her, dragging her upright. "I should have killed you in your bed."

Chloe's spine slammed against the iron post of the gazebo. The back of her skull smacked metal, leaving her dancing on the edge of nausea. When her eyes finally focused, she saw a man looming over her, pushing his face close to hers. She tried to turn away, getting only an impression of a closely trimmed beard and stale fish breath.

"Did you miss me?" Crushing her into the iron post, he managed a full-body grope. He was taller, so his crotch ground against her belly. "I nearly had you, little princess."

Sam shot you that night. Next time it'll be me, and I'll finish the job. Chloe clung to the thought, but her whole body broke into a trembling sweat.

He'd pinned her hands behind her, between her back and the post. *Helpless.* Or not. She had a knife in her ankle sheath. *How do I get it into his ribs?*

"Your friend has the dress. What do you want with me?" She forced the words to snarl, using anger to stave off tears.

"Guess." He yanked open the zipper of her fleece jacket and grabbed for a breast. He squeezed hard enough to make her give a sharp cry. "That's more like it," he said in a hiss that was half a purr.

She took sideways glances at him, dodging his face as he thrust his just inches away from hers. Yet every time she moved, so did he, their noses nearly touching. "Get away from me!" she snapped.

"Baby, I'm the last thing you'll ever see."

Like hell. Her one advantage was the wound in his shoulder, where Sam's bullet had struck. She could see the bandages showing above the collar of his sweatshirt. They were stained with fresh blood—all this running around must have opened the wound. Good to know. He favored that arm as he moved. His left side was weaker.

He was using his weight to pin her, which put him off-balance. He also assumed she was too petrified to fight back.

Try again. She hooked a foot around his ankle and swiveled her shoulder to his left, using the post behind her for leverage. When he tried to step back, he fell.

She scooped up her gun, gripping it with both hands. Her elbow still hurt, but her fingers worked again. Chloe turned, pointing her weapon at the man who had tried to smother her in her own bed.

An arm grabbed her from behind. "Not so fast, little girl."

This was someone new. She couldn't see his face, but he had a long, shining bowie knife.

Chloe screamed, letting her voice rip through the darkness. Then she swiveled the muzzle of the SIG Sauer down and shot him in the foot. With a surprised yell, he flung her forward.

It wasn't like the first guy knocking her down. This time Chloe flew through the air, as if an immense tennis racket was vaulting her forward. Instinct made her cover her face. Training made her bring her knees up, so that she landed in a roll.

It was not a good landing. It was hard and graceless and it hurt. The air left her lungs in a rush, but she managed to keep rolling until she slammed into a tree.

But she was alive.

Get up! Her mind screamed at her, urging her to run.

She couldn't. Sick and dizzy and aching, Chloe couldn't make her limbs obey.

Her eyes would only open to slits. The one who'd thrown her was braced against the gazebo, cursing and bleeding. The other was picking himself up off the ground. In about five seconds one of them would decide to finish her off.

"Kill her," the second man commanded.

Sam was in a maelstrom of rage. Winspear had escaped. Sam knew he was faster, but Plague was resourceful and clever.

Leaping over a fallen tree, he scrambled up the next rise of ground, searching the darkness for any sign of the doctor. There was nothing. *If he'd really wanted me dead, he wouldn't have missed that shot to my head.* Whatever his plan, Winspear was playing a longer game than just a diamond heist. Killing Sam and Chloe tonight wasn't part of his script.

There were worse things a centuries-old assassin-turned-physician could do. Already, he'd effectively separated Sam from Chloe by making himself too immediate a threat for Sam to ignore.

Sam's greatest fear was that Winspear had somehow doubled back to find her. He'd barely admitted this to himself when he had heard Chloe cry out. When he broke through the trees he could smell blood, both human and undead, but no one was in sight. Without breaking stride, he leaped to the top of the octagonal gazebo, landing silently on all fours.

He could see much of the garden, the winding paths like pale gray tracery through the dark lawns. He could smell vampire blood but couldn't see one anywhere. Whoever was bleeding had left or was hiding. And where was Chloe? His gaze tracked in a slow arc, searching every shadow.

Then he spotted her, huddled under the low branches of a rhododendron. A man was reaching down as if to drag her to her feet. The same man who had nearly killed her in her bed.

Fury swept through Sam, a white-hot need to defend. It wasn't just chivalry. There was a territorial edge to the impulse that sprang from his primal core. Baring his fangs, he surged into the air.

Bullets flew from west of the building, skimming the skin from Sam's back. Pain licked past his spine, but was forgotten the instant he grappled with Chloe's attacker. Momentum carried them into the bushes. Sam grabbed the human in one hand, tossing him back onto the paving stones as if he were no more than a sack of oatmeal.

Incredibly, the man rolled to his feet, lurching into a run. Sam sprang after him. The man was quick, charging up the side of the rocky hill, but Sam bounded upward, caught his ankle and yanked him back to the earth. The man landed with a hollow thump.

Sam's first instinct was to bite, but Chloe was there, her eyes already wide with fright. Instead, he pounded his fist into the man's face. Again. And again. He could have broken his neck, snapped it with one blow, but Chloe was watching. Muted violence would have to do.

Sam finally planted his boot on the man's chest, pinning him to the ground. "Where did the vampire go? The one who's hurt?"

"He's gone," the man croaked.

"He can't have gone far. Someone shot at me just now, and it wasn't you."

"You'll get nothing from me."

"We'll see about that." Sam bent, grabbing the front of the man's shirt. He gave a hard, sharp jerk that made the man grunt with pain. The cloth ripped, baring the man's chest. There, just below the notch of his collarbone, was a tattoo of two blades crossed over a twining serpent.

The mark of the Knights of Vidon. *Winspear is working with the Knights?* It still seemed impossible. No one on the planet loathed the vampire slayers more. Sam swore under his breath. Whatever was going on, he was going to get to the bottom of it.

The man was watching Sam's face, reading every expression. "I'm not telling you anything."

"Oh, you will." Sam knelt, leaning forward. He felt a cold smile curl his lips as his rage found a target. "Let me introduce myself. They call me War."

Chapter 20

But Chloe was Sam's first priority. His prisoner could wait. Within seconds, Sam had zip ties around the man's wrists and ankles, then gagged him with a strip of his own shirt.

Chloe was sitting under the bushes, her face smeared with dirt. He knelt beside her, pushing a lock of hair from her eyes. "Are you hurt?"

"I'm a little banged up, but nothing's broken." Her voice sounded detached, as if she were shell-shocked. Her fingers were shaking as the adrenaline left her system. "I dropped my gun."

Sam rose to his feet and looked around, found it within moments and put the safety on. He handed it back to her, his chest tight. She didn't look good. "Are you sure you're not injured?"

"Thanks." With slow, awkward movements, she took

the SIG Sauer and holstered it. "Uncle Jack said you should always know where your weapons are."

In an almost unconscious gesture, her fingers went to an ankle sheath, and Sam saw the hilt of a respectably sized knife. He noticed she had night vision goggles, too, hanging from a strap around her neck. She'd come prepared. He had to admire that much, but by the nine hells this was no fight for a civilian.

Sam gave in to the impulse to check every inch of her for broken bones. He dropped to his knees beside her, checking along her arms and legs for bumps or tender spots, every sense tuned for the faintest whiff of blood. The feel of her soft, warm form under his hands roused his protective instincts. She'd risked herself. It was unthinkable. He wasn't sure if he wanted to kiss her or shake her until her teeth rattled. "What did you think you were doing?"

Chloe's eyes snapped into focus. "I told you I need to know what's going on. I told you that just hours ago, but apparently that doesn't matter to you one little bit."

Sam felt an answering spike of anger, struggled to bite it back. "If I didn't tell you, there was a good reason." He found the camera in her pocket and pulled it out. "Did you take any pictures?"

"One."

He stuffed it in his own jacket, then zipped the pocket shut.

"Hey!" She grabbed for it. "That's mine!"

He caught her hand. "Stop it. Just. Stop. Now."

Her anger spiced the air. She was clearly furious, the pulse in her wrist pounding against his fingers. Guilt raked him, but he knew his reasons were good.

Sam sucked in a deep breath, reminding himself that yelling wouldn't help. "You want information? How about this—if I'd been a minute later, I don't know if you would still be alive."

"And I shot the guy pointing a gun at your head, remember?"

Sam had to give her that. "Good shot, too, but that's not the point." With a slow sense of wonder, he realized this frail mortal woman had tried to save his life. *She* had done her best to save *him*. An uncharacteristic feeling of humility besieged him. "Thanks for that, all the same."

All the tension went out of her, her forehead sinking to rest on her knees. "I've never shot a man before."

He'd won their argument, but it didn't solve a thing. Sam released her hand, tucking the whole of her under his arm instead. "Sucks."

"Yeah." She was softly crying.

Sam squeezed his eyes shut, feeling her pain all the way to his own heart. "I'm sorry."

She leaned into him, the silk of her hair under his chin. He wished there was something he could do, but once a person pulled the trigger at another being, there was no going back. He kissed the top of her hair, smelling the sweetness of her shampoo.

"Following you was the stupidest stunt I've every pulled," she muttered.

"Not that I'm encouraging you, but I've seen rookies do worse."

"I thought I'd be safe."

He heard the anger in her voice. Anger at herself. He knew she prided herself on being sensible, but she'd taken a bigger risk than she'd anticipated. He'd seen it before, people caught up in the heat of the moment. An unfamiliar queasiness passed through him when he imagined what might have happened.

But he kept that to himself. "You're safe now."

He shifted uncomfortably, adrenaline and his protective instincts colliding with a sudden wave of pure, primitive lust. Her breasts pressed into him, soft and warm, her pulse throbbing in her throat. Her top had pulled up, leaving a strip of bare, silken skin free to brush his wrist. The next kiss he gave her was on her lips. He shifted, knowing he had to end this. His fangs itched to come out.

There were too many primal emotions ricocheting through his blood to make holding her a good idea. Any moment, the hunger for her blood would blossom from a dull ache to an unbearable thirst.

He broke the kiss. She looked up at him, her eyes unfocused. Her small, pink tongue darted around her lips. They were swollen, glistening like ripe berries in the uncertain light.

The only thing that pulled him back to the present was the stirring prisoner. Sam sucked in a deep breath, clearing the confusion from his lust-addled brain.

"I get it. You'd be stupid not to wonder what was going on. But this goes far beyond a regular crime," he said softly. "I can't tell you much. I wasn't briefed myself. I don't have that clearance."

"I get it," she mumbled. "I think."

"Good." But if he held her much longer, he'd confess whatever she wanted to know. Nine hells, he'd make a story up if she just kept looking at him like that. "You need to get back to the house. And I've got to get this guy into custody."

Chloe lifted her head, turning to look at him. Tears had made trails through the dirt on her face. He kissed the tears, tasting the salty echo of her blood. By the gods, she was sweet. Her lips found his, forgiving him, begging him to get closer.

He wanted her. By the changing scent of her skin, she

wanted him, as well. Chloe's lips were flushed, her eyes dark with desire. Sam felt his self-control slithering away like a soft, silken robe falling to the floor.

"Sam," she murmured.

He teetered on the brink of losing himself utterly. He ached with a primitive need to take her right there on the dew-spangled grass. *Mine. Now.*

He cursed silently, struggling as a last vestige of good sense prevailed. Setting her aside gently, he moved before their prisoner got far more of a show than he'd bargained for. Chloe sank back on her heels, looking up at him as he rose. The dirt stains and disheveled hair made her look like an urchin, both innocent and wise beyond her years.

"There were more than just the man you caught," she said. "There were two that found me."

Sam frowned. "Our friend there said the other guy ran away. Did you see him?"

She shook her head. "He attacked me from behind. He was horribly strong. He threw me like I was no more than a dishrag."

Winspear. Sam felt a grim foreboding. "I'll kill him for that."

Chloe blinked. "You literally mean that, don't you?"

Sam didn't answer, not trusting himself to sound like a mere human right then. *Of course I mean it. You matter too much to make empty threats.*

Chloe trailed a step behind as they returned to the house, Sam carrying the man over his shoulder like a sack of potatoes. Sam's face darkened with every step. He was obviously unhappy that she was anywhere near his prisoner, but he hadn't been prepared to let her walk back to the house on her own. When they approached the door to the laundry room, she ran ahead to open it. Sam's burden was awake and starting to struggle.

"Get me something to tie him up with." Sam's tone was harder than Chloe had ever heard coming out of his mouth. It startled her enough that it took a moment to obey.

"Now!"

The man thrashed in Sam's hands. Sam thrust him into a folding chair beside one of the dryers. The chair's aluminum legs skidded across the tile floor with a squeak. Chloe looked around desperately, then tore down a length of laundry line that had been strung from the ceiling. It was too long, but Sam used it anyway, winding it around the prisoner several times before knotting it behind the chair.

Chloe stared first at the battered face, then at the tattoo on the man's chest, half-hidden in the blood from his reopened wound. "What's that?"

Sam hesitated a moment, but then answered her. "His—I guess you could call them a gang—all wear that mark. If you see someone with it, run."

Chloe looked again, memorizing the design. She edged toward the man, at least until Sam put out a hand to keep her from getting too close.

"It's not a gang," the man said, bloody lips curling away from his teeth. "We are the Knights of Vidon."

"Be quiet," Sam ordered. "I'll let you know when it's time for you to speak."

Chloe narrowed her eyes, taking in every detail of the tattoo, the clothing. If this was the enemy, she wanted to know how to recognize their kind. In return, the prisoner gave her a long, long look that lingered on her skin like rancid oil.

She felt her cheeks heating. "What's your problem?"

"You keep staring at me." He had an accent. Not Italian, but not entirely unlike that, either. "You like what you see?"

"You almost killed me in my own bed. I'm trying to see that in your face."

He gave a bark of laughter. "Every one of us is a killer. Every face is a killer's face."

"I don't believe that."

"Then you haven't suffered enough."

A flash of rage curled her fingers into fists. "I've never done anything to you!"

"You're with *them*. That is enough." The look he gave Sam dripped with loathing so virulent that Chloe instinctively reached for the butt of her gun. He was tied up, but that much hate had power.

Sam had gone pale. "Chloe, you should leave."

"Why?"

"You don't need to hear his nonsense."

"How do I know it's nonsense?" Her voice was bitter.

The man in the chair laughed. "She has no idea what she might learn, does she?"

Sam glanced at her quickly, not taking his eyes off the prisoner for more than a second. "Trust me. Let me handle him. I've done this before."

"I haven't," Chloe said. "But if he killed Jack, I'll hold him down for you while you ask questions."

The man stopped laughing. A sick satisfaction shot through her. She had spoiled his mockery. Or had she? A sly look came over his face.

"You don't know what he is, do you?" The words were for Chloe, but he looked at Sam as he said it.

Sam's fists balled tight. "Silence!"

"He's the one who saved my life," Chloe said quietly.

"For now. It won't last. Sooner or later, they always show their true faces. Killer faces."

Sam's hand moved too fast to see. He struck open-handedly, the crack of skin on skin echoing in the small room. The man's head snapped to the side, the chair rocking with the momentum.

"Sam!" Chloe gasped, then felt foolish.

Sam had slapped him. It was nothing, given that the man had tried to kill her. But that didn't make it any easier to watch.

"What's your name?" Sam demanded.

"Pietro." He spit blood to the floor, missing Chloe's shoes by inches.

She felt sick, a hot wave of dizziness rolling through her. "Pietro what?"

He closed his eyes, swallowing hard. "We perform our mission to keep the throne of Vidon free of the Devil's influence." The toneless statement sounded like the equivalent of name, rank and serial number.

"Then why are you in league with Winspear?" Sam snarled, clearly struggling for control of his temper.

"Winspear?" Chloe backed away. "What are you talking about?"

Sam gave her a pained glance. "He was the one who took the dress."

Chloe reeled. She'd hardly spoken to the doctor. He'd been too solemn, too withdrawn to invite even casual interaction, but he hadn't seemed treacherous. *Every face is a killer's face.* Could that be true?

She didn't know because she hadn't seen her attacker's face. She'd exchanged so few words with Mark Winspear that she wouldn't recognize his voice. But the doctor wasn't as big as Sam, and whoever had thrown her had been incredibly strong.

Sam grabbed the man's jaw, forcing him to look straight into Sam's eyes. "How is Winspear involved?"

"I don't know what you're talking about." The words were distorted by Sam's hand.

Chloe watched Sam's expression. There was deep sadness in his face. Her chest ached for him. "Are you sure that was Dr. Winspear? I couldn't see his face."

Sam gave a single nod. "I'm sure."

Chloe took a step back. She tried to picture the doctor shooting at Sam, and it just didn't fit.

"How did you know the diamonds were here?" Sam asked Pietro, removing his hand from the man's face.

Pietro worked his jaw as if it hurt. "Little birds listen at keyholes. For a price, they may open the door."

"Will Tyler?" Sam named the security guard who had become the getaway driver, and then had become dead.

Pietro's head was hanging forward, his chin on his chest. He looked up, moving only his eyes.

Sweat trickled down Chloe's sides, slithering over her ribs. Had Tyler known Pietro would try to kill her?

The prisoner laughed. "That kind always wants more than they have. For a price they'll leave the door unlocked." His gaze slid toward her. "But believe me, sweet girl, that's not the worst of your problems. This movie is far from over."

The words made Chloe draw in a quick breath that caught Sam's attention. He took her hand, pulling her to his side. It was a wordless gesture of comfort, putting her securely in the circle of safety he offered. She locked her fingers through his.

Sam pulled out his phone and thumbed a key. Chloe heard someone pick up and thought she recognized Faran's voice. "I'm in the laundry room, with Chloe. Where are you?"

Chloe locked eyes with Pietro, trying to read his face. All she could see was spite. She couldn't trust a thing that came out of his mouth.

Sam was still talking. "Then get down here. I've got a package." He put the phone away.

Package? She wasn't sure if she should laugh or shudder at the innocent-sounding phrase. She turned to Sam. "What happens now?"

Sam leaned against the dryer. "Now? Now Kenyon comes."

"He's not...like the doctor." She remembered Lexie's warnings about Faran.

"No," Sam replied. "He'll take you back to your room."

"Does he know about any of this?"

Sam frowned. Thoughts she couldn't read flitted across his features. "Don't say a word about what you've seen here. Not even to him or to your photographer friend. Anything you might say puts them deeper into danger."

Chloe's skin went cold. "Okay."

The prisoner gave a derisive snort.

Chloe's eyes narrowed. "Are you going to go on questioning him?"

Pietro tried hard not to look up at Sam, tried to pull his chin down and stare at the floor some more, but fear won out. Sam continued to lean, looking almost bored.

"I'll find out who killed Jack. I'll give you their heads on a platter."

The way he said it make Chloe shiver. "Where do the police come into this?"

Sam looked at her, his face like stone. "I am the police."

"What?" She pulled away, tingling with surprise. "I thought you worked security for Uncle Jack."

"Call the FBI or the CIA. Ask for someone who deals with international crimes. Mentioning Jack's name should get you someone in charge. They'll confirm that I have authority to handle this."

That shocked her. "Seriously? Jack never said anything about ties to those agencies."

"Because you aren't supposed to know. It's that simple."

Chloe swore under her breath. That explained so much—Jack's secrecy, his obsession with weapons, and his connection to men like Sam. *And I've been trying to spy on these guys?* A sudden wave of embarrassment heated her cheeks.

Sam straightened, scowling down at the man tied to the chair. "Chloe, the business with the diamonds is the tip of an iceberg. There's a lot more underneath."

The prisoner tilted his head back to look Sam full in the face. "Good luck figuring it out."

Sam smiled. "I have all night."

Unfortunately, Sam's night got more complicated.

Kenyon came, clearly curious, but took Chloe back to her bedroom. Moments later, Carter arrived.

Sam's maker strolled around the laundry room, hands behind his back. He was hiding a slight limp, but Sam knew Carter well enough to see it. An injury? Unusual, for a fast-healing vampire. One might say a coincidence.

Ugly suspicions fluttered through Sam's mind.

"So, you've got yourself a plaything, my boy," said Sam's sire. "Do you think he will be tasty?"

"Knights never stay with me. I'll want another in half an hour."

"Perhaps we can arrange something." Carter paused to consider Pietro as if he were a steak on the grill.

The prisoner was starting to look less defiant and more fearful. He tracked Carter's every move.

"So your ruse with the wedding dress worked?" Carter asked.

"Yes. And you were right," Sam replied, keeping his voice controlled and even. "Winspear took it."

"Did he now?" Carter's thick eyebrows drew together. "I'm sorry to hear that. He was a good agent until this. A bit fond of having his own way, but he always got the job done in the end."

"I thought he was my friend."

Carter shook his head. "Since when do monsters have friends? We have honor. We have duty. The rest is only memory of what we were."

"This one has a ladylove, boss man," Pietro said, sneering. "She doesn't know what he is."

"Be quiet!" Sam snarled.

Carter gave both of them a sharp look, but settled his piercing eyes on the prisoner. "I would hold your tongue until we ask you to speak. You'll be singing soon enough."

But Pietro was done with obedience. He returned Carter's gaze, eyes wild with fear and hatred. "You're going to kill me anyhow, right? I may as well ask a few questions of my own. Who is this Winspear? What's he got to do with anything?"

"You think he'd give you his real name, you clot?" Carter rested a hand on the man's head and looked up at Sam. "So who is the woman?"

"I've been keeping an eye on Jack's niece."

"You know the rules."

"I do. There is nothing between us."

"You've always been a terrible liar."

Pietro sniggered. "But that's what you're all best at,

isn't it? Everything about you is a lie. Isn't that right, boss?"

"I wish you would be quiet," Carter sighed, and snapped the man's neck.

The sudden *pop* startled Sam. "I needed to question him!"

Carter gave a faint smile. "He didn't seem the helpful type."

Sam stared at the limp body, slumped against his bonds. "As you say." He had the sudden conviction that Pietro, helpful or not, knew far more than Carter had liked.

Sam was going to have to play this carefully. Carter was old and wily and knew him far too well.

"About that dress," Carter said, wiping his hands on the thick twill fabric of his pants. "I could take it now if you like."

"I don't have the combination to the safe," Sam replied. "Only Jack's niece has that."

He couldn't have been that bad a liar, because Carter bought it.

Chapter 21

Chloe didn't know what to think.

Last night had been something of a turning point, or maybe it was simply a realization.

Sam wasn't just a bodyguard, a security expert. He was something more. Incredibly dangerous, for a start, with the blessing of some of the most powerful crime-fighting agencies in the world. Being close to him was, as the old saying went, like having a tiger by the tail. It was a wild, perilous ride.

Who is Sam, really? That was the question of the hour.

Restless, Chloe picked up her laptop and wandered through the house, looking for someplace that didn't remind her of darkness and danger. She drifted until she found the breakfast room. It was more a glassed-in porch than a proper room, filled with plants and light. Chloe sat down at the wicker table, enjoying the warmth of a sunbeam on her back. A window was open, and she smelled the clean, fresh scent of greenery as the wind ruffled the curtains.

It was exactly what she needed. Chloe closed her eyes and pressed her fingers to her eyelids, trying to stave off the headache threatening to invade. Her head still hurt from whacking it against the iron post of the gazebo.

"Hey," said a husky female voice.

Chloe looked up at the sound, blinking the room back into focus. Alexis Haven stood in the doorway, holding a cup of coffee. Chloe started in surprise.

A grin spread over her friend's face. "Gotcha."

"Lexie!"

"Live and in person. How are you doing, Chlo?"

Chloe jumped up with a whoop, throwing her arms around her friend and just about spilling the coffee. "I'm so glad to see you!"

"Right back at you!"

Chloe released her friend, holding her at arm's length for a good look. The photographer was tall and slender to the point of skinny. It wasn't from dieting so much as moving too fast for any ordinary metabolism to keep up. She had bright hazel-green eyes and a fall of dark red hair that swept her hips. With the artless grace of the true bohemian, she wore no makeup, a shapeless khaki tunic dress and hiking boots that laced up to her knees—and somehow managed to make it look fabulous.

"How are you?" Chloe asked, giving her another hug before she let her go. "How was your flight?"

"I'm fine." Lexie's smile was crooked. "I tried to call last night, but kept getting your voice mail."

"Sorry, I was out."

They sat at the table.

"Good time?" Lexie asked.

"Hard to say. I don't remember a lot of what happened."

In truth, her memory was fine until she got to the part where she was on top of the gazebo shooting at Jack's so-called friend who had turned out to be one of the villains. Then it just seemed like a bad dream. *Mark Winspear? How is that even possible?* She was usually better at reading people. The doctor was a bit scary, but he hadn't struck her as evil. Somehow his betrayal had made more sense last night, when she wasn't sitting in a sunny, bright room.

"Sam and I were chasing bad guys last night."

"Whoa!" Lexie set down her coffee and scrunched her eyebrows together. "You and Sam, huh?"

"Yes." Chloe waved her hands helplessly. "I don't want it to be real. I don't do that kind of thing. I'm the girl who spends hours worrying about centerpieces and place cards."

"I'm not so sure that's all you are. I remember your uncle was pretty nuts about making sure you knew how to take care of yourself. You're a better shot than me."

Queasiness lurched through her. "I'm not sure I want to talk about shooting right now." How many people had she hit? One? Two?

Lexie was watching her face, clearly trying to read her thoughts. "We all have sides of ourselves we keep locked away until they're needed."

"This guy…" Chloe stopped, considering how crazy she wanted to sound. "This man threw me through the air like a toy."

An angry flush crept over Lexie's cheeks. "Are you hurt?"

"Bruised."

"Did you lose consciousness?"

"Almost, but I don't think I have a concussion."

But what about her memory of Sam leaping on top of the gazebo? Sam running faster than her eye could follow? That flash of sharp, sharp teeth? Those had to be hallucinations. She was turning him, in her panicked imagination, into some sort of avenging beast. *That's it. I'm finally cracking up.*

Lexie reached across the table and felt Chloe's forehead. "I don't know, Chlo. You look pale as a mushroom. You feel a little feverish, too."

"I'm tougher than a bump on the head. I've been orphaned. I've been left at the altar. I've faced down Iris Fallon."

Lexie laughed at the last one. "Okay, Iris Fallon is proof positive you can take whatever life dishes out."

Chloe made an exasperated noise. "Until I met Sam Ralston. He's turned me into a basket case in a matter of days."

Lexie's mouth curled into a feline smirk. "He's got a little more oomph than you usually go for."

"Oomph?"

"You know. Swagger. Danger. Suits cut to hide the sidearms. It's an acquired taste, but you never go back."

That was what she was afraid of. "I always wanted a nice, quiet guy who liked antiquing and family picnics."

Lexie kept a neutral face. "Nice."

"I like nice."

"Nice is good. Nice is underrated."

"I think I want…" *I want my avenging beast.*

"Not nice?"

"A garnish. A bit of spice on the side." Chloe held up her thumb and forefinger, showing a sliver of air between. As she thought about Sam, the space widened. She wanted more than a little of whatever made him…him.

Lexie rolled her eyes. "Whoa, look at the wild child bursting out of her shell."

"Don't mock."

Her friend was suddenly serious. "I'm not mocking. I'm worried, Chloe. You had a close call. You got into something deeper than you were expecting. Remember I said I didn't trust your uncle's friends? Spice comes with a price."

Chloe shivered. Serious wasn't Lexie's style. Normally she would have carried on, making one off-color pun after the next. *What's going on? I don't know how much more I can take.* "If it hadn't been for Sam, I would have been chopped to steak tartare. He's saved my skin more than once."

"We need to talk, Chlo. These guys aren't as squeaky clean as you seem to think."

A flush of anger heated Chloe's skin. She could feel Sam's strong arms picking her up, the shield of his body between her and danger. She wanted to defend his honor. She owed him that much loyalty.

Lexie must have seen it on her face. "Don't get mad at me. I'm trying to help you."

She was too tired to fight down her emotions. "Like I said, Sam saved me. I don't want to hear anything against him."

"You're defending him?"

"He defended me."

"You're the one who always wants information. Maybe now is the time to listen."

Chloe looked up, meeting Lexie's adamant gaze. She wanted to face whatever her friend had to say now, but she shied away. Too much had happened; her courage had been used up last night.

Lexie leaned close, putting her lips close to Chloe's

ear. "How much do you know about Faran and his friends?"

"Only that they've been great. Mostly." Chloe suddenly wasn't sure what to say. "It's complicated."

Lexie put her finger to her lips. "Can we talk privately here?"

They leaned across the glass-topped table so they could speak softly.

"What's so hush-hush?" Chloe asked. Lexie hadn't wanted to talk on the phone, and now she was acting like Oakwood was littered with listening devices. Well, given the Gravesend Security connection, maybe it was.

Lexie bit her lower lip. "How much time do you have right now? For any of what I have to say to make sense, I have to go back to when Faran and I met. There's a lot to explain. *They're not people.*"

As if on cue, Faran walked in the room, his head bent as he finished texting on his phone. When he stopped and looked up, he froze, phone halfway to his pocket.

Chloe swore under her breath at the horrified look on her friend's face.

And Faran had seen Lexie. No, *seen* was the wrong word. From the bald pain that flickered across his face, it was more as if his soul smashed against the windshield of her sudden frosty reserve. The moment lasted long enough for Chloe to squirm. She'd warned him his ex-girlfriend would be in town, but he hadn't expected her here.

"Lexie." He drew himself up, chin lifting, his aspect suddenly one of studied calm. For all his laid-back manner, he showed iron control.

"You," Lexie said softly, but that one quiet word held a universe of anger. "What are you doing near my friend?"

"My job. I'm in security, remember? One of the good guys?"

"I hardly think that's possible."

"Lexie!" Chloe exclaimed.

They both glared at her, expressions nearly identical.

Her friend's stare was the more ferocious of the two. "Stay out of this, Chlo. What's between him and me, that's our business."

"Don't get involved," Faran said at almost the same moment. "It's old history. It doesn't need to be dragged up and turned over like old compost."

Chloe heard Lexie's indrawn breath. "Nice, Kenyon," she snarled. "Nice to know what we had rates the same as coffee grounds and kitchen scraps."

His eyes went an icy blue. "You broke it off."

"You lied."

Faran's eyes narrowed. "You pushed. I told you there were some questions I couldn't answer. I had no choice."

Her friend looked away. "Forget it. If you can't see the flaws in that picture, nothing I can say will make a difference."

Silence ached through the room. Chloe made a T gesture with her hands. "Time-out. I'm a wedding planner, not a couples therapist."

"And from what you said on the phone, you have a huge wedding to plan." Lexie stood, smoothing her skirt. "I'll get out of your hair."

Faran followed her every gesture, pain etched into his face, then looked away. Lexie paused, studying his profile, her mouth drawn into a tight line.

Chloe wished she could fix whatever was wrong, but didn't have a clue. "Lexie…"

"We'll talk later, Chloe," her friend said briskly. "Let's

set something up at the hotel. I'm all yours for as long as I'm in town."

With that, she walked out. Faran seemed stranded in the middle of the floor, not sure what to do with himself.

"I'm sorry," Chloe said gently. "I had no idea it was that bad."

"No, I'm sorry. You didn't need to see that. I'm going to go for a walk." His voice was oddly throaty. "I think I need to eat something, and then I'll be all right."

"Blood sugar?" she asked.

Faran smiled wanly. "Kind of like that."

"Then take care of yourself."

"Yeah. Whatever."

His hands were clenched as he stalked from the room, shoulders hunched. Chloe watched him go, wondering what in blazes had happened between the handsome young man and her best friend. She realized she was sweating, her stomach in a tight, hard knot.

They're not people.

What the blazes did that mean?

Chloe opened her laptop and waited as the screen sprang to life. She was back in Jack's office. Outside, the light was fading.

For the past few hours, she'd been too upset to deal with Sam, Faran, Lexie or any of the rest of that part of her life. Instead, she'd spent the afternoon making wedding arrangements. As always, work helped calm her.

Her staff had been doing the legwork to fulfill Iris Fallon's every desire, but Chloe still had to make decisions. Phone calls to and from her suppliers kept her focused and busy, but now most businesses were closing down for the day.

Finally, her mind was free to roam back to the question of Sam Ralston. *Who is he, really?* And why did Lexie think he wasn't "people"? Did it have to do with the whole international Men-in-Black thing?

She clicked on a search engine and sat frowning for a moment. *What am I thinking? Do I have the right to check him out like this?*

Just because Lexie had warned her to stay away? Just because he'd done his best to keep her ignorant of everything he was doing? Just because he'd admitted he was an agent of some kind? *Um, yeah.* Just because she understood there were things about his work she couldn't know, that didn't make her any less curious about who he was as a man.

She was willing to believe that Sam thought he was doing the right thing. She did not believe she knew a quarter of what she ought to know about him.

She typed his name into the search engine. A bazillion hits came up and most looked relatively useless. A smattering of them, however, seemed to relate to a news story. She selected the first of those. She immediately saw a black-and-white portrait of a pretty blonde twentysomething wearing a fascinator. The caption below the picture identified the woman as Lady Beatrice Concarra. She stared at the picture for a moment, feeling an irrational jealousy. What did Lady Beatrice have to do with Sam? Then she read on.

Assassination Attempt at Emerald Sea

Lady Beatrice Concarra, eldest daughter of the famed shipping magnate, Arnaud, Duke of Nulanne, was fatally shot at 1:15 a.m. on Tuesday. The incident occurred at Emerald Sea, a dance club located in the Marcari capital. Lady Beatrice had arrived at the club around midnight as part of Princess Amelie's retinue.

Palace security has not yet released the name of the attacker. The gunman fired directly onto the dance floor, striking Lady Beatrice in the heart. Sam Ralston, security chief for the palace, claims the attack was an assassination attempt on the princess. Security at the dance club was reportedly breached, although no one in authority would give specifics. According to Ralston, "There are hostile elements we have been watching for several weeks now. The tragedy is that Lady Beatrice suffered as an innocent bystander." The palace would not comment on whether those "hostile elements" are Vidonese nationals.

However, unnamed sources claim the ancient feud between Marcari and Vidon is heating up again in reaction to the proposed marriage between Princess Amelie and the Vidonese crown prince, Kyle. Separatists on both sides protest the prospect of unification of the two kingdoms.

The article went on and Chloe read the rest with a growing sense of shock. Sam Ralston was security chief for Princess Amelie of Marcari? *Seriously? He's part of the palace staff?*

That explained so much. Guarding royalty? The responsibility was staggering. No wonder he took the whole bodyguard thing to the max. A lapse could be fatal. Look what happened to poor Lady Beatrice.

When he'd said being a bodyguard could go wrong, this must have been what he meant.

And this surely had some bearing on what had happened to Jack. Would his security work have included

working for the Marcari government? Then of course security agencies would know about him because he was
in the business of keeping crowned heads alive. And the
wedding dress? A connection to the princess went a little
way to explaining why he had it. *Why didn't you tell me
any of this, Uncle Jack?*

She clicked on a few more links, but they all seemed
to be about the same shooting. Otherwise, Sam Ralston
kept a very low profile. Or, *her* Sam Ralston did. There
was also a Sam Ralston, car dealer in Utah; a physics
professor in Toronto; and, a twelve-year-old playing the
drums on YouTube. But now Chloe's curiosity was going
at full steam.

Never mind snooping on the internet for information
made her feel like a love-struck teenager searching to
find photos of her latest crush.

She tried *"Samuel Ralston"* and got the less-than-help-
ful hits again. Then *Samuel, Ralston* without the quotes.
That resulted in a bazillion hits to the power of ten. Chloe
just about closed the laptop and walked away, except
she spotted a row of thumbnail images partway down
the screen—all pictures of various Samuels. She clicked
the command to show her only images. The screen filled
with tiny squares.

And there he was, in an old tintype photograph. A
shock of recognition made her breath hitch as she sat up
straighter, angling the laptop screen for a better view.

Same eyes, same chin, same delectable mouth. He
was wearing a Union officer's uniform and that frozen
expression people got from holding still for the old, slow
cameras, but it was definitely Sam. Chloe zoomed in on
the image until it started to blur. It had to be him. Even
his long, dark eyelashes were the same.

She sucked in a breath, snapping herself out of the

realm of impossibility. No, it was his ancestor, surely, but the family resemblance was marked. She clicked the link and it took her to a page hosted by a Pennsylvanian historical society. Ralston Samuel Hill had been a lieutenant colonel in the Civil War. Son of a career politician, graduated from West Point, married to Amy Weston, father of two sons and one daughter. Presumed killed in action, 1862.

They look so much the same. But that was silly. If he'd lived, he'd be how old? Over 180, anyway. Chloe stood up, pacing around the room to burn off a sudden burst of nervous energy.

Sure, the names and features were similar, but there was a good explanation. Sam must be a descendant of one of the children. That was all. And it was easily proved.

Chloe sat down again and logged into a genealogy database she sometimes used when a couple wanted a family tree in their wedding album. She looked up Ralston Hill there, but the only new information she could find was that his widow had remarried and the children had taken her new husband's name. There was no easy link between Sam's historical double and his present-day self.

The only useful thing she'd found out was that he'd been there when tragedy struck Lady Beatrice, a young girl who'd gone out to dance away the Mediterranean night.

That death was the only key she had to Sam's history. Otherwise, the internet had little to say on the present-day Sam. When a guy showed up only when someone died or was in danger of dying, she had to wonder just how much more she wanted to know.

But I think I'm falling in love with him.

Chapter 22

Sam stormed back into the house two hours later. Chloe wasn't absolutely sure he hadn't left sometime in the middle of the night. Wherever he'd been, it hadn't made him happy.

Long ago, her mother had advised Chloe, in a rare mother–daughter conversation, never to confront her man when he first got home from the office. He should have a drink and a relaxing moment alone with the newspaper before being presented with domestic problems.

As old-fashioned as it sounded—and a bit odd coming from a woman who had been about as domestic as a bobcat—it wasn't bad advice under certain circumstances. Chloe waited an entire hour before tracking Sam to his lair, Scotch on the rocks in hand. Her quarry was in the games room, chalking a pool cue with the air of Vlad the Impaler sizing up his next victim.

"Home from the office, dear?" she said sweetly, handing him the Scotch. She tried not to think about what Sam's workday might have entailed.

He put down the chalk and cue, an unsettled expression on his face, and took the drink. "Thank you."

"Bad day?" Chloe started a circuit of the pool table, giving him distance.

He didn't answer.

"You questioned that man, Pietro, after I left last night, didn't you?"

He didn't answer. It felt like a wall had sprung up, dividing the room between them.

"I know you probably took an oath of secrecy or something to do with your job. I get that now. And if you can't tell me what the creep said now, just say that someday you will tell me, so that I'll understand why my uncle died."

"Chloe—"

"Don't *Chloe* me." Her tone was sharper than she intended, and she took a deep breath to soften her words. "That man tried to kill me."

He watched her walk around the table for a beat, tracking her movement with his eyes. Chloe felt the wall between them pushing outward now, crowding her away.

He looked both sad and wary. "I know he did."

"Did he tell you anything useful?"

A dark expression crossed Sam's face. "No. So don't push. This time, it's not worth the effort."

She watched him take a sip of the drink, then set it down neatly on a side table. "That's it?"

The corners of his mouth twitched down. "I spent today tracking down where the Knights were staying. We tried before, but this time I finally found them. They were in a campground trailer park some distance away. They left around three this morning. They're in the wind. We have men trying to locate them again."

Chloe's breath caught. He was giving her real information. He was letting her in as far as he could. That was all she could ask. She took a step closer to him, wanting the discomfort between them gone.

Something slid behind Sam's careful expression. It looked to her like hurt and confusion. "Winspear's gone, too. No one knows where he is. I don't trust very many people right now."

She was going to take his hurt away if she could. If she could get close enough. "I just want to know one other thing. What's going to stop the thieves from coming back here?"

"The dress and the jewels go back to where they belong. If they're not here, there is no motivation for anyone to bother Oakwood."

"And when is someone coming to get the dress?"

"I'll take care of it." His eyes were hard and flat as iron. "I don't trust anyone else. That doesn't seem to work out for me."

She knew he wasn't referring to her; he probably meant Winspear. But his words still bothered her. "You can't judge everyone by what's happening here."

He braced his hands on the pool table, glaring at the green surface. "It's not the first time I've trusted when I shouldn't."

"Is that what happened with Lady Beatrice? You trusted people to help out with security and they failed?"

He looked up sharply. "I don't talk about that."

Chloe folded her arms against the sharpness of his gaze. "I'm sorry."

"Where did you hear about that?"

"The internet. It said the boy in the club wasn't the only one you caught. In the end three conspirators were charged and convicted. They found the bodies of the assassins torn to pieces in their cells. All but the boy who fired the gun." Her voice shook as she said it. The description of the scene was nauseating.

The tension in the room spiked. "Leave it alone."

"What happened?" Chloe replied, her fingers trailing along the polished edge of the pool table as she circled it slowly, working toward him. The hard, glossy wood felt a bit like the conversation—there was substance there, but it was slippery and hard to grasp.

"Leave it alone."

She stopped, close enough that they could reach out and touch. Proximity acted like magic. The wall between them crumbled. She couldn't explain how she felt it, but she did. They'd somehow reached an unspoken agreement. He would tell her what he could. She could ask for more, but agreed to accept it when he had to remain silent.

Sam gave a heavy sigh. He picked up the drink and took another swallow. "Lady Beatrice made the princess laugh. I think she was the only real friend Amelie had. I was supposed to keep both of them safe. I brought in others to help. Lady Beatrice died because I trusted them." He stopped abruptly, seeming to stop himself before he said more. "I don't like to talk about it."

"I'm asking because I want to know you. I'm not finding that an easy task."

"Yes, I know." The words were soft. "And you can't seem to get it through your head that I'm bad for you. If you have a type, I'm probably not it."

"French fries are bad for me, but I eat them anyway."

"Chloe." Her name was a growl.

Her whole being grinned, though she struggled to keep it off her face. "Now you sound like my dad."

This time he came toward her, moving in slow, prowling steps. Chloe watched him, not quite sure if she was excited or apprehensive. Either way, a fizz of anticipation settled in her stomach.

When Sam finally stopped he was so close that his pant legs brushed her knees. He leaned forward, putting one hand on either side of her, gripping the table. Chloe let her eyes drift closed so that she looked up at him from under her lashes.

"You're playing with fire," he said. "When it comes to you, I can't hold back."

The low tones of his voice resonated in her belly. She closed her eyes altogether for a moment, breathing him in. He smelled like whiskey and cool dusk in the lush green grass. He'd spent time outdoors that day.

"I know you're not going to stay," she said, words snagging in her throat. "You belong beside your princess. You have obligations."

"It would be worse for you if I did stay."

"You don't have a high opinion of yourself."

"I know what I'm talking about."

Chloe opened her eyes then. She stared right into his. She'd always known they were gray, but now she could see the individual streaks of dark and silver. A shiver ran up her backbone, something in her primitive brain sensing a danger her rational mind couldn't quite place. At the same time, desire for him ran hot in her blood. Whatever happened tomorrow, she wanted him tonight.

Fire and ice swirled inside her belly, goading her to lure him in. "So are you bad for me all the time, or just sometimes?"

"I'm bad for you right now." Sam took one hand from the chair and stroked her cheek. "Because I'm going to take what I want. I can't resist you."

"It's about time."

Sam didn't move at once, but let his fingers trail down the line of her jaw to the sensitive spot just below her ear. A trail of electricity followed his touch, leaving a tingling path. Chloe arched her neck against his cool fingers, wanting to feel more.

The next moment, his lips began the same journey, weaving tiny, quick kisses in a chain along her flesh. Chloe's breath hung suspended as he moved, unwilling to disturb the spell. Every press of his mouth sent a charge along her nerves, igniting sensations through her whole body. As he finished, the last kiss lingered, his lips soft and almost cool over the pulse in her throat. Shivering, she finally gulped in air, almost tasting the attraction between them.

Her hand cupped the back of his head, pulling him down so her mouth could find his. Thick and hot, her pulse felt slow, almost drugged. As she finally tasted him, a sweet ache infused her entire body. *And yet all he did was kiss me.*

Either Sam Ralston was a new gold standard of lover, or she'd been alone far, far too long. Only one way to be sure.

Chloe summoned her sweetest smile. "Are you going to aim for the eight ball, or do we get to find a bedroom first?"

His gaze raked over her as if weighing the inconvenience of relocation. It looked like sex on the pool table was winning the argument until finally something filtered through the lustful haze. "Bed."

Monosyllables would do. She gave his chest a shove so she could straighten up. He caught her around the waist, as if mere inches of airspace was a very bad thing. His thick sweater rubbed softly against her bare arms. She

cuddled close, letting his arm wrap around her posses-
sively. "My bedroom is closest."

"Go."

Holding hands, they stole up the stairs. Chloe dared
not look at Sam, afraid she'd start to giggle. This was
too much like a flashback to her school days, when she'd
unsuccessfully tried to sneak boys up to her room under
Uncle Jack's nose.

"Are you sure no one saw us?" she asked once Sam
closed the door behind them.

"Yes."

"Not even your wolf?"

Sam's expression was a curious mix of horror and
embarrassment.

"Forget about him." Sam slid onto the comforter next
to her, pressing his mouth to hers, drinking in her mirth.
Chloe melted into him, working her hands under the hem
of that soft sweater, feeling the hard muscle underneath.
She raked her fingernails lightly over his skin, earning
a murmur of pleasure as she kissed him back.

His hands stole up her rib cage, lingering over every
inch until he finally cupped her breasts. His thumbs
brushed her aching nipples, making her arch against him,
seeking more pressure to satisfy the pain. He pulled her
onto his lap and she felt the hard evidence of his own
ache. She reached down, but he brushed her hand away.

"Not yet. There's no need to rush."

She was about to rap out a snappy rejoinder, but he'd
found the buttons down the front of her dress, and his
mouth was on her breast. Chloe's head fell back as she
gave herself over to the delicious feel of his tongue exploring the lace cups of her bra. The brush of his hair
against her sensitized skin brought gooseflesh down her

arms. As he closed on her nipple, her thoughts turned to the snowy blankness of a TV that has dropped its signal.

Somewhere in the following minutes, she lost her clothes. At the same time, she worked on Sam's, determined to find the beast within. She'd seen his chest before, but the sight bore repeating. He must have done some serious weight lifting, because muscles like that didn't happen by themselves.

She finally got the right angle to pull down his zipper. Sam rose from the bed, sliding off his jeans. He wasn't wearing anything underneath. Chloe wasn't sure where to look first. In the soft glow of the bedside lamp, he seemed made of marble, pale and sculpted, the shadows blurring the hard angles of his muscular flesh. As for the individual details—well, maybe there was some truth to the whole monster thing. As he fished in his wallet for a condom, Chloe sank back into the pillows, feeling like Christmas had come early.

The next moment, Sam was beside her. He held a lock of her hair between his fingers, teasing her skin with the ends. He brushed it over the curve of her breast, seeming fascinated by the roundness of it. Chloe ran her hand down his chest, pausing to circle his nipple in a mirror image of his movements.

"You are so beautiful." He let her hair fall free, pulling her close. At the same time, his fingers found the soft core of her, slipping inside to stroke the most sensitive places. Chloe writhed against him, wanting more, aching for completion. He brought her close but pulled away just shy of the brink. She wriggled closer, demanding, plunging against him.

The third time, Chloe ran a hand up the length of his shaft, and his attention shifted like the gears of a well-tuned race car. He trapped her in the cage of his limbs and entered her in one long, hard stroke.

Chloe cried out at the sensation. He was large enough that it was almost uncomfortable. He pulled out, and pushed in again, drawing another gasp. She shuddered, close to her peak but hanging on, taking him in and making it last as long as she could.

He seemed to read her thoughts, making the next stroke so long and delicious that she detonated. He had done too good a job preparing her, and she crumbled beneath his assault. She was his.

Falling to pieces was just the beginning, for she was adrift in a euphoria that seemed to spin endlessly. Chloe could feel Sam inside her, feel him working and pushing, possessing her as she had never been before. Like a territory to be conquered, no part of her went untouched, no inch untasted.

As he drove her again to climax, her muscles seemed to move entirely to his will, her body nothing but an instrument of desire. His own movements were growing faster, more ragged. She grabbed his shoulders, pushing to meet him, her skin a slick of sweat.

With a ragged cry, Sam gave a final thrust, spending himself inside her as she fell under another wave of mindless pleasure.

But not so mindless that she missed the fangs sinking into her throat.

Chapter 23

Chloe awakened with a start, her whole body gathering itself to spring free of the sheets. Her mind came online a beat later, befuddled by the adrenaline surging through her system. She rolled onto her side, groping for the edge of the big bed and tangling herself in the blankets.

"Hush!" A hand touched her bare shoulder.

Chloe froze, staring into the dim atmosphere of the bedroom. Enough sun leaked around the curtain to show it was morning, but not enough to make the room light. *Naked. Bed.* Her thoughts scampered like panicked mice. *Sam.* Memory returned with all the subtlety of a sledge-hammer.

She flipped over, staring into the steel-gray eyes of the man beside her. "You bit me!"

It was out before she could stop herself. Fear skittered over her skin, and she stayed perfectly still for a long moment, barely daring to breathe.

Finally, he gave a slight shrug.

Chloe pushed the hair out of her eyes. "That's just rude."

"I didn't leave a mark."

Chloe's hand went instinctively to her throat. She was sure he'd drawn blood, but there was no soreness, no heat of a fresh bruise. *Impossible.*

"Not even a hickey," he said calmly.

"What did you do?"

He arched a brow. "Sorry, I thought you were enjoying it."

She had. Oh, yes. Chloe's insides turned to syrup at the suggestion. She felt the echoes of her last climax, shadows that could surge back to full force at any moment. Even the memory of his tongue and teeth was enough to send her over if she let herself revel in it.

A sigh escaped her before she could stifle it. His eyebrow quirked.

Not fair. Fear started to morph into irritation. *You just don't bite someone without their say-so!*

She tried to rise to her knees and keep the sheet drawn up around her at the same time. Unfortunately, that pulled the covers off Sam. There was suddenly more of Sam visible than she was prepared to deal with right then.

She twitched the coverlet over him, feeling a flush creep up her skin. "That was something else."

"You say that like it was a bad thing."

"It wasn't completely bad." She tried to keep a straight face. He was teasing her, the slant of his gaze a little bit mischievous, a little bit guilty. This was a different, playful side of him, and she wasn't sure she was ready for it. "But you..." She trailed off helplessly.

"You've got a good imagination."

"No. Forget the whole denial dance. That wasn't a

daydream. You had fangs. It wasn't the first time I saw them."

The teasing started to look ragged around the edges. "What are you saying?"

He's strong. Fast.

"I don't know." *Hates the sun. Looks exactly like a picture that's a century and a half old.*

Oh, no way.

She put a hand on his chest. There was no heartbeat under the cool skin. "Are you dead?"

Annoyance twisted his features. "Excuse me? Did I seem dead last night?"

She'd spent too much time with Uncle Jack's mouldy manuscripts and plastic fangs to avoid the obvious conclusion. "You're a vampire!"

He sat up so quickly she had no time to scoot back. They were nearly nose to nose. Chloe felt her remaining blood drain from her face.

"Do I look like a vampire?" he demanded.

She studied him. She had no clue what to say. "You've got the broody looks down."

He collapsed back onto the pillows, covering his face with his hands. Chloe was glad for the moment of privacy, and hopped out of bed to grab her bathrobe. She wrapped the thick terry folds around her, hands shaking so hard she could barely knot the belt. Panic sang through her bones, locking muscles. Her jaw ached with it.

Vampire? Was she nuts? There were no such things as vampires. Not literally, anyway.

But, come on. She knew what she saw. She'd felt his teeth. Sure, the sex was good and all that, but did it cause hallucinations? Sex didn't make her see fireworks or flowers opening in slow motion and it sure as Vlad didn't make her see vampires.

She marched to the foot of the bed and gave him a furious glare. She felt oddly detached, as if she were floating above her own body.

"Don't you guys warn your lovers?" she snapped. "That's like the ultimate STD."

Sam emitted an exasperated groan, somehow still managing to look masterful while wearing nothing but bedclothes. "I thought I'd hypnotized you. You're not supposed to remember that part."

Chloe huffed. "Well, that's nice, isn't it? Snack and go."

"It was for your own good. I'm just not…the mind control talents are not my strength."

"Mind control?" she repeated in freezing tones. "What are you? Straight out of a B movie?"

He scowled back. "You're taking this rather calmly. Most people get hysterical."

"Most people?" His words riled her temper another notch. "Think about my last week, Ralston. My uncle was murdered. I inherited a wedding dress covered in stolen diamonds. Everyone who owns it winds up dead. I was attacked in my bed. Bad guys. Wolves. A wedding in three days. I don't mean to bruise your ego, but one night of hot sex with the living dead isn't as much of a shocker as you might think."

And then she burst into tears. Chloe jammed her fingers into the thick tangle of her hair, horrified by the hot ache in her eyes and the wetness trickling down her cheeks. She couldn't say another word. All the fear and anger since Jack's death jammed in her throat, choking off any explanations. All she could do was cry.

She heard the rustle of sheets, and then Sam was in front of her. Tenderly, he wrapped her in his thick, muscular arms and tucked her head under his chin. She fit there perfectly, her body cradled against the strong curve of his chest. Rhythmically, he rubbed her back, almost as if she were a colicky baby.

"Hush, sweet one." He kissed the top of her head, then tipped her head up to put gentle kisses on her eyelids. "Hush."

His touch was hypnotic, soothing the shivers from her limbs. No words, no excuses, no telling her how to think or feel—he simply held her. It was exactly the right thing. As his lips touched the spot just under her ear, she gasped, every cell in her body suddenly yearning for him. He slipped the robe from her shoulders, sliding his hands down the line of her back.

Chloe arched into him feeling his body wake, long and thick, against her. *He's a vampire!* But in the next moment, all she could remember was that he was Sam.

"I'm sorry, Chloe. I didn't mean for that side of me to come out. The more I want somebody, the harder it is to control. And I want you far too much."

She made a yearning noise deep in her throat. He grew harder, and his hands slid down to cup her backside. Chloe forgot everything but the taste of his mouth. "I need to know you."

"Now you do," he murmured. "You know everything."

Whether she fell back onto the bed or he pushed her was hard to say. He was on top of her, beside her, and then she was on top of him, taking possession of Sam.

His stomach tensed as she tasted him, letting her tongue linger in a slow circuit of his tip. Now he was the one making the throaty noise.

Yes, she was getting to know him. Getting to know exactly what he liked. She closed her lips over him, sucking and teasing him with her teeth.

"Chloe!" he protested through gritted teeth.

She bit down carefully, figuring turnabout was fair play. The salty taste of him grew stronger, the muscles in his thighs hard under her hands.

He shuddered, obviously at the edge of his control. Peeking up through her lashes, she could see his face. And there they were, the tips of sharp, white fangs just visible through his parted lips. Pleasure made them come out.

Fear and excitement knotted inside her. She released him, dragging herself forward in one long, continuous movement, using as much of her skin as possible against the sensitive, engorged member.

Sam grabbed her, rolling her under him in a swift, predatory pounce. He was breathing hard, his nose buried against her neck. "You smell of fear and desire."

Chloe was beyond words. Instead, she arched her hips against him. And then he was inside her once more, stretching her, filling her, driving her to insanity. She felt the rhythm of her body milking him hungrily, responding with intensity she hadn't thought possible.

She could feel his teeth against her again, but this time he didn't drive them home. "Do it," she whispered.

"Too soon."

His words were nonsense to her. "Do it. Do it, please."

And he did. It wasn't painful, but an explosion inside her that seemed to come from deep in her belly, a sun of pleasure going supernova. Chloe cried out, tears of release trickling down her face.

"You're mine, Chloe." He stopped her cries with his mouth, and then thrust one last time, reaching his own climax. "All of you. Everything."

They lay boneless, exhausted. Chloe rolled into his arms, burying her face in his shoulder. "So. Vampires, huh?"

Her mind roamed to her uncle and his collection. The fact that he had it, that he'd shown it to her, was no coincidence. Just like the target practice, he'd been preparing her for something.

She sat up suddenly. "Uncle Jack was like you!" That explained so much—his strange hours, the secrets, the mysteries and the tasteless collection of rubber bats. "He never said anything."

Sam sighed, pulling her back down beside him. "We're not supposed to exist."

Her head spun. An insane desire to giggle rattled through her. She swallowed back the nervous laughter. "Are there many of you?"

"Maybe a thousand in the whole world."

Chloe sniffed, the storm of her emotions finally abating. A thousand. That was barely any, compared to billions of humans. "Don't you make more of your kind?"

"Not often. It's not as easy as it sounds, and not very smart if you're trying to stay invisible."

"How did you get to be Princess Amelie's bodyguard?"

Sam slipped his arm under her, curling her even closer. "Do you remember I told you about the two kings, and how they went to war when their brother brought the gems back from the Crusades?"

"Yes."

"The eldest brother, Vidon, loved his army and soldiers and dreamed of great conquests. Marcari, the younger, followed the path of alchemy and spells. Each secretly recruited magical beings—vampires, werewolves and demons. When they went to war, they used their magical creatures in the fight."

This sounds like a fairy tale. Yet Chloe paid attention. Fairy tales, it seemed, could come true.

"Many—human or not—were destroyed in the war. Staggered by guilt and remorse, Vidon blamed the supernatural creatures on both sides for the scale of the massacre. He demanded an oath from the Knights of Vidon, making them swear vengeance on nonhumans for all the generations of his royal house."

"That's where the Knights come in."

Sam nodded. She felt the motion of his chin rather than saw it. "Marcari offered the magical creatures protection instead, blaming himself and his all-too-human greed for his part in the war. Aching to atone, he swore to keep such madness from the earth forevermore. Recognizing his sense of honor, the vampires who survived the war banded together and pledged allegiance to Marcari."

"And you're still the princess's bodyguard."

"Not exactly *still*," Sam said with a smile in his voice. "The crusades were definitely before my time. I was born in 1830."

She pondered that. "How come you're tall?"

"Pardon?"

"I thought people were short in the old days." Perhaps it was an odd thing to ask, but she needed something to make sense. A hard fact she could hang on to.

He was silent for a long moment. "Size and strength are some of the gifts that come with the change."

"Oh."

His arms tightened around her. "Other things change, too. We're not men anymore. We're beasts."

Beasts? She pulled back just far enough that she could look into his face. His eyes had gone dark, the gray lost to the blackness of his pupils. Some of it had to be the dim light of the bedroom, but some of it was his obvious interest.

"Exactly what do you mean?" she breathed.

"For one thing, we don't choose our women lightly. Bedmates, yes, but not anyone we'd spend the night with. When we choose, we choose forever."

"You slept with me."

"Yes. And not lightly."

A shiver ran through her at the sound of his voice, half rasp, half growl. It was as if he'd let his human mask fall away, not needing it one second more. It left her with a cocktail of dread and thrilled anticipation.

You're saying I'm more than a one-nighter. That was supposed to be a good thing, but it made her break into a light sweat. *What does* forever *mean to a vampire?*

"And what do you do with your chosen women?" The words shook, her tone a little too high.

He gazed down at her, his eyes both hungry and tender. "Everything we can."

Instinctively, she reached up, caressing his cheek. He grasped her wrist gently, pressing a kiss to her palm. The gesture reminded her of the night he'd stopped her attacker and the first time he'd kissed her fingers. That was Sam, too. Courtly. A beast. Both, and more than both. He had claimed her. Somehow she'd claimed him, too.

He still had her hand, but now it was folded in his, pressed to his chest. His skin was cool, but not cold. Not at all unpleasant.

"What about this bite, then? Does it have any after-effects?"

"No. Not unless I feed off you regularly."

"So you didn't hurt me."

"I'd never hurt you. I'm here to protect you."

She heard the fierce note in his words, the time-honored declaration of the male selecting his mate. He hadn't done anything—bite aside—she hadn't invited, but there was something savage a millimeter under the surface. *The men who shot Lady Beatrice were torn to pieces in their cells.* Was their killer the same man who held her now?

"What if you did feed off me a lot?" She had to know.

"There can be a psychic bond between a vampire and its human, um, friend."

Does the, um, friend happen to be named Renfield? She'd read plenty of vampire books that involved human servants and mind control.

"No, it's not like that," he said.

"You read my mind?" she asked sharply.

"No, but you had the question written all over your face." One corner of his mouth turned up. "I'm not like that, Chloe."

But the hunger was in every line of his body. Not blood hunger, or at least not entirely that. Chloe could see so much more in the set of his head and shoulders as he leaned toward her, the tension around his eyes. It didn't take a lot of imagination to fill in the details. He wanted her in ways without number—the touch and warmth of a woman, the answering voice when he called out in the dark. He'd been alone a long time, and for some reason he'd placed that loneliness at her feet. He'd picked her to banish it.

But what would have happened if she hadn't remembered the bite? How long would he have let her go on thinking he was an ordinary man? Would he have walked away, taking his loneliness with him? His very nature was something he could not share. This was the secret behind everything about Sam Ralston. And yet, she had found him out.

She sat up, putting distance between them. "And if I say I can't handle this, what then?"

By now he understood her fears. *What you don't know could kill you. In this case, vampires.*

"When a human finds out what we are, erasing those memories is standard protocol," he said softly. "Standing orders. It's considered easier in the long run."

His expression said it wasn't going to be easier for him.

"You wouldn't," she breathed.

"I don't want to."

That wasn't the same thing as a *no.* Then she remembered he'd already tried. A cold, sick feeling surged through her. She slipped out of the bed and found her robe where Sam had let it fall to the floor.

She stared at him where he lay, dark hair and dark eyes stark against the white sheets. She knotted her robe shut with quick, sharp movements.

Guilt pinched the lines of his face. It wasn't hard to read.

"You're going to do it, aren't you? You're going to try again to wipe my mind."

"You're resistant. An expert would have to do the job." His voice held a world of unhappiness. He didn't want to face this any more than she did. But she knew enough about Sam to know he didn't flinch from duty.

"But you'll follow orders. Or try to. You—or your supersecret spy network—think you can make choices for me." Chloe drew herself up, gathering the shreds of her dignity. "Get out of my bedroom."

Chapter 24

Sam had to get out of this dilemma. He was supposed to be a straight arrow. Somehow, he'd wound up in knots.

It was hours later. Chloe stood across the room from Sam. Jack's study was quiet, the rain turning the day to a false twilight. For once she'd been the one to find him there, rather than vice versa. He'd been lingering amongst the old books and paintings, hoping she'd come. He'd made himself swear to leave her alone, but if they met by accident?

Be honest. He was stalking her like a lion in the long grass. He knew where the gazelle would wander. *She's mine.*

But that was the fastest way to get her forcibly brain-washed or killed. Humans who knew too much were considered enemies of the Company.

She was dressed now, her hair rolled up in that neat, elegant twist she had been wearing the day the wedding dress had come out of Jack's safe. The memory of it wrenched him. They'd come full circle, from shared mystery to mutual discovery to passion to...whatever this standoff was.

When we choose, we choose forever. He meant it. It had been dangerous to say it, but every word was true, regardless of the Company's rules.

"We have to find a compromise." Her voice cracked, all the vibrancy sucked out of it. "There is no way on earth I'm letting some stranger mess with my brain."

Sam kept his face a neutral mask. When it came to erasing memories, "let" wasn't usually a consideration, but he wasn't going to point that out. He remembered the feel of her in his arms, and his groin began to ache. She was his. The instinct to keep and claim warred with logic. Above all else, he had to keep her safe. "The Company isn't easy to fool."

"Who or what is the Company?"

"The group of us who serve the King of Marcari."

"Your boss." Red was creeping up her cheeks, her eyes turning from a soft summer-blue to a frozen winter sky. "Your friends. That fairy tale story about the king and his loyal vampires. They're the Company, aren't they?"

"Yes."

"This is madness." She paced to the window and back, her face pale as paper.

Sam's face was numb, grief and guilt crushing whatever spark kept him walking the earth. *You'd think a hundred-and-fifty-year-old could keep his fangs zipped up.*

But he owed her truth. She had railed against those who sought to protect her by keeping silent. He wasn't going to make that mistake. "The Company's reach goes further than you know. If they find there has been a security breach, they'll come after you. It doesn't matter where you are."

That caught her up short. "What?"

"You heard me." He said it gently. "They'll want to take your memories or your life."

Her eyes went round. "Kill me for just knowing you exist?"

"Yes."

She spread her hands into the air, a gesture of resignation. "Tell them to take a number. There are *already* people trying to kill me! And tell me this—How am I supposed to watch my back if I don't know about the Knights and the vampires and whoever else is out to get me? You're setting me up to die!"

"No!" Sam reached for her, but she shrank back. He dropped his arm to his side, his cold, still heart breaking in his chest.

Her mouth tightened, her eyes growing too bright in the half light of the room. The Company would kill him, too, for permitting the breach to occur. The rules about mating with human women were clear. But Sam didn't mention that. It was almost irrelevant. He wasn't sure he was going to exist if the memories of their union were erased from her lovely eyes.

Self-loathing scorched him. He had betrayed her the moment they kissed. He hadn't been able to control his yearning for her. He still couldn't. His body burned to feel her against him. From her scent, he knew she felt the same fire.

His world pivoted on its axis, changing utterly. Duty was everything, but his first obligation was to this woman who had held him in her slim, soft arms.

Words scraped through his aching throat. "I said I wouldn't let you come to harm. I mean it."

"How can I believe that?" Her eyes were bright with unshed tears. "You're asking an awful lot of trust for someone who's lied to me since the instant we met."

For a moment, Sam could find nothing to say. For the first time in his long existence, he was floundering. If he was going to solve this, he was going to have to break from everything he knew.

He grabbed her arms, pressing her back against the wall, capturing her body with his. He felt her breath on his face, the softness of her breasts against his chest. It was an act of pure possession. "Is this a lie?"

He crushed his mouth with hers, plundering the warmth of her with his lips and tongue. He left kisses along the corners of her mouth, her eyelids, the delicate line of her jaw. She tasted sweet, but there was also a trace of salt on her skin. She had been crying.

He broke away. No one made his woman cry. "I will protect you. I swear it. I am War. I am the strongest."

She studied him, her gaze flicking back and forth over his features. Her lips trembled for a moment. "How can you fight the whole Company by yourself?"

"I refuse to let you suffer for just knowing me."

"I'll suffer if you're hurt. Did you think of that?"

It was an effort to hide the stab of grief her words delivered. No one else worried if War was hurt. And yet standard orders said to wipe away her feelings like fog obscuring the clear window of duty. How could anyone ask that of him?

He set his hands on her shoulders, his touch as gentle as he knew how to make it. "My beautiful Chloe." *Forget obedience.* "I will take the two kingdoms apart stone by stone before I will allow anyone to touch you."

"I don't think that's a solution."

"Then what do you propose we do?"

Her jaw clenched, as if she were the one who was going to do the biting. "We don't do anything. We don't say anything. I have a wedding to put on here. I have to sell this house. You have to take the dress back to Marcari. We say goodbye. No one needs to know."

Sam narrowed his eyes. This plan required patience. Not his favorite thing. "You can keep me, the Company, everything a secret?"

"Of course I can." She swallowed hard. "I have to. Otherwise we'll have to find another end to this situation where I don't end up a victim, and you don't have to fight the entire world." Her eyes pleaded with him, willing him to accept her plan.

This means I will disobey orders. He was the straight arrow, never deviating from his path. But breaking the rules made perfect sense. It would save them both—if she could keep his secret.

He growled a conditional acquiescence. "We walk away, then what?"

She hung her head, all the strength seeming to seep from her frame. "Are the rules going to change?"

"No." The word stuck in his throat.

She lifted her eyes to his, pain and anger mixed in her face. "Then nothing."

Nothing. If he loved her, if he wanted to be sure she was safe, he had to keep his distance. Never call her. Never touch her soft, warm body again. Never taste her again. *Unthinkable!*

He took her mouth again like a drowning man seeking a last gasp of air. He knew she was right. Carter was already suspicious that there was something between them. Until he had a better plan, silence was the safest course. But still…

"Forgetting isn't the worst thing that could happen,"

he said hoarsely. "Remembering will be a thousand times worse."

Her brows pulled together. "What's the alternative?"

He had no answer. No other plan. At least, not yet. He wanted to rage, beat something. Put his fist through a wall. Roar. "I will solve this."

"How?" She gave him a look that skewered him where he stood. It held despair, sadness, every raw and bloody feeling that was tearing him apart, too.

"I don't know yet, but I will take care of it. Trust me."

"I trust you to be wise and careful." Her eyes were gentle as she pulled his hands from her shoulders, kissed him chastely on the cheek and walked out.

Sam's first instinct was to haul her back, force her against the wall and mark her as his own all over again. She *had* to be his.

Except that way was disaster. That impulse to possess, to dominate was what got him in this mess in the first place. He was too much the vampire. Now she was at risk.

He watched her slim form walking away. *Wise and careful.* Careful wasn't his prime skill set. Battle was more his style. But for her, he could be anything.

Then, across the widening distance between them, he heard a sharp intake of breath. Chloe had been unspeakably brave, but she hadn't managed to stifle her tears.

No one cried for him. No one until now. *Nine hells.*

War had never shied away from battle. This was no exception. He *would* find a way to win.

Chloe drove to the Eldon Hotel, the SIG Sauer on the passenger seat. If she'd been pulled over it would have been a huge problem, but not as big a problem as angry vampires. Everything was relative.

She wondered if the rain-darkened sky meant all the

undead could come out and play in broad daylight. Sam seemed to be able to get around in the day, but clearly didn't enjoy it.

Sam. Her eyes prickled again. She'd cried and cried until there were no more tears, but the pain of that last conversation hadn't dimmed one bit. She knew what they had was incredible and wonderful and, in effect, she'd said goodbye. And, at the same time, begged that she'd be allowed to remember she'd done it. How messed up was that?

There was no way she could say this outcome was for the best. It was just that the alternatives were worse. Die. Forget Sam. Or, be miserable but at least remember their brief time together. Door number three sucked the least.

Chloe blinked tear-filled eyes and turned into the El-don's parking lot. Rain left the hotel grounds looking dark and drab. She wondered what Hope's Reach looked like on a day like this. The memory of her lunch there with Sam sent a fresh wave of pain through her stomach.

There was too much she didn't know about the vampire world. Why did they mix with humans at all? Just for food? Or was there something else they gained from the contact? How big an impact did their kind have on the mortal realm? Chloe burned to know. Yet, if they had their way, she wouldn't have the time to ask questions before her memories were ripped out. *Over my dead body.*

Well, apparently that was an option.

When Lexie opened the door to her suite, she looked Chloe up and down with mounting dismay. "What happened to you?"

"It's raining out." Chloe stepped inside the living room of the suite. Done in pinks and greens, it looked like every other hotel anyplace, anywhere.

"I'm not talking about the weather. You look like you've just watched Bambi's mother die."

Chloe grabbed Lexie in a hug. "I just broke up."

"With Sam?"

Chloe staggered back, fighting off a fresh wave of tears. "He's a vampire."

Lexie looked sad and a little angry. "Like I said, they're not people."

"I had no idea what that meant."

"And how would you? We never had a real chance to talk. Is Sam aware that you know?"

She nodded. "How much do you know?"

Lexie sucked in a ragged breath. "Faran. Why we split up. Faran is a werewolf."

"Fido!"

Her friend gave her a puzzled look.

"That's what Sam called his wolf."

"Fido? Seriously?"

"That was Faran!" Chloe flopped onto one end of the overstuffed couch. "He turns into a wolf. How the blazes does that even work?"

Lexie put a hand to her forehead as if staving off a headache. "It's hereditary. The whole biting-contagion thing is a myth."

"Are you sure?"

"Yes. Faran has a lot of flaws, but he wouldn't out-right lie about something like that." Lexie's face was serious. "You're in a lot of trouble, Chlo. You know about the whole memory-wipe thing?"

"Yeah. How come your memories were never erased?"

"No one knows I found out."

"Doesn't Faran?"

"We agreed to pretend it didn't happen. He was okay with that. He was never a rules kind of guy. We met at this resort in Cannes. I was photographing a swimwear collection and he was hanging around in the Casinos. I didn't find out till much later that he was working undercover. I thought he was just a rather nice part of the scenery."

Chloe gave her a long look, thinking how different Sam was from his friend, and yet they had ended up in the same predicament.

Faran, who was a werewolf. *I petted him!* And she'd sprayed him with Aunt Mavis's hair products. *Good grief.* "Faran trusts you not to spill his secrets."

"About that, yes." Her voice was thickly buttered with irony. "We had other problems. I couldn't deal with the wolf."

They were both quiet for a time. The rain beat against the window of the hotel room. Chloe's whole body ached with tension. She was incredibly grateful to be able to talk to Lexie, but then they'd always kept each other's confidences. They were closer than sisters, and Chloe had never needed her friend more than now.

She finally broke the silence. "Sam and I have decided to pretend I don't know. That nothing important ever passed between us."

"Do you believe he'll stick to that?"

"That wasn't his first thought. He was more concerned about the power of the Company. He could change his mind or, worse, try and take on the whole world for my sake."

Lexie was curled up on the other end of the sofa, her long legs tucked under her. "I don't think it's as simple as whether he trusts you, or whether he thinks of the Company's power first. The fact that he even questions his duty shows how much he cares for you."

"Was Faran the same way?"

Lexie shook her head. "He's aware we've chosen a dangerous path, but Faran is a lone wolf. He obeys orders because he chooses to for the time being. Vampires are different. With them, it's all about hierarchy and obedience. If Sam picks a fight with the Company, it won't end well no matter who wins."

Chloe buried her face in her hands. "I can't believe this. What a nightmare. And yet I don't want to forget."

"The whole supernatural thing is pretty amazing stuff." Lexie gave a lopsided smile. "I don't, either."

"It's not that. It's Sam. I don't want to forget *him*."

"Also amazing stuff?"

"Very." Chloe felt a tremor pass through her. It was more than memory, or just the replaying of sensation. It was her body's knowledge of Sam, bone-deep and howling with loss.

Lexie waved a hand in the air. "Then run for it. Don't wait."

"Before this wedding? I'll ruin my career, my business, everything I've worked for."

"So choose what's more important."

Chloe gave her a furious look. "This is ridiculous! Why am I in this position? Why should I have to choose?"

"Has Sam said anything to his friends?"

"I don't think so. Not yet."

"Good." Lexie drummed her fingers on the arm of the couch. "Watch out for that doctor, Mark Winspear. He has expert brainwashing skills. Apparently not all vampires can do it well. In that little pack of theirs, Winspear's the eraser. Once he played a trick on Faran, completely removing his memory of eating dinner so that he prepared and ate the complete meal over again three times. I wish I'd seen that."

Chloe huddled deeper into the cushions, anxiety pulling at her. The vampires had it all organized. There were chosen personnel who specialized in tearing apart human memory. *Sam wasn't exaggerating. They're serious about keeping their secrets.* "Winspear is on the outs with them. He's missing and Sam thinks he's working for their enemies."

Lexie raised an eyebrow. "Good to know."

"What does the Company think I'm going to do, anyway? Alert the media? They'd think I was crazy."

Lexie pushed back her long red hair. "The nonhumans have survived by being careful. If enough people spoke up, eventually the media would have to pay attention."

Chloe buried her face in her hands. "I hate this. I can't just walk out of my life. I've worked too hard to let everything go."

Her friend's face puckered with worry. "It's your brain. What do we have besides our memories? It's kind of who we are."

"What if I just went home? Finished the wedding and left? Do you think Sam would stick to the plan?"

"You know him better than I do."

Chloe swore under her breath. She couldn't keep herself from remembering his first response had been to try to wipe her memories. How could she trust him? "This is insane."

"That's why I ended it with Faran. I couldn't live with all the cloak-and-dagger and, well, furriness."

"Sam knows tampering with my memory is the last thing I want." Yet the worm of doubt wouldn't quite lie still.

"Then give him a chance to be on the side of the angels. If he agreed to pretend nothing happened, he might just be honorable enough to do that."

Chloe nodded, her throat too tight to let her speak. She

knew Sam wanted to find a better solution to their problems, but she couldn't imagine what that would be. In
some ways, it would be a blessing if *he* forgot she existed.

"If you want to hedge your bets, leave before he ex-
pects you to. They can't erase your memories if you're not
there. If you go just before the wedding wraps up, right in
the middle of all the goodbye confusion, you can simply
vanish. Lay low somewhere for a while. Give the bloodsuckers a chance to start worrying about other problems.
Once the dust has settled, you can slip back home and
carry on like nothing happened. If he's the right guy, no
one will be the wiser and the Company will never darken
your door again."

Is he the right guy? Of course he was. If he wasn't,
would she be so desperate to remember him?

"I know, we'll go together," Lexie said. "I'll make sure
you get away from the wedding. Plus, I have friends everywhere. We can be on the road forever without using
a credit card or registering in a hotel. We'll be ghosts in
the wind."

It was a terrible idea for a million reasons, but it was
still better than having her brains vacuumed. Plus, it
would still allow for her to keep her obligation to Elaine
and Leo. "You make running away sound like a big adventure."

"Isn't it?" Lexie said with relish, leaning forward to
poke Chloe's arm. "We've got to show the boys in black
that we've got ideas of our own."

This was Lexie all over. Bolting was her number one
way of dealing with difficult situations. There was a reason she was a globe-trotter, working freelance and living out of a suitcase.

Chloe drew her knees up to her chin. She hated the
plan for the same reason that it was necessary: it took

her away from Sam. They'd agreed to be apart, but these were concrete steps for putting miles between them. Her insides felt cold and heavy, as if someone had turned them to lead.

She sucked in a breath and her chest hurt with the effort. "Will you take a picture of Sam and me together at the wedding, just in case? If they do catch up with me and take my memories, I'll have something to show we were together."

"You want to remember him that much?"

Chloe rested her forehead on her knees, hiding her misery. "Whatever else he is, Sam is the once-in-a-lifetime guy."

Chapter 25

The rehearsal dinner was over, and all Chloe could think about was the fact that thirty-six hours from that moment, the wedding would be over.

Iris Fallon had been enchanted with the plans for the hors d'oeuvres. She had been okay with the dais and pavilions putting holes in Jack's garden lawn. She had been critical of everything else. Chloe had been at some pains to explain why poising a concert harp on the diving board of the swimming pool, while it would project the sound just dandy for the reception, would be objectionable to the harpist.

Some people are the clichés. Chloe closed her bedroom door behind her, kicked off her shoes and gathered up her supplies for a long bath. Unlike her old bedroom, this one didn't have an ensuite. She padded down the hall barefoot, reliving memories of Faran sliding across the floor in wolf form, of Sam coming to her rescue, gun drawn. That night seemed a thousand years ago.

Vampires. Werewolves. Okay, that's freaky. But I don't really care as much about that as I do the fact they have stupid rules keeping us apart. She'd finalized her plans with Lexie to leave during the wedding. If all went according to plan, she'd soon be far away from Sam, her memory intact and her heart in tiny pieces.

She shouldered through the bathroom door. It had a claw-foot tub deep enough to float in. A soak, a sleep and then she'd hit the ground running before the crack of dawn. Jack's mansion was stuffed with guests, staff and contractors. Even the palfrey was in the barn, having his hooves painted gold.

Chloe was stupefied with exhaustion. All she wanted was some quiet time. She wanted to sleep for a thousand years, without dreaming of Sam. She pushed the stopper into the drain of the tub and turned on the water, making sure it was good and hot.

She slipped off her clothes, donning her terry towel robe while she waited for the tub to fill, then lit a candle that sat on the counter. When she turned off the overhead light, the flame shimmered against the tiles and bounced off the mirror.

"Chloe," said the deep voice behind her.

She started. Big hands clamped her shoulders, holding her before she could wheel around to face the intruder.

"It's just me," said Sam.

"How did you get in here?" she demanded.

"I'm very good at sneaking around."

"It's a small room. I should have seen the door open!"

"I wanted to surprise you." He kissed the back of her neck. "No one knows I'm here."

Chloe hugged the robe around her, feeling more like she was wearing nothing at all. "Are you sure?"

His mouth was busy on her shoulder, tasting every inch of skin. "I'm not ready to let you go. I don't think I'll ever be ready." He turned her around. She could see his eyes now, black in the dim light. They held a world of promises.

His mouth crushed hers. It wasn't a kind or gentle kiss, but devouring. Reflexively, Chloe's hands flew up to fend him off, but she only managed to press her palms against his chest. That gesture turned to a caress as he held her, pulling her so close against his body that only her toes touched the floor.

There was no room for talk in whatever Sam Ralston had planned. He parted her robe with one flick of his hand. A voice in the back of her mind protested. She had told him to leave her bed, and that applied to more than just that bed on that night. It had cost her all her courage to tell him they had to part. Now she would have to go through the agony of goodbye all over again.

Unfortunately, the small voice was drowned in the rush of her desire. Her body knew Sam, knew what he could do. Future pain didn't matter to her flesh, only the promise of pleasure.

She was already slick between her thighs. All it took was the sight of him, that musky scent of his, and she was ready. With a mind of their own, her fingers were unbuttoning his shirt. The touch of her skin against his, so slight, was enough to send shivers down her arms.

He nuzzled her neck, and she all but cried out in need, her nipples aching to be touched. He bent, his mouth closing around her breast. The warm, wet sensation mixed in her head with the rushing taps. She was drowning in the sensation of him, of the dark, warm room, of the wetness inside and outside of her body.

As he sucked, the sweet tension low in her belly was sharpening to hunger. She pressed against him, her body begging for more. He moved from one breast to the other, making his possession complete.

His shirt slithered to the floor. Chloe dragged her nails lightly down his back, feeling the curve of hard flesh, the sleek angle of his ribs. Sam truly was built like a god of battle, his chest deep, shoulders thick, his waist trim and ridged with muscle. She used her own tongue on his flat, dark nipples, flicking them to life.

Sam lost the rest of his clothes. When he sprang free from his pants, he was thoroughly armed for battle. A pleasant, tingling weakness passed through her, the breath of ecstasy to come. Sam turned off the taps of the tub. The sudden silence was broken only by the gentle lapping of the water and Chloe's own breathing. Sam climbed into the bath.

"Get in," he ordered, his voice a growl of desire.

She did. The tub was huge, deep enough that the water provided some buoyancy. Sam caught her around the waist, positioning her so that her back was to his chest. The hot water stroked her breasts, adding more fingers to the teasing sensations invading every nerve. She felt slightly weightless, tingling from heat and heightened sensitivity.

Sam angled her just so and entered her from behind. The size of him brought a sound of surprise from her throat. His hands closed over her breasts as he thrust, the lapping water echoing his motion. Chloe came on the third stroke.

Sam felt the pulses of her climax pulling at him, but he willed himself to resist his own climax. He pushed forward, bracing himself now on the edge of the tub, thrusting at a new angle, touching her inside and out in ever-changing ways. He could feel the tension building in her again, bringing her to the crest once more.

Was he being unfair, rekindling the fire they'd agreed to bank for the sake of safety? Perhaps. But he would not walk away from her. He had too much to lose. He had waited through lifetimes to find a woman like Chloe. Every instinct he had demanded that she stay glued to his side. *She's mine.*

Dimly, like a will-o'-the-wisp of reason in the wilderness of his pleasure, Sam knew he was lost. When vampires made up their minds about a mate, they claimed that person with every fiber of their souls. This had never happened to him before. In fact it rarely happened to anyone, but when it did, vampires were little better than wild beasts until their women accepted them.

I'm in trouble. He no longer belonged to himself. If Chloe was his, he belonged to her in an equally absolute equation. The Company's rules were no more than cobwebs to be brushed aside. Easier said than done, but there was no place in his brain for that now.

He thrust, and she dissolved around him, warm, sweet slickness milking him hard. Sam's fangs were out, the hunger for her blood—hers and hers alone—a painful cramping in every cell. As her mate, he was addicted to her.

His mouth found the softness of her neck and bit. Salty blood welled from the bite, filling his mouth with life. Chloe moaned, melting around him yet again. His saliva held the key to her pleasure, venom filled with erotic stimulants that also completely healed and hid the wound from his teeth. In hours, not even a discoloration would remain.

The pleasure cut both ways, giving to him as well as her. Sam felt aching, tightening and then an explosion that seemed to last an eternity of infinite, brilliant bliss. It tore him apart, killing him even as he was made new. He came long and hard, with everything he had.

He had never experienced orgasm close to this before. *Chloe!*

He rolled back to slouch against the tub, pulling her with him. He was sated, the raging need inside him fading down to a few glowing coals. Her blood churned inside, branding him with the very code that made her. That thought stiffened him enough that she moaned. He had to be careful. She was only human. The vampire male was next to insatiable. His lust could hurt her.

Chloe lay quiet against him, lost in an exhausted haze between consciousness and sleep. Her breath fanned across his chest, teasing his nipples until the skin around them prickled with gooseflesh. The water was cooling now, the air of the bathroom seeming to grow colder with every drip of the tap.

Sleep. He was nowhere near the mind sage Winspear was, but he could guide her the rest of the way into slumber. *Sleep, Chloe.*

Her limbs grew heavier where she lay. He shifted, grabbing a towel to blot the water from her face. She was so beautiful, it made his chest ache. He pressed the towel gently to her cheeks and forehead, squeezing the water from her hair gone dark with its soaking.

When he had gazed his fill, Sam lifted her from the water, setting her gently on the thick white bathroom carpet. He dried the rest of her, and wrapped her in the robe he had dropped to the floor. Without bothering to do more than tie a towel around his hips, he carried Chloe to her bed and tucked her in it before she could catch a chill.

It was midnight. The witching hour.

Sam stood beside her bed, knowing what it was to be thoroughly bewitched. He had gone to Chloe planning to reassure her, to tell her somehow they'd stay together, even if that meant disappearing to places not even the Company could follow. War was still the best.

They'd never got to the talking part.

Surely she'd understood what he'd meant.

Chapter 26

Sam returned to the bathroom to dress. In the process, he found his phone and dialed a number. He started picking up wet towels while the cell rang, putting the bathroom back in some sort of order.

"Carter," came the gruff voice of his maker.

"It's Sam."

"When can I get the dress?"

The memory of Pietro's cracking neck bones came flooding back. *Why do you, the director of the Company, want to take it back on your own, with no escort?* That made no sense.

Sam had every intention of taking the dress back himself. If Carter was on the level, he would be annoyed but content as long as the dress made it home safely. If he wasn't—well, Sam didn't much care if he was angry, then. They'd be locked in a battle to the death.

The fact that he could even think that about the man

he honored as a second father said too much about Sam's suspicions.

"I need to talk to you about something."

"You know I'm always here for you, boy." Carter's voice took on a homey singsong. A simple man with simple loyalties, it seemed to say.

"Had you ever met Pietro before?"

"No, of course not." His voice said clearly this wasn't the conversation he wanted to have.

Sam hung up the last towel. "He seemed to know you. He kept calling you boss. He didn't know Winspear's name."

"Like I said, Winspear must be using an alias. Winspear *is* an alias. You know as well as I do he's a Johnny-come-lately to the Company."

"Then how would the Knights know his information was of any value? You would think a strange vampire appearing at their doorstep would be staked. He must have credentials of some kind."

Carter was silent for a moment. "Winspear played a game darker than any of us really know. He was a trained assassin from the time of the Borgias. I'm sure he has credibility with all kinds of lowlife."

"True."

"Of course it's true."

"Unfortunate that Pietro died before we got more answers." Sam pushed a window open to let out the steam from the bath. The air smelled like Chloe's perfume.

"Don't criticize, boy. We were never going to get anything of value there."

How do you know? You broke his neck the moment he accused you of being a liar. Sam's gut knotted to a hard lump. "I worry Winspear is going to return here. He knows the layout. The staff trust him."

"You're worried about the girl."

"Chloe? Yes. She doesn't deserve any of this."

"She's a human and irrelevant. Vampires who moon after mortal women lose themselves."

"What does that mean?"

"They mate them. They feed so often they turn the women." Carter's voice was thick with disgust. "Female vampires. No better than succubi."

But that woman and her mate are together forever. His heart lifted.

But Carter wasn't done. "And the men are useless afterward. Their loyalties are always with their women first. What good is that to the Company? They should owe their loyalty to me first and always."

Sam froze, really listening to what Carter was saying. Carter had made the rules about fraternizing with humans. The real reason he didn't like his warriors finding mates is because it eclipsed his authority. It was a question of power. *You keep us alone because you want to keep us obedient.*

Anger burned through Sam, his muscles tightening to the point of pain. Why hadn't he seen this before? Mind you, the only other time it had come up, Sam had barely become a vampire.

There had been his wife, Amy. He'd loved her fiercely, and still did. She'd been a woman of her time, gently raised and groomed to be a pillar of polite society. She'd had him wrapped around her delicate white fingers from the time he was in long pants.

After he'd been turned, he'd tried to go home, to find his wife in the country retreat up north where she'd taken the children. It hadn't worked. At the time, the thrill of having his new powers was impossible to conceal. After Carter had worked his dark magic, Sam had not only the semblance of life, but the strength of a Titan. He'd reveled in it. He hadn't tried to hide it.

His reunion with Amy had been the disaster of a single night. By dawn, she'd fled with the children, terrified that her husband had been possessed by devils. In some measure, she'd been right.

Carter intervened, blurring Amy's memories. She'd spent the next year in a nurse's care. Grief, they'd called it. She'd only imagined that he'd come home because she wanted it so badly.

It had been then that Carter had given him the script. War wasn't made for love. Amy's mental breakdown was Sam's doing. And his children? Sam had watched them grow and have children of their own, but he hadn't dared come near them. What evil might he have sown in their lives? He had no choice but loneliness. He would destroy every human he loved.

Carter had known what damage a newly turned fledgling could do. He'd helped Sam convince himself of his own beastliness.

For centuries, Sam had felt a grief so deep it had no words.

"About the dress," Carter was saying.

Sam snapped back to the present, his gut a knot of hot, hard fury. "I can't get it right now. The place is crawling with humans. There is a wedding here in the morning. It will be much quieter after tomorrow."

Carter was silent for a moment. "We'll be in touch."

The line went dead, the silence filling Sam with disquiet. Personal issues aside, there were too many things that didn't add up. For one thing, if his maker had the authority of the King of Marcari behind him, why didn't he simply come forward openly? And where did Winspear fit into this? Were they working together?

He is my maker. He gave me life. He made me War.

The loyalties of so many years didn't die easily. His chest felt heavy, as if his heart had suddenly turned to a lump of iron.

Sam slipped back into Chloe's bedroom. She was curled on her side like a kitten, her knees drawn up into a ball. *We could be together forever.*

Carter forbade it.

Unless I break every rule in the book. Unless I find a way to be with her. Unless he turned his back on the Company. He would always honor the Throne, he had always been Marcari's ultimate champion, but how could he follow a maker who condemned him to darkness?

Maybe it was time War chose his own battles. It meant breaking every other bond he had, but what would he not give for a chance at real happiness?

She's mine. Did he seriously think he could give Chloe up? *Not bloody likely.* Straight arrows could have different targets, ones of their own devising.

Sam turned that idea over the way one might a candy melting on the tongue. Slowly, leisurely, tasting the pungent sweetness of disobedience.

He slid under the covers, curling around her, and held her as she slept.

Chloe woke alone. If her memories were befuddled for the first sixty seconds, her body was quick to remind her exactly what she'd been doing and how many times. For a moment, her breath left her, staggered by the memory. She fell back on the pillows, luxuriating in the sensations replaying themselves through her every cell.

The wedding!

She sat up so fast her head swam. Chloe stumbled to her dresser, groping for her phone. She hadn't set the alarm and panic was starting to ramp up inside her. What time was it? She had a wedding to put on.

At the same time, Sam's words replayed in her head. *I'm not ready to let you go. I don't think I'll ever be ready.*

Okay, so that was pretty straightforward, but what did it mean in practical terms? The mind-blowing sex was lovely, but when her life and her brain were at stake, she needed specifics. She had to talk to him.

She finally found her phone and thumbed it to life. Seven o'clock. She'd meant to get up at four. *Geez!* Chloe ran for her closet.

When she reached the teeming kitchens, Faran was already there. He'd been better than his word, not just helping with the menu but helping to cook it, too. His whites were splashed with food and he was piping something into tart shells at lightning speed. "These are savories," he said with a grin. "My own recipe. The venison is locally sourced. I, uh, hunted it myself."

Racks of finished tarts were set out to cool. They looked and smelled delicious, the crusts exactly the right shade of golden-brown. Chloe gave him her best smile, refusing to grapple with the image of Fido versus Bambi. *I hope there aren't any dog hairs in it.* "They smell fabulous," she said.

"Thanks." With only a cloth to protect his fingers, he pulled an enormous pan of the tarts out of the oven, releasing a mouthwatering cloud of warm spices. "I'll serve these with a piquant currant coulis."

"Sounds perfect." She had to shout over the clamor of pots and urgent voices bouncing off miles of stainless steel. It was at least a thousand degrees in there.

"The cake arrived," he put in. "It's in the walk-in for now."

"Did you look at it?"

"It's a bit purple, but it's a bit late to do anything about it."

Chloe took a look inside the fridge. *Okay.* The cake was huge, and when assembled would create a castle a good five feet tall. Chloe had asked for something in a mauve, but Faran was right. The baker had got into the spirit of the moment. The cake was a psychedelic purple, the surrounding hill a lime-green. The dragon clinging to the main tower was every bit as tall as the castle itself. When the dry ice was activated, curls of smoke would drift from the creature's nostrils. It was playful, color-ful and full of personality. Elaine was going to love it.

Faran pushed through the crowd and stood beside her, wiping his hands on his apron. "When do you need to serve this?"

"It has to be on display by three o'clock. That's when the reception starts."

"All you can do now is embrace it's quirky spirit." He was staring at the cake, doing his best to keep a straight face.

"Mrs. Fallon is going to freak."

"Well, she likes unicorns. Unicorns *might* live in a bright purple castle."

Chloe kissed his cheek. "I've got it covered. I found dozens of tiny medieval toys. Knights. Unicorns. Fair ladies. The display is going to be a fabulous tableau."

Faran gave her a high five.

Outside, the sky was hazy with cloud, but it looked like the kind that would burn off after a few hours. Her staff was putting up the ribbons and bunting, decorat-ing the chairs where the ceremony would be held, and setting up sound equipment under one of the pavilions. The champagne fountain was going to be a popular spot, so Chloe ordered another few cases be brought up just in case. Then she stopped to change the location where the string quartet was supposed to go. At the last minute, Iris Fallon had fired the harpist, since she wouldn't play suspended over the pool in a mermaid costume or wearing angel wings. The string players had thankfully been left unmolested in their tuxedos.

Chloe stopped in the barn to check on the faux unicorn. The horse, despite the shiny gold hooves, looked reasonably content. All in all, things were going fairly well.

By the time the ballroom, large dining room and the retiring rooms for the wedding party were perfect, the clock had jumped forward to noon. Guests were arriving in droves. Chloe felt like a mechanical car racing around a track, moving faster with every lap.

The wedding party was arriving. *Oh, crumb.* That meant Mrs. Fallon was on-site.

Chloe got the bride and her maids into their dressing room, ducked Iris and scurried off to make sure the group of madrigal singers knew where they were supposed to go.

One group of security had set up by the twin oak trees at the gate of the drive. They were stopping every car that came in, checking identification against the guest list. It was more stringent scrutiny than any other wedding Chloe had managed, but with the diamonds, the cream of the business and social worlds, and stray maniacs on the loose, it seemed prudent. Thankfully, the visitors were accepting it with good grace.

As she passed the gate, Sam caught her arm. He was wearing his industrial-strength sunglasses, and she realized they no longer bothered her. Now she understood exactly why he wore them. According to everything in

Uncle Jack's vampire memorabilia, the undead were nocturnal creatures.

"How are you doing?" he asked, his voice like a caress.

"Good." Chloe leaned in to his touch. She wanted to talk about last night, but now wasn't the moment to discuss it. Until the ceremony had started, she would barely have time to think, let alone wrap her head around something as important as their future. "The guests are coming thick and fast. How's the security? Do we have enough bodies?"

Sam nodded, slipping back into guard mode. "I've called Gravesend to send out a few dozen more. I think we have enough on-site, but I'd rather overdo it. After all, Oakwood has two hundred acres to keep track of. As it is we can't cover the whole perimeter. I'd rather set up patrols just in case."

Whatever Sam thought was a good idea was fine with her. "Perfect. Thanks. I'll find you later." She kissed him lightly and hurried off, leaving him alone in the shadow of the shattered oak tree where Jack had died.

She checked her phone again. Half an hour until the ceremony started. Everything was in place. Now she just had to cross her fingers and hope. She started back for the house, taking the shortcut between the overflow garage and the building where maintenance had its workshop.

A man was leaning against the side of the garage, smoking a cigar. She didn't recognize him, but given the crowd that wasn't a surprise. She nodded and smiled. He smiled back and stepped into her path.

"Hello, my girl," he said in a gruff voice. The man had a mane of gray-streaked hair and sunglasses much like Sam's. "Are you Chloe, Jack's niece?"

She stopped, wanting to get past him so she could begin herding the bridal party into place. Something always went wrong at the very last moment. But she fell back on good manners. "Yes, sir, I'm Chloe Anderson."

He rolled his cigar between thumb and forefinger. "My name is Aldous Carter. I was a friend to your uncle as I am to young Sam."

Chloe tensed. Anyone who described Sam as young either didn't know him very well, or was himself one of the undead. "I'm pleased to meet you."

"I'm sure you are." He took a puff on the cigar, the pungent scent of it tickling Chloe's nose. "Jack left you something I want. Sam seems reluctant to get it for me."

Chloe's alarm bells went off. It was too far to run back to the gate, especially in the shoes she was wearing, and the space between the two buildings was hidden from view. Anyone making a circuit of the grounds was sure to walk past without noticing.

Chloe decided to brazen it out. "I'm sure I don't know what you mean. I am organizing this wedding, Mr. Carter. I need to get back to the house. The ceremony is going to start shortly."

She started forward, prepared to shoulder her way past, but he raised his arm, planting his hand against the side of the workshop. Chloe stopped, her way effectively barred.

"I don't think so." Carter smiled. "You're my bargaining chip. Sam won't listen to me, but he wants you badly. If he's as far gone as I think, a fortune in diamonds is nothing compared to a chance to get between your legs again."

Chloe gasped, not at the vulgarity of what he said, but at the feel of cold iron against the back of her dress.

"Oh, yes," said Carter. "I brought some friends with me. I think you already met the late Pietro. Let me introduce you to his brothers."

"You were working with him?" she gasped. They'd all thought Mark Winspear was the traitor, but they'd been wrong.

He leaned forward, his face an inch from hers. "Still pleased to make my acquaintance, little girl?"

The words, and the way he said them, resonated through her. This was the man she'd shot in the foot the night she'd followed Sam into the garden! Chloe's throat closed with terror.

Chapter 27

Where am I?

Chloe gasped as the hood was pulled from her head. The air was stale, but far better than the sour-smelling cloth that had been jammed against her face. Her momentary relief was almost instantly replaced by fresh apprehension. Wherever they were, it was dark and damp and all too dungeonlike for comfort.

Anger choked her before she could frame any questions. Anger, laced with panic. Chloe struggled against the zip tie Pietro's brothers had used to bind her hands. They'd mercifully left her feet unbound, but she wasn't running anywhere. They'd shoved her into a chair, and Carter was looming over her, a flunky to either side. She was a bird surrounded by hungry cats.

"Now down to business," he said.

Her mind groped for what business that might be. She'd been standing by the garage, and then she was here, in this tiny dark room. She didn't remember anything in between. Zero. Nada. They'd taken her to their lair, and she had no idea where that was.

Disorientation swam through her. "Did you mess with my mind?"

He gave a sardonic smile. "I thought you might prefer hypnosis to being knocked over the head. It worked just as well on the security Sam had posted on the north gate. Good men. No match for me."

Chloe wasn't prepared to accept any of this. "There had to be hundreds of people at Oakwood. You can't just kidnap a person from the middle of a crowd! Somebody would have noticed."

He tsk-tsked. "People see what they want to see. Typically, they ignore anything that will cause inconvenience. Don't think the cavalry is going to come charging in to save you."

"Sam will."

"Will he?" Carter snorted. "True enough—I can smell Sam's presence on you. You've been his dinner before this."

"So?"

Carter's eyes widened, and she realized she'd made a mistake. She should have been doubtful or horrified, not accepting. She wasn't supposed to know what Sam was.

"Interesting." The tone of his voice made the flunkies stir. They'd been so quiet she'd almost forgotten them. "Sam, Sam. The boy never listens."

"What do you care?" She was growing colder, but she couldn't tell if it was the room or just the frozen depths of her fear. Her lips felt numb, too clumsy to work properly.

He fell back a step, face clenched in a look of pure frustration. "You should ask rather why *you* should care.

As long as I direct his actions, the world is safe from him. You are safe."

"Who are you?" she asked, fighting to keep a quaver from her voice.

He ripped off the sunglasses, revealing furious, ice-blue eyes. "I *made* him. I found him all but dead, a great soldier shackled by the obligations of his species. He put everything between his potential and the great things he could achieve. A woman. His mewling brats. The poxy rabble he called his men. In the end, those obligations dragged him into the mud, his guts on the ground. I freed him of that. I made him War."

He grabbed a fistful of her hair, dragging her head back so that she was forced to look up at him. Chloe cried out, pain and fright struggling for supremacy.

"He's mine. He belongs to me. I hold his leash."

That made her blink. "His leash?"

"Vampires aren't house pets, my dear. They are machines of destruction, dedicated to the great work of the Company. But without a dominant influence, they are simply monsters. I do what I can to teach my boys the face of their evil, but learning can be slow. I never thought Sam would go back for seconds. Not after the first time."

"The first time?"

"His wife went mad." Carter released her, stomping in an agitated circle.

Chloe's head snapped forward, her scalp throbbing where he'd grabbed her hair. *His wife went mad.* She remembered. Amy, the wife of Ralston Samuel Hill. Sam's wife. *What happened to the poor woman?* "She eventually remarried."

"I took her memories."

Chloe shuddered, her own mind reeling. A wad of panic was trying to work its way up from her stomach. Already, her heart was starting to pound too fast.

Carter was pacing, his flunkies watching him. One had an automatic rifle cradled in his arms. Suddenly Carter wheeled, glaring at her. "You don't understand. What makes us powerful makes us beasts. It is the influence of demons. Only evil can come of this infection. Our souls are long destroyed."

"But Sam is a good man!"

"None of us is good." His face was a horrible mask of agony, as if he saw something that cracked his reason into splinters. "When the bloodlust was on me, I slaughtered my own wife and brats."

Chloe cringed, as much from the pain and rage in his voice as from what he said. She heard Pietro's brothers shift uneasily.

Carter leaned down, bringing his face far too close to hers. "I can't let Sam slide down that unholy path. I must bring him to heel. And you, you are too much temptation. He forgets his duty to me."

She could do nothing but stare back into his glassy eyes. She wasn't even sure he was seeing her, but might have been gazing on some spectacle from the sewers of his own brain.

The flunky with the gun pushed forward, breaking his trance. "Then take your revenge on him, or on her, I don't care. But do it later. Right now, we have a small opportunity to retrieve the diamonds."

Carter didn't take his eyes from her, but his expression focused to something more sane. "Where is the dress?"

Forcing herself to take a deep breath, she tried to still the tiny earthquakes of fear shaking her insides to pieces.

"I'm not going to tell you. Once you have the dress, I'm as good as dead."

She watched him digest this. As long as she kept this maniac talking, that gave Sam more time to find her. He would find her. That's what Sam did.

But she miscalculated. He was done with conversation.

Carter's blow knocked her sprawling from the chair. One of the flunkies had to jump aside to avoid her body as it hit the floor.

Sam looked at his watch.

The natives were getting restless. He could hear their muttering all the way down at the gate. According to Chloe's timetable, the ceremony was about to start. All the guests seem to have arrived, because no cars had come by for a good quarter hour.

He looked up at the shattered tree, wondering what Jack would have thought of turning his place over for a wedding like this. He probably would have liked it. Jack had always been up for a party.

Sam, however, was not enjoying himself. He was worried about Chloe. She'd greeted him warmly enough just now, but the look in her eyes spoke of unfinished business, of serious conversations yet to be had. Maybe she still thought he was going to erase her mind and abandon her, no matter what he had told her with his body.

Sam heaved an inward sigh. Women were so bad at interpreting wordless devotion. With them it was always talk, talk, talk. In his youth, they had begged for letters and poems. Sam had received a good education, but no schoolmaster had prepared him for writing love poetry. By the nine hells, he was thankful modern women were over that fashion.

He turned to the security guard standing a dozen feet away. "I'm going up to the house."

"See if they can send down some sandwiches and water," the guard suggested. "This is going to be a long day."

Sam agreed and started up the road. He entered the house as soon as he could to get out of the penetrating sun. Most of the crowd had shifted to the lawn where the ceremony was to take place, but Iris Fallon was still at the house, storming from room to room. She wore a peach chiffon pantsuit that billowed as she moved. It made him think of old paintings of the Furies, drapery aflutter as they chased their victims down and ripped off their heads.

Iris slid to a halt in front of Sam, her heels scraping on Jack's hardwood floor. "Where is that chit of a planner? Where is she?"

Chit? "I don't know, ma'am," Sam replied, centuries of good manners forcing him to be polite. "I last saw Chloe about an hour ago." *Call her a chit again and I'll forget that I was raised to be a gentleman.*

"I need her here now!" she seethed. "I've had the security men look everywhere for her. This is insupportable. I'm paying her to be on the spot!"

"I'll find her," Sam said soothingly. He was looking for Chloe anyway.

"And bring that unicorn from the stables."

Sam didn't reply to that one. Despite his calm tone, doubt nagged at him. He knew how important this event was to Chloe. If she wasn't here, where was she?

Taking a guess, Sam headed for the kitchen. Kenyon was there, filling trays with tiny bites of this and that. "Have you seen Chloe?"

The werewolf looked up. He was dusty with flour but

looked completely happy. "She was here a while ago." He glanced at the clock on the wall. "She should be with the wedding party."

Sam felt his doubts grow sharp claws. "She's not there. It sounds like they've looked everywhere."

A strained look came over Kenyon's face.

"What?"

"Chloe's under a lot of pressure, what with the thieves and the wedding and…whatever."

Sam grabbed the front of the werewolf's whites. "What are you saying?"

Kenyon's eyes held pools of sadness. "I'm sorry, I've been where you are."

"What are you talking about?" Sam forced himself to let go of his friend.

"I just can't help remembering what happened when Lexie and I got close."

"What do you mean?"

He almost saw Kenyon clam up, as if a steel wall had slammed across his face.

"What do you mean?" Sam growled.

"Well," he said carefully. "When things didn't work out, Lexie took off. Dropped off the face of the earth for months and months. You know those two women are like sisters, right?"

Sam just stood there, feeling whatever semblance of life he had draining away.

Kenyon looked around the room as if checking for eavesdroppers, and then leaned close. "Is there any chance that Lexie might have talked Chloe into running away?"

Chapter 28

Pain shot through Chloe's shoulder as she landed, followed moments later by a burning in her jaw. Tears leaked from her eyes as she clutched the floor, afraid to get up in case he knocked her down again.

Her mind was a turmoil of fear, but anger had taken control. They could take her life, but she could cling to her will—at least for a little bit longer. Yes, everyone broke eventually, but Jack Anderson's niece was going to make them work for it.

Rough hands heaved her up and dropped her back into the chair. It was one of Pietro's brothers. "Where is it?" the man asked in heavily accented English.

Chloe tried to open her mouth, but her jaw hurt too much. She started to cry from pain and exhaustion. Mortified, she pressed her bound hands to her face.

"This is useless," Carter grumbled.

The other Knight spoke up. "Can't you pull it out of her mind?"

"I can erase something. Finding a fact is different."

"Is it impossible?"

"It takes time. Once something passes from short- to long-term memory, it becomes hard to find."

The one with the gun broke in. "Don't worry about being neat. Do it, then kill her."

"No!" Chloe managed to get the word out. *The least you can do is let me die with my mind in one piece!*

Someone pounded on the door. The men fell silent.

"It's security! Anyone in there? We're looking for Chloe Anderson."

Chloe took a breath to cry out. The next instant, one of the Knights clamped a hand over her mouth. He bent, putting his mouth to her ear. "Wrong move."

The security guard turned the door handle and rattled it, but it was locked.

"You got a key?" someone asked.

"Not to this room," another voice answered.

The pressure of the Knight's hand pained Chloe's bruised jaw. She whimpered, tears leaking from the corners of her eyes. With a shiver, she felt the cold iron of a gun under her right ear. The others stood silent, barely breathing, until she heard the footsteps of the security guards move away.

The Knight with the gun growled. "Try and call out again and you can watch your brains redecorate the wall."

She squeezed her eyes shut, giving herself the blessed relief of not seeing those three horrible faces. She was on the edge of throwing up. But a thought niggled—security men had been just outside that door. Where was she?

With her eyes closed, she could hear how badly her breathing rasped with tension. For a moment that filled her world, but another sound began to press in on her. Voices. Many, many voices.

Chloe opened her eyes and studied the wall in front of her with renewed interest. It was old, unfinished concrete, but there was shelving along one side. She let distant memory fill in the rest of the scene. Once, that shelving had been full of wine crates. *We're beneath Oakwood!*

That meant the voices she heard were upstairs, probably in one of the reception rooms. Now things were beginning to make sense. There was an underground utility passage from the basement to the workshop where they had grabbed her—it would have been easy to bring her here unseen.

Relief, almost a fierce joy, revived her dwindling will.

She worked her jaw to see if it would move. It was still horribly stiff, aching worse than any root canal she could remember.

The man with the gun dug the barrel into her skull. "Where is the dress?"

"It's in the study," she mumbled.

Carter's head snapped in her direction. "The study?"

"In a safe. Behind the painting of a soldier."

There was indeed a hidden compartment in the study. The dress, however, was in the safe in Jack's bedroom. But she was in the business of buying time, not providing accuracy.

"What's the combination?" Carter demanded.

"It's written down. I don't remember." *Where is Sam?* It was past time he put his superhero tights on and showed up.

"I can get anything open," said the smaller Knight. "The problem is getting through the house unseen."

Carter looked thoughtful. "This is a big wedding. There are so many strangers and workmen in the house, no one will notice a few more. Not even men carrying tools."

The men looked at each other. The Knight with the gun spoke. "One cracksman, two lookouts minimum in a busy location. Someone has to watch the prisoner. We're a man short."

She watched Carter's face and could see him make the decision. "You'll have to make do with one lookout. Tie her to the chair and go. If she's wasting our time, I'll shoot her."

Sam was stunned. Would Chloe leave?

He stormed out of the kitchen, ignoring the sunlight that slammed against his skin like the blast from an oven. Iris Fallon swooped down on him.

"Mr. Ralston, where is Chloe?"

He stopped short, struggling to put his fangs away. The woman was in his way. He barely stopped himself from sweeping her aside. "I don't know."

"Well, who is going to fix this?"

"Fix what?

"The madrigal singers are wearing green. I distinctly said the color theme of the wedding was mauve and gold."

He felt his instinctive manners unraveling at a dangerous rate. "Are they any good?"

"Of course they are. I chose them."

He clenched his jaw a long moment before he spoke. "Then no doubt people are listening too hard to notice the outfits."

She inhaled in short, jerky gasps. Sam could tell she was about to start crying, or perhaps shrieking with rage. In time-honored male fashion, he looked around for another woman to handle it.

Elaine was standing in the hall, touchingly beautiful in

her wedding gown. She looked lost. "Chloe was supposed to tell me when to start the procession. They've seated Grandma, Leo's there at the altar, but—" She waved her hands helplessly.

Sam swallowed. He knew the look. He'd seen it on soldiers who needed a leader. They knew what to do, but they needed somebody to point them at the target. "Now. Do it now. You're the bride. Everyone will follow your lead."

"But I can't get on that horse without help! Not in this skirt."

Sam thought of Chloe, and how badly she'd wanted this wedding to work. Fixing this was the least he could do.

"Come with me," he said to Elaine, giving her his arm.

They walked onto the lawn. Elaine's father was holding the head of the white horse. The stuffed unicorn horn Mrs. Fallon had demanded was thankfully absent. Against all odds, good taste had prevailed.

"Hang on," Sam said to the bride, and lifted her onto the saddle.

Elaine settled easily, obviously comfortable with horses, and lowered her veil. "Thank you, Mr. Ralston."

Iris appeared at Sam's elbow and handed up the bouquet. She stared at her daughter a long time, her expression growing soft.

"You're beautiful," she said. "Never forget that."

"Thanks, Mom," Elaine said in a quavering voice, and her father led her away. The horse began the long procession that would lead it to the aisle. The whole path was strewn with flowers, the way marked by tall, ribboned poles crowned with tumbling sprays of roses.

Iris stood for a moment, her lower lip trembling. Then

she swallowed. "That cake is purple. And it has toys on it."

"Forget the cake," Sam said. "You're going to miss the wedding. Go watch your beautiful daughter get married."

Iris gave him a long look. "You're right."

And she went to watch the ceremony she had so meticulously planned.

A few minutes later, the wedding was under way. Now that it was in motion, the event would unfold as it should. Chloe had organized everything down to the last ice cube.

Sam slipped from the back of the crowd, ready to resume his search of the grounds. He caught the flash of a camera. Lexie Haven was darting around the sidelines, catching the candid moments between the bride and groom. If she had planned to leave with Chloe, it hadn't happened yet.

Then Chloe is still here! Sam quickened his pace, moving toward the house. The Fallon woman said security had looked "everywhere." Jack's security guards were human, though. They weren't him.

Sam stopped cold. There was a man standing in the shadow of the porch. *Winspear.*

The doctor beckoned.

Suspicion, anger and worry collided. Sam stormed toward him with the brute fury of an avalanche. He hadn't seen him since the night of the firefight at the gazebo. The night Winspear had snatched the fake wedding dress.

He grabbed Plague by the front of his shirt and slammed him against the side of the porch. "What in the nine hells are you up to?"

The doctor looked tired, his already pale face bonewhite with strain. "Hello to you, too, Sam."

"You've gone over to their side. Why?"

"Have I?"

"You shot at us. You shot at Chloe!"

"And the little minx shot back and actually hit me. Believe me, if I wanted you dead, you'd be pushing up daisies. For centuries I earned my livelihood taking out oafs like you."

There was every chance that someone could pass by and see their argument, but there was no one around right then. That was good enough for Sam. He closed one hand around Winspear's windpipe, lifting him enough that his feet dangled free.

Sam realized the low, vibrating growl was coming from him. Fury swirled in his gut. Chloe was in danger, and so much of it seemed woven around the doctor's betrayal.

Within seconds, Plague began to struggle, a strangled noise rattling from his throat. Suffocation wouldn't kill him, but a crushed windpipe would be painful. Severing his spine would finish the job.

"Wait!" he managed to croak.

Sam released him, but just enough so that he could speak. With a violent push, Winspear broke the hold the rest of the way.

"Listen to me, Ralston. Two Knights are ransacking Jack's study. They're looking for the diamonds. I caught a glimpse of Carter, too. He's the leak. He's betrayed us to the Knights."

Sam had suspected it, but Winspear's words still fell like a blow. "So have you."

"No. I've been working both sides to find out who the informant is. That's why I was at the gazebo. When the grapevine hummed with word that you were going to hand off the dress, I had to know who showed up. I also wanted to make sure the diamonds were safe."

Irritation flashed through Sam. "The dress was a decoy. I'm not that stupid."

"I couldn't take that chance. You've always followed orders to the letter."

"It seems we're getting bad orders these days."

"I'm sorry. I know Carter was your maker. I couldn't take the chance that you'd side with him if I decided to take him down. You're loyal, Sam."

Sam's brain was righting itself, feeling as bruised and sore as someone who'd fallen down a long flight of stairs. Winspear had been undercover. It made sense. It was also a huge relief. Something unknotted in his heart, and he stepped back, giving the doctor room.

"I'm loyal to the Horsemen."

"Good." A smile flickered over Winspear's face, and was gone.

Sam gripped his friend's arm, an apology without words. "Carter knows our names, how we work, everything. If he tells the Knights of Vidon…"

Winspear nodded slowly. "Our vulnerabilities will be exposed. He wants to take the diamonds and run. If he slips through our fingers today, we may never catch him."

Sam spoke the words that had been pounding through him like a pulse. "Chloe's missing."

Winspear's face grew paler still. "They think she's the key to the dress. We have to find Carter *now*."

Chapter 29

Carter prowled the room. Chloe followed the restless movements, her stomach squeezing a little tighter every time he changed direction. It was as if he were winding himself up, the spring of his nerves—and hers—cranking tighter with every circuit.

Carter was her only guard. Before they'd left for the study, the two Pietros had lashed her feet together and bound her to the chair with thick nylon rope. Then they'd cut the zip tie binding her hands and then secured her hands behind her with her own silk scarf. Someone had forgotten to bring extra zips. It didn't matter. They knew their business; there was no way she was loosening the knots.

Carter went back and forth. He looked as if he was as tense as she was. Unless he snapped out of it, all those demons he ranted about might come out and play.

Chloe took a shaking breath. "Mr. Carter?"

His head snapped around in a disturbingly snakelike motion.

"Why are you working with those men? Pietro's brothers?"

He was silent long enough that she thought he wouldn't answer, but then he spoke in a quiet voice. "I have worked for the Company for centuries, but nothing changes. I would say that whatever experiment Marcari has run has been allowed to go on long enough."

"I don't understand."

"Vampires, even with the most rigorous discipline, cannot be wholly tamed. They've been allowed to exist long enough. My intention is that the Knights of Vidon prevail."

Chloe didn't pretend to understand, but she grasped enough to almost feel pity. Carter had murdered his family, and his sense of guilt had eventually driven him crazy. Somewhere in the kaleidoscope of that madness, he'd decided controlling other vampires with an iron fist was no longer enough. Only the ultimate act of control— killing them—was going to satisfy his self-loathing. It would mean destroying himself, but not until he'd done as much damage to the Company as he could.

But she still had one question. "What do you want with Princess Amelie's wedding dress?"

The overhead light cast harsh shadows over the rough-hewn lines of his face. "To level the playing field. Marcari has monsters. Vidon has few resources to match that. The diamonds will go a long way to buying humankind a fighting chance."

As he spoke, he'd moved closer and closer until she could feel the brush of his clothes against her. By the look in Carter's eyes, his demons were feeling frisky. Involuntarily, she jerked, scooting the chair an inch to the right.

He didn't seem to notice, but just stared down at her like a bird sizing up a worm.

I have to keep him talking. "Then where did my uncle fit in?"

He scowled, distracted.

Good.

"Jack? He suspected what I was doing, so I stopped him before he could interfere."

Her brain stopped for a moment, frozen by sheer fury. Then heat began creeping up her body, like a flame of rage rushing up from her belly. "You killed him!"

She flung herself against her bonds.

"No." Carter's look was almost a sneer. "But I caused it to be done."

Her chest shredded inside. The pain and loss felt like pieces of her soul falling away, leaving only an ache in their place. "I hate you." Her voice was dull, the words spoken without much emotion at all. She hurt beyond ranting.

Carter's eyebrows lifted slightly. "It's an understandable reaction. Nevertheless it had to be done."

"I loved him. He looked after me." All of a sudden her anger began to rush back. Her throat began to close, choked by a need to scream and cry. Maybe tear Carter's head off his shoulders.

"When faced with true darkness, love doesn't matter."

Chloe looked into his face, studying it hard. There wasn't any remorse. *He's crazy. Absolutely mad.*

A cold, clinical need to survive took over. Rage wouldn't help her. Her wits might. "What about Jessica Lark?"

Carter shrugged. "I don't know who killed her. I don't know why. She didn't have the diamonds when she died. Lark didn't matter anymore."

"Did you know Uncle Jack had them?"

"Not until you pulled them out of his safe, little girl. That was one deadly inheritance."

"How did you know out about the safe?"

"We had a man on the inside."

The one Sam had found dead in the car. *So many dead.* Chloe swallowed down fresh horror. Details were falling into place, but there was no time now to think about what they meant. Not unless she wanted to join the body count.

Carter reached out to touch her, maybe put a hand on her shoulder. Chloe jerked again, the chair skidding farther to the right. Carter stepped forward, reaching, and she tried to repeat the motion. Instead, the chair overbalanced, tipping her over backward.

Chloe yelped, trying to tuck and roll. Bound as she was, she was helpless as a doll. The impact drove the slats of the chair into her back. Pain fountained through her hands as they were crushed between the chair and the floor.

Nausea swam through her, not helped by the fact she was nearly upside down, her head toward the wall and the empty shelving partially obscuring her view. They'd tied her feet together, but hadn't bound them to the chair legs. They dangled awkwardly, her right foot minus its shoe.

Carter loomed over her, hands on his hips, but she couldn't see anything above his collar. "I think we've talked enough, little Chloe." His hands moved to linger over the weapons strapped to his sides.

Sam, now would be a good time to rescue me.

A twitch of Carter's fingers sent adrenaline rushing through her. Her feet kicked up, knocking the long wooden shelves from their brackets. Chloe angled the move forward, so the clattering boards flew at Carter. He jumped back to avoid them. A few of the brackets unhooked from the strapping, falling to the floor with a ring of metal. One skidded under Carter's heel, sending him tumbling to the ground.

The move also rolled the chair. The knots in the fat nylon rope slipped enough to let her wriggle upward, working the loops of rope over the top of the chair. She tucked her legs up, catching her heels on the seat of the chair and pushed. The chair scraped along the floor, and then she was free of it. The entire maneuver took no more than seconds.

She managed to push herself to her feet. Her ankles were lashed too tightly together to do more than wobble. Bracing herself against the wall was the best she could do.

Carter was already standing, watching her with grim amusement. Letting the mouse run a bit before he batted it with his paw. *Fine. Let him.*

"Hope can be such a sad emotion in the end," Carter said, reaching her in two strides.

He grabbed her throat and began squeezing. He could have shot her, but something in his face said hands-on murder would be so much more satisfying. He would drag it out by inches.

Chloe felt her pulse pounding, echoing through her skull. Breath wouldn't come. She writhed, feeling the delicate architecture of her throat begin to crush. She made a gagging, gurgling noise she'd never heard any creature make before.

He was just too strong to fight back.

I'm going to die.

They caught two Knights of Vidon in Jack's study, sizing up the safe. Moments later, Sam and Winspear were dragging the two down the service stairway.

"Where's Carter?" Sam tightened his grip on the captive man's arm to a crushing pressure. "Where is Chloe Anderson?"

The question reverberated in the empty stairwell. Sam was aware of the distant murmur of voices, the smell of cooking, the pale beige paint of the walls. Most of all, he was conscious of the bruising flesh beneath his fingers. Soon, it would be breaking bone.

He had to find Chloe.

The man let out a ragged groan. Winspear's Knight winced, his eyes flying wide at the sound. "Stop it! You already killed one brother!"

Sam saw his opportunity. "Who?"

"Pietro!"

"I didn't kill him. Carter snapped his neck to keep him from talking."

"Impossible!"

Sam met the man's gaze. He had limited sympathy for slayers, but Carter had murdered their brother when he was helpless and then lied about it. That offended his sense of honor. "Believe what you like, but I'm telling you the truth."

The Knight doing the talking didn't say another word, but grew deathly pale.

Sam knew he had him. "I'll let this brother live if you answer my question."

One word escaped the bloodless lips. "Basement."

Sam released his grip, feeling his prisoner sag in relief. "Let's go."

Once they were down the stairs, it took little encouragement to extract which room Chloe and Carter were in.

"How about we use their heads for battering rams?" Sam growled when confronted with the storeroom's locked door.

"Too mushy." Winspear banged it open with one well-planted kick.

Sam tossed the Knights through the door. They flailed nicely until the floor stopped them. Mark drew his weapon, training it on the men. Sam pushed past them, a half dozen strides taking him into the cellar. As he moved, he swept the area with the nose of his gun. There were shelves and metal brackets strewn across the floor.

Sam turned just in time to see Chloe dangling from Carter's hand. She crumpled to the floor when Sam's maker released her throat.

He froze, not wanting to comprehend what he was seeing. *Chloe!* Memories, feelings, hopes smashed together, leaving him blind and deaf for a split second. Everything he cared about was plummeting into the abyss, about to shatter beyond repair.

She wasn't dead—yet—but she was badly hurt, breath rasping through her horribly bruised throat. And, with Carter armed and only inches away, she was still in terrible danger. Sam ached to run to her, but first he had to destroy the threat.

His fangs came out. *"You hurt my woman."*

"You're mine," Carter said. "My tool. My War."

"Never again." Sam's voice came out in a rasp.

"Your duty is to me."

Words. Words didn't have a place in Sam's head right then. Rage reared up inside him like a dragon unfurling huge, black wings.

Carter didn't seem to understand that he was about to perish. "You know I'm right. You're the straight arrow."

"You betrayed us to the Knights. That makes you the target."

Sam moved in a blur, closing the distance between them and smashing his fist into Carter's face. He didn't hold back. In one wrench, he tore his maker's shoulder holster apart, flinging his weapons across the room. The move had been easy because Carter had not expected it. The older vampire blocked the next blow, showing his teeth in a savage hiss. The fight was on.

It had to end quickly. Chloe was hurt. Drawing his gun, Sam aimed for the head, but Carter kicked it from his hand in a move even Sam's vampire sight didn't catch. A roundhouse kick followed, forcing Sam to fall back. Behind him, Mark was yelling something. Sam could feel the tide of the fight struggling to turn against him.

No. He dove forward, ducking under Carter's guard to grapple him. For a moment it was a battle of raw power, strength against brutal strength. Sam had the physical advantage, but Carter had fought him time and again on the training field. There were few moves he didn't know.

Except Carter didn't practice with a werewolf. Sam twisted, thinking to fling the other man down. It was the same move he had used on Kenyon the last time he'd run the testing field.

But Chloe sat up. Sam's heart leaped with relief.

It was the distraction Carter needed. He slammed Sam to the ground instead. Sam's teeth rattled with the force of the blow. Carter's eyes were wild as he tried to pin him, but Sam rolled, breaking Carter's grip. Cold metal pressed into his hip. He groped, hoping for a blade.

It was a metal bracket, the type that held up cheap shelving. Sam barely registered the fact before he plunged it into Carter's throat. Blood spurted, showering Sam, the floor, the walls and ceiling.

A wound to the throat wasn't enough to kill a vampire, but it would slow him down. Or so he thought. Carter pounced. This time Sam grabbed him, wrestling his maker to the floor like he had the wolf. This time, there was no mistake.

He wrenched the bracket from Carter's throat, and then plunged it into the vampire's heart. Rage began to separate into distinct thoughts and images. The wreck of Jack's car. Carter's lies that night at the Salmon Tail. Chloe crumpled on the floor.

Mark kicked Sam the gun he had dropped. He picked it up. "No one hurts my friends." Sam aimed the piece. "And no one hurts the woman I love."

Carter's head exploded. The blast rang through the tiny room like a grenade. Sam rose and looked down at his handiwork. Not even an undead was coming back from that.

Instantly, he went to Chloe, who was staring at him with wide, amazed eyes. She had pulled herself to a sitting position, propped against the wall. She held herself stiffly, taking quick, shallow breaths. She was obviously in pain. He fell to his knees beside her. "You need a doctor. Winspear!"

"Holding bad guys prisoner over here. If you want to cover them, I'd be delighted to help."

Sam wanted to go and needed to stay. He wrenched apart the silk scarf binding her wrists. Chloe clutched his sleeve, her grip weak as a baby's. He covered her chilled hand with his own, feeling the ache in her swollen, red fingers like it was his own.

"Just hold me," she whispered. "That's all I need."

"I'm filthy."

"I don't care." She leaned into him, and he gathered her in his arms and held her as she wept out the aftermath of fear and pain. "You came when I needed you."

"Always." He pressed his lips to her hair and clung to the light that had finally broken the chains of his lonely darkness.

Chapter 30

This is Gossip Quest TV News Magazine, *bringing you the latest update on the surprise event of the season. Kidnapping! Stolen diamonds! Who knew that a wedding could be the scene of so much derring-do? A week has passed, and we still have so few facts. Will we ever find out what was really behind the supersecret showdown in the basement of Oakwood Manor? Every branch of law enforcement this news reporter contacted refused comment.*

What we do know is that this event has made the front page of bridal magazines everywhere. As drama unfolded below ground, an utterly fabulous event was happening in Oakwood's gardens. News cameras could not help capturing the decorations, the food and that fabulous cake! According to those in the know, society weddings haven't seen such fresh and natural elegance in decades. You can bet that Chloe's Occasions, the wedding design

*firm responsible for the spectacular nuptial event, is now
on every bride-to-be's speed dial....*

Chloe clicked off the TV, silencing the hyperventi-
lating news anchor. A brief, rueful chuckle escaped her.
Ironically, after planning the so-called event of the season, she had missed most of the actual wedding.

After a stay in the hospital—the injuries to her neck
and throat had given the doctors pause—she was finally setting her old bedroom to rights, removing the
last traces of the night she was attacked. The housekeeper
had replaced the mattress and bed linens, and sunlight
poured through the curtains, turning everything bright
and cheerful. It looked as though nothing had happened.

Except that it had, and things kept happening. This
afternoon, she had received a request from Mark Winspear to meet her in Jack's study.

*Is this the moment when Mark erases everything about
the Company and its personnel from my mind? Or just
parts of it? Who decides what I get to keep?*

Her stomach clenched with anger. It was unfair. For a
moment she envied Lexie, but there was no way she could
point to her friend as an example of a human woman who
could keep a secret. That would get Lexie and Faran in
trouble, too.

Nevertheless, she would somehow prevail. If she'd
found a compromise between Iris and Elaine, she could
negotiate a compromise with the Company. They owed
her that much after their director had kidnapped and
nearly strangled her.

Slowly, painfully, Chloe pulled on a light linen jacket
that hid the multicolored bruises on her arms. Some of her
fingers were taped, the joints sprained and a few small
bones fractured when she'd fallen on her bound hands.

Her neck was badly bruised, too, but a soft scarf hid the worst. She had no intention of looking like a victim.

Just before she left her bedroom, she slid a small digital recorder into the pocket of her jacket. If Mark Winspear did tamper with her memory, she meant to have some clue to follow so that she could reconstruct these past few weeks.

She walked into Jack's study as firmly as her aching body would allow. A glance around told her that Mark was alone, sitting at the desk with his dark head bent over a sheaf of papers. He rose when she entered the room. To her surprise, she saw the wedding dress draped over one of the overstuffed chairs, diamonds shimmering in the dim light.

"What are you doing with that?" she asked tightly. "Why isn't it in the safe?"

"I thought you might want to say farewell," Mark replied. "Half a dozen of the most trusted palace guards will be here tonight. With your permission, Faran and I will return with them as escorts for the dress."

"Not Sam?"

Mark was silent. She crossed the room to where the dress lay, touching the soft layers of silk and lace. It was good to think she'd fulfilled her uncle's request to see the gown returned to the princess, but watching it go would be like saying goodbye to Jack all over again.

"I thought we should talk," he added. "I'm leaving tonight, and there are things you and I have to settle."

He walked around the desk to face her. She reached into her pocket and switched on the recorder.

"It seems strange talking to you," she said quietly. "I thought you were the evil genius behind everything."

He gave a bark of laughter, turning his face away to hide who knew what emotion. He wasn't an easy man to read, but the moment gave Chloe a chance to study his body language. He was more slightly built than Sam, but no less deadly. A rapier instead of a broadsword. And every line in his body said he was more than a little uncomfortable.

Finally, he shrugged. "I don't blame you for being suspicious."

He reached over, plucked the recorder out of her pocket and switched it off.

"I was working both sides of the game," he said. "And by the way, Vampires can hear these things working. I wouldn't try that again if I were you."

Chloe colored and took the recorder as he handed it back to her. "You were a double agent?"

"More or less. Your uncle and I knew something was wrong. I was the logical choice to go undercover."

In the past few days, Sam had told her about Jack's role with the Horsemen. It had made her proud and sad. She wished she could talk to her uncle about what he'd done and seen. "Not Sam?"

"No one would believe Sam as a turncoat."

Which implied they would believe it of Mark. She couldn't quite tell what he thought about that.

She waited a beat, wanting to get on to the subjects that interested her most, like whether he was going to scrub her brain. He didn't say anything but seemed to be waiting for her to speak.

Finally, she asked a question just to break the silence. "Did you know it was Carter from the start?"

"Not at first. We knew there was a leak at Company headquarters. We began to suspect half the scandals around the prince's love affairs were untrue, created to damage his reputation and his relationship with Princess Amelie. Then there was an attempt on the princess

right after the wedding was called off. It served its purpose to finish destabilizing the truce between Marcari
and Vidon."

Despite herself, despite the reason she was there, that
piqued her curiosity. "When Lady Beatrice was shot?"

Mark gave her an appraising look. "Yes."

"I read about it." She shifted painfully from one foot
to the other. She was still in too much discomfort to
stand for long.

He caught the gesture and motioned to the couch.
"Please, sit. I am forgetting all my courtesy."

They both sat, each in one corner, with a neutral distance between them. Mark still looked uneasy but carried on with his story. "The shooter was mesmerized
by a powerful mind. There aren't many of us who can
do such a seamless job. That's when I began to wonder
about Carter. The fact that the shooter got by Sam's security net was suspicious in itself. He doesn't make that
kind of mistake."

"Why didn't you warn Sam?"

"Warn him of what? I had no proof. Carter was our superior. I don't accuse anyone of treason without solid evidence. Accuracy is serious when the wrong word could
cost a life. So I did what I could. I went to find answers."

Chloe heard the edge of steel in his words. "I see."

"Perhaps." He didn't sound convinced. "Perhaps your
adventure in the cellars gives you a glimpse of what kind
of danger we deal with."

"I don't kid myself that it was more than a glimpse."

"Good. If you'd answered any other way, I would have
thought you a fool." He gave her a long, narrow look.

She didn't know Mark Winspear, but something told
her he would be a bad enemy to have.

"Will putting an end to this affair help smooth things over between Marcari and Vidon?" she asked.

"The Knights will not tolerate a truce with Marcari, regardless of what treaties are signed. The King of Vidon plans to break publicly with the Knights once a purge of the palace guard is complete. I'm sure the treachery will be harder to stamp out for good, but at least it will not continue under the palace roof."

"Is there any chance the royal wedding might go ahead?"

Mark's dark face was thoughtful. "I don't know."

She nodded, looking down at her bandaged hands. "It would be a shame for that dress to go to waste. A lot of people put themselves on the line to get it back to the princess. Who will take Carter's place?"

"I don't know," Mark replied. "There will be an inquest, but no one blames Sam for what he did. Once that is over, the King of Marcari will appoint someone new."

A silence fell between them.

"I want you to know something," Mark said quietly. "Vampires are not human. We do everything more intensely. When we make war, entire cities die. When we love, it's forever and with every cell of our beings."

The intensity of his words rattled her. "You sound like you know what you're talking about."

He pressed his lips together, giving a slow nod. "I see what's going on between you and Sam. I've lost one good friend this month, and I don't have many left."

Apprehension quivered in Chloe's chest. "I don't understand."

"You know it is my job to erase your memories of the Horsemen."

The words fell like a hammer blow, and she felt her insides coil tight. She should have listened to Lexie. She should have run before the wedding. She could have run after, but she had foolishly believed shedding her own blood to protect the dress would make the vampires spare her.

Chloe nodded, unable to speak. If she did, her pride would fail her. She would grovel.

"Carter made those rules." Mark said the name as if it tasted foul. "He believed vampires were intrinsically evil. Much of that fear came from his own early experience. He had been turned and abandoned by his maker. There was no one to help him make the transition, things went horribly wrong and that trauma festered over time. Yet there was a certain truth to his beliefs."

"How so?"

"A vampire in love is more than a little crazy. He will find it hard to put anything before his beloved. In effect, he would give up everything for her sake."

Chloe finally found her voice. "Humans aren't that different."

Mark raised an eyebrow. "Would you leave everything for a man you love?"

"Is that a trick question?"

"No tricks. I'm just curious."

"I believe in love that strong."

Something in his face grew harder. "Would you leave everything for Sam? If we asked, would you give up everything to be with him?"

The odd tone of his voice made her turn around, her injured neck protesting at the movement. Sam was standing in the doorway, his face carefully schooled, not a shred of emotion showing.

Anger sliced through her. "What does it matter what I am willing to give up if you're going to steal my memories?"

"It's the only thing that matters," Sam said, his rough voice giving away the pain his face was hiding.

Chloe weighed what she was going to say next. She was here to have her memory wiped. Until that was off the table, nothing else made sense. "I don't want to say goodbye to you, or Mark, or Faran. It's like an entire world has opened to me. I'm living and walking and talking with miracles."

"I've not been called that before." Sam gave a wry smile.

"You are miraculous. You've saved my life time and again. You kept Elaine's wedding from falling to pieces. You defend the people you love and protect things you care about. That's more than wonderful all on its own. So you're a creature of legend. That's gravy."

"I bet you've not been called 'gravy' before, either," Mark said dryly.

"I'm not going to talk about sacrifice." Chloe rose, circling the room to face both men. The movement put her next to the dress. She reached out and stroked the frothy skirt. "I know my job. I know what makes couples work. Every relationship is a compromise, but love doesn't count costs. If you feel that bad about what you're giving up, you'd better take a step back and ask yourself if you're really in love after all."

She turned to Sam and touched his face with her bruised, bandaged fingers. Everything she felt, every pain, every joy throbbed in her voice. "I don't think the real question is what I give up, but what I bring. What you bring. We're infinitely richer by being in love. We don't lose by being together."

Sam caught her hand so gently that she barely felt the pressure of his touch. And then he kissed it, pressing his lips to her damaged fingers with infinite care. "But you might lose. Carter was only one person. There is an entire army of Knights."

"I know," she replied softly. "But I will manage as long as you don't keep secrets from me. Don't shut me out."

Sam blinked. "I promise not to do that."

"Then believe in the joy we'll have, and we'll take the rest as it comes."

Sam's gray gaze caressed her. "Nine hells, I love you, Chloe Anderson."

Chloe turned to Mark. "Does this mean you're not messing with my head? I mean—"

The doctor held up a hand to stop her words. He looked as if he wished he could vanish under the couch. "Those were Carter's rules. I don't feel obligated to rescue Sam from your depraved clutches."

Chloe released the breath she'd been holding. With a low chuckle, Sam pulled her to the safe space within the circle of his arms.

Mark shook his head. "I think he likes those clutches just the way they are."

Chapter 31

Later, Chloe and Sam went for a walk in the moonlit garden.

She was as irritated as a woman madly in love could get. "Mark had no intention of wiping my memories. Why on earth didn't you just say so?"

Sam was quiet for a moment. "Lexie left Kenyon. It was entirely possible you'd want to back out of any association with the Company. There would have been more to consider then."

"I hadn't thought of that." She was suddenly sorry for Lexie. What had gone on that the two of them couldn't work it out?

"I'm glad you didn't walk away."

"Just glad?"

He turned to look down at her. "Ecstatic."

"Well, you said you'd find a way for us to be together. You did it. You solved the case, and more."

Nothing more needed to be said. They walked a little farther, moving slowly to compensate for Chloe's bruises. The night was silent but for their footsteps on the gravel path, the odd sound of something small rustling through the grass. She had a thick shawl pulled over her shoulders. Even though it was summer, this close to the ocean the night breeze was cool. Above, the sky was strewn with stars, a half moon pinned in the velvet dark.

"I'm going to be sorry to leave this place," she murmured. "Uncle Jack loved this garden."

"He did." Sam was silent for a few steps. "He was a good friend."

"How long did you know him?"

"Since the Great War."

She tried to imagine Sam and Jack, flying biplanes or airships or strolling beneath the crystal chandeliers of the great luxury steamers like the *Titanic*. "You shared a lot of history."

"Yes."

"And with Carter, too."

"Yes."

The set of his mouth told her there was loss and pain he didn't want to talk about. It wasn't that he was keeping secrets; part of him was still Ralston Samuel Hill, born in a time when men didn't share their feelings the same way they did now. She'd work on that, right along with training him to give answers of more than one word.

"Chloe," Sam said. "About your parents. I asked some questions. Did you know what they were working on when they died?"

"All I know was that they were biochemists with a drug company. They died in a home invasion."

"But you've always believed they were killed because of their work."

"Yes. The house was torn to pieces, but as far as I could tell, nothing was taken. Mom's jewelry was still there. No one had touched Dad's wallet. Most of the damage was in the home office. The killers were looking for something, and judging from the mess they didn't find it. I have no idea what they wanted. My parents never discussed their work with me."

"They couldn't. They were protecting you. They worked for the Company."

She stopped. "What?"

Sam put an arm around her shoulders. Someday, he vowed, he would find out who took Chloe's family from her. He would see justice done. "Jack knew how talented they were. He convinced our research and development department to take them on, even though they were human."

"What were they working on? What was so important that they were killed for it?" Chloe suddenly realized that Sam probably couldn't tell her, either. "Generally speaking, of course."

He gave her a wry smile. They started to walk again, drawing near the gazebo. "Mark could give you a more informed answer. I'm not the science guy. As I understand it, they were trying to figure out, biologically, what makes a vampire a vampire."

"Dreamy eyes and a rockin' cape?"

Sam winced. "They were separating myth from fact. We're fast healing, not technically dead even though we are often at death's door when we're turned. Although it's rare, vampires can produce children."

Chloe's step hitched, realizing that they'd used a condom only the first time they'd been together. After that, she'd assumed it wasn't an issue. *Sam's babies?* Her whole body flushed with the idea.

"Your parents believed we're actually a separate species, genetically altered through union with a symbiotic microorganism."

Chloe caught her breath, fascinated. "Were they right?"

"As far as anyone can tell me, they barely scratched the surface of the question. There is as big a mystical component as a scientific one."

She shivered, and Sam pulled her closer. "But why kill them for researching that?"

"Sometimes people fear information as much as they desire it. People like the Knights. They would love to know what makes us tick so that they could kill us more efficiently. Or maybe they want to know how to make themselves just as fast and strong."

Chloe thought about her parents, and how she had sometimes resented their silence. "So it was volatile enough information that they couldn't risk telling a teenaged girl."

"No. And Jack couldn't tell you about it, either. He broke all kinds of rules just showing you his collection of vampire knickknacks."

"I'm glad he did. I think my head would have exploded in these last few weeks if he hadn't prepared me to consider the existence of vampires."

He bent down and kissed the top of her head. "Just so you know, not all the Company are vampires. There are a handful of werewolves like Kenyon and one or two humans like your parents."

Chloe thought about that. "Was Jessica Lark one of you?"

"She worked for the Company on special assignment. That's really all I know. We may never find out exactly why she died, or…" He trailed off, eyebrows drawing together.

"Or?"

"I saw a picture of her with somebody I know. I'm just wondering if there was more to it than I assumed."

"Are you worried?"

He shook his head, his face clearing. "No, it's someone I trust."

They'd reached the gazebo, which hadn't been Chloe's favorite spot since the night they'd captured Pietro. She tried to look at it now with fresh eyes, willing the bad associations away. Sam mounted the steps, holding Chloe's hand. It was warmer there, the rock face behind it blocking some of the wind.

"A private spot," Sam said approvingly.

"There are still security guards roaming the grounds."

"But not here."

He guided her to one of the wooden benches with the ornate, wrought iron frames. Chloe sat, glad of the opportunity to rest. She kept forgetting how much her encounter with Carter had taken out of her.

Sam sat beside her, cuddling her close. "I, um, suggested to the guards that they leave the patrol of this area up to me tonight."

"Are we patrolling?"

"I'm your personal guard. Forever."

She poked his side playfully. "Be careful what you wish for. That means a steady stream of wedding clients to deal with."

He smiled, but it was quickly replaced by his serious face. "When we bond, it's as much biochemical as emotional. The two get mixed together. We're as good as addicted. I'm going to need you always."

She felt the weight of his solemn mood. "I'm mortal. I won't last."

Sam took a deep breath. "I love you, Chloe. More than anything. But you should know that if you stay with me, you will become like me."

She wasn't even sure of everything that becoming a vampire would mean, but she knew she wanted Sam. She could handle the rest. She'd proven she could survive when the going got tough. And being with Sam? That was the opposite of tough.

She leaned close to whisper in his ear, not because it was a secret, but the words were meant only for him. "I promise to love you and be with you always."

Sam held her close, burying his face in her hair. She recalled Carter's words: *When faced with true darkness, love doesn't matter.* It deserved a rebuttal.

"When there is love, there is no such thing as true darkness," she said. "When there is love, darkness doesn't matter."

They made love in the grass, Chloe's shawl spread out beneath them. Sam moved tenderly, taking care not to touch the bruised places on her skin. As he peeled back the fabric of her blouse, her skin pebbled where his breath fanned across it. Her nipples rose hard beneath the silk of her camisole. With so many bumps and bruises, she hadn't been wearing a bra.

He cupped her face in his, tasting first one lip, then the other, leaving kisses at the corners of her mouth where her dimples lay sleeping. And then he plundered her, bold as any pirate, stealing the secrets of her kiss. She moaned beneath him, tasting him, capturing his tongue with hers.

Sam's hands were busy with other buttons and zippers, so he pulled down the tiny strap of the camisole with his teeth. Chloe's shoulder was lovely, a perfect feminine roundness, neither too plump nor too slender. He wished he could draw just so that he could capture that graceful curve.

He captured it with his lips instead, proving he was an artist in another medium. The smell of her skin made him slightly dizzy, as if every synapse in his brain were firing at once. "Chloe," he said to the butter-soft skin of her shoulder.

"Hmm?" she replied, fumbling with the belt and button of his trousers. The roughness of her bandages making an interesting friction in male places. It was a phenomenon worth experimenting with in future.

"Chloe," he repeated, following the scalloped neck of the camisole to that heavenly hollow between her breasts.

His fangs were down, and he let them scrape along the curve of her breasts, not so hard as to injure, but enough to make her squirm with the sensation. The squirming did little for his self-control. The ache in his groin was enough to stop his breath.

Chloe pulled down the zipper of his pants. It gave some relief, but that only encouraged his lower brain to hurry things along.

"I want you," she demanded.

In the moonlight, her skin looked pale as milk, almost luminous. The patch of lawn they had claimed was surrounded by roses, their scent lingering like the memory of sun in the air. He plucked one, a full-blown white bloom tipped with a pink core.

He straddled her, knees on either side of her slim waist, and touched the petals to her skin. She shivered enticingly, her hands on his as he trailed the flower over the curve of her belly to the slick folds below. Her hips arched beneath the silken touch, aroused and sensitive. She was ready, wet, inviting.

Pulling her legs around his waist, he found the core of her with his tip. She took him greedily. The hot slickness of her engulfed him, and he pushed more and more. Each thrust earned him a little moan. Those sounds were almost more than superhuman strength could bear.

He stopped thrusting. Her eyes opened, wide and unfocused, searching his face. With the rose, he stroked her cheek, trailing the petals across her lips. Then he bent to taste her mouth. There was nothing innocent left in their kiss. They ate at each other hungrily, all but heedless of his sharp teeth.

His hands found her breasts, kneading them, suckling the nipples. Chloe's back arched to meet him, the movement nearly shattering his control. His hips moved in response, triggering the pulsing of her first climax. Sam's breath was ragged, his thoughts shredded to nothing but skin and sweat and desire. He thrust again, fighting the impulse to finish, wanting to draw it out, but needing, wanting, aching to make her his.

Chloe cried out beneath him, and he could hold on no more. His body shuddered with the need to move, the urge to feel her flesh tight around him. He pushed, and pushed again, falling into a rhythm as ancient as birth and death. *Chloe. Chloe. Chloe. Chloe.*

He roared as his own release came, taking her with him. Her body pulled at him, milked him, sucked him under a mindless wave of possession and surrender. Sam let himself drift on the feeling, aware of the stars above, the grass beneath them.

"You're mine," he said again, speaking the words before the witness of heaven and earth. He sucked in a great breath of air, feeling the power of his claim.

When they had finished, he curled around her, wrapping the shawl over her to keep her from the cold. This time, after tasting her blood, he pierced his own wrist, offering it to her.

"It will heal you," he said, stroking her hair.

There was a moment when he was not sure if she would turn away, revolted, or trust him enough to take it. Then she wrapped her hands around his wrist and bent to the wound, lapping at what he offered.

The sensation of it made him hard again, but he waited patiently, drinking in the scent of the rose they had crushed beneath their weight.

Chapter 32

They woke the next morning in Chloe's bed. The first thing she felt was Sam's arm curled over her hip. The second was an absence of pain.

Slowly, carefully, she stretched each limb. She didn't hurt anywhere. Whatever magic was in Sam's blood had cured her wounds. In fact, she felt wonderful.

Oddly excited, she rolled over, curling against the hard slab of his chest. The scent of him made things clench low in her belly.

"Hello," he growled in her ear.

"Hello." She gave him a kiss. "I had an idea."

"I have a lot of ideas." He rolled her onto her back, following so that he landed on top, braced on his elbows.

It didn't take an anatomist to guess what his ideas involved. He pressed against her with distracting emphasis.

Chloe cleared her throat. "I could help you."

"Indeed you could," he purred with a smile.

"With your spy stuff."

The smile deepened a touch. "Planning all our weddings? You'd better bring unbreakable dishes for the werewolves."

She narrowed her eyes. "I'm serious. Think about how many people go to weddings, anniversaries, whatever. What better cover to get into places? To get into homes where you'd never otherwise secure an invitation?"

Sam's eyebrows drew together. "We don't need invitations to cross a threshold. That's myth."

"You know what I mean! You could show up and do your spying while you were mixing drinks. Bartenders hear everything. Or mix in the crowd serving appetizers. It's a no-brainer."

"It's not a bad idea. In my youth, the best spies were the servants. They had an excuse to go anywhere, overhear any conversation. They were invisible."

"Then you'll think about it?"

"It could be a useful tool." One corner of his mouth curled up. "It would give us plenty of opportunities to work together."

"Exactly."

They had just finished a thorough kiss when Chloe's phone went off with the ringtone that said there was an emergency at the office. Sam swore as she rolled over to grab her cell from the bedside table.

"Hello?"

"Check your email," said her assistant's voice. She sounded stressed. "This is one I can't handle."

"Why not?"

"It's from the Crown Prince of Vidon. I didn't think I should open it myself."

Chloe hung up and switched on her laptop. The message was actually a video clip. She set the laptop on the bed so Sam could watch, too.

The clip started with a sweeping view of the Mediterranean. White beaches. White buildings framed by palms. Blue sky. Blue water. She could just make out the top of a railing made of swirls of black iron.

"That's from the balcony of the palace in Marcari," Sam said. "What's he doing there?"

The camera pulled back to show a young couple sitting at a table for two. She recognized them at once. Kyle Alphonse Adraio, Crown Prince of Vidon, looked more like a striker for one of the Italian football teams than he did royalty. He was dressed nicely, but his clothes were casual. His brown hair curled past his collar, and his mobile mouth looked ready to laugh. She could see why he had a reputation as a charmer.

Beside him sat a slim, dark-haired woman Chloe recognized as Princess Amelie. The most striking feature of the princess was her large, thick-lashed violet eyes, which made her look meltingly vulnerable. The two were laughing and lifting flutes of champagne toward the camera.

She caught her breath. "They're together."

Sam rolled onto his elbow to get a better look. "She looks happy. That's good."

Prince Kyle smiled broadly at the camera. "Greetings, Ms. Anderson. And to Sam Ralston. My informants tell me where I find one of you, I shall find the other."

"Salut!" the Princess chimed in, clinking her glass against Kyle's.

Amelie spoke in a charming, soft accent. "First of all, thank you so much for your part in seeing the dress home safely. It arrived this morning, along with Plague and Famine. And you deserve to know a piece of the puzzle we discovered here in Marcari. The idea to put the diamonds on the dress came from my grandmother."

"By all nine hells." Sam made a noise of both amusement and exasperation. "That's the dowager for you."

Amelie went on. "She envisioned her granddaughter sparkling on worldwide television as she walked down the aisle of the cathedral. Spectacle. Theater. A billion cameras snapping. My grandmother was ever the genius when it came to the showmanship of state."

Chloe was still a beat behind. "The dowager queen removed the crown jewels without telling the rest of the royal family?"

Amelie answered as if she heard the question. "It was the dowager's taste for a surprise that started this whole affair. She knew the king, my father, would never risk the gems by removing them from the treasury, so she convinced Jack Anderson to spirit them out of the castle and take them to Jessica Lark. He was just enough of a rogue to agree. So you see, this is how my wedding dress came to be in the eye of this storm."

She gave Kyle a significant look, and the camera shifted slightly toward him.

"I have two points of business," he said. "First, I have made an offer on Oakwood Manor. I have every reason to believe it shall be accepted by your solicitor, the esteemed Mr. Littleton. He shall make the title deed out to you, my dear Chloe. Please accept it in thanks for your generous, brave spirit and the courage you showed protecting my Amelie's treasure. I have a feeling, with your business going so well, you will need a place befitting your future station in life."

"I can't accept that!" Chloe gasped.

"Of course you can," Sam said calmly. "You don't say no to a prince."

"Second," Kyle went on blithely, with what seemed a cheerful certainty that no one could deny him, "our wedding shall be on Valentine's Day."

He stopped to kiss Amelie. They were a beautiful couple, the Mediterranean wind twining their dark locks together. It would be nice to get a wedding shot of them, just like that.

Sam's hand closed over Chloe's thigh. If he kept that up, whatever Kyle had to say next would rapidly diminish in importance.

Kyle resumed in the nick of time. "We heard what an incredible job you did on the Venuto-Fallon wedding, and what professionalism you showed in extremely trying circumstances. So highly have your praises been sung, we want you to plan our wedding."

Chloe's heart stopped in her chest. "Huh?"

"You can do it," Sam said, patting her leg.

Amelie leaned into the frame. "We hope you will bring that rogue Samuel Ralston with you. Perhaps you would consent to be our guests for your own Mediterranean wedding?"

Chloe's jaw dropped. "Do they have spies or something?"

"Yes." Sam's hand traveled up her thigh.

"Remember," said Kyle. "Valentine's Day. Send your reply as soon as you get this."

The clip ended as they both lifted their glasses in a toast. Sam closed the laptop and set it on the nightstand before the last word was done. "He can wait."

Chloe slid into Sam's embrace. "A royal wedding. What do you think?"

Sam gave her a devouring look that promised her reply to Kyle would be very, very late. "I think Marcari is the perfect place for a honeymoon."

Afterword

For a number of years, I played with several Celtic and early music ensembles that performed at weddings—occasions big and small, formal and costumed, in fancy hotels and backyards. It was great fun, even though I always tear up during the vows, whether or not I know the couple—go figure—and that is definitely not a helpful habit when trying to read music.

Each wedding was unique, but there were some especially memorable moments, like the time a bagpipe-playing uncle insisted on a duet. Yes, those pipes are excruciatingly loud up close.

Through it all, I came to completely respect the heroic individuals who organized those wonderful celebrations, whether they were professional planners or dedicated family and friends. Let it be said that the stories of the Four Horsemen of the Apocalypse are fantasies. Even with all her contacts, Chloe Anderson puts on a huge wedding in a sliver of the time that it would normally take. All I can say is: you go, girl. Why should vampires get all the superpowers?

And while we're asking questions, how did Mark Winspear know Jessica Lark? What did the Knights of Vidon plan on doing with the money from the stolen diamonds? Princess Amelie has her dress back, but what happened to the designs for the rest of the bridal trousseau? Although Sam and Chloe found each other, the story of Amelie and Kyle's star-crossed royal wedding has just begun. Be sure to look for *Possessed by an Immortal,* available next month.

Please visit me at www.SharonAshwood.com. I love to hear from readers!

* * * * *

POSSESSED
BY AN IMMORTAL

This book is for those wonderful readers
who have stuck with me through the years. Those
emails, Tweets, posts and visits at my signing table
mean more than you know.
Hugs to you all.

If you press me to say why I loved him,
I can say no more than because he was he,
and I was I.

—Michel de Montaigne,
French philosopher, 1533–1592

Chapter 1

Don't drown my boy!

Seawater soaked Bree up to the waist. When the rocky shore slammed into her knees, she wasn't sure if she'd fallen or if the choppy waves had thrown her. Her arms automatically folded around the child sheltered against her chest. Jonathan whimpered, his voice achingly small in the darkness. She scrabbled forward, hauling him with her in a one-armed crawl until she reached a scruff of grass and ferns. It was hard going, half stumbling, half climbing as the shore rose sharply from the beach.

Bree tried to look behind her but from where she knelt, she couldn't see the man below. For a fat, old, whiskery fishing guide, Bob was strong. And a coward. And cruel.

Curse him! She clung there for a long moment, palms smarting from clambering over the sharp rocks. Vertigo seized her, the tug of the surf still haunting her blood and bones. *It's okay. We made it, at least for now.* She cradled Jonathan, trying to give the four-year-old a comfort she didn't feel.

They'd left the ocean below, but not water. Rain pounded against her back and shoulders, dripping through her hair and down her face to mix with tears and sweat. The only light came from the boat below, where Bob was turning the craft around. She was still panting, still needed to rest, but she couldn't let the moment pass. Bree stood and wheeled around, instinctively pulling her coat closer around Jonathan.

"You promised to take me to town!" she screamed toward the bright light of the boat. It was a useless protest, but Brianna Meadows had never been the demure, silent type.

"Count yourself lucky!" Bob bellowed back. "I saw you to dry land."

"They'll kill us!"

"Better you than me. I'm sorry for your boy, but you're nothing but trouble."

"But—"

He said something else, but the words shredded in the rain and wind. The motor roared as the boat picked up speed. It was a small, agile craft a shade too light for the brewing storm. She'd paid him well to get her to the mainland, where she could have found a bus going south. Instead, he'd dumped her ashore at the first hint of danger. Bob was used to tourists in pursuit of salmon. He wasn't cut out for dodging villains with live ammunition.

Maybe she should have warned him. Maybe she should have gone to the police back at the beginning. But then again, some of them were on the wrong side, weren't they?

You're nothing but trouble. The old fishing guide wasn't the first to say it.

Bree watched the light from the boat shrink to a blurry splotch on the rainy sea. Wind shushed through the massive cedar trees overhead, making her feel tiny. All of her efforts had been spent keeping Jonathan out of the freezing waves. She'd been hot with exertion when she'd crawled ashore, but now the knife-edged wind on her wet clothes made her shudder with cold.

At least Bob had waited for shallow water before he'd forced them out of the boat, but then he'd done it so fast she had no time to fight back. The thought triggered Bree's fury all over again. *How could you leave me here? How could you do this to my baby?* She was literally at the end of the earth. The west end, with the Pacific Ocean gnawing at the rocks below.

She licked her lips, tasting salt and rain. She was a city girl. Her survival skills involved flashing a gold card at a five-star hotel. "Don't worry, I'll figure something out."

Jonathan looked up at her from the shelter of her coat, his eyes dark shadows framed by curls of damp hair. He didn't speak. He'd stopped talking months ago. It had been a call to a clinic that had given her away and started the chase all over again. Seeking help had clearly been a mistake, but what else could she have done?

Scraping wet hair from her cheeks, she tried to blink the scene into better focus. Bree took Jonathan's hand and moved under the shelter of the trees, their thick, astringent scent enfolding her. The ground was soft with rotting needles, her feet silent. All she could hear was the drumming of the rain, weirdly amplified by an utter absence of light. Scalp prickling with nerves, Bree made a slow turn, barely able to see her hand in front of her face. She snuggled Jonathan closer, afraid she wouldn't be able to keep him warm enough. *Oh, please, I need a miracle!*

No doubt she'd used up her stock of those long ago. Like when she'd escaped her pursuers in the Chicago airport. Or that incident in the Twin Cities. She was probably in miracle overdraft by now.

Except…as her eyes grew used to the gloom, she caught a faint glimmer of yellow light if she shifted a smidgen to her left.

Someone lived in this forsaken wilderness! But her

enemies were clever, and she'd been fooled before into thinking she'd found safety. A walk through the woods could save her life, or lead her straight into the monster's cave. As if sensing her indecision, Jonathan squirmed against her, letting out a weak whimper.

That was the problem with being a mother. Risk didn't mean the same things when your baby was at stake. Bree would dare anything if it meant Jonathan lived through the night.

Mark Winspear listened to the sounds outside his cabin, hearing each rustle of branch and bird. The cabin was sparsely furnished, the only light an orange glow spilling from the cast-iron stove. The dark wood walls disappeared into the shadows, giving the impression of a cave. Mark tossed another log into the stove's maw, watching as crimson sparks swirled. In a moment, fresh yellow flames licked at the wood. He settled back into his threadbare easy chair, letting the worn fabric embrace him.

The scene was domestic, even dull, but it was overdue. Out here, in the back of beyond, he could be what he was: a wild beast and solitary hunter. A vampire. Most of all, he could be alone. After five hundred years plus, he'd become less of a people person.

He willed his shoulders to relax, but his instincts forbade it. Tonight, something was different. His vampire hearing was on alert, the night birds and small furred creatures whispering of something new. An invader. Mark's fingers gripped the ragged arms of the chair. *Who dares to come here?*

He rose, gliding to the cupboard beside the stove. He unlocked it using a key he hung around his neck. Inside, he kept a rifle and a pistol—a Browning Hi-Power—

and a curved kukri knife. Logic said to take one of the guns, but it would be infinitely more satisfying to hunt as a vampire with fang and hunger, and not with human weapons. Still, there were other hunters who knew exactly how to kill his kind. As a compromise, he picked up the knife and relocked the cupboard.

He did not leave by the front door. Instead, he climbed the narrow staircase to the loft and raised the sash window. Clean, cold air rushed in on a gust of wind. Mark crouched by the sill, listening. He zeroed in on the disturbance within seconds. Footsteps. Human. Coming this way, no doubt drawn by the firelight in the cabin window.

Mark searched the darkness for any sign of movement. Feathery cedars, tall pine and thick fir trees blended their heady scents in the pounding rain. Enemies aplenty hunted him, many of them professionals. Trapping him here at the cabin, when he was alone, was a logical choice.

Whoever came would be the best—or they would be dinner. He worked for the Company, what his friend Faran Kenyon laughingly called an army of supernatural superspies. Kings and presidents called when their own experts failed. Solving kidnappings, thefts, smugglings and every other kind of nefarious plot was the bread-and-butter work of Company agents. Dr. Mark Winspear preferred healing people, but he had other skills that came in handy more often than he cared to admit.

In a single smooth move he was perched on the window frame, and then sprang to a nearby tree. The wet, rough bark scraped his palms as he moved from one tree to another, positioning himself for a view of the intruder. Where the limbs were too soft to bear his weight, he used his vampire abilities to fly silently from trunk to trunk. Branches snagged his hair and shoulders, dripping rivulets of rain down his neck. Mark ignored the discomfort and focused on the ground below.

Territorial instincts triggered a wave of hot anger. These were his hunting grounds. Whoever dared to enter would feel his wrath. He leaped, silent and agile as a cat, barely a branch crackling as he moved.

A rare smile played on Mark's lips as he caught a whiff of warm blood. Warm female blood. It made his mouth water. Clever, to send a female assassin. No doubt she was a seductress, meant to disarm him. He knew better. Women killed just as easily, sometimes better, than their brothers.

Nice try. After a steady diet of black-tailed deer—well, he was ready for dessert.

Then he saw her, stumbling through the trees. She'd found the deer track that passed for a path and was making good progress, but she didn't move like someone accustomed to the woods. He leaned a little farther, balancing in the perfect spot to peer between the branches. The hood of her coat was pulled up, so he could tell little outside the fact that she was tall for a woman, around five-nine. No flashlight. Obviously, she was trying to sneak up to the house.

Mark shifted his weight, poised to drop on top of the woman as she passed beneath his tree. Then shock rippled through him as he saw she was leading a small child by the hand. In his surprise, his foot nearly slipped. Who took a kid through the woods on a night like this?

A cougar stole through the brush a dozen yards behind. Adrenaline tightened his muscles. *No!* One rush and a spring, and the cat would have the child.

Mark dropped between the woman and the cat. His boots landed with a hollow thud on the needle-strewn path. The woman stumbled, letting out a yell of surprise.

Mark rose, turning to see both her and the cougar. The cat padded backward a few steps, ears flattening.

A need to protect his domain flashed through Mark. He gave a warning growl, hoping the cat would turn and run. Compact and muscular, this male was nine feet from nose to tail-tip and as heavy as a grown man. Mark suspected it was also every bit as smart.

Except tonight. Instead of running, the cougar bared its fangs in a rattling hiss.

It was too much for the woman. She bolted, dragging the child with her, tripping and crashing as she went. The cat lunged forward, but Mark was there in an instant, crouched in its path. The cougar swiped a huge paw. Mark caught it before the massive claws touched his flesh. The cat strained against his grip, rearing up. Mark grabbed both front legs, struggling against the steel of its muscles and tendons. If he had been human, the cougar would have flayed him in a heartbeat.

With a roar, Mark thrust the cat away, the force of it making the creature slide and skitter into the brush.

"Not tonight," he said evenly, using a touch of vampire compulsion. "This prey is mine."

The cougar gave a long, slow blink, ears flat against its head. Mark waited. The moment stretched, the cat lashing the ground with its tail, its emerald eyes sizing Mark up, choosing whether or not to obey. Mark raised the knife, letting the cougar see it. The cougar hissed again, a nightmare of long, ivory fangs.

Go. I don't want to kill you. The moment stretched, Mark still and silent, every muscle poised to strike.

At last the tension broke. With a disgusted swish of its tail, the cougar wheeled and stalked away, shoulders hunched with displeasure. Mark watched it go, relieved to avoid the fight. *Good hunting, brother.*

He retreated a step, then two, making sure the cat did not change its mind. At last, Mark turned and sprinted after the woman, dodging roots and low branches. She hadn't gone far. Mark caught another wafting cloud of warm, human blood-scent, now spiced with extra fear.

She ran, too much like a doe fleeing through the woods. Mark's instincts to chase and devour sparked and flared, roused by her slender, panicked form.

Chapter 2

Mark grabbed the woman's shoulder. She gasped, making the sound of someone too scared to scream. He spun her around, her feet slipping on the wet ground. His grip tightened as she started to fall, but she sprang back with another noise of pure terror, pushing the child behind her.

"Stop!" he commanded, putting a snap into the word.

She obeyed, hunched against the rain, face hidden by the hood except for a pale, pointed chin. Her feet were planted wide, as if to launch herself at him if he so much as twitched in the direction of her child. The cougar had nothing on a mother protecting her young.

"Please," she demanded, voice shaking. She didn't say what she pleaded for. There was no need. They both knew he could be a threat—he knew exactly how much.

Mark didn't answer at once, but took the time to study her. She was wearing a tan trench coat with half the forest stuck to its sodden hem. Her boots were sturdy tan leather, scuffed and splotched with mud. The only other feature he could make out was her hands, long fingers ending in short, unpainted nails. Capable hands. They were half curled, ready to lash out.

"Where's the cat?" Her voice was nearly lost beneath the sound of the rain.

"I scared it off. What are you doing here?" he asked in turn, his voice deceptively soft. She smelled so good, his stomach tightened with desire and hunger.

"What does it matter to you?" she snapped back. "I mean, do you live here? Where's the road to the nearest town?"

She was trying to sound brave, but he could hear her pulse racing with terror. To a predator, fear meant food. He barely resisted the urge to lick his lips. "You're trespassing."

"My bad. It's kind of dark out."

"A person doesn't just take a wrong turn out here. The next house is miles away."

"We walked up from the beach."

That puzzled him. "You came by boat?"

"Yes."

He hadn't heard a motor, but the pounding rain might have drowned it out. Still, something was very off. She was extremely wet, the skirts of her coat soaked through and stinking of saltwater, as if she'd waded to shore.

The child peered around her legs, his small, white face pinched with cold. Mark felt a stab of anger. "You took your boy for a sail on a night like this?"

The woman's chin lifted to a stubborn angle. "I made a mistake."

"I'd say so."

Mark was growing impatient, rain trickling down his collar. He'd been expecting assassins. He'd never met a professional killer with a child in tow, but such things weren't impossible. Some would do anything to make a target drop his guard. All that fear he smelled didn't make her innocent.

He lunged forward and yanked her hood back, wanting to see the woman's face.

"Hey!" She blinked against the rain, her mouth opening in a startled gasp. It was a nice mouth, wide and soft and giving her features a vulnerable, unconventional beauty. Her face was more long than oval, framed by squiggling tendrils of rain-soaked hair.

"Who are you?" he demanded. She was lovely. Desire rose in a sudden heat, but this time it held more lust than appetite.

"Back off!" She crouched, wrapping her arms around the boy and scooping him onto her hip. The fiercely protective gesture put her body between Mark and the youngster. The swift, selfless courage pulled at his instincts. Whoever this woman was, she was magnificent.

But the child made no more sound than a ghost, and that silence dragged Mark's attention away from the female. *The boy has to be sick or exhausted. He's cold and wet and it's dark and his mother is frightened. Most kids would be crying by now. This one hasn't made a peep.*

"I apologize." Mark frowned, his tone making the statement a lie. "Who are you?"

She backed away. "Bree. Who are you?"

"Mark. Is that your son?"

"Yes." She shifted uncomfortably, rain trickling down her face. The moment dragged. "Is that your cabin?" she finally asked, her tone torn between need and reluctance. "It's cold out here."

Mark bristled, edgy. No one came to his property by accident—it was too far from civilization. Then again, his unexpected guests weren't going to survive the night without shelter. *Kill or protect. Food or willing flesh. Be the vampire, or be the healer.* For centuries, the debate had worn on Mark, eventually driving him to his island retreat. He wasn't a monster when there was no one to kill. He liked it that way. This woman was interrupting his peace.

Still, a good hunter never harmed a mother with fragile young. "Come inside. Your boy needs to get out of the rain."

"Thank you." The woman bowed her head, her expression a mix of relief and new worries. She didn't trust him. Smart woman.

Mark took her elbow, steering her down the path rather than letting her walk behind him. He might be taking pity on the woman, but he still didn't trust her. After climbing the wooden steps to the cabin and opening the door, he gave Bree a gentle push inside.

After shuffling forward a few steps, she stopped, reminding him of an automaton winding down. Water dripped from her clothes, puddling on the old, dark wood of the floor. She shivered with cold as she let the boy slide from her hip to stand clutching her thigh. He saw the child, at least, was dryer, as if she'd done her best to keep him out of the water.

Mark knelt to stoke the fire in the stove, keeping one eye on his visitor. The cast-iron door squeaked as he opened it, a blast of hot air lifting the hair from his face. Bree drifted closer, lured by the heat. Pressing himself to her side, the boy clung to her hand.

The firelight played on her skin, highlighting the gentle flare of her cheekbones. She unbuttoned her coat with her free hand, then pushed back her long, wet tangle of hair. The gesture was slow, almost listless. Bree was a woman at the limit of her strength.

"The fire feels so good," she said softly. She lowered the khaki backpack she carried to the floor. It sagged into a damp heap.

Mark studied her, his curiosity every bit as hot as the fire. "How long were you out there?"

"I'm not sure. It felt like hours, but it couldn't have been that long."

"Where did you sail from?"

She didn't reply, but stared into the burning core of the stove. A few wisps of hair were already drying, curling into pale waves.

Mark waited in the silence. He could use vampire power to compel the answer, but he chose to be patient. Something else had drawn his attention. Crouched before the stove, he was level with the boy. The child was good-looking, dark-haired, but thin. Mark caught his gaze just long enough to see a lively intelligence before the brown eyes shied away. Once again, Mark noticed that the boy never spoke. Was he simply afraid? Or was it more than that?

Dark circles ringed the child's eyes. He was exhausted, thin and probably anemic. Mark had medical training, but any vampire could have diagnosed as much. The boy's scent was wrong. "Your son is ill."

Bree pulled the boy a fraction closer. "Jonathan's just tired." A look of chagrin flickered across her face, as if she hadn't meant to give even that much away.

"I'm a doctor," Mark said. "You'd better let me take a look."

Bree looked at him sharply, her full lips parting as if to protest, then pressing into a tight line. "No."

The refusal didn't surprise him. The protective arm

she had curled around the boy's shoulders said everything, but Mark didn't give in. "I might be able to help."

"I've taken him to a G.P. already, and they sent me to a specialist."

"And?"

"They were no help."

Mark offered a smile. "Whoever they were, I'm better." Suddenly, illogically, it was important to prove it. It had become a challenge. *Beware your pride. It would be easier to just send her on her way.*

Her brow furrowed, as if she didn't know how to reply. As Mark rose to his feet, Bree tilted her head slightly to watch his face. He was half a head taller, so he had to look down into her eyes.

Beneath the scent of woods and ocean, there was the warm, earthy smell of female, sweet as sun-warmed peaches. The cabin, with its shabby chair and dark shadows, seemed slightly shocked by the female presence. Or maybe that was just him. Somewhere in the past few minutes she'd morphed in his mind from food to mother to woman. It had been a long time since he'd thought about a mortal female that way. It was almost a novelty.

"First, let me take your coat," he said, remembering he had once possessed a gentleman's manners. He was fine with patients, but now the conversation felt painfully stilted. He never had guests, much less mortal ones. Vampires differed little from humans on the surface, but there were a thousand ways he might betray himself. For instance, it was a sustained effort to remember to breathe when he wasn't talking.

As if sensing his unease, she clutched the collar of the garment for a moment, but then gave way with a sigh. "Thanks."

She surrendered the wet trench coat silently, letting

go of Jonathan's hand just long enough to free the sleeve. Mark hung the garment on a peg close enough to the stove that it would dry.

"Come into the kitchen," he said. "We can find you two something to eat."

It was a mild deception. As he'd planned, the mention of food caught her attention.

"It's been a long time since Jonathan had dinner," she said.

"I'll take care of that. It'll be my pleasure."

Her eyes flicked to his at the last word, imbuing it with extra meaning. Then, she looked away quickly, as if regretting that moment of connection.

Mark smiled to himself. He hadn't lost his touch after all. "This way."

Wordlessly, reluctantly, Bree followed him, Jonathan at her heels.

"Can I get you a drink?" he offered.

"I don't drink." She bit the words off as if he'd offended her. Fine. Whatever.

Mark turned on the overhead bulbs, washing the room in stark brightness. Bree followed, blinking at the bright light. Suddenly, she was in color. Her face was dusted with golden freckles, her eyes shifting between green and blue. A few strands of hair had dried around her face, morphing into long, tawny ripples. He put her somewhere in her mid-twenties, younger than he'd first thought. Hers was a face meant for summer afternoons.

Mark washed his hands in the chipped enamel sink. Then he bent and lifted Jonathan to sit on the battered wooden table.

"What are you doing?" Bree demanded.

Mark ignored her. The boy inhaled, but didn't protest. Mark bent to catch the child's eye again, using a tiny push of compulsion to calm him. "Hello, Jonathan. How old are you?"

"Almost four," Bree answered on his behalf.

Mark frowned. Now that there was good light, he could see the child's pallor. "How long has he been sick?"

She looked about to protest, as if to say she'd already refused medical advice, but then surrender washed over her features. "Just after his third birthday, I noticed he couldn't play for long without getting breathless. Then about five months ago, he stopped talking."

"Fever?"

"Off and on."

"What other symptoms?"

"There have been no rashes or anything like that. He's not in pain that I can tell."

Now that they'd begun, her voice was brittle with worry. Mark wanted to reach over, brush the curve of her cheek in a gesture of comfort. The blood hunger leaped to life, drawing his eyes down the V-neck of her cotton sweater. He forced his gaze away. "Let's get these wet clothes off him. They can dry while I do the exam."

It was a good plan, but doomed to frustration. Mark had brought his doctor's bag to the cabin, but it was meant for emergencies, not laboratory-level diagnoses. Some of Jonathan's abdominal organs seemed to be tender, but it was hard to tell when the patient couldn't speak. He asked many more questions, but Bree's answers could only help so much.

"He needs tests. The nearest place that does that kind of work is in Redwood. I can arrange it if you want." Mark watched her carefully. Her gaze lowered, but he could still see her weighing the odds, her son's health against—what? "Is there a problem with insurance?"

For a moment, she looked as if she was in physical pain. "It's more complicated than that."

"How can I help?" The question came instantly to Mark's lips, surprising him a little.

"You can't."

"I can see your son gets the treatment he needs."

"That's not your decision." She sounded almost angry.

Mark's temper stirred in reply. "Don't the child's needs come first?"

She cursed so softly he almost missed it. "I need to think." She scooped Jonathan into her arms and walked back to the front room, cradling him against her shoulder. The boy's dark eyes watched Mark from over his mother's back.

The sudden silence in the kitchen jarred. Mark stared at the litter of doctor's instruments on the kitchen table and cursed. He was trying to help, but something wasn't right. Too many questions crowded into his mind, and he had a feeling none of the answers were pleasant. *Why involve yourself with their troubles? You were at peace with just the other beasts for company.*

But the one human attribute that still plagued him was curiosity. Bree and her son obviously had a story, and he wanted to know what it was. With speed born of long practice, he tidied away his medical equipment. After that he found some cans of tomato soup in the cupboards. He never had visitors, but kept a small stock of human food for emergencies. He probably should have offered food first, but he'd forgotten many of those small courtesies. Such were the hazards of living mostly among his own kind.

Mark returned to the sitting room, about to ask if he could make tea or coffee. Bree was slouched in his chair, Jonathan—now in dry clothes—asleep in the curve of her arm. Mark's step hitched, caught for a moment by the peaceful tableau. Mother and child. It never got old.

She rose to her feet, a graceful unfolding of her long, slender legs. Mark watched with appreciation until she brought his own Browning pistol into view, aiming straight for his chest.

A lightning glance saw the weapons cupboard standing open. She'd picked the lock. *By all the fiery hells!* Shock soured to bitterness. "So you are here to kill me."

"Paranoid much?" He could hear fear in her voice. "Don't flatter yourself. I don't need to kill you. I just want your car keys and all your cash."

Chapter 3

Nerves dried Bree's mouth to cotton, making her words clumsy. The cold metal of the gun chilled her hand, driving every scrap of the stove's warmth out of her blood.

The doctor named Mark stood frozen in the kitchen doorway, stark surprise on his handsome face. Disappointment flooded his dark eyes, making Bree's throat clutch with regret. He didn't deserve this. *I'm sorry. You're kind, and I'm horrible, but I have to run.*

Mind you, this was the guy who'd dropped from the trees Tarzan-style and scared off a cougar. He was six-foot-plus of steely muscle, and she was very glad she had the gun.

His face dropped back into what seemed to be his usual expression—a wary, keep-your-distance frown just shy of an outright scowl. He'd cheered up when he was dealing with Jonathan, but the frown was going full blast right now.

"You're robbing me?" he said, voice heavy with incredulity.

A flicker of annoyance bolstered her resolve. "Duh. Yeah."

His upper lip curled with disdain, ruining the line of his perfectly sculpted lips.

Bree gulped, fighting her dry throat. With that face, he could have been a male model. Wavy dark hair, olive skin, perfect nose, dimpled chin. And a doctor. Even her mother would have approved, except—what was he doing out here? Dancing with wolves?

Though gentle with Jonathan, whenever he looked her way Mark was too intense, too raw. He scared her even as he fascinated. And just to complicate matters, she was coming to believe that he really meant to help. But there were always strings attached—strings she couldn't afford.

Involving anyone else in her headlong flight meant trusting them. Trust meant risk. She would make fewer mistakes if she worked alone, and Jonathan would be safer—and her son's safety was the bottom line.

The nose of the gun shook. To cover, she pulled the slide back, remembering it was a single-action pistol and she had to chamber a round. She knew the basics, but was no marksman. She frowned, doing her best to look tough.

"Have you done this before?" Mark asked in that silky tone he'd used in the woods. "Is this a new kind of home invasion?"

"Uh-huh." Her heart pounded so hard her head swam. Behind her, Jonathan stirred anxiously. Her free hand groped behind her, catching his hand. Images flicked past. Bob the fishing guide who'd left her to freeze. The men who'd chased her from New York to these wild islands in the north. Her best friend and employer murdered, the studio where they'd worked burned to the ground. She'd heard Jessica scream that night, the sound coming shrill through the phone. The memory made her stomach roil.

This wasn't a game. If Bree faltered, she'd be dead and Jonathan right along with her.

Dr. Bedroom Eyes didn't know any of that. He just looked annoyed and—embarrassed? He'd probably never been threatened with his own gun before.

"You shouldn't have wasted my professional time," he said with deceptive coolness. "You should have just robbed me straightaway."

Anger rose, and Bree's hand stopped trembling. "I'm not an idiot. I know I need to find proper medical care. I was hoping you could just give Jonathan some medicine."

"I can't even diagnose him yet."

"I thought you said you were better than the other doctors."

His dark eyes flickered dangerously, sending a chill up her neck. There was menace just below that handsome facade. "I need the proper equipment. For that I need a hospital. *You* need a hospital."

What Bree needed was someone—anyone—to understand. "Hospitals need names."

Comprehension crossed his face. "You're on the run. You're in some kind of trouble."

"You have no idea." Men with guns. Men who would cheerfully take what she had and kill both her and her boy.

Mark took a step closer.

"Stay where you are!" she warned.

A second later, he was inches away from her, grabbing her gun hand and twisting her facedown against the back of the overstuffed chair. How had he moved so fast?

The edge of the chair back dug into her flesh. His hands were cool and horribly strong. Rough cloth grazed her cheek as her arm was wrenched behind her. The gun slid out of her tingling hand.

"Jonathan!" she wailed. Where had he gone?

With an inarticulate cry, her son threw himself against the doctor, pounding his fists against the man's legs. Jonathan's face was twisted with fury, tears streaking his cheeks.

"No!" Bree forgot the pain snaking up her arm.

Jonathan kicked the doctor's ankle. With a curse, Mark released her, stepping back and removing the clip from the pistol in a single move. Then he ejected the cartridge from the chamber with practiced ease. "Enough!"

Bree fell to her knees and grabbed her son, who was ready to relaunch his attack. "No, baby."

Jonathan threw his arms around her neck. With a mother's instinct, she knew he was offering protection and needing comfort at the same time. She closed her eyes, her heart squeezed with dread for whatever was going to happen next.

Her arm and shoulder throbbed. "I'm sorry. Please, please don't take it out on him." She looked up at the doctor, putting her soul into her eyes. "Let us go."

His gaze narrowed, his expression unreadable. "I'm going to ask questions, and you're going to answer me. I'll know if you're lying."

Bree balked, but she had no cards left to play and everything to lose. "Okay."

She stood, setting Jonathan in the big, stuffed chair. The boy slumped into the cushions, his face still red and wet with tears. She kissed his cheeks dry. Then Bree turned to face the man she'd held at gunpoint moments ago.

"Why are you running?" he asked.

"I witnessed a murder." It wasn't the whole answer, but it wasn't a lie.

"When?"

"A year ago."

"You've been running all that time?"

"And hiding. I was safe for a while, until—"

He interrupted with an impatient gesture of his hand. "A doctor ran your insurance card, and somehow that let the bad guys find you."

She nodded, and that perfect mouth of his twitched down at the corners.

"I get it." He paused a moment, and she could almost see thoughts chasing through his head. After drawing a long breath, he thrust the empty gun into his waistband. The gesture was slow and reluctant, as if he wasn't sure he'd made the right choice. "You're lucky I came along. That cougar wasn't going to back off because you asked nicely."

Frowning, he looked at the clip in his hand. "If you're on the run, how come you don't have your own weapon?"

Bree stiffened. He had a point. She could have used something like the Browning when Bob had forced her out of the boat. "I'm doing the best I can, but it's not easy. I can't travel with a four-year-old boy and a loaded gun. That's just bad parenting."

He didn't answer, but made a noise that sounded as though he was choking back a laugh. Heat flared across her cheeks.

The doctor closed his fingers over the clip. The gesture mesmerized her. She remembered the hard strength of his hands, and the delicate touch he'd used when examining Jonathan. With unbidden clarity, she imagined them skimming her limbs with the caress of a lover. Desire simmered under her skin, and it shocked her to realize that she wanted that touch with an ache so sharp it stung.

She'd been alone too long.

His voice snapped her back to reality. The menace had gone out of it, but it wasn't warm. "Why are you here, in these woods?"

"I hired a boat to take me to the mainland. When my ride found out we were being followed, he dumped me on your beach."

He took a step forward. "Who's following you?"

Bree suddenly realized she'd brought danger to his door. She'd been so focused on getting Jonathan to shelter, she'd missed that point. "I don't have names, but they're bad news. If they catch up with Bob, he won't play the hero. He'll sell me for gas money."

"Knights in shining armor are few and far between."

She folded her arms. "No kidding."

He shrugged. His expression was stone, hard and unwelcoming. "Knights were overrated, if you ask me. If you want to protect a treasure, ask a dragon."

Mark had spoken without thinking, but the look she gave him was significant. He was the fierce predator, the dragon; her son was the treasure. Even if she didn't realize it yet, Bree was counting on him to get Jonathan someplace safe.

No. No women and children, not ever again. I'm not that man. Mark recoiled. He understood the primitive instincts of pack and cave. He knew why Bree looked to him for protection. He was three-quarters beast, only a shred of humanity still tying him to the civilized world.

Family would be his nightmare reborn, history mercilessly repeating itself. Sure, he could play doctor, whether it was with one small boy or a country ravaged by flood and fire. But as a medical man, he could come and go at will, getting involved on his own terms.

A family man had no escape from their needs and his failures. *I am not your dragon.* Still, he had to do something for her, if only to get her out of his cabin— and maybe after centuries of woe and slaughter, he was ready to see someone like her win.

Nevertheless, this would only work if he set limits. He was a vampire, and far, far from a saint. "I'll take you as far as Redwood. I have hospital privileges there. I can run tests off the grid."

She stared at him with something like wonder. "Why are you doing this for us?"

"After you threatened to shoot me?" And, as the most ferocious creature in the room, he would just skip past the fact that she'd got the drop on him with his own weapon.

"Well, yeah." She had the decency to look abashed.

"I'm a doctor. You seem to need help. It's what we do."

"You're very kind."

"Not so much. Getting to Redwood is the matter of a phone call." And if she was being followed, it made sense for them all to leave. He folded his arms. "Where did you learn to pick a lock like that?"

"My dad's liquor cabinet. All it takes is a paper clip."

He remembered she'd said she didn't drink—but obviously she had once. "Very resourceful."

"I have to use what I've got."

Don't I know it? She was beautiful. He might be a monster, but he was still male, moved by her grace and her courage. Despite himself, Bree's desperate protectiveness had made him care. *A dangerous woman.*

"Stay here," he said, removing the rifle from the cupboard where he had—emphasis on the word *had*—locked his weapons. He began mounting the stairs to the second floor. "I don't have any other firearms sitting around, so don't bother looking for another gun to finish me off."

"I would never…"

Turning on the staircase, he gave her a look that made the words fade from her lips, reminding her that he was the dragon, not the knight.

Still, the anger between them had eased. Jonathan had grown comfortable—and tired enough—to have fallen fast asleep in the tattered armchair. Mark turned before Bree could see him smile.

Once upstairs, he found his cell phone and the spot by the window that caught a signal. This far out in the country, cell coverage was spotty and he exhaled with relief when the call connected. It was the middle of the night, but in the supernatural community, that was business hours.

"Fred Larson."

"It's Mark Winspear."

"I didn't expect you to call for weeks yet. You've barely been out there a month."

"Something came up."

"Business?"

"Yes and no." It wasn't Company business, but Larson didn't need to know.

"Must be serious to call you back to civilization early."

"My bad nature precedes me."

"Just a bit. What can I do for you?"

Mark studied the horizon. The rain outside had slowed, now pattering instead of pounding on the roof. Light was already turning the horizon to pearl-gray. Bree's pursuers were probably lying in wait, biding their time for sunrise to make a search of the island easy. "I need to get into Redwood as soon as possible."

"Today?"

"I'm talking hours. There will be passengers besides me. A woman and child."

The ensuing silence vibrated with curiosity, but Larson knew better than to ask. Mark wasn't just Company, he was one of the Horsemen, a small team of elite operatives. As a doctor, they'd nicknamed him Plague, his two friends War and Famine. Death, ironically, was dead. A pang of sadness caught Mark. He treasured the few friends he had. Losing Death—whose real name had been Jack Anderson—had cut deep.

"I can have the plane in the air at first light," Larson replied, mercifully breaking into his thoughts.

"Be careful. There's a good chance we have hostiles in the water nearby."

"I'll keep my eyes open and my powder dry."

"Good. See you then." Mark thumbed the phone off.

And then winced. *First light. By the fiery pit.*

Larson worked for the Company, but he was human. Daylight flights were no problem. Vampires could function during sunlight hours, but only under protest. It felt like stumbling around in the blare of a zillion-watt floodlight. *Bloody hell.*

Mark pocketed his phone and started for the stairs.

A square of white paper lay on the floor. As he stooped to pick it up, he saw it was an envelope. He had obviously passed by it on the way up.

The cabin didn't have a mailbox, much less delivery straight to his bedroom. He tilted the envelope to the faint light falling through the window. The handwriting read *Dr. Mark Winspear.*

Curious, he ripped it open and slid out a folded letter. The salutation inside used his real name: *to my Lord Marco Farnese.*

He sucked in a breath. No one had called him that in

hundreds of years. Seeing that name written in modern ballpoint pen gave him an odd sense of dislocation, as if he were neither in the present day nor the past.

He clicked on the bedside lamp, welcoming the puddle of light. The message was only a single line: *I haven't forgotten you.*

He flipped the paper over, studying the blank side, then turned the page print-side-up again. He was annoyed more than disturbed. Except…there was a human woman and child downstairs. Whoever came for him would kill them first. They were easy targets.

Just like before. He'd played this game long ago, and lost.

A second thought crowded in. While he had been out playing pat-a-cake with cougars, his enemies had been in his house. Standing over his bed. Territorial rage swept through him, leaving his fingers shaking.

The signature on the letter was a crest, the inky impression of a signet ring used like a rubber stamp. It hadn't worked very well—the ink had run, making the whole thing look smudged—but Mark could make out the serpent and crossed daggers of the Knights of Vidon. Below the crest were the initials N.F.

Nicholas Ferrel.

Vile memories ripped through him, old but undiminished. *He killed my wife. My children. He burned them alive.*

Mark had slaughtered Ferrel, Commander General of the Knights of Vidon, back in the fifteenth century. Then he'd torn every Knight he could find flesh from bone.

Mark clenched his teeth. Vengeance had solved nothing. Ferrel's sons had sworn a vendetta. They'd sworn their service to the vampire-slaying Knights, as had their sons after them. Back then, the Knights were a breed apart, stronger, faster and resistant to a vampire's hypnotic powers. The Ferrels were the foremost among them.

None had killed Mark, but a good many men, human and vampire, had paid for the feud with their lives. Was this new Nicholas a descendant eager to perpetuate the fight? Why leave a note and not just, say, drop a bomb on the cabin?

Mark glanced at the horizon again, calculating how long it would take the plane to arrive. Two hours at most. He crumpled the letter in his hand.

Assassins had come before, but this time was different. These had been in his bedroom. These had used Ferrel's name.

And that meant Mark had more than himself to protect. History was repeating itself. There was a woman and a boy, and they were depending on him for their lives.

Bree's enemies weren't the only ones he had to fight. Now there were his, too.

Suddenly two hours to dawn was a very long time.

Chapter 4

Dawn clawed its way into the sky. It came stealthily at first, a lighter shade of steel that threw the craggy trees into sharp relief. Then the sky erupted in streaks of crimson and orange, a flame that started low in the forest and slowly climbed as a rising wind shredded the clouds.

To Bree, the light brought little comfort. Jonathan was asleep in the big chair, buried under blankets, but she was too restless to sit still. As the fire in the stove burned down, the circle of heat around them grew steadily smaller, as if the cold, wet forest pushed through the cabin walls.

Mark moved about the small space with quiet efficiency, packing a large nylon knapsack with clothes, books, weapons and a whisper-thin laptop. He wrote a note and left it on the table for someone who was coming in to ready the cabin for winter. He spoke little and checked the window often, a sharp crease between his brows.

"It's time to go," he said at last.

His low voice startled her. She turned from staring out at the fiery sky. The light inside seemed a thick, pearly gray—neither day nor night. His scowl was deadly serious. Not the face of a healer, but of something far more dangerous. She prayed he would keep his word. She prayed he was really on her side. If she guessed wrong, it would be Jonathan who suffered.

"Okay." She pulled on her coat. It was still wet in the folds, but most of it was warm from the stove. "Is it far to the plane?"

"About a ten-minute walk."

With Jonathan, it would take twice that. The boy was asleep and not ready to be disturbed. She started putting on his shoes. They were cold and damp to the touch, and must have felt awful. He woke up with a noise of protest.

"Sorry, baby," she said, crouching down before the chair so she could get a better angle.

He jerked his foot back, his lower lip jutting and his eyes resentful.

"C'mon, we've got to go."

Bree reached for his foot again. She was exhausted, with a numbness that came from no sleep all night. She felt as though she were moving underwater.

But her fingers closed on air as Jonathan's feet disappeared under his bottom like darting fish. As she reached under him, he curled into a ball, drawing the blanket into an impenetrable cocoon.

"Jonathan!" Her voice held an edge she didn't like.

The wad of boy and blanket shrank tighter. She rested her forehead on the arm of the chair for a moment, summoning patience. Forcing the issue would simply start a

struggle that would last half the morning. Her son—oh,
bliss—had inherited her stubborn streak.

She changed tactics. "If you're good and put your
shoes on right away, we'll find waffles for breakfast."

There was no response.

"With syrup and bacon." Bree studied the blanket ball
for signs of surrender. It was hard to read. "I'll count to
three. If I don't see your feet, no waffles for you."

She poked the blanket with a finger. That got her a
giggle. *Good sign.*

"We have to go." The doctor's voice was urgent.

"In one minute. I have to get his shoes on."

"Now." Mark picked up the boy, blanket and all, as if
he weighed no more than a stuffed toy, and braced him
against his shoulder. Jonathan made a protesting noise,
but not for long. Mark hushed him, one large hand ruf-
fling the boy's hair. He gave Bree a look made inscrutable by a pair of dark sunglasses. No hint of a smile.

She tried not to notice how well the dark glasses
showed off the fine sculpting of his lips and chin. She
wasn't sure she wanted to like him, much less lust after
him.

"You bring his shoes and my medical bag," he commanded.

Bree obeyed, stuffing the shoes in her pack, but every
instinct wanted to rip Jonathan out of the doctor's arms.
That was her son. He had interfered. Still, she followed
Mark out of the cabin into the damp morning air.

Jonathan seemed perfectly content loafing against the
man's shoulder. That stung, too. She had grown used to
being her son's only protector. Hot, tingling anger crept
up her cheeks, barely cooled by the mist.

Mark led the way beneath the trees, moving in a
swinging stride that made her trot to keep up. The sun

was up now, slanting across the dew-soaked greenery. Where autumn had kissed the leaves, golds and reds shone like scattered jewels. Her temper eased. It was hard to hold on to anger in the face of such beauty, and she was too tired to make the effort.

Easier by far to watch the lithe movement of his body through the forest. It was like watching a panther on one of those nature shows. The play of his muscles against tight denim did something to her insides.

As the path began to angle downward, she heard the distant purr of the plane's motor beneath the incessant chatter of birds. The sound made her heart lift. On the mainland, they could get a decent meal, a bus to civilization, medical help, a new place to hide. Bree didn't know what she would do after that, but there *would* be an after, thanks to that plane.

And thanks to Mark. He stopped at the edge of the trees, Jonathan still propped against his shoulder. He held the boy one-handed, which impressed Bree. Her son was getting far too big for her to do that for long.

She followed Mark's gaze to the sky, now kissed a fading pink that reflected in the silvery water. Ropes of mist shrouded the end of a wooden pier. This spot was farther south than where she had landed last night.

"Where's the plane?" she asked.

"There," Mark said, nodding his head to the southeast.

Bree drew a step closer, suddenly far too aware of being near a good-looking man. It wasn't just his handsome face that unsettled her. It was the fact of his physical being: tall and broad enough to shelter her from the searching breeze; strong and alert enough to offer protection. And yet—that was a problem in itself. It felt like an ice age since she'd noticed a man, and it felt risky. She'd shut down that part of herself for far too long. How good was her judgment? *You're better off alone. You know that.*

And yet, solitude had its own vulnerability. Standing next to Mark reminded her how raw her loneliness had left her. Every kindness left her close to tears. *But what if trusting him is a mistake?*

She didn't see the plane at first, but in a moment or two, it emerged above the trees right where he indicated. The stubby body made the craft more of a duck than a swan, but it made a graceful enough landing. It began gliding toward the shore, leaving a glittering wake behind its pontoons.

Bree took a step forward, but Mark grabbed her wrist. "Wait."

High above, a raven croaked.

"What?" she asked, the sun losing all its warmth.

"Your friends from last night have joined us," he said quietly. "Or maybe they're here for me. Either way, they're not bringing roses. Wait until the plane docks before making a move."

"How do you know they're here?" she said under her breath. "How did they know the plane was coming?"

A sudden wave of panic hit her. Did he call them? He was holding Jonathan. Was this a trap? She wanted to grab her son and fade back into the woods, gathering the sheltering green around her the way Jonathan had hidden under the blanket.

For a split second, Mark studied her from behind the dark glasses, somber and silent. As if sensing her uneasiness, he handed her Jonathan. The boy settled on her hip, and the doctor tucked the blanket around him with practiced efficiency. For a fleeting moment, she wondered if he'd ever had a child of his own.

Holding Jonathan calmed her instantly. The next moment, Mark had drawn the Browning from under his jacket and was checking to make sure it was loaded. She clutched her son closer, glad that the walk had lulled him back into a doze.

The plane glided closer, turning to one side before the pilot cut the motor and drifted in next to the pier. Bree watched as a tiny arched door opened just behind the wing. A man jumped out, using one pontoon as a stepping stone before hopping onto the pier and grabbing a mooring rope. Using one foot to stop the drift of the seaplane, he anchored the craft securely to the pier.

Mark stepped from the tree line, motioning Bree to stay put. A bullet slammed into the rocks at his feet. Bree gave a startled cry that woke Jonathan. She clutched him, backing into the trees as he started sobbing in her ear.

Mark dropped to one knee, returning fire. He was angling the shot upward and to the right. Whoever was shooting was higher up on the rise. Bree saw the pilot of the floatplane draw a gun, scanning the land behind and above her. Even from this distance, she could tell he was hesitating, not sure what to do.

Bree's heart sped, suddenly thumping double time. A jumble of thoughts raced through her brain, most of them focused on the open stretch of beach between her and the plane. How was she going to get Jonathan across without both of them getting killed? *How did the gunmen know we'd be right here?*

Another shot came from Bree's left. The pilot fumbled with the gun a moment and finally returned fire.

Bullets were coming from the right and left. Two shooters! Bree's breath stopped. She was no strategist, but to her it looked like the gunmen had them caught between pincers. And even if they got across the beach, a stray bullet in the plane's fuel tank could cause an explosion.

Jonathan's sobs were escalating to a hoarse, breathy wail. Bree cursed herself. He was frightened by the noise, but even more by her terror. She had to calm down. She took a gulp of air, forcing herself to breathe.

Mark wheeled. "When I start firing again, run for the plane."

"Are you crazy?" Her voice was high and thin, choked with panic.

"Larson and I will keep them busy."

"But—"

His mouth was a grim line. "It's your one chance. Now, go!"

He started firing a deadly, insistent barrage of bullets. *Blam! Blam! Blam!* She understood what he meant by keeping the enemy busy. They'd either be ducking or aiming at him—and too busy to worry about her.

"Go!" he repeated, his voice on the edge of a snarl.

She ran, covering as much of Jonathan with her body as she could. It felt like a crazy game show, or a terrible episode from some thriller movie. It just didn't seem real. Her. Bree. Bullets. She tried to pretend she was just running for the bus. It was about the right distance, half a long city block, maybe.

A bullet whizzed by her ear. She stumbled, Jonathan's weight dragging her down. Somehow she got her feet under her and kept moving. *Go, go, go!* If she thought about what she was doing, she'd be too terrified to move. *Only a few yards now.*

Larson went down with a scream. Blood bloomed on his leg, staining his khaki pant leg crimson. Jonathan was wailing in her ear, a steady tearing sound that made her want to scream herself, to snarl at him to just shut up so she could think. She was so terrified, her breath was coming in wheezing gasps because her body was too tight to function.

Her feet hit the wooden pier, the pounding echo of her footfalls adding to the din. A black haze was clouding the edges of her vision, but whether it was fear or lack of oxygen was hard to tell. Another bullet skimmed her elbow, a lick of heat telling her it had grazed her skin.

She stumbled up to the plane. The pilot was on the pier, one hand pressing on his wound, the other still holding his gun. She crouched next to him.

"Get inside," he ordered. "Fast."

Bree looked for stairs, or a ladder, and then remembered he'd used the pontoon. A strip of ocean gaped between the plane and the pier, wavelets making the pontoon a moving foothold. She might be able to climb over the watery gap, but not her son. Fresh panic engulfed her.

"Go!" Larson barked, then let off another volley of shots.

"I'll go first." Mark was suddenly behind her.

Bree jumped as he touched her, her nerves wound too tight for surprises. But she was insanely glad he was there and in one piece. He jumped onto the pontoon, his movements quick and sure. Then he grabbed the handhold by the door and made the long step inside without hesitation. He turned. "Pass me the boy."

Apprehensive, Bree rose from her crouch, still cradling her son. The pier was only a few feet from the edge of the plane, but it seemed miles. She put one foot on the bobbing pontoon and angled her body to shorten the distance between Jonathan and Mark's outstretched arms. Her son protested, digging his fingers into the cloth of her coat and catching a handful of her hair into the bargain.

A bullet rammed into the plane, inches from Mark's

head. She jerked in fear, but he had Jonathan firmly in his hands. For a moment, she thought everything would be fine.

And then her foot slipped off the pontoon. Bree's hands clawed for the handgrip, the edge of the door, anything, but she was falling. Another bullet smacked into the plane, just above her groping hand. Her knee hit something, and she was deafened by a loud, shrieking sound.

Her shoulder jerked in its socket, stopping her in mid-drop. The noise stopped, and she realized it had been her. As her mind cleared, she realized Mark had caught her under the armpit and was keeping her out of the water with the strength of one hand. Frantically, her feet scrabbled to find the pontoon again. Then, with both hands, Mark lifted her through the door.

"Are you all right?" The words were brusque.

"Yes," she answered automatically. She didn't actually know yet, but he was out the door again before she could reply.

She shoved the pain aside. She could still use her arm, so her own injuries were the least of their problems. The shooters were finding the plane a much easier target than humans running around the beach. It was only a matter of time before they hit something important.

There were four seats behind the cockpit, two rows of two, and some space for cargo. She put Jonathan in one of the seats and helped Mark pull the pilot inside. Larson was white-faced and sweating, letting out a steady stream of profanity as the doctor heaved him through the door.

"Lay him down," Mark ordered as he left the plane one last time so he could release the mooring lines.

Bree helped the man to the floor behind the seats. Mark hopped in behind him and went to the controls, pausing only long enough to fasten a seat belt around Jonathan.

"Can you fly this thing?" Bree asked anxiously. Obviously, Larson wasn't going to get them out of there.

"Yes," he answered, starting the engines. "There's a first aid kit in the back. Do you know any first aid?"

"I do." She'd taken a course when she first found out she was going to have a baby. She'd been so determined to be a better parent than hers had ever been.

"Apply pressure to the wound. Elevate the leg. It didn't hit an artery, so you should be able to hold him until we reach Redwood."

"How long?" Bree asked, but the sound of the motors drowned out her question. Another bullet pinged against the side of the plane.

"Don't worry," Larson said, wincing as he shifted on the floor.

"Don't try to talk." Bree was hunting for the first aid kit, trying to ignore the rattling vibration as the tiny aircraft taxied toward open water. She'd been left in charge of a bleeding man, and her hands were shaking and sweaty. *Don't you dare die on my watch!*

Mark was a doctor. It should have been him doing the first aid, but she couldn't fly the plane. Irrationally, she scolded herself for never taking pilot lessons. If they got out of there in one piece, that was going to be high on her to-do list.

The waves bumped under the pontoons. The plane felt to her like a toy powered by a rubber band. Her stomach began protesting against the motion.

Finally, Bree spotted the familiar red cross painted on a white tin box. She pulled it out from under the right-hand seat. "You'll be okay," she said a little too heartily. "I promise."

"Oh, I'll be fine." He winked, as if to give her courage. It would have worked better if he hadn't been as pale as death.

He had a nice face and sandy-brown hair. She knew the type—a little past his prime, a little overweight and a lot of good, kind heart. He looked as if he would have been happy sitting in a bar telling fishing stories to his buddies.

"You don't need to worry about the plane, either," he added. "It's got the best lightweight bulletproofing money can buy."

Bree's hands stalled partway through unlatching the lid of the first aid kit. The plane didn't look like anything special. Neither did Larson. *Bulletproofing?* What was he, a smuggler? That would explain why he seemed to be a pretty good shot once he finally decided to start shooting.

"I don't want to know," she replied, digging through the kit for scissors. She found some with rounded tips, made for cutting away clothing, and bent to slice through his blood-soaked pant leg. "I just want to get out of here with everyone alive."

"I can get behind that." He winced as she worked around his wound.

"At least they didn't seem to be very good shots."

"Don't underestimate how hard it is to shoot a moving target in a stiff wind. They got me and they clipped you from a good distance. That's better than you think."

Bree didn't want to think. She peeled away the cloth from his wound, exposing the bloody mess the bullet had made of his thigh. Stomach rolling, she turned away, searching in the kit for sterile pads. She wasn't normally squeamish, but this was worse than anything she'd ever seen. Sweat trickled down her back.

She found a sterile pad and ripped open the pack. "I'm sorry if this hurts."

"I've had worse." Still, he sucked in his breath as she pressed down on his wound. He pushed her hand out of the way, and then pressed down twice as hard himself. It was a necessary evil. They had to stop the bleeding. Bree found a triangular bandage and tied the pad in place, knotting it tight but not so tight that the circulation would stop completely.

"Is there water on board?" she asked. "You need fluids."

"Cockpit," he ground out. "If you find anything stronger, bring that."

Just then, Bree felt the plane lift from the water, a lurch as if she had leaped into the air herself. She grabbed the back of the seat, casting a glance at Jonathan. He was fine, his nose pressed to a tiny window. A typical boy, in love with anything that had a motor. She hoped he had no sense of just how much danger they'd been in.

Rising carefully, she shuffled forward between the seats. Mark was completely focused on the instrument panel and the scene below. That awareness of his presence rose again, and she made herself look out the cockpit window and not at him. *Focus on what's ahead of you. Don't get distracted.*

The view out the cockpit stopped her in her tracks. The scenery was breathtaking, a cluster of pine-covered islands scattered over silver-spangled ocean. The warmth of the sun through the glass touched her face, making her realize her skin was itchy with the salt of tears.

She raised her hand to wipe them away, but it was crusted with blood. Swallowing hard, Bree wiped it on her pant leg, which was already smeared, and then bent to scrounge around the floor for bottled water.

"How is he?" Mark demanded. Beneath his sunglasses, he looked even paler than Larson. Deathly pale. "I smell a lot of blood."

Bree wrinkled her nose. She could smell it, too, but not enough to gauge quantity. Maybe that was a doctor thing. "Working on it. I'm looking for water."

"Behind the copilot's seat." He caught her arm, reminding her that her shoulder was sore. "That's your blood I can smell. Your elbow. It's fresh."

The way he said it sent a shiver through her, despite the warm sun streaming through the windows. She twisted to look, and vaguely remembered the bullet grazing her. Her sweater sleeve was soaked, but after Larson's wound, it seemed trivial. "That's nothing."

"I'll look at it when we land." He turned back to the controls, his movements slow and deliberate, as if he were fighting to concentrate on one thing at a time. He must have been tired, too.

She moved to get the water and then paused, aching to satisfy her curiosity. "How did you know those men were on the beach?"

He didn't answer right away, but finally relented when she didn't move. "Better to ask how they knew we were coming."

"I'd settle for that." The answer was simple, no big surprise. Someone had betrayed her. Someone always did. That's why she worked alone. The moment she didn't...

"There was only one other person who knew I was leaving the island," Mark said.

Bree turned to the back, where Larson lay. The man had been shot. The man had kind eyes, and up until that moment, she would have sworn Mark had trusted him. "So much for friends."

The doctor stared out the cockpit window, not saying a word.

Chapter 5

Late that night, Mark stormed into the office he shared with two other part-time physicians at Redwood General Hospital. He slammed the door behind him, beyond frustrated. Larson wasn't talking.

At first, it had been understandable because he was unconscious. The wound was serious, but Mark had tended to it and thankfully Larson would recover.

But once Larson was awake, he hadn't talked because he was afraid. Someone had threatened his grandchildren. Someone he feared more than Mark—and that was saying something.

The phone rang. Mark snatched it up. "What?"

There was a beat of silence. "I see someone had their grumpy pills today."

It was Faran Kenyon, werewolf and fellow member of the Horsemen.

"What?" Mark snapped again. He wasn't in the mood

for Kenyon's antics. His skin itched like the devil. He'd been exposed to too much sun on the plane and now he looked pink. He'd already used half a tube of medicated cream and smelled like the victim of a bad diaper rash.

And the scent of blood on the plane had gotten to him badly. As a doctor, he was used to it, but Bree had been bleeding. The blood of strangers was one thing. The blood of a woman who had caught his notice was something else. Dangerous. Tantalizing.

"Next time you send a top-secret report to the captain, blind copy me," Kenyon said, breaking through his thoughts. "Otherwise, all I get are bits and scraps. I heard about the damsel in distress showing up and you deciding to get her and a sick rug rat to town, but why the shootout in the bush?"

"I was tracked. I found a letter inside my cabin."

"Who from? The health department?"

"The Knights of Vidon."

Kenyon swore.

"Indeed," Mark said with wry humor. "Vampire slayers apparently take no vacations. Therefore, I don't get one, either. Unfortunately, the letter was from one of my longtime fans. It was a surprise. I haven't heard from that family for a very long time."

"Who?"

"Nicholas Ferrel. I knew the taste of his ancestor."

"Creepy. How long ago was that?"

Mark sat down at the desk, and was greeted with stacks of files plastered with sticky notes. Sign this form. Initial that one. Complete another mountain of logs and charts. He shoved them aside with a sweep of his arm. "Five hundred thirty years, give or take."

"And his descendant still holds a grudge? What in blazes did you do?"

"It was a different era. Listen, I'm sending some blood samples by courier. I've addressed them to you, but would you send them over to the lab when they arrive?"

"Sure. Anything I should know?"

"They're for the boy. There's something about his case that worries me. Redwood is just a small regional hospital. I want the Varney labs on it."

The Varney Center in Los Angeles was the West Coast hub of the Company and the North American headquarters for the Horsemen. As well as the usual mountains of data intelligence, spy toys and black ops coffeemakers, it had an exceptional medical facility. There were few things that made Mark go weak in the knees, but those labs counted. The fact that he got to work there was one of the main reasons he had joined the Horsemen.

"Not to sound like the trolls in accounting, but he's a human, right? Should we be using our resources for this?"

"Do I ever ask for favors?" He knew very well that the answer was negative.

Kenyon sighed. "Dare I ask why now?"

"The woman has insurance issues. If there's a hassle, tell them to take it out of my pay."

Kenyon was quiet for a moment. "If you're that involved—"

"I'm not involved," he said quickly. "I can't figure out what's wrong, and that frustrates me. I became a doctor for this kind of science." Not to mention atonement for all the lives he'd taken.

Kenyon's voice was cautious. "The boy's really sick, isn't he?"

"Maybe. Probably." Closer examination had confirmed his earlier fears. Whatever was wrong was chronic and debilitating—almost certainly something in his blood. He could smell it. "But I don't want to say anything until I'm absolutely certain. I don't want to put his mother through any false alarms."

He swiveled the chair around so that he could look out the window. All he got was a view of the parking lot, growing dim in the fading light. Besides sending a brief report to L.A., he'd spent hours treating Larson, then more time testing Jonathan and looking in on some other patients he had in long-term care. He'd lost track of time, and now the clock said it was after six in the evening.

A whole day back in the human world. He already missed the green of his island retreat, where he didn't have to fight to wear a civilized mask. Where choices were easy.

"I have bad news," Kenyon said. "You don't get to hang around up there playing Dr. McGrumpy. The boss wants you in L.A."

"Now?"

"Right now. He's sending a plane to pick up Larson. Raphael got the copy of your statement."

The boss. Raphael. "His timing is inconvenient."

"Sorry. He wants you on the plane. He's scooping up Larson's family, bringing the whole lot of them in so that they'll be safe. Then he's going to question Larson again. He wants you present for that."

We'll see. Mark had never liked having his leash yanked, and thoroughly resented it now. "Then I need you to do one more thing. I want an ID on this woman. Her name is Bree. The boy's name is Jonathan. He's almost four years old."

"Last name?"

"I don't have one. I suppose Bree is short for something."

"Uh-huh. Date of birth? Place of birth? Maybe a Swedish accent to give us a clue?"

Mark considered. "I'd say Californian."

"Californians don't have an accent."

"They do if you're Italian." California hadn't even been discovered when he was born in 1452. By the time Columbus sailed for the New World forty years later, Marco Farnese had been Undead for a decade. *"Parlo la lingua del canto e della seduzione."* I speak the language of song and seduction.

Kenyon gave a short, dry laugh. "Right. Like I'd call you for phone sex. There's something sad about an Italian vampire. All that great garlicky cuisine going to waste."

Mark grunted. "Call me when you find something."

"When is optimistic. Stick to *if."*

"Nonsense. You're a bloodhound."

"I'm a werewolf. Hear me howl in dismay."

Mark swiveled back to the desk and hung up the phone without saying goodbye. His mind was already racing ahead to what Kenyon might find out, and how that would connect with any of the other puzzle pieces.

Larson's refusal to say who had frightened him so badly was a problem. Mark's enemies had been close by—close enough to play mailman.

And why had Ferrel resurfaced now, after so many years? After generations? Mark had let down his guard enough to take a position at a hospital filled with vulnerable patients. If the Knights of Vidon found him on the island, how long would it be before they showed up here?

And that was only half his problem. There was Bree and the boy, with their own set of gun-toting maniacs. Whose enemies had been the ones shooting at them? His or hers?

Mark swore softly. Even if he was being summoned to Los Angeles, Mark had a responsibility to the boy and his mother. He couldn't just dump them and go. At the very least, he had to get the boy into adequate care.

That didn't mean he was involved with them in the warm-and-fuzzy sense. It was just that there were some occasions when he had to be a doctor first, and a vampire later.

Mark pushed back from the desk, trying not to see the paperwork glaring up at him. So much for a paperless world, where everything was digital. He swore every time he looked at the stack of files it was bigger. Worse, it didn't care if he was a supernatural being of immense power. Growling never made bureaucracy run away.

He left the office, closing the door behind him. The corridor was narrow, painted the usual nondescript hospital-beige. A nurse in scrubs hurried by, giving him a nod and the professional half smile of someone with too much to do. He nodded back, then strode toward the ward where he'd left Bree and her son.

Like everything at Redwood General, the pediatrics area was small, but the staff made the most of it. It was the one place with bright colors. Mark found the kids' TV room, where Bree waited with Jonathan. A swarm of cardboard bees covered the walls, smiling down at the tiny patients. Jonathan was playing on a giant red sea monster that doubled as a slide. Skinny arms flung wide, he scooted down the curve of it as Mark walked in.

It always fascinated Mark how even the sickest children still had the impulse to play, but healthy adults quickly forgot how.

They were the only ones in the room, and Mark saw Bree before she saw him. She was hunched over, her chin propped in her hands, watching a cartoon with the dull expression of the exhausted. Nevertheless, she'd angled her body so that she could still see her son. That vigilance of hers never, ever slipped.

As if she could sense his presence, she raised her head. She was disheveled, her eyes bruised with shock and fatigue. He'd bought a different jacket for her from the gift shop because her trench coat had been bloody. This one was ice-cream-pink and fuzzy—not something he guessed was her usual style—but it was all the store had. She'd pulled another pair of jeans from her backpack, and this pair had threadbare knees. The woman had nothing but the clothes on her back, and they were in sorry shape. And yet, she was lovely.

As their eyes met, hers widened, expectant. Mark's chest squeezed, a half-forgotten feeling waking inside. It had been so long since someone had waited for him. It was something he'd never take for granted—to walk out of a room, and have it matter to someone if he ever walked back in. He'd lost the right to expect that from anyone long ago.

Yes, she was beautiful with her soft hair waving around her face, like a painting of an angel. Not the Christmas-card type, but the angels from his day, with swords and arrows and smiles that woke the sun and broke armies of war-proud kings. That kind of sweetness remade worlds.

And destroyed vampires like him. Innocents invited tragedy because, well, beasts would be beasts and angels would ultimately suffer. Mark tried to freeze his heart as he strode forward, but the bitter lesson of his memories melted like cobwebs in the wind. Hunger rose in his blood.

The corners of Bree's mouth quirked up in a hesitant greeting. He was struck with yearning to kiss those wide, generous lips. He could tell they were warm, just like every part of her he'd already touched.

He squashed that thought before it took flight. A kiss would only end in complications. Neither of them needed that, especially when he might have to tell her she was going to lose her precious son. *Please, no.*

"Bree," he said softly, sitting next to her in the row of molded plastic chairs.

"Mark." Her hands twisted, fingers lacing and unlacing. "Or should I call you Doctor here?"

"Mark is fine." He reached over, stilling her hands. The bones felt delicate beneath his fingers. "I'll be honest. I still don't have a diagnosis for you, but I've sent some blood samples to an excellent laboratory in Los Angeles. They'll run whatever tests I ask for and not ask any questions."

Her eyebrows lifted, expressing skepticism and hope in one gesture. "Really?"

"Yes. It's a start. Depending on what those tell us, there are some other things we will probably want to do—we just don't know yet."

Her eyes clouded and she pulled her hands away. "We can't stay here. Those men who were following me—they'll check hospitals."

Again, Mark wondered if they'd been shooting at him or at her. "Who are they?"

She looked down. "Like I said, I don't have names. I'm really sorry you got caught up in this. You're kind. You don't deserve it."

"You said you witnessed a murder."

She shifted in the chair. "You don't understand how powerful they are."

You don't understand how powerful I am. "Tell me."

She bent her head, avoiding his eyes. "It's been like

this all along, from one coast to the other. And there
have been close calls. Jonathan and I got cornered in the
Chicago airport. They stuck both of us with needles full
of some sort of sleeping drug. The only thing that saved
us was that they got the dosage wrong. They didn't give
me enough. I woke up in the back of a van and managed
to get out with Jonathan. I was so scared." She covered
her face with her hands. "He didn't wake up for ages. I
started to wonder if he would."

Fury washed through him in a hot tide, followed by
hard suspicion. Why drug Bree and Jonathan and not
just kill them?

Her expression was bitter. "They're getting closer
every time they strike. One day we won't get away."

"You need a bigger city."

"Maybe." She looked away. "I've been through most
of them."

"I could take you to Los Angeles."

She shuddered slightly. "No, I— No. Not Los Angeles."

Clearly, something bad had happened there. "Seattle?"
She chewed her lip. "Maybe. For a while."

The implication being that it wouldn't work indefi-
nitely. No hiding place would. *What does she have—or
know—that someone wants so desperately?*

"I'll take you there," he said, almost before he had
made a conscious decision. "I need to catch a plane, anyway. I can do it from there." He'd just miss the one Raphael was sending for him and Larson. Oh well.

"You're going away? And here I was getting used to
personal service." Her tone was careless, but a lift in her
voice betrayed a hint of dismay. Then she laughed, shaking her head as if to clear away unwelcome thoughts.
"No, I travel alone."

"So do I." He gave a slight smile. "But it's just to Se-attle. A couple hours, then I'm on a plane and out of your life. I can leave you a contact number so you can call me to get the results of the tests. No matter what, I'm still your son's doctor."

She was silent.

"Are you okay with that?" Mark asked. "Am I being too pushy?"

"Of course you're not. I'm sorry. I'm not really this antisocial," she said, flushing.

"But the men with guns totally ruin cocktail hour. I get it. Take the ride, no strings attached."

"You're a kind man." She lowered her eyes. "Okay."

Then she looked up from under her lashes. Her gaze caught his, holding it while his gut squeezed with guilt. *Fiery hells, she's beautiful.* And she had no idea what he was. She was running away from one kind of killer and accepting help from another.

And right when Nicholas Ferrel was back in the pic-ture. It was like Mark's nightmare was unfolding again, and he was helpless to stop it.

Well, he'd get her settled in Seattle, and that would be it. There were other agents there who'd keep an eye on her if he asked. This didn't need to be complicated. It couldn't be.

Just then, Jonathan ran over, flopping into his moth-er's knees with a giggle. Bree laughed, too, her waves of honey-gold hair swinging with her as she scooped her son into her lap. The sound eased the tension in Mark's gut. If she could still laugh and Jonathan could still play, there was hope for them.

His cell phone rang. Mark rose, walking out of the playroom to get away from all that domestic bliss. He thumbed it to life. "Winspear."

"Hey." It was Kenyon.

"You have something?"

"I've just gotten started, but before I go any further, I have a photo for you to look at. Is this your girl?"

Mark's phone pinged. He tapped the photo and it filled the screen. He felt his eyes going wide. It was Bree, but looking very different. Her hair was the same, but she wore a lot of makeup and a very tiny sequined dress. He was tempted to head back to the playroom for a detailed comparison of all that smooth, white flesh. What would she feel like, warm and alive, half-naked and in his hands? He felt his fangs descending, his mouth suddenly filled with saliva.

He sucked in a deep breath, crushing those thoughts. "Yes, that's her."

"Holy hair balls," Kenyon groaned.

"Why?"

"You pick 'em, Winspear."

"I don't pick anyone. What are you talking about?"

"If there's a train wreck within a million miles, you'll put yourself on the scene."

"Stop talking and say something," Mark growled in icy tones. "Who is Bree?"

"Brianna Meadows. Daughter of Hank, also known as Henry Meadows of Henry Meadows Films."

Mark knew the man's work. Gorgeous sets, huge budgets, historical epics of doomed courage and noble sacrifice. Genius stuff, if you liked that sort of thing. Having lived the real deal, Mark didn't.

"And of course that's only the half of it."

Mark waited through a beat of silence. "Which means what?"

"Don't you ever watch *Gossip Quest TV News Mag-*

azine? She's the ex-mistress of Crown Prince Kyle of Vidon. That kid of hers is rumored to be his illegitimate son. She's unofficially on the Vidonese most-wanted list."

Chapter 6

Vampires were not made for road trips.

The red Lexus IS F Sport luxury sedan had specially tinted windows to block the sun, climate control, a V-8 engine that did zero to sixty miles in five seconds and a sound system calibrated to please extrasensitive hearing, but it was still a metal box on wheels. Mark needed to be outside, with the wind and sky. Free. Alone. He'd lost a good deal of patience along with his humanity, and what remained had been whittled away by the centuries that followed his Turning.

Speed was his only consolation, and the 416 horsepower motor of the Lexus was begging to give it. Except there were humans in the car, too fragile to risk on the twisting roads. Bree was dozing in the passenger seat next to him. Jonathan, wide-awake but silent in the back, clutched a stuffed duck.

Mark hadn't let on how much he knew, or that he was taking them straight to the Company safe house in Seattle, where they could be protected. Explaining about the Company without revealing the existence of the supernatural was a delicate business, and he wanted the right environment to do it. Bree had to be convinced the safe house, with its guns and rules and guards, wasn't a jail. If he got it wrong, she might bolt at the first gas station they stopped at, her ailing child in tow.

Mark cast a glance in the rearview mirror. The booster seat—pilfered out of the hospital lost and found—brought Jonathan just into view. The child met his eyes in the mirror. Mark was struck again by the watchful intelligence in that gaze. The kid didn't miss a thing.

He tried to see Prince Kyle in the boy's face. The dark hair and brown eyes were similar, but that was inconclusive. Maybe the shape of the eyes was the same, or the way his hair fell across his face, but he didn't exactly have a poster of the Crown Prince of Vidon taped to his locker door. He couldn't remember every feature.

Mark made himself smile at the boy and turned his attention back to the road. The sun was up but it was still early, the world fresh and tipped by frost. The rolling land was a rumpled blanket of evergreens patched with gold. The sky was a rich autumn-blue. It was going to be one of those fall days that seemed a parting gift from summer—and all that sun was giving him a splitting headache.

Mark had used the night to get Larson ready for his flight to Los Angeles and to attend to the files on his desk. Larson would be fine—at least from the bullet wound—but the hospital administration might perish from shock when they saw the completed paperwork the next morning.

The wait had served two other purposes. It gave Bree and Jonathan a real night's sleep, and surveillance teams were less likely to see them leave during the morning shift change. Mark had remained on the alert, but had seen nothing suspicious. If their pursuers were watching the hospital, hopefully they'd given them the slip.

Bree opened her eyes, stifling a yawn. She was still pale with fatigue, the freckles across her nose standing out. "Where are we?"

"We just passed through Sequim." He focused his attention on the ribbon of highway, ignoring her soft, female smell. Or trying to. He was getting horny and hungry, and wasn't sure which impulse was in the lead.

She turned around in her seat, checking on her son. "We should find a drive-through for breakfast."

The scent of woman was one thing. Tantalizing, dangerous, but good. Mark imagined the stench of human food trapped inside the car, and nearly shuddered. "No."

"Kids need to eat."

"Kids are sticky."

"He'll be hungry."

"I'm the driver."

Bree gave him a sharp glance that reproached him and acknowledged his position of power at the same time. "Fine. It's your car."

It was. With a dove-gray leather interior. And she'd managed to make him, a centuries-old monster, feel bad about it. He winced. "We can stop at the Gleeford Ferry. There's better food in town than just drive-through."

She sank back, turning her face to the side window until all he could see was her long, waving hair. Even it looked disgruntled. "This road we're on is barely a highway. Wouldn't it be faster to pick up the I-5?"

"Someone put Puget Sound in the way."

She made a small noise of impatience. "I guess we're farther out than I expected."

"We've only been driving an hour."

"It feels longer."

He realized she was nervous, but it was coming across as demanding. He stifled a growl. Being alone on his island was much easier. "There are fewer cars here. I can spot someone following us on this route."

With no further comments, Bree pulled a magazine out of her backpack and started flipping through it. From the corner of his eye, he saw it was one of those thick fashion rags. Each page turn was a sigh of impatience.

Flip. Flip. Flip.

Mark gripped the steering wheel, trying to ignore the sound. To make matters worse, Jonathan was humming tunelessly, thumping his stuffed duck against the car door. He clenched his teeth, summoning inner strength. *You are the lion. The hunter that strikes in the night. You have the patience of the leopard in the tree.*

Thump. Thump. Flip. La-la-la.

I'm not a thrice-damned cab driver. Another few hours, and he'd be alone again. Breathe deeply. No, then he smelled tasty woman. Open a window. Yeah, that was it.

This was his nightmare. Once before, he had been responsible for a woman and her young. The Knights of Vidon had destroyed them. *And I tore the first Nicholas Ferrel and his animals to pieces in retribution.* The centuries that followed had been a bloodbath, an endless feud of vampire against slayer as one act of violence demanded payback, then another.

But Mark had taken a different path since then, one of healing instead of death. He desperately wanted to stay on it.

Bree stopped turning pages, gazing out the window again. Her long fingers gripped the magazine so hard the tendons stood out along the backs of her hands. "You don't think anyone's following us now, do you?"

Mark cleared his throat. "Not that I've seen."

"What have you seen?"

"Two logging trucks and a pickup full of produce. Unless the gunmen are disguised as squash, we're safe for the time being."

"Good." The word was as packed full of meaning as her glance had been. "It's been a while since I had a few hours."

He looked over at her. He was wearing dark glasses despite the tinted windshield, and they washed the color out of her, leaving her in shades of gray. "You mean a few hours to not worry?"

She gave a quick, rueful smile. "To worry about one thing at a time. To focus on normal mom things, like breakfast. Clean clothes. I've been carrying this magazine around for weeks and haven't got past the first ten pages. Getting to read it feels like a scandalous luxury."

Something made Mark glance in the rearview mirror. Jonathan was watching his mother, picking up every word. Mark wondered how much of it he understood. Probably everything. Kids in trouble grew up fast. Maybe princelings on the lam grew even faster.

"Where's Jonathan's father in all this?" he asked.

"Nowhere." Bree said it quickly, opening up the magazine again. The word was the next best thing to a slamming door.

Mark watched the road, keeping his face turned straight ahead. They were getting near the ferry that would take them to Seattle. He should start laying a little groundwork to prepare Bree for the safe house. "It's a lot, raising a child on your own."

"Sure it is. But you do it, whether you're ready or not." Her voice was quietly matter-of-fact.

"The guy's a prince. He can afford child support."

Her hands froze midflip. "You know who I am."

Got you. Mark shifted his hands on the steering wheel, as if closing his grip on more than the car. "I figured it out."

"How?" She pulled herself straighter in the seat. "How did you know?"

"I have a good memory for faces." Which was true, though he'd made no connection between this woman and the celebutante who'd graced Crown Prince Kyle's arm four years ago. But now that he'd met Bree, there was no chance he'd ever forget her.

She slumped. "Sue me. I had my fifteen minutes of fame."

"You weren't the last girl Kyle showed a good time." There had been others, including the infamous Brandi Snap, who had nearly wrecked Prince Kyle's engagement to the much-beloved Princess Amelie of Marcari. "Does Kyle know about Jonathan?"

She gave him a dirty look. "They've never met."

"That's not what I asked."

"Oh, but everyone knows about him, don't they?" Her tone was steely enough to draw blood. "I worked hard to keep a low profile for a long time. Lived my life, raised my son. Then one day the paparazzi must have been having a slow week, because all of a sudden it was all over the papers—the prince's bimbo had a baby."

"Is that who you think is after you?"

"Photographers shoot with cameras, not guns." She toyed with the edges of the magazine, riffling the pages. "And Kyle isn't the one giving the order to chase us. He's a good guy, prince or not."

Mark was inclined to agree. As one of the Horsemen, he had crossed paths with the crowned heads of several kingdoms, including Prince Kyle. He'd seemed pretty levelheaded—but the fact that he'd had this woman and then let her get away—well, that was just foolish.

Mark turned her story over in his mind, still trying to match the glittering arm candy with the serious, frightened young woman next to him. "Let me play devil's advocate for a moment. A royal court is a well-oiled machine. Kyle is only one piece of it."

"What does that mean?"

"He might be a nice guy, but there are plenty of people at court who aren't. It's not just all parties and polo. Vidon has been at war with its neighbors off and on since the Crusades."

"But he always knew he would marry Princess Amelie from the kingdom next door. Their families have been fighting forever. He wanted to end the war and, from what he said, so did she. Marriage would unite Marcari and Vidon."

Her matter-of-fact tone surprised him. "You don't mind that he's marrying another woman?"

She shrugged. "He's a prince. He has to marry a princess. Besides, we were just friends."

Just friends. Not the statement he'd expected, but relief eased his shoulders. A silence fell over the car for a moment, leaving only the sound of the road and Jonathan's aimless humming. Mark struggled to tune it out. Whatever kept the kid from talking, it wasn't his vocal cords.

They passed through a tiny hamlet that was nothing but a gas station and a place that sold pies. A bored-looking horse swished flies and stared morosely over a broken-down fence. Mark checked the rearview mirror. Still no one tailing them.

"Your son can still be used as a pawn, even if he's not a legitimate heir."

Bree snapped the magazine shut. "He's not the heir. He's not Kyle's. I wish people would believe me."

"There are people who might benefit from saying he is."

"Seriously?" she scoffed. "These are tiny kingdoms. Nice, lots of Mediterranean beaches and all that, but Texas could swallow them both and leave room for snacks."

"Neither country is big, but the income from tourism, especially gambling, is huge."

"Still, how would kidnapping Jonathan help anyone?"

Mark wondered how much he should say, but decided she deserved the straight goods. "Not everyone wants the match between Vidon and Marcari. Their feud is so old, it's become a way of life for some people. Even a means of making money."

And then there was the whole supernatural issue. Amelie's father, the king of Marcari, had an old alliance with the vampires. The Company and the Horsemen had his personal support. But right next door, the vampire-slaying Knights of Vidon had kept the feud between the two nations alive—and had most recently left a fan letter in Mark's bedroom.

Which meant the his-and-hers sets of gunmen were probably the same people. Mark had to get her to the safe house, whether she liked it or not. He turned to Bree, who was biting her nails.

"Think about it," Mark said softly. "What if people believed Jonathan was the only heir? What if someone stopped Kyle's wedding to Amelie so there would be no real heirs?" *Or what if they killed the royal couple?* But Mark didn't want to say that out loud.

Bree gave him a look packed with excitement, reluctance and another emotion he couldn't name. "I didn't put everything together before now. What you say makes more sense than I want to admit to."

"Why?"

Her grave eyes held a glimmer of something he hadn't seen before—trust. "Someone tried to sabotage the wedding before. I was there, firsthand."

Mark tensed, his gut mirroring the conflicting emotions on her face. Knowing her story would connect them. Part of him wanted that. Another part wanted to run free, back to his island, untethered.

But that wasn't an option. He had a duty as a Horseman. Even more than that, Bree's vulnerable expression made him push on. "Before?"

"I used to work for a design firm. We got the commission to do the wedding clothes. Weird, eh? I was working on the outfits for my friend's celebrity wedding. My ex-boyfriend, if you believe the tabloids."

Mark nearly veered off the road. He knew this part of the story already. "There was a fire in the design studio. It destroyed the whole collection, except the wedding dress. That was found later." Mark had been one of the Horsemen who'd returned the gown to Princess Amelie. Jack Anderson, the Horseman called Death, had died doing it. *By all the fiery hells!*

Bree closed her eyes, suddenly looking excruciatingly young. "Yes, all the clothes for the wedding were burned up. Except for the dress." A tear leaked out from under her lashes.

"What is it?" Mark asked gently, although he felt a wave of anticipation surge through him. He was finally getting somewhere with her.

She opened her eyes, giving him a long, steady look. "You don't need to get any more involved than you are."

"The dress wasn't the whole story, was it?"

She sighed, giving in. "No. There was something else, another reason they might be tailing me besides Jonathan. My boss, Jessica Lark, was murdered before the fire was set."

So that was the murder she'd witnessed. Mark felt a chill go through him. "There were rumors that Lark had an assistant, but the name on the payroll records was a fake. There was no way to find out who you really were."

"I was hiding from the press. Jessica kept my real identity off the books as a favor, especially when it turned out that we were the ones working on the wedding designs. I wanted my work to be taken seriously and not regarded as fluff because I was a rich girl playing with fashion."

Mark felt a knot of suspicion forming in his gut. "You realize that doesn't look good. Everyone thinks you're the prince's ex. The wedding was sabotaged. Lark was murdered. You would have been the prime suspect."

"Yeah," she said, her voice growing hard. "I would be if you don't know the whole story. But think about it. The police are good at their jobs. The whole thing with Jessica's records slowed them down, sure, but the police should have been able to get past that."

"So why didn't they?"

She turned her face toward the window, speaking so softly he barely heard her, even with his excellent hearing. "The murderers don't want me in police custody. For some reason, they want me and Jonathan for themselves. And to keep hunting all this time, I think they must have a lot of resources."

Mark shifted his grip on the steering wheel. He had to get her to the safe house, and now it wasn't just for her safety. Jessica Lark had been one of the Company's agents. There would be questions. "Tell me the whole story."

Bree's mouth quavered and she bit her lip. "I was on the phone with Jessica when it happened. I heard the whole thing."

Chapter 7

"What happened?" Mark demanded. Jessica Lark had been his friend long ago. Long before Bree would have joined Lark's studio.

But Bree turned away, as if regretting her words. "Look, there's the ferry. We must be in Gleeford already."

"Tell me." His voice was nearly a snarl.

Her eyes were shuttered. "I've said too much already."

He wasn't sure how to answer that. When he thought of Lark, it was as more than a coworker. Mark didn't connect with people; he was too old, weary and wary both—but she had been different. "Jessica Lark loved animals, hated housework, didn't trust banks and was allergic to any kind of jewelry that wasn't pure gold or silver."

Bree made a sound that might have been a laugh. "She loved pretty things."

"She was a creative genius who everyone wanted to know but most found a little frightening. Anyone lucky enough to land in her bed quickly bored her but she was too soft-hearted to send them away. Does any of this sound familiar? Do you believe that I knew her and that she was important to me?"

Bree made a derisive noise. "All the men were in love with her. You, too, then."

"Not in the way you mean. But yes, I loved her. We knew each other a long, long time."

He caught her glance for a moment, and it was like seeing some small, frightened animal backing into its burrow. Bree was pulling away, giving in to her fear. Silence and running were the only survival tactics she knew.

Frustrated, Mark turned at the sign for the ferry. Ticket booths guarded a parking lot filled with cars waiting for the next boat to arrive. Puget Sound stretched before them, a broad silver swath of water rimmed in dark forest.

Mark pulled up to a ticket booth and lowered the window. "Two adults, one child."

"The next sailing's at ten twenty-five. You've got a forty-minute wait." The man took Mark's cash. He looked cold despite a Cowichan sweater under his coat. The wind off the water was brisk. "You may as well park and go for coffee."

"Where's a good place?"

"There's a shop that does its own roasting right over there." He pointed up at the road. "Good cinnamon rolls, too."

Mark thanked him and pulled ahead. There were about a dozen cars ahead of them already.

"Breakfast," Bree said, unbuckling her seat belt before the car had come to a full stop.

Mark caught her wrist. "I have questions."

She shrugged him off. "I need to eat. So does Jonathan. We can talk after."

Mark hesitated but gave in because she was right. Besides, he seemed to have her trust for the moment. Everything was going according to plan. There was no good reason to insist they stay with the car.

He waited for her to unbuckle Jonathan. The boy bounced out of the car like a joyous puppy, banging into Mark's knees. He caught the child before he could zip in front of a moving SUV. Automatically, he hoisted Jonathan into the air, making him gurgle with laughter, the wind tossing the waves of his soft, fine hair.

Memories. He'd done the same thing long ago in Parma—picking up his own son in the stable yard, keeping him out from under the horses' hooves. His son had laughed in just that way.

The image caught him off guard, a jab under the ribs that nearly made him stumble. He slammed into grief and anger he had long tried to forget. He set Jonathan back on his feet, but the boy clung to him as they walked toward the street, the feel of his tiny hand chaining him to the past. Mark wanted to pull his hand away, but stopped himself. The child was innocent. It was up to Mark to swallow down the pain.

Fear made another lap through his imagination, repeating what he already knew. The first Nicholas Ferrel had killed his wife and children over five hundred years ago. Now his descendant was prowling around, just when Mark had found this woman and child. *Surely I'm smarter now. Surely I can stop him this time.*

The threat could be anywhere. Mark tensed, opening his vampire senses to scan the quiet scene, tasting the wind for any hint of an enemy. A low growl thrummed deep in his chest. Jonathan gave him a curious look.

Fortunately, Bree didn't hear him. "This is the cutest town ever. And there's a quilt shop."

"I thought you wanted breakfast."

"Some women need pretty fabric the way others need air." But she turned into the coffee shop.

It was a long, narrow space with a few wooden tables and chairs. Most of the space was taken up by the coffee bar and glass cases of buns and pastries. Jonathan pressed himself against the glass like a determined squid.

"Isn't there anything with protein?" she muttered. "Too much sugar isn't good."

"There's milk," Mark suggested. "And I don't think one pastry will hurt. Surely his grandparents have spoiled him once in a while?"

"No." Her answer sounded cold and final.

No doting grandma and grandpa, then. Mark pondered that, and the frown that suddenly darkened her face. Bad memories?

Jonathan bounced on his toes and pointed to a tray of buns thick with nuts and frosting.

Bree huffed a sigh. "I shouldn't be feeding him that stuff. At least at a drive-through I could get something with eggs."

"Forgive yourself, and make the best choice from the available options."

"You sound like a self-help book."

"Does that mean I'm quotable?"

"Only when I'm feeding my child his own weight in sugar. Remember we'll be trapped with him for miles and miles while he burns it off."

Mark grunted in acknowledgment. "I'm sure I have duct tape in the trunk."

"Hey," said the young man who took their order. He was looking at Bree closely. "Are you somebody famous? I know you from somewhere."

She laughed easily. "My kid thinks I'm a rock star, but that's it, I'm afraid."

Mark shouldered his way forward to pay, blocking the young man's view of her. Bree picked up their tray and claimed a table for the three of them. As Mark waited for change, he watched Bree with fresh interest as she arranged food and drink and boy, every gesture quick and graceful. Jonathan sat down, grabbed a sticky bun as big as his head and tried to eat it all in one bite. Bree moved in for the rescue, napkin in hand.

Mark chose the chair closest to the shadows and sat down. He took a swallow of thick, strong coffee, feeling the caffeine hit his finely tuned vampire metabolism. Jonathan wasn't going to be the only one climbing the walls, but Mark needed to be on full alert.

Bree heard Jessica Lark die. How many people knew? Was there more to her sudden appearance on his island than met the eye? "The man named Bob. Your boat driver."

Bree looked up from cutting Jonathan's bun into socially acceptable chunks. "What about him?"

Mark waited while a man in coveralls shuffled past their table, bag of pastries in hand, before he answered. "I wonder if he knew Larson."

"He knew everyone. He knew every inch of every island."

Which meant he probably knew Mark's cabin. "I think he meant for me to find you."

"I found you, remember?"

"Whatever. The fact that we met drew both of us into the open. A sweet package deal. I think the reason he dropped you where he did, and the reason I was motivated by a letter I received to leave the cabin—well, it made somebody's work a lot easier. Now they get a two-for-one."

Bree frowned. "What are you saying?"

"We might both be targets. I knew Jessica Lark. We worked together. Not on fashion, but on other things."

Her eyes grew wider. "What kind of things?"

"Things that interest men with guns. We, uh, did a bit of freelance undercover work." It wasn't information he ever shared, but Bree's life, and Jonathan's, depended on getting out of this mess. The least he could do was sketch in a few details to help her. As a vampire, he could always erase her memory later.

"You mean you two were like spies?"

"Sort of."

Before Mark had joined the Horsemen's team, he and Lark had done a fair number of assignments together—a fey and a vampire posing as a beautiful couple, infiltrating the rich and famous. It had been easy for Mark, who had spent his youth as a courtier. Lark had been fun, vibrant, beautiful and very unpredictable. Not an ideal operative, but a fascinating female.

Bree leaned across the table, lowering her voice. "What else are you besides a doctor?"

"I have varied interests." He leaned forward, as well. It put her face only inches away, the blue-green of her eyes so clear that he could see the subtle shading of the irises. She smelled of warmth and life.

"You could have killed me when I pulled a gun on you."

"Yes."

Her lids lowered, her lashes sweeping the dusting of freckles that crept over her cheeks. He'd meant to reassure her, but it wasn't working. Tension pulled at the corners of her mouth. She was so afraid.

"Bree."

Those thick lashes lifted. Mark was aware of the chatter of other customers, the hiss of the coffeemaker, but that was all distant backdrop. He kept telling himself that he didn't want to become tangled in her story, but here he was—tangled. She seemed to step right over the circle he drew around himself. "I can protect you."

The hunger in Mark welled, reminding him that he wasn't just a human, and he wasn't just a healer. There was a flip side to him, a darkness that destroyed. That was his natural state, what lay beneath when the surface was scratched. He was appetite without end.

He never let that creature loose anymore. But now it battered against its iron cage, yearning to take the woman whose mouth was right there, so close he could already taste her. Her lips were wide and generous, giving her face an oddly vulnerable cast. Loneliness rose from her like a scent. Any predator could see she was cut off from the herd, alone and unprotected.

The temptation was too much. He let his mouth brush hers, a bare graze that mingled breaths more than flesh. His fangs ached, ready to spring free, but he held on with sheer will. This was not the time to feed, but only to sample.

He brushed her mouth again, this time catching that ripe lower lip in a playful tug. The sweetness of icing burst on his tongue, and beneath that the lush taste of woman. His whole body quickened with need, every cell urging him to savor her however he could.

As if catching his urgency, Bree turned the moment into a real kiss, moving her mouth under his. It was shy, almost chaste for a woman who had dominated every scandal rag on every continent. It was almost—Mark searched for the right word—innocent.

He clamped down on his hunger, forcing it away like an unruly cur dragged back to its kennel. He broke the kiss, suddenly light-headed, as if he had been starving for months and just been denied another meal.

Her blue-green eyes were watchful, as if considering what that kiss might have cost her. Not so innocent, then. Mark gripped his coffee cup, unable to drag his gaze from her face.

"That was unexpected," she said softly.

"I'm sorry." His voice sounded rough in his own ears.

Those lips quirked. "No apology necessary, but I'm not on the market."

"Neither am I. Just consider it a close call."

She laughed at that, not understanding the truth of his words.

Mark's cell phone rang and he nearly bolted out of his chair. He pulled it out and saw the caller ID. *Kenyon.* "I have to take this."

The cool air outside struck his face. Vampires rarely felt the cold, but this time it was almost soothing. He thumbed his cell to life. "What's up?"

"Where in the inky blackness of hell are you?"

"Gleeford."

"And you are not on Raphael's plane because?"

"I'm taking Bree and the kid to the safe house in Seattle. It'll be easier for them to hide there." But even as he said it, he knew that wasn't enough. It wasn't as though he could drop them off and wish them a nice life—especially not after that kiss. "She's in trouble. More than just because the Knights are after the kid."

Kenyon made a disgusted sound. "More than that? It must be bad. Those guys are like silverfish. They get everywhere."

"She was Lark's assistant."

There was a moment of silence before the werewolf replied. "Say that again. *The* assistant? The one who disappeared?"

A wave of impatience sharpened Mark's tone. "I thought you were running her profile. You didn't see anything that shows her involvement with Lark?"

"Not so much. From what I can see, she stayed pretty much off the grid after the break with Kyle. In fact, it looks like she more or less vanished."

So that much of what she said was true. "Bree claims she was on the phone with Jessica Lark when she was murdered."

The silence on the line was profound.

"I haven't been able to get more out of her than that," Mark added.

Kenyon cleared his throat. It sounded odd over the phone. "You have to bring them in."

"I'm taking them to the safe house. We should be there in a few hours."

"Good. I'll make sure they're ready for you. Whatever's going on, we're Bree's best chance."

Mark knew Kenyon was right. Still, he was beginning to realize the situation had risks—and he was the danger. He was too powerfully drawn to Bree. She wasn't just any woman—he could resist most with no problem. But she had inspired something deeper than ordinary lust or hunger, and that was treacherous for them both. He should walk away—leave before he took her, body and blood. Head back to his island.

He paced along the sidewalk beside the little row of shops. Awnings shaded a scatter of molded plastic chairs. Water dishes sat out for dogs, and flags fluttered in the steady cold breeze from the sound. It was all so normal, so human. So unlike the fractured creature he was—half demon, half hermit.

"Mark?" Kenyon's voice prodded.

He stood at the corner, watching the street. A silver Escalade was crawling down the road toward the ferry dock. Moving like the eyes behind the tinted glass were searching the streets. Instinctively, Mark stepped farther into the shadows. "I need you to run a license plate for me."

He rattled it off, waiting as keys tapped at the other end of the line. Kenyon gave a low whistle. "It's a 2011 Cadillac Escalade registered to Pyrrhus Enterprises. That's owned by Nicholas Ferrel."

Mark said nothing, letting his mind race.

"What are you going to do?" Kenyon asked.

Mark hung up before he thought of an answer.

Chapter 8

Mark dashed through the doorway of the café, nearly crashing into a couple carrying their lattes to go. Bree looked up, her face changing as she saw his expression.

"They're here." He didn't need to offer more explanation than that. She nodded once.

"Time to go," she said to Jonathan.

She reached for his arm, but the boy jerked away, not willing to leave the rest of his sticky bun behind. His glass of milk went tumbling.

But the boy caught it before more than a drop spilled. Mark stopped in his tracks, frozen by what he'd just seen. The boy had moved faster than even his vampire sight could follow. Intent on getting Jonathan into his jacket, Bree seemed not to have noticed. Mark shoved it from his mind. There were more immediate problems. As Bree was gathering up the last of their things, he herded them out of the coffee shop.

It wasn't fast enough. The Escalade had parked, and four men were emerging from the silver vehicle. They were fanning out, looking around for their quarry. Although he had never seen the man at the head of the group, Mark recognized Nicholas Ferrel at once. He was the exact image of his ancestor.

Ferrel was tall and fair, a hard expression making his face older than his years. The breeze ruffled his hair as he strode across the street on long legs. With an experienced eye, Mark spotted a holster beneath Ferrel's jacket and another at his ankle. In another time and place, Ferrel's ancestor had swaggered just so, his sword swinging from his hip. *He looked just like that before he took Anna and the boys. I mocked him that day, but he had his vengeance in the end.*

A stew of emotions flooded Mark, rage, weariness and dread for Bree and Jonathan. Mark stepped in front of them, using his body as a shield. *I will bleed them all before that happens again.*

"Go," he said to Bree. "Get Jonathan out of here. I'll keep them busy."

She gave him a startled look, but thankfully didn't argue. She was already in motion, throwing their coats over one arm and taking Jonathan's hand in hers. Smart woman. She was used to improvising. Wordlessly, she turned and vanished down the narrow alley between the café and the quilt shop, Jonathan in tow.

Mark turned to face the threat.

Bree's heart galloped with anxiety. Sweat trickled behind her ears even though the air was cool. And she wasn't moving quickly. There was no running fast with a four-year-old. Jonathan was too big to carry for long and too little to keep up with even a brisk walk. And he ran out of breath so fast these days.

She cast a glance over her shoulder. Through the narrow gap of the alley, she could see Mark, his tall, broad-shouldered stance radiating thinly repressed violence. He was squaring off with a tall blond man she thought she recognized—one of the men who had pursued her before—but Mark wasn't letting him pass.

Prickles of alarm ran up her back, a primitive response that held both fear and gratitude. She hurried faster. Why was he helping her? It made no sense. And yet, Jessica had been the same way, looking after her and her baby in a way no boss really needed to. Mark and Jessica seemed cut from the same cloth—a little too good-looking, a touch too perceptive and much too involved in a world of trouble. *Things that interest men with guns.*

She swore under her breath. *I can't help him. I'm not like that.* She would have to run off and leave him behind. That was clearly what he had in mind.

But that rankled even worse. If Mark was putting himself on the line for her, she could do no less. *But then what about Jonathan?*

She turned left at the end of the alley. Jonathan turned, tugging at her hand and pointing back at Mark.

Bree shook her head. "We have to go. He wants us to run away."

Jonathan frowned.

"He'll catch up."

The boy shook his head, curls flopping. Bree bit her lip. She didn't want to leave Mark, either, but there weren't a lot of options. Besides, she worked alone. If she'd stuck to her solo act, Mark would still be safe in his cabin. Of course, she and Jonathan would be dead of exposure or kidnapped by their enemies.

She crouched in front of Jonathan, groping for a plan. "We have to get to the car, but to do that we'll need to be very quiet and sneaky. Can we do that?"

Jonathan nodded, squeezing her hand in both of his. Bree felt a catch in her throat. Sometimes it was as if he'd lost his ability to speak only to grow more expressive. She pulled Jonathan close and hurried onward.

Bree turned the corner. This side of the street had mostly businesses, but there was a souvenir shop on the corner. She ducked inside, buying a baseball cap with a ferry on it. Then she stopped outside the store, letting everything she was carrying slip to the ground while she organized her thoughts. She pulled the cap on, stuffing her hair inside. Then she slid Mark's leather jacket over her fuzzy pink fleece one. If anyone was looking for a woman in pink with long blond hair, that at least was changed. Mark's sunglasses were in the pocket of his jacket. They were too big, but they hid her face well enough. Finally, she pulled out her cell phone.

"Okay, kiddo, let's go." She took Jonathan's hand again, ambling slowly toward the parking lot where the cars waited for the ferry. She could see the boat now, pulling up to the dock. Passengers were coming from every direction, finding their cars and preparing to leave. She didn't have a lot of time.

The Escalade was parked beside the entrance to the lot. One man was still inside, watching the road. Bree held her phone to her ear, blocking her face and carrying on a pretend conversation. She kept Jonathan on the other side of her, away from the lookout.

"Don't hurry," she said to the phone. "Don't rush, don't look around. Pretend you don't care what's happening around you. You have no cares in the world. None at all. Nope."

Jonathan pressed close, his little body almost a weight against her side. She slid an arm around him, taking comfort from his warmth. Sometimes she wasn't sure who looked after whom.

They were getting close to the Escalade. The sight of it made breathing hard, as if its sinister presence froze her lungs. She tried to force her mind to other things—the gulls in the sky, the splash of red in the sumac. Bathed in autumn sun, the town could have been a postcard come to life. But Bree only saw the silver car with its dark windows, and the shadow of the man inside.

She sauntered by, forcing herself to keep her pace relaxed as she talked nonsense into the phone. Her fingers were cold enough to chill her where they touched her cheek. *Steady, steady.* At any other time, she would have put some distance between her and the car by walking on the road, not on the sidewalk. But now, she dare not arouse their suspicion and forced herself to stay on the path. She half expected a hand to reach out and drag her inside the SUV. Every tug of the wind made her nerves skitter. The Escalade was so close, her sleeve brushed the mirror as she passed. Jonathan's short steps faltered. She stroked his hair, letting him know she understood.

They had gone halfway down the row of cars when she got up the nerve to glance over her shoulder. The Escalade door was open, the man standing behind it, watching her. She turned back, checking her location. Mark's vehicle was five cars ahead.

She pretended to end her call and started walking faster. Mark's car was three ahead now. Another glance told her the man was headed her way, with two more on his heels. She suddenly realized the Escalade had an extra row of seats. If she was counting right, they'd stuffed seven villains inside. Just her luck to get the bonus pack of baddies on her tail.

Bree was jogging now, dragging Jonathan behind her. They were at the Lexus, and she grabbed the door handle. Locked. Mark had locked the car. She needed the keys. She looked around, realizing how tightly packed the rows of cars were. They were locked out and blocked in.

Jonathan started to whimper. Bree looked up and realized their pursuers were bearing down in long, purposeful strides. They must have been watching the car, waiting for her to return. Her disguise had only bought them a few moments. Bree cursed her stupidity, stuffing her phone into the pocket of Mark's coat.

And feeling the brush of a key fob against her hand. Her ribs suddenly expanded as if the iron band of fear fell away. She'd clicked the fob before she even got it out of the pocket. The door locks clunked, and she pulled the back door open, lifting Jonathan inside and buckling him into the booster seat in record time. Then she scrambled around to the driver's door. Now the pursuers were only two cars away.

She slammed the locks shut and pushed the starter. The motor purred to life, obedient to her touch. Once upon a time, she'd had a Mercedes she'd driven around town like a bat out of Hades. Mark's sleek car gave her some of that attitude back. Bree pressed her lips together, relishing the spark of defiance suddenly fizzing in her veins.

Now was the moment things changed. Bree shifted into drive and started turning the wheel. She'd been running and running from one side of the continent to the other, and she was sick of it. She worked alone, but that didn't mean she'd abandon the one man who'd stuck his neck out to help her. These goons hadn't beaten her down that badly. Not yet. Not ever.

All she had to do was get the car back to the place she'd last seen Mark. He couldn't have gone that far. Not in this short a time.

So there wasn't a whole lot of space to maneuver the car out of the ferry line. She'd do her best. It would be too bad about the paint job, though.

Bree glanced in the rearview mirror at her son. "Mommy's going to run over the bad guys now. Are you ready, sweetie?"

Mark could scent Ferrel's apprehension. *Good.* Nerves made Ferrel sharp, but they also might make him leap to conclusions. Mark could use that. Anything to buy Bree and Jonathan a bit more time to get away.

He studied his enemy, the beast in him searching for weaknesses. The leader of the Knights, ancient order of slayers and sworn servants of the Royal House of Vidon, looked as if he had stepped out of a Ralph Lauren catalog—neat, pressed and casual with an edge of sophistication. His artfully windblown hair glinted gold in the autumn sun, the two-day beard shadowing the line of his jaw. Only his angry eyes looked raw and real. There was hate in Nicholas Ferrel. The rest was just packaging.

The hate made Mark's beast stir. It would be the man's strength and a weakness that Mark could exploit. For now, though, he had to string him along.

Ferrel's henchmen ranged themselves on either side of their leader, a tall man and a redhead to Mark's left, one with a Vandyke beard to the right. Mark barely registered their faces—not because they weren't impressive specimens, but Ferrel seemed to absorb all the energy around them into his rage. No one else counted.

The street was busy and none too wide for a show-down. Pedestrians carrying waffle cones passed behind Mark, chatting and laughing as if a vampire and four wannabe Van Helsings weren't glaring at each other like growly dogs. The four Knights stood along the line of parked cars, facing Mark. Someone pulled up, parking a Hummer. It forced Vandyke to step away from the curb, ruining the quartet's symmetry as he nearly collided with a baby stroller.

That was good. Anything to gain the psychological advantage.

Mark made a show of looking Ferrel over. "So you're the new head of the Knights. Congrats on the promotion."

"Spare me your pleasantries. Where are the woman and her child?" Ferrel's voice was pleasantly pitched, fluid as a radio announcer's.

"They are elsewhere." Mark bit out the words, investing them with all his wrath.

"You cannot hide them for long. We have eyes everywhere. Technology has granted humankind powers almost equal to yours, demon kin. You are no longer the supreme hunters. The Knights even undergo training that boosts our natural immunity to your hypnotic powers."

Cold crept through Mark's bones, as if the shadows were plucking at him. His answer came in a low, quiet rasp. "Remind me of that when I'm bending your neck to my teeth."

Ferrel gave him a frown. "Spoken like the devil you are."

A passerby with a camera around his neck gave Mark and Ferrel a curious glance. Neither looked at the tourist, but Mark reminded himself to watch his tongue in front of the humans. This was a public place. He had to use his brain, not his fangs.

"I could tell jokes if you like. How many zombies does it take to change a lightbulb?"

"Silence!"

Mark wondered how far Bree had gotten. He wouldn't be able to keep Ferrel talking for very long. "Would you prefer knock-knock jokes? Or go old school with quotations from Punchinello? After one has lived as long as I have, one amasses quite the repertoire."

"Silence!" Ferrel repeated. "You will tell me what I want to know."

Try me, slayer.

As if reading his thoughts, the one with the Vandyke beard tried to edge past Mark. With a grunt of satisfaction, he sidestepped into the man's path and roughly shoved him back. The sheer physicality of it felt good. Doing was always better than talking—and deep inside he remembered that he was designed to kill.

"Is that the best you've got, Ferrel?" he snarled. With part of his mind, he realized the people on the street were giving them a wide berth now. Their showdown was attracting attention. *Be careful.*

Ferrel bristled. "I'm better than you, bloodsucker."

"At knitting?"

The man's hand lingered around the lump under his jacket. A holster. Knights of Vidon used silver bullets, good for anything: human, vampire or werewolf. Mark's beast stirred, restless beneath a fresh wave of anger.

Mark dropped his voice. "Why do this, Ferrel? Why send me the note? Why not just kill us all on the island?"

"Because that's not the object of the game," Ferrel replied in a tone that said he was stating the obvious. "I want the woman and her son alive, and I want you to know they're in my power because you failed, vampire. You've already brought them to me. You've played right into my hands. All that's left is your shame and destruction."

Weariness and rage overtook Mark. "Because I killed your ancestor five centuries ago? And then your kin killed my family? And I killed more of yours? Or did I get the order of events wrong, and your kin killed mine first? It's been too long to make any difference. Give it up."

"No difference in your mind, perhaps," Ferrel replied. "The Knights have a longer memory."

"That was hundreds of years before you were born. Vendettas went out of style, right along with codpieces and hats with bells."

Ferrel's face went colder still. "Vendettas? This is more than a family feud. I am a Knight of Vidon, and you are demon-spawn. I am sworn to end you. The blood spilled between us just makes it personal."

If anyone had a personal stake in this, it was Mark. He'd been there—not that fact mattered in the ceaseless battle between vampires and slayers. They were two wolves locked in a fight neither could win. "We don't have to do this." The words had to be said.

"Do you think so? Do you think playing doctor will cleanse your sins, vampire?" Ferrel smiled, but it wasn't happy. The next words were so quiet, Mark would have missed them if he had been a human. "If I locked you in a cage with no one to prey on, how long would it be before you'd drain the first human unlucky enough to wander too close to the bars? Days? Weeks? No more than that."

Mark was too aware of the people all around. Kids. Mothers. A man walking briskly along with his briefcase. "Not the place for this conversation."

Ferrel drew his gun. So did his three sidekicks. Mark's beast seized control of his reactions. He sprang over their heads, landing on the roof of the Hummer. He crouched, tension thrumming through him, ready to leap and run. If he drew his own weapon, that would start a firefight. Someone would get shot, maybe killed. Probably some local kid.

Unfortunately, three of the very humans he was trying to save were pulling out their smartphones. If he wasn't careful, he was going to star in an online video.

Tension built in the air, like a brewing storm or static electricity. It pulsed through his skull, making his molars ache.

"But you enjoy the violence, don't you?" Ferrel said softly. "It's more than the blood you want. You all have a taste for the kill. So do we."

Ferrel pulled the trigger. A woman screamed as the Hummer's windshield fell to a rain of glass chips. Mark was already in the air, then landed on the roof of the coffee shop, rolling to his feet to see the Knights wheeling around in consternation. The car alarm began blaring into the chill, sunny morning. Crouching as low as he could, Mark sheltered behind the false front that ran along the roofline. The bystanders were running now, cameras forgotten until they found cover.

Mark swore viciously. Shooting in public? Was Ferrel just extracrazy—which appeared to be a given—or had the Knights given up the tacit agreement to keep the war between the supernatural and the slayers out of the public eye? Or did he think bystanders meant that Mark wouldn't fight back? That was true, up to a point.

Mark reached for his own gun, wondering how to make an exit. Every human had vanished, or so he thought. Then his eye caught what had to be the local lawman, hurrying down the street with a too-much-mac-and-cheese swagger. *Oh, crap.*

"What's your damage, Ferrel?" Mark bellowed. "How can we end this?"

"Where are the woman and child?"

I want you to know they're in my power because you failed, vampire. Ferrel meant to give the feud between them renewed viciousness. Mark said nothing, a hard, cold anger clogging his throat. He had backed away from the endless cycle of revenge. Became a doctor. Gone to his island. That didn't mean he was over what the first Nicholas Ferrel had done to his wife and boys.

Ferrel was aiming at the roof. "Hand the woman and her brat over. You have no right to them. They're not yours to protect!"

Up till that moment, a piece of Mark had done his best to believe that. But from his vantage point, he saw his Lexus screaming the wrong way out the entrance of the ferry parking lot. Mark blinked, not quite believing his eyes. Uniformed men were piling out of the ticket booths, waving their arms. The car swerved a fishtailing right turn and tore down the street toward them.

The driver was wearing a baseball cap, but Mark's sharp eyesight caught the features. He'd know the determined set of that wide, expressive mouth anywhere. Bree's face was swiveling side to side, searching the street. Looking for him. By the darkest hells, *she* was coming to save *him*. Amazement blossomed in his chest, and he almost laughed out loud.

"She's just made herself mine to fight for," he said under his breath.

He waited, calculating the exact second the Lexus passed. His muscles ached with the urge to spring too soon, the beast's desire to be free, but he forced himself to obey. *Control.*

The lawman was getting closer, shouting into a radio strapped to his shoulder. Bree was getting closer, but now Mark was pinned between the police and the enemy. He would have to be quick and accurate. He would have to count on Bree's steady nerves. He silently pleaded with her to look up, to see him there on the roof.

The lawman was yelling at Ferrel and company. Now everybody had their guns out. Mark's muscles twitched.

At last, the Lexus was almost directly ahead. Bree glanced up, nearly driving into a lamppost when she saw him on the roof.

He leaped, landing on the hood. The car skidded, making him grab on so hard his fingers dented the metal.

"They're human," Ferrel shouted. "You'll destroy them in the end!"

But Bree kept speeding toward the road out of town. Another volley of bullets splattered the street, followed by sirens. The local lawman had apparently called his friends. Mark flattened himself on the roof. If he was stuck on top like a roof rack, a high-speed chase would suck.

Then the passenger window hummed open. Relief washed through him.

Jonathan squealed in delight as Mark swung his legs inside and slid into the seat. At that speed, it was a very good thing he had a vampire's brute strength and agility.

"Nice move," Bree said, steaming onto the highway out of town with a squeal of rubber.

"Thanks." Superhuman or not, he reached for the seat belt. She was driving like a werelion on catnip.

"Sorry about the paint job," she added.

"We'll talk about that later."

She shot him a sidelong look, but Mark ignored it,

staring moodily out the window and listening to the sirens. *You'll destroy them in the end.* A sudden weakness made his stomach roll. *No.* It didn't have to end that way. Not again.

Chapter 9

Bree stepped closer to the counter at the convenience store, straining her ears to catch the news report about the incident at the ferry terminal. It had only been hours ago, but already a confused account was circulating about how the villains had got away despite the police. Apparently Ferrel had given the cops a merry chase after Bree had blown the scene. She was almost sorry she'd missed it.

The sound of the reporter's voice, live from the scene, made her stomach tighten. She hated, hated, hated reporters only slightly less than she hated every idiot with a cell phone camera and the notion that they were entitled to play paparazzi at her son's expense. Not that any of the bystanders at Gleeford knew a thing about her son, but her protective instincts surged to the fore. She kept listening, waiting for any mention of Jonathan, but there was nothing. They did mention Mark's dramatic leap to freedom, though. That was almost as bad.

Unfortunately, the bottom line was that Nicholas Ferrel and his happy band of psychopaths were still on their tail. *Nicholas Ferrel.* All this time, the men chasing her had been shadows, nameless bogeymen hiding under the bed. Now they were individuals. Knowing Ferrel's name did nothing to ease her fears.

The broadcast changed to a cheerful country song as Mark paid for their bag of groceries. Jonathan peered over the edge of the counter to watch the clerk bag the prefab sandwiches and containers of yogurt. The man kept giving the boy sorrowful glances. Even he could see her son was ill. Bree closed her eyes, feeling as though she was dying by inches.

To make matters worse, there was a security camera on the wall above the till. Assuming the thing worked, it was just one more way someone could track where they'd been. This was a nightmare. There was no way she regretted saving Mark, but her actions had drawn the attention of the police. They were fugitives from them now, too.

The only plan they'd made so far was to get as far away from Gleeford as they could, which meant heading west.

Brows drawn into his habitual scowl, Mark pocketed his change, picked up the bag and walked toward the door. Jonathan was on his heels, playing with a plastic dinosaur.

"Did we pay for that?" she asked her son as they drew near. Jonathan was at that age where ownership and theft were still fuzzy concepts.

"I did." Mark pushed open the door, making the bell ring. "He liked the T. rex best."

Jonathan made a gleeful roaring noise, baring his teeth.

Something about it put Bree on edge. She was already anxious, not sure where she stood after what had just happened. Kissing. Shooting. A wild escape. Nothing in the dating advice columns on how to handle that one. Oddly, it was the kiss her mind kept returning to, the feel of his lips caressing hers. She had always been confident with men—okay, confident that men wanted her—but had been pretty good at handling herself once she'd gotten out of the disastrous high school phase. Mark was a different case. She'd done her best to avoid getting involved, and now she felt like she had stepped off a cliff. She could picture herself floundering, arms flailing as she hurtled toward disaster.

It made her uneasy and snappish. "When I was his age, I had a stuffed lamb."

"He's a boy," Mark said with almost a laugh. It was the first sign of amusement she'd seen since they'd started this journey.

"He's a baby. And he's sick. I don't want him…"

"Pretending to be a monster?" The statement had a cutting edge, though she wasn't sure why. "Be grateful it's dinosaurs and not guns."

"Why does it have to be anything violent at all?"

They stopped a few feet from the car, taking the moment to truly look at one another. Mark was still radiating a muted ferocity, as if he hadn't quite calmed down from the confrontation with Ferrel. His hands were at his sides, his fingers so tense they were half curled into claws. His eyes were hidden behind the shades, but his jaw bunched as he clenched his teeth. Was this the same man whom she had kissed? She edged forward half a step, putting a hand on his arm. The muscle beneath his sleeve was ropy with tension. "I'm sorry. I didn't mean to sound snappish."

"It's okay. It's been a busy day." His tone was ironic.

Bree shifted uneasily. "I wouldn't blame you if you wanted out. You don't have to risk yourself for our sake."

He made a sound of impatience, stepping away from her touch. "I have to make a call. We need to change cars."

Fine. An ache of confusion wrapped her chest, making her sigh hurt. Bree looked around at the tiny town they'd stopped in. There was the gas station, a few houses and what looked like a saloon. There were even hitching posts in front of it, but no rent-a-car business or even a sign to say where they were.

Mark prowled out to the road, talking on his cell while Jonathan walked the T. rex up the side of the Lexus and made growling sounds. He'd taken to Mark. Perhaps a smart mother would keep him away from her son, try to cushion the inevitable shock when Mark went his way and they went theirs. But she'd made a different choice by going back for the man. She just prayed it wasn't a bad one.

Bree watched the two males, one tiny and vulnerable, the other anything but. Mark stood at the edge of the road, one hand on his hip, his shoulders tensed as if he wasn't pleased with the conversation. She wouldn't have wanted to be whoever was at the other end of the line. She couldn't make out the words, but she heard the gruff tone of his voice.

He turned the phone off and stalked toward her, his mouth a grim line.

"What's wrong?" she asked.

He gave a quick shake of his head and pulled open the car door. "We're going to have to change rides farther on. There's no place here with anything besides tractors for rent."

His disgust was almost comical. She buckled her son into the backseat. "Doesn't your secret spy agency or whatever it is you work for have vehicles stashed all over the place?"

"Yes. In Paris. Toronto. St. Petersburg. Places bigger than your average flyspeck." He started the engine. "James Bond wasn't forced to buy ham sandwiches at a Dodgymart in the back of beyond."

"And Ursula Andress didn't have to live on ham sandwiches and animal crackers." Bree dragged the shopping bag out of the backseat and rummaged inside. "Or cheese twirls or cola. I thought doctors were into nutrition."

"There's milk and yogurt," he said, still sounding grumpy.

She pulled out one of the yogurts. Coffee-flavored. Jonathan would never touch it, so she peeled off the foil and found a plastic spoon. The stuff tasted like something she'd use to clean the sink, but she wasn't going to whine. "Thank you."

"You've got to eat."

And she was just about out of ready cash, and that slim wad of bills was all that was left of her savings. Sure, her parents had money, but she'd learned the hard way that she couldn't trust their staff. They'd give her away to whoever offered them the next promotion, the phone number of an agent—heck, the latest in handbags. There was no looking to home for help. The thought disappointed her, but she was used to it. She'd never really gotten help there.

"It's more than just feeding us," Bree said, wanting to show her gratitude and yet afraid of ruining their tenuous alliance by saying too much. "You're going above and beyond."

He gave her one of his inscrutable glances. The dark

glasses hid his eyes, but not the tension of his sharply angled jaw. "I'll be frank. I will protect you, but I've been in this position before. These are very, very bad men."

"So I've noticed." *He's afraid of screwing up.* No wonder he was in such a bad mood.

"If you're so bent on thanking me, then how about some payback. Tell me how you got into this mess."

She tensed, sitting up in the seat so that her back barely touched the upholstery. "Um."

"Surely you trust me by now?" Mark said, sounding resigned.

Without thinking, she put her hand on his arm again. This time, though, he didn't pull away. The car didn't leave room for that. "These aren't all my secrets. Some of what happened isn't mine to share."

"At least tell me what you think won't make a difference."

"Like what?"

The corners of his mouth turned down as he thought. Her lips twitched, tempted to brush away that frown.

He had kissed her, and it had been wild and hungry. The memory of it made her ache with wanting the moment all over again. The men she knew didn't kiss like that—as if the soul of a wild mountain cat had taken the body of a man while in search of its mate. Maybe she could tame him with sweetness, and he would hold her and make her feel safe again. Yeah, right. Like that ever really happened. She wanted to believe it so badly, her chest hurt.

"How did you meet Kyle?" he asked.

This time, his hand reached out, tentatively brushing her knee. She could feel his fingertips through the threadbare cloth, a hint of skin on skin. For a moment, her mind went blank. "Kyle?" she repeated numbly.

How was he relevant? But then she realized that meeting the prince was the beginning. That was when her life had started to change.

About six years ago, she'd first met Kyle at one of her father's parties. Her dad had invited the world and then some, celebrating the triumph of his studio's latest blockbuster release. Her mom was doing her international corporate lawyer thing in The Hague. At loose ends, Bree was free to amuse herself among the rich and famous.

Kyle Alphonse Adraio, Crown Prince of Vidon, looked more like a soap opera star than he did royalty. Breathtakingly handsome, his clothes were casual, his brown hair curled past his collar and he was always ready to laugh. According to the gossip magazines, he was an avid sportsman. However, from what she'd seen so far that night, his main hobby seemed to be women.

"Greetings, Miss Meadows," Kyle had said in accented but otherwise perfect English. "I am very pleased to find you here. I am hoping you will spare me a moment of your time."

"And what would you want with me?" she'd replied. "Your Royal Highness." Her tone had been dry as the bartender's best martini.

One corner of his mouth had quirked up even as his eyes roved over the silver sequins of her dress. "You do not wish me to buy you a drink?"

"First of all, this is my dad's party. I can have all the alcohol I can hold and then some, except I don't drink anymore. And second, the women here aren't on a buy-ten-get-one-free punch card. You don't need to pick up every girl in the room."

His expression had gone from offended to surprised to amused. "You've been watching."

"You're kind of an artist. In a sleazy way."

"Princes aren't sleazy."

"Oh, c'mon." She'd picked up her mineral water, giving him a cool glance over the rim. "Look around the room. Everyone here is sleazy. You're just fitting in."

And he'd laughed. They'd spent the rest of the night laughing, and every night after that. Kyle was good, undemanding company—not at all the spoiled princeling she'd expected. Then again, he'd been at a turning point in his life, too, moving from playboy to young statesman.

Watching him come to terms with his own future had made her think about what she was doing with her life. She'd gone through art college, earning a diploma, a few DUIs and rehab. She was going nowhere fast.

"What about your parents?" Mark interrupted, nearly startling her.

"What about them?" Bree tried not to think about her folks. "They didn't care what I did with myself. It was my friend Adam who got me into a program when I came home drunk once too often. He made me stay sober, and I kept my promise." It was the last promise she'd ever made to him.

"Oh?" Mark's tone was curious.

She could satisfy that curiosity, or she could go on with the story. She picked door number two.

On a whim Bree went with Kyle to New York for the February fashion week, and there they had met Jessica Lark. Bree had taken one look at Jessica's runway collection and been smitten.

"I want to do exactly what she's doing," she declared to Kyle. The tipping point had been the green silk ensemble with the harem pants and passementerie detailing. It should have been too much, but Lark had made it look so casually elegant Bree's mouth had actually watered.

"Don't you have to go to school to do that?" he asked mildly.

Her reply was instant and passionate. "I can draw. I know clothes. I can do that."

"Then let's talk to her," he said with his characteristic shrug, and took Bree's hand to steer her through the crush of fashionistas.

By the time they'd walked out of the venue, Kyle had talked Lark into giving Bree a job in her atelier. Royalty had its privileges. The rest, he'd said, in the nicest way possible, was up to Bree. That was Kyle. He was generous to a fault, yet somehow managed to make people deserve whatever he gave them.

"It was the happiest time of my life," Bree finished. "I grabbed that chance and worked like a mad fool. Jessica was strict, but for once I had something to be proud of. She taught me everything, and I was good."

That made what came after all the harder, when all her dreams had died on the other end of the phone.

Bree realized she was sobbing. She looked over her shoulder, afraid Jonathan would be upset, but the boy was asleep, lulled by the motion of the car. Mark pulled over to the shoulder of the road, his face as neutral as ever. She'd never cried about any of this, not until now. She'd loved Jessica, but she'd had to be strong for Jonathan. If she'd faltered, they might have died. There had never been a safe moment to grieve. There had never been anyone like Mark.

He turned off the motor. "Bree."

She couldn't look up. Memories were pounding at her, and she could only sit still and mute, praying they didn't crush the armor she'd built around her heart. If they did, it would end her.

She heard the rustle of clothes as he reached over, then felt his touch, sure and firm and gentle as his arms slipped around her shoulders. There was nothing tentative now, no pulling back. He drew her close, folding her against him with rough tenderness until her tears were done.

It made a new memory of the soft, worn leather of his coat against her cheek, and the gentle stroking of his fingers in her hair.

Chapter 10

Worn-out from crying, Bree let her eyes drift closed and missed the name of the next place they stopped—but it had a car dealership. When she came out of her doze, Mark was making the arrangements to rent a vehicle and to park his Lexus until someone could pick it up. From the snatches of conversation she overheard, Bree was fairly sure he was using fake ID.

Who is he, anyway? She was still reeling from her tears and the way he'd held her. He was a doctor, yes, but there was nothing of the laboratory and white coat in that moment. Nor had that been the embrace of the man with the fake ID and cabinet of guns. For a moment, she might have glimpsed something unguarded, the real Mark behind all his carefully crafted identities. She wondered if it would ever happen again.

She let Jonathan out of his car seat for a trip to the little boy's room. He'd been quiet for the past hour. It had been a relief. Children his age were rarely completely silent, always squirming or singing and always at play. Or healthy children were.

Now Jonathan was listless with dark circles that stood out like bruises under his eyes. Worry clutched her with sharp talons.

"He's spiked a fever," she said anxiously, pushing the boy's dark hair away from his flushed face.

Mark stuffed the rental papers for their next car into his pocket and crouched beside them in that eerily graceful way he had. The grim set of his face softened, though it was still serious as he felt for a pulse.

He rose, pulling out his phone. Bree watched his face as he continued the cursory exam one-handed, waiting for someone to pick up at the other end. His expression changed when someone answered. "Are the labs back yet?" he demanded before even saying hello. Then he listened with a crease between his eyebrows. "Are you sure about that last result? Who logged that test?"

Bree bit her thumbnail as she waited, helpless. She could feel the pressure of tears behind her eyes as she watched her son let himself be prodded and poked with the mute acceptance of the sick. He'd been doing so well ever since the plane ride, but that boost of energy had obviously faded. Jonathan blinked wearily, the plastic dinosaur clutched in one hand. With a wrench of guilt, she thought how he had been growing sicker in the backseat while she prattled on about Kyle, reliving the glorious time before she was responsible for anything but her own future. Some mother she was.

Mark got off the phone.

"Is there anything we can do for him? What did the tests say?" The words came out in a panicky rush. Then came more tears, silently rolling down her cheeks. She brushed them away angrily.

"Hey." Mark slid back into the car. "Not all the test results are back yet. I don't want to say too much until I have all the facts."

"Can you say anything at all?"

He hesitated. "There's anemia. We can treat that, but we can't determine the cause until we know more."

"That's it? That's all you found out?" Bree heard her voice going shrill. Frustration clawed at her.

Mark touched her hand, his cool fingers gentle. "I have theories. They're useless without hard data. But so far I have no reason to believe that I can't cure Jonathan. Okay?"

Mark's voice was soothing, almost hypnotic. He took off the sunglasses, squinting against the bright sun. His skin looked flushed, as if the sun bothered it, but his eyes were a lovely, liquid brown, darker than chocolate. More like the near-black of pure, strong coffee and just as much a grown-up drink. Even as he looked down at her, his expression sympathetic, her body responded in a very adult way. It brought heat to her face, half of it shame. Her boy needed help. This wasn't the time to worry about how she felt about the doctor—or spy, or whatever he was—as a man.

But his face was so close to hers, she caught the scent of his skin. It was unique, musky and very male. She needed to move away before she forgot everything else. He reached up, brushing away her tears with his thumb. Then he leaned over, kissing the place where the wetness had been. Bree caught her breath, suddenly electrified, but the kiss was over before she could do more than gasp.

"If you move our luggage to that car," he said, nodding toward a bland-looking station wagon and handing her the keys, "I'll head to the drugstore. I think I can come up with a mix of things that will help until we get where we're going."

"Which is?"

He dropped his voice. "I need to make one more phone call, then I'll have a plan."

Bree nodded mutely, willing to put her fate in his hands, at least for another five minutes. They barely had any luggage, so moving it and the car seat was a short job.

The wagon was one of the few cars on the lot with a tinted windshield. Still, it had been sitting in the sun, so she opened a window to let in some fresh air. The warmth made her want to lie down and sleep. Instead, she sat in the backseat, Jonathan stretched out with his head in her lap, and waited for Mark to return.

She stroked Jonathan's hair, her gaze lingering over his features. They were so familiar, and yet they changed almost daily as he made the inexorable march from child to man. She could see so much of his father there, in the chin and the set of his eyes. Jonathan stirred, his eyelids flickering in that twilight zone between sleep and waking. Bree wished she could curl herself around him, shelter him with her own blood and bone against every shadow.

And the shadows had come thick and fast in his short life. The first years in New York had been good, when she had worked for Jessica and cared for her baby.

Telling Mark about Kyle had opened a floodgate. She wanted to close it back up, push away those memories, but they were part of this terrible present. She would not be on the run if it hadn't been for what happened back then. Jonathan wouldn't be so far from help.

The first signs of trouble came when they had started work on Princess Amelie's trousseau. Jessica had told her people were watching the atelier. By then, Bree had changed her appearance and her name, vanishing from the public eye. She had assumed whoever was hanging around were just fashion hounds, trying to get the scoop on the design of the wedding dress. Annoying, but hardly life-and-death.

Or so she'd thought. Like many designers, Jessica had kept a sketchbook of her ideas. When she'd started one for the wedding clothes, she'd begun locking it up every night in the safe. No big surprise there. The wedding was the media event of the year. Whatever Amelie wore would set the trend for years to come, and the first company to manufacture look-alike garments would make a fortune.

But then came the bad night.

Bree's mind veered away from it, not wanting to open that door again. Every time she did, it left her cold and shaky—and yet remembering held the key to what was happening now. She had to face it.

No. Bree looked out the car window at the bright autumn sunshine. Mark was handing over the keys to the Lexus. As always, he was keeping to the shadows, a habit she'd noticed almost at once. He burned easily and said the sun gave him headaches, with a stabbing pain through the eyes.

Someone else had said that—Jessica's friend, Jack. He'd worn the exact same style of dark glasses that day in New York. *The memory won't leave me alone.*

Jessica had met with Jack Anderson that day. Unlike most of her meetings, the office door had been closed. When he'd left, the man had been upset, almost angry, though he had been scrupulously polite to the staff. Curious, Bree had cornered her boss before she'd had a chance to close her door again.

Bree could still see her now, just as vibrant as the last time Bree saw her. Jessica Lark was a slim, elegant woman with a tumble of mahogany hair. She was sitting very upright, almost dwarfed by the antique desk. Behind her, the large windows of the old building filled the wall. The summer light was fading outside, the glittering marvel of the city skyline winking to life as Manhattan traffic rumbled and honked below.

"What did he want?" Bree had asked.

"Jack's doing me a favor," Jessica had said with a quick, bleak smile. "I've given him the wedding dress."

Thunderstruck, Bree had sat down in one of the office chairs. "Why?"

Instead of answering, Jessica had pushed the design book across the desk. "Take that home with you tonight."

Bree had drawn a breath, about to ask why again, when Jessica's look had stopped her.

"Just do it," Jessica had said. "Do it for me."

Bree had. The atelier had burned to the ground that night. Somehow Jessica had known and had saved the collection. Unfortunately, she hadn't saved herself.

Mark rapped on the windshield, making Bree jump. Jonathan woke with a whimper. The door opened and the doctor leaned in. "Is he awake enough to drink something?"

Bree sat Jonathan up. Mark had a half-pint carton of chocolate milk and was crushing pills into it, using just his fingers to pulverize each tablet to a fine dust. Bree blinked at that, stunned by the strength in his long, fine fingers. Then he pinched the top of the carton tight and shook it up before sticking a straw in the top and giving it to Bree. "Make sure he drinks it all."

"What did you put in it?"

"Mostly iron. His count is extremely low. It should help."

"For how long?"

"Long enough to get where we're going. I know you said you didn't want to go to Los Angeles, but it's his best chance." His grim expression was back. "The clinic there will have the equipment I need for conclusive tests."

"Los Angeles?" It had been the scene of so much unhappiness in her life.

His tone gave no room for argument. "It's where we'll all be the safest."

Bree's heart pounded with alarm. Would they make it that far? She tried to keep her voice level as she guided the straw to Jonathan's mouth. "That's a long way."

"We can share the driving till my friend can arrange a plane or a chopper to pick us up."

"Why not just get a regular flight?" But she knew the answer the moment she said it. After the incident at Gleeford, the police wanted them for questioning. They'd never make it through an airport.

"By car we can stay off the beaten track." He turned to look at her and Jonathan curled up in the backseat. "Buckle up. After my car, this ride is going to suck."

Bree got Jonathan settled into the car seat. Mark got in the driver's seat and turned the key. The station wagon sputtered to life with a cough like a pack-a-day smoker. She couldn't help smiling at his disgusted expression. "It's an honorable man who will abandon his Lexus in the service of the greater good."

Mark flinched. "I'm not abandoning her. I'm keeping her out of harm's way. Her paint's already been wounded."

They rode in silence for a few minutes as Bree got the rest of the chocolate milk into Jonathan. For all Mark's complaining, the wagon moved at a good clip.

Mark caught her gaze in the rearview mirror. "Did

you ever meet my friend Jack Anderson?" The question sounded wistful.

"The one who took the dress. Yes. He seemed nice." And then he'd died. Another sad story.

"How did he come to have it?" Mark asked. "If you don't mind. Like I said, he was a friend."

She stroked Jonathan's hair. He'd fallen asleep clutching the plastic dinosaur Mark had given him. The little toy snarled back at her with painted white teeth. *If you want to protect a treasure, ask a dragon.*

She knew who her treasure was. She still wasn't completely sure about the guardian. They'd only just met. "Like I said, these aren't all my tales. I don't have the right to say everything."

But Bree had already started to tell her story. Now she felt the rest of it pressing against her, wanting to get out. She was at a crossroad where secrets weren't helping her anymore.

"Jessica gave him the dress for safekeeping," she said. "The bodice was covered with the Marcari diamonds."

"I know," Mark said softly. "But it wasn't just the diamonds they were after, was it?"

"No," she replied with a sigh. This was it, the secret she had sworn to keep. But if something happened to her on the road, who would ever know the truth? Mark was a mystery, but had done his best to keep them alive. Maybe she did owe him some trust. "It was all about the book."

So she told Mark about the day his friend had come to meet with Jessica, and how Jessica had given her the journal. Bree had taken it home, as Jessica had asked, but grown more and more uneasy as the night went on. Caution was one thing, but Jessica had clearly been afraid.

She'd finally given in to her nerves and called the atelier.

"It's Bree," she'd said as soon as her boss picked up.

"Take the book and leave town," Jessica had said in a rush. "Find Jack and give the book to him. Don't give it to anyone else. No one, do you understand? Only Jack."

"Where is he?"

"He's gone." Jessica's voice had dropped to a whisper. "Now they've come for it. They're here now. Jack will know what to do. Please, Bree, find him. It's important. It's up to you."

Jessica's voice had risen in a wild, enraged cry that finished in a shriek of pain. Then the line went dead.

Bree had left town with her baby before first light. The next morning, news of the tragic death of designer Jessica Lark had been buried by a media storm about the surprise discovery of Prince Kyle's illegitimate son. The DNA reports were fiction. The timing looked like clever manipulation of the press. The public, and most officials on the case, never gave Lark's supposed death by fire a second thought.

Bree was panting when she finished, but she was done with tears. All she felt now was a hot, red ache in her chest. She closed her eyes, shutting out the late afternoon sun that sank lower on the horizon. They'd made it back to the coast and were nearing the Oregon border.

Jonathan nestled against her side, holding tight.

"A sketchbook," Mark mused. "Did you ever call Jack about it? Did you ever tell him what was in it?"

"No. I had no idea where he was. I could have tracked him down, but I had other things on my mind. The moment I tried to leave New York, the scandal magazines started running stories about Jonathan's paternity. Suddenly the paparazzi were everywhere, hunting for me.

Skip private detectives and surveillance cameras, those photographers are worse than bloodhounds."

"What about the police? Did you go to them?"

Bree gave a choked laugh. "They demanded I turn over the book. When I phoned a few days later to check the names and badge numbers of the detectives I'd talked to, it turned out they didn't exist. Right after that, they caught us in the airport. I'm pretty sure that call was what gave my location away. They were tracking the calls I made from my cell phone. I got a disposable one after that."

"Is that when your pursuers tried to drug you? At the airport?"

"Yes. And this is where it gets even more confusing. I overheard a few of their conversations when they thought I was knocked out." Fresh anxiety made her scrunch farther into the station wagon's lumpy seat, pulling her son close. "They weren't just after the book, or Jonathan. Not one or the other. They wanted both."

Mark met her gaze again in the mirror. He had his sunglasses back on, so she couldn't read his eyes, but his mouth was a firm, uncompromising line. "They won't get him, Bree. Not Ferrel. Not whatever is making Jonathan sick. Nothing gets past me."

Her gut uncoiled a degree. She desperately needed that reassurance. She'd held it together, all on her own, for far too long. She wanted to thank him, but remembered he hated that.

"Did they ever find out who killed Jack Anderson?" she asked in a small voice. "I wonder if they thought he had Jessica's sketches."

"They were caught." Mark's voice was firm. "They were brought to justice and the bridal dress was returned to Amelie. I gave it to her myself."

That surprised her. *Who is Mark Winspear, anyway?*

"Now there is one thing you must tell me." This time his voice was softer. "Where is the book?"

Bree's mouth fell open. She'd promised Jessica never to give it away.

Chapter 11

The moment Mark asked the question, he was distracted by what he saw in the rearview mirror. Like a blip on the horizon, a silver Escalade ghosted far behind them. *By the fiery hells.*

"I don't have the book anymore," Bree said. "I had another bag, one I lost when they kidnapped us."

It was just more bad news. He swore under his breath. Would she have really lost something so important to her freshly murdered mentor? Mark clenched his teeth, wondering if she had lied—but this wasn't the moment to question her about it.

"Our friends are following us again," he said.

Bree turned to look out the back window. "How do you know it's them?"

Mark's beast stirred, wanting to fight the men who threatened the woman—*my woman,* the beast whispered—and her young. "A hunter always feels his prey."

"Aren't we the ones doing the running?"

"Not forever. My turn will come."

Bree sagged back into her seat, looking small. "We changed cars. How did they find us?"

Mark swore softly, remembering what she'd said about her call to the police. "Because I'm an idiot. Do you have a cell phone?"

"Yes." She'd bought a new one when she'd hit the road again. The old one had been dead for months. "It's just a burner. I keep it switched off, though."

"Take the battery out."

"What?" Bree fumbled for her cell.

"It might be a burner, but somehow they're tracking it. Maybe they got the number from a call you made. They've got the technical skills to do it."

Bree swore under her breath.

Mark gave a rueful grimace. "Keeping it switched off doesn't always work, but if there's no battery, there's no signal."

"What about yours?"

He handed her his cell. "This one, too."

She stared at the batteries in her hand. "How do we call for help?"

"We're on our own." He struggled to keep the strain from his voice. "We can't make a call without giving ourselves away. Not on our own phones, anyway."

"Great. Just great."

The Columbia River was catching the fiery sunset, flashing back pinks and golds. Despite the beauty, his heart felt cold. *Isolated.* He could fight alone, but he had grown used to having the Company at his back, and Kenyon always there whenever he dialed the phone. Perhaps he was not such a hermit after all.

More important, he had Bree and Jonathan in his

care—and with them, whatever traces remained of the secrets Lark had tried to pass on to Jack Anderson. He had to get them to safety, for far too many reasons. His friends had died for what was in that book.

Bree was the only one who knew what was in it. *And she knows more than she's saying.*

And in the meantime, he had to come up with a plan. Well, this wasn't the first time he'd had to play fox and outwit the hounds. His eyes narrowed as he hit on an idea.

"I know how to lose them," Mark said, stepping on the gas. "We just have to keep our distance for a while."

They drove another three hours, Mark biding his time with his questions. Centuries of practice had made him a stealthy hunter, and nothing would be gained by spooking Bree, who was already crawling out of her seat with anxiety.

They arrived in Depoe Bay well after dark. The town advertised itself as the world's smallest harbor and seemed to cater to seaside tourists. Mark parked at a motel, gathered up their things and led the way to another place three long streets away.

"We should keep going," Bree said, carrying a sleeping Jonathan. "I could drive if you need to rest."

"I don't need rest," Mark said gruffly. "We need a different car. This is where we lose our tail."

She looked around uncertainly. "How? I don't see any car rental places around here."

"Patience," he urged. "I've done this before." He'd pulled a similar trick during the French Revolution, but she didn't need to know the particulars.

They went in the front of one hotel, through the lobby and out the back exit. A few minutes later, they were walking up the driveway to a slightly shabby motel, so bland and average that it looked like the set for a Stephen King horror story. Mark shouldered open the glass door, holding it open while Bree carried Jonathan inside. He then strolled up to the desk, renting a room for Mr. and Mrs. Anderson and their son, Kyle, freshly arrived from the nearby bus depot and looking for an inexpensive seaside holiday.

By the time he'd finished, Bree almost believed him. He lied with charm and ease, and that set her on edge. *He saved me. He held me while I cried for Jessica. And he wants her book.* Could he have wanted it all along? Was he just setting her up? She was tired and confused, unable to separate what was real and what was the paranoid babbling of her fear. The dark night outside pressed in through the lobby doors. Not far away, the Escalade was hunting them.

Mark turned, ushering her to the elevator. Wordlessly, Bree followed.

Room number six was one story up and faced the pool at the back. Despite the decor needing a push into the twenty-first century, it was clean and quiet. There were two double beds. Bree laid Jonathan down on the one closest to the door. The boy was still dead to the world.

"He's slept since you gave him medicine," she said.

"Good."

She rounded on him, giving vent to her anxiety. "I may not be a doctor, but I know sleeping pills aren't good for children."

He lifted a brow. "I didn't give him any."

"Then why is he still asleep?"

Mark sat down on the bed next to Jonathan, feeling his pulse and the temperature of his skin. The boy had been feverish earlier, but he was cool to the touch now. Almost too cool, Bree thought uneasily. She watched the doctor carefully, trying to see past his professional mask. Mark's face didn't give anything away.

"His pulse and breathing are good. I don't see anything here to be alarmed about. Children can sleep very deeply when they've been ill. It's nature's way of recharging their batteries."

She folded her arms protectively across her chest. "Are you sure?"

"I am, for now. Rest in a proper bed is the best thing, at least while we prepare for the next leg of the journey." He put a hand on Jonathan's head for a moment, a gesture that seemed almost paternal. "I'll watch him carefully."

"Did you ever have children?"

His head jerked up in surprise. Their gazes met, and his look was guarded. She'd struck a sore spot. Nevertheless, he answered. "A long time ago. I had two sons."

His tone was like a slamming door, raising the fine hair on the back of her neck. His bitterness curled through the room like a wisp of dragon's breath. He got up, pacing to the sliding glass door that looked over the pool. "That incident in the airport—you said you were given a knockout drug with a syringe."

"Yes."

"Were you sick afterward?"

She thought back. "I was sick to my stomach. It felt like the flu."

"For how long?"

"A couple weeks. Hard to say. I was running for my life at the time, so I wasn't really paying much attention to aches and pains."

He crossed the room to her with quick steps, catching her hand and drawing her to the pool of light thrown by the bedside lamp. One hand cupped her chin as he turned her face to the light, his dark eyes searching every inch of her features. He tipped back the shade impatiently. The bulb dazzled her, making the dim room seem cave-like by comparison.

"What?" she asked, a vague sense of threat gathering around her.

"Open your mouth."

She obeyed as he tilted her head back for a better angle. The only comment he made was a considering grunt, then he took her pulse. "You're healthy enough."

"Were you expecting something else?"

"It was just an idea."

He looked down into her eyes, serious. Some of the gruffness had left him, replaced by a concern that was easy to read. It was what she needed to see right then, giving her courage.

"What idea?"

He gave a slight shake of his head. "Something in the shot. But you're fine."

She bit her lip, wanting to scream in frustration.

"Hey," he said gently, touching her cheek.

"Jonathan's like a piece of me that broke loose and is suddenly on its own," she said, her voice rough. "It's not under my own skin where I can protect it. It drives me crazy."

Mark gave a slow nod. "That's what children do to you."

"Yours?"

"Hush." He leaned forward, his dark, liquid eyes that much closer. She'd been aware of them under those sunglasses all day. They'd been like a veiled weapon, but they were out in full force now, shadowed by long, dark lashes. No man had a right to lashes like that.

Bree swallowed, telling herself they were an accident of genetics, not an excuse to lose her wits. And still they affected her like one too many glasses of wine. But she didn't drink anymore. That way led to danger.

Danger. Maybe his mouth was the culprit. For once, it wasn't pressed into an impatient line. It was full and soft and right there, just inches from hers. She already knew what it tasted like, and her belly twisted in anticipation. She wanted to taste him again but couldn't. Jonathan was fast asleep, but she had no business taking her attention from him for one second.

But there wasn't another moment to think of that. Mark's lips were on hers, hard and yielding at the same time, exactly the way a man was supposed to be. A perfect combination of gentleness and command. He caught the fullness of her lower lip with his teeth, tugging, demanding entry.

Good sense said she should pull back, end the moment. Things were complicated enough without adding a lover to the mix. It just wasn't wise.

But instead, she plundered him, seeking with her tongue. Heat flamed up through her core, burning her with its hunger. His body tensed as she responded, meeting her need for need. But then he relaxed, drawing her closer. Bree leaned into him, fitting perfectly against the curve of his strong chest.

He was still wearing his leather jacket, supple with long wear. She ran her hands under it, finding the soft cotton of his dark green T-shirt. It fit tight over the muscles of his chest, letting her hands follow his smooth outline all the way down to where his shirt met the waistband of his jeans.

He nipped her tongue as she stroked him with it, distracting her as his hands found her hips, then her backside. And then the tables were turned, and he was the aggressor, taking her mouth with the boldness of a pirate.

Bree gasped, no longer holding the advantage. She was suddenly at his mercy, desire lancing through her with the acuteness of a blade.

It was more than she'd bargained for. She broke the kiss, pushing away to put air between them. She could feel the pulse in her lips, a throbbing ache from his bruising demands.

Bree took another step back. Mark's eyes were still dark, but the lamplight seemed to dance in them, as if fire flickered within. His face had gone still and tense, locking down whatever was going on in his head. Bree felt suddenly cut off, even though it had been her backing away. The distance between them left her cold, as if he had absorbed every scrap of heat from the room. She glanced guiltily at her sleeping son, relieved for once to see the child was still asleep.

"I'm sorry," she whispered.

"Was there a problem?" Mark's voice was so low and soft, it was almost a growl.

Nothing, except that she could fall into his embrace as if it was a drug, losing herself in that sensual power. "Bad timing. I want to stay focused."

That much was true.

He reached out, the movement slow and controlled, as if it was all he could do not to grab her. His cool fingers traced her cheek, lingering with a butterfly touch. It would have been so natural to turn her lips to those fingers, to rub her chin against him like a cat marking her territory, but she didn't dare. If she made one move, her restraint would fail. She would be his, forgetting all else in her desperation to be touched like a woman again. It had been so very, very long, and her imagination toyed with everything he could do to her.

Heat flickered in his eyes. "There's no need to worry. I can protect you. I can protect him."

She shook her head. "I'm sorry. I can't. Not right now."

He finally pulled his hand away, fingers curling into a fist. The air pulsed with tension. Some of it was sexual, but there was wildness underneath it, almost violence. Bree's stomach fluttered, suddenly unsure. What did she know about Mark Winspear, anyway?

He took a step toward her. Instinctively, she fell back and for a fleeting instant wondered what she could use to defend herself. But then he turned away, this time the one to put distance between them.

The tension broke, and she took a long, shaking breath, feeling foolish. He had kissed her and wanted more. That was what men did. She knew that much to her sorrow.

When he turned to face her again, he was standing by the door. She took another breath, yearning to touch the hard, strong muscles of his chest, but held herself in check. Mark Winspear was a peril all on his own, and not a man to be toyed with. If she said yes to him, she had better mean it.

The woman in her wrestled with the urge to call him back, but Jonathan was asleep and helpless. She couldn't ignore that for an instant.

"I'm going out for a few minutes," Mark said. The words were casual, but his glance was not. For an instant, she was seeing the cougar in the woods again, this time staring from behind his dark, liquid eyes. Her head had known he was just as dangerous as Nicholas Ferrel. In that instant, her gut knew it, too.

Anything she might have said stuck in her throat.

Chapter 12

Mark, restless and weary, roamed the perimeter of the block where the motel sat. His mind inched back to Bree and the scene that had almost happened, and then ricocheted away. He knew he should not become involved with her. She had a young child. She was vulnerable. He was doing his damnedest to be a doctor, not a killer.

And yet she tempted him like sin itself. In that moment of madness, he had reveled in the smoothness of her skin, the perfume of her desire. For an instant, he had felt as fragile and urgent as a mortal, grabbing at life before the flame snuffed out.

She was keeping secrets. Had she really lost Jessica's book of designs? He doubted it, yet knowing that she had probably lied to him didn't dull his yearning. If there was a measure for his idiocy, that was it.

Now he stood alone on the corner, just out of the glow of the streetlight. The darkness felt good after the punishing sun, his flesh itching lightly as it healed itself. Saltwater washed the air, mixing with the bitter scent of the old gasoline soaked into the surface of the parking lot. The restaurant across the street was frying onions and burning the coffee. Two lovers stood at the side door, hidden behind the Dumpster but he could hear them whispering and laughing. Only minutes ago, he'd almost had what they now shared.

But everything had been wrong. Bree had wanted him to hold her. He had wanted to possess her with all the savagery of a bloodthirsty beast. Mark clenched his fist, though what he threatened was a mystery. Fate? Love? His own incapacity for feeling?

No, that wasn't really true. He had wanted love in that instant. He had felt that unwelcome wrench under his ribs, a pang of loneliness he dreamed she could kiss away. *Foolishness.*

And something of a surprise. He wasn't a mortal, safe and warm and capable of keeping a woman's affection. Not once she truly knew him. He had ethics—or at least his own code of morality—but he was a monster. He had been since the day the first Nicholas Ferrel had burned his wife and little boys at the stake for harboring the undead. Five hundred years later, he could still hear their screams. Was it any wonder he'd taken revenge on the Knights of Vidon?

The memory flared, but he pushed it back into the dark places inside him. Surrendering to a lust for vengeance had never eased his pain. And he had plenty of problems in the present: murder, a book of secrets, slayers and a vulnerable woman and child.

Mark paced the boundaries of the motel again, but caught no sign of their pursuers. Staying put made him nervous, so he had to find a new vehicle soon. But not too soon. The woman and boy needed rest. He had slipped the child a few drops of his own blood at the hospital and then again when they had stopped to change cars. That was what had made Jonathan sleep so hard this afternoon. A tiny dose of vampire blood had curative powers—at least enough to keep the boy from getting any worse until they reached Los Angeles. For a little while, rest could be a priority.

As for Mark, he needed to hunt. Spending his day locked in a car with a beautiful human female he wasn't supposed to bite was the next best thing to outright torture. And while he could survive on the hospital blood stores or the deer around his cabin—well, there was a difference between surviving and dining well.

He drifted through the shadows, searching for what he wanted. There, he saw a family arriving at another motel, tired and stretching out the stiffness of too many hours behind the wheel. There, he saw a young man leaning against a back stairway, smoking a cigarette. And there, a waitress from the diner throwing garbage into the trash. None of them stirred his appetite.

He wanted Bree. *No.* For so many reasons, no.

Then he saw the Subaru Forester pull into the motel lot. Not a scratch on it. He could smell the new-car scent all the way to the corner. With barely a moment's hesitation, he walked toward it as it parked. He took in the tinted windows, cargo space and roof rack. Not a tired station wagon, but a compact SUV with good mileage and all the safety features. A perfect family vehicle. *No one ever called me a poor provider.*

A man was getting out. The raincoat and briefcase said businessman. Despite the darkness and the distance, Mark could still read the convention badge clipped to his lapel: Brian MacNally, Seagirt Insurance. Someone breaking the long drive home from a professional conference? With silent steps, Mark closed the distance between them.

The stink of sex and cheap perfume clinging to Mac-Nally's clothes said there'd been after-hours adjustments that had nothing to do with homeowner policies—yet a wedding ring flashed on the man's left hand. A sudden flash of rage overtook Mark. He would have given anything for the man's way of life: a job, a home, the family that went with the family car. And this Brian MacNally was risking it for what? Relief from boredom?

Mark put one hand on the hood of the car, blocking MacNally's path. "So, does this vehicle have childproof locks?"

He'd moved quickly, using the bad light to disguise his approach. MacNally jerked with surprise. "What?"

"Childproof locks?"

"Of course."

"Good."

The man looked confused. "What do you want?"

Mark stepped into the pale glow of the streetlight, catching MacNally's gaze. The man was on the cusp of middle age, turning pudgy from too much paperwork and quitting-time Scotch. In another fifteen years he'd be old, fat and facing diabetes. Mark could smell the incipient condition in his sweat. He pitied the man's wife. He looked like a whiner.

"I noticed your convention badge. Do you have a business card?" he asked.

MacNally reached into his breast pocket, whipping one out with a practiced flourish. "I do all kinds of insurance, but I specialize in life. It's never too soon to think about the future. Have you spoken with anyone about your coverage?"

"Truthfully, no." Mark kept the man's gaze, slipping

his will over the man's mind like a glove. All vampires had some talent for hypnotism, but he was what the Company called a Cleaner: one who could control human memories with a surgeon's precision. Cleaners took care of the mess when an ordinary human got tangled in their affairs.

The talent was also extremely useful when hunting. "Stand on your left foot and hop in a circle."

MacNally did as he was told. *Good.*

"Give me your car keys."

MacNally complied, and Mark handed him the keys to his rental car. "There is a brown station wagon in the lot of the Sleepytime Motel three blocks east of here. The wagon is a loaner from a repair shop you visited because of a crack in your windshield. You will ask no questions now or in the future, and you will not remember meeting me here tonight."

MacNally nodded weakly.

"In a few days' time, a man will return your Subaru to you. You will give this station wagon to that man. I repeat, you will ask no questions. Furthermore, you will stop cheating on your wife." That wasn't any of Mark's business, but he was in an unforgiving mood. "And you will adopt an effective diet and exercise plan. Lose twenty pounds and stop drinking. Do you understand me?"

MacNally nodded again, a faint look of relief in his eyes, as if he was happy that someone had seized control of his will. "Yes."

The beast in Mark tightened its grip on the man, ready to move in for the kill. Mark kept an iron grip on the impulse. Vampires could give sexual pleasure with their bite, but this sure as hell wouldn't be one of those times. He would feed, but only as much as he needed to take the edge off. The blood he truly craved belonged to a woman with tawny hair and eyes the shifting color of the sea.

A woman he was sure was still keeping secrets from him.

Bree lay beside Jonathan on the bed closest to the door, leaving the other conspicuously vacant. She was wide-awake, comforted only by the fact that Jonathan seemed to be sleeping normally, if deeply.

She should eat something, but there was too much to think about. She wanted to use her phone, maybe surf the net looking for more news of the incident at Gleeford Ferry, but she'd pulled the battery out for a good reason. Still, the thought left her feeling isolated. Losing contact with the phone and internet was almost like being deaf and blind.

A perfectly good landline sat on the bedside table, a sticker on the side telling her to dial nine to place an outside call. Surely a call from an anonymous hotel number was different from her personal cell phone? No one was going to listen in here. Except, who was she going to call? She'd kept her own secrets and everyone else's for so long, she had cut herself off from the world.

She stared at the phone, and it stared back at her. *There is no one.*

That was crazy. Mark was taking them to Los Angeles. *Home.* The word sounded almost odd. Sure, she kept up on what her family was doing—they were nothing if not publicity hounds—but she'd left for New York and never looked back. She'd slammed their big front door.

Now here she was, just hours from her childhood home, and she wasn't sure how she felt about that. Bree's mother had sent her to boarding school when she reached fourteen. She'd been seeking attention in inappropriate ways—stealing things, sneaking out at night. The kiddie shrinks had recommended discipline. Bree would have prescribed real parents—ones who kept an eye on their daughter when her dad threw a bash for his movie friends.

Poor, innocent Brianna, they'd used to say. Bree had become very good at dodging their hands and sliding away, as quick and deft as a ferret. That had started when she was nine.

She'd been running then, too.

A good mother would have noticed that Bree's first boyfriends were too old for her. Or that she'd come home with her clothes torn, or drunk, or with a bloody lip. Some men didn't understand no.

She'd assumed it was just the way things were. All the starlets in her father's world expected to be used—or at least it seemed that way to her inexperienced eye. She was a lot older before she understood that some of it was just games.

Looking back, her father probably assumed she knew, if he had thought about it at all. Hank Meadows, motion picture genius, was anything but malicious, but his only child was just part of the landscape, like the potted orange tree in the front hall.

A twinge of old anger snaked through her. She'd never ignore Jonathan that way, ever. When they'd found the place on the coast, surrounded by trees and water and good people, Bree had settled in to raise her son. It didn't matter if they had no money and the locals thought fashion was a clean pair of jeans—no one asked questions. It was safe. She had been prepared to give up everything to stay.

The idyll had lasted almost a whole year, until she'd been stupid enough to hand over her health insurance card. Then they were on the run, there was Mark and here she was.

Mark, who was man enough to listen when she said no. She had to respect that. Not all men had that kind of honor.

Bree looked down at her son's sleeping face, her gaze tracing the familiar lines of his nose and chin. She tucked the blankets around him a bit more tightly, as if that could erase the stamp of illness from his face.

Her folks had never even met Jonathan. Regret filled her, followed by a sliver of guilt. *They'd want that, wouldn't they? Don't people want to see their grandkids?* Her parents had never made the move, never suggested that they visit her in New York. *Were they giving me space, or do they really not care?*

Or was it because Bree had promised never to come home again? Their last family meeting made high noon at the O.K. Corral look downright friendly. Bree had been free at last, on her way to a real life and a real career. She had taken that final chance to lash out at the people who had hurt her so badly. But leaving would never ease the ache inside her. Against all reason, she still wanted their love.

Before Bree knew it, her hand was on the telephone receiver, putting it to her ear. She dialed her dad's private cell number.

It rang. Bree held her breath, her heart beating fast. What would she say? That she would be in town and wanted to see him but she was being followed by lethal madmen so maybe next time? Would her dad think she was crazy or ask for the film rights? Or call out the National Guard? It was hard to predict.

It went to voice mail. It wasn't even his voice on the message. She hung up.

Bree stared at the phone again, wondering if she should try her mom. She picked up the receiver again, trying to remember her mom's number. Althea Meadows was an expert in international corporate law and more often than not was on a plane. In more ways than one, Bree had given up trying to reach her long ago.

"I'm on the road," her mom would say when she was little. "Ask your father."

Bree would reply that he was on location, filming in Nevada. Or Africa. Or Iceland.

"Then ask the nanny."

The dial tone went to a steady beeping. She still hadn't called her mother, and the welling discomfort inside told her she probably wouldn't.

Jonathan shifted and mumbled while Bree glared at the phone, frozen with fury. *Why wasn't I important enough to protect? What was the matter with me?*

But then Bree heard footsteps in the hall. She replaced the receiver as quietly as she could and nestled down into the pillow, closing her eyes. She slowed her breathing. Long practice as a kid had taught her how to fool her caretakers into believing she was sound asleep.

The lock clicked and the door swung open. Bree opened her eyes just enough to peer out from under her lashes. Only the dim glow from the bedside lamp took the edge off the darkness, but Mark moved through the room with sure-footed ease. He paused, looking around, looking at her, and then picked up her backpack, quietly sliding the zipper open.

"Hey!" she said, sitting bolt upright. "Get your hands off that!"

Without a word, he upended it on the bed, dumping

out socks, underwear, a hairbrush and Jessica's priceless book of wedding designs.

"You really are bad at keeping secrets," he said.

Chapter 13

Mark hadn't been fooled for an instant by her sleepy-time act. Bree's heart had been thumping like a drum kit while she did her best to avoid him. *Fine.* So he was a monster for wanting to kiss her. Little did she know just how much of a beast he really was.

She bounced off the bed and lunged at the book. "You have no right!"

He snatched it away. "I'll be the judge of that."

She fell back a step, gathering her dignity. "How did you know I even had it?"

"Unless you were utterly brain-dead, you kept it as a last-ditch bargaining chip, just in case you needed to buy your safety from Ferrel." He saw her pale face, pinched with fear, and wanted to swear. He wasn't the enemy. "Don't bother. His type use words like *honor* and *promise,* but they'll break a deal if it suits their plan."

The book was the size of a thick hardcover, handmade

and bound in brown leather. It was fastened with a leather thong that wound around an elaborate brass stud on the front cover. It made him think more of medieval fantasy than fashion designers. It was all very…Jessica.

Bree looked from the book to his face. "So this is what you're really after?"

He could see her constructing an elaborate plot in her mind—one where he befriended her for the sole purpose of stealing the dress designs. He nearly laughed. "You're the closest thing we have to a witness to Jessica's murder. Of course I'm interested in this, and you. I want justice."

Without saying another word, he unwound the thong and opened the cover. The paper was thick and rough, more beige than white. There were watercolor sketches of gowns and coats, hats and handbags, all labeled with Lark's flowing handwriting. He had little interest in clothes, but could tell they had the trademark elegance of the fey. No wonder the humans had paid top dollar for her work.

He turned page after page. The paper rustled, sounding dry and strangely brittle for a book that shouldn't have been older than a year or two. Bree watched him, all but crackling with anger.

The last few pages of the book were blank. He flipped backward, pausing when he recognized the sketch for a wedding dress. Yes, it was the same one Jack Anderson had kept hidden in his house. "This is Princess Amelie's bridal gown, diamonds and all."

"Yes."

"I can tell it's Jessica's work." He tried to find the right words to take the fury out of Bree's eyes. "The designs have panache."

But clothes were just clothes, even if they cost a lot of money. After five and a half centuries, he'd seen every kind of heel, wig and corset for both men and women. Was the book really worth killing for? Maybe he'd believe that if Bree was being chased by a pack of couturiers, but as far as he knew, the Knights of Vidon had about as much taste as a block of tofu.

And yet they had chased her. They'd even mobilized the paparazzi with that story about Jonathan's paternity to slow her down. Why?

He closed the cover, ready to hand the book back to Bree. But then he caught a whiff of it. It smelled musty. Or was that glue? Cautiously, he sniffed the binding.

"What are you doing?" she demanded.

He turned the book on end and peered down the spine. The stitching that sewed the binding together looked new, but the edges of some pages looked oddly waffled, as if they'd been left in the rain. But not every page. Very, very carefully, he opened the book as far as it would go.

Bree had silently come to his side and was peering over his shoulder. "What is it?"

He felt along the edge of the page where it disappeared into the crease. His fingers found telltale unevenness in the paper. Using his fingernail, he peeled away the corner of the page covering the real page of the book. It lifted with a sound like crunching leaves, but his hands tingled as if he'd thrust them into an anthill. *Magic.*

With an intake of breath, Bree bent to see more closely. "There's more handwriting underneath!"

So there was, in thick, dark ink. Mark kept peeling, separating the hidden page from the page of sketches that covered it. Fey magic prickled all the way up to the nape of his neck, but there was no burst of sparkles or beams of energy to show it was anything more than a particularly clever scrapbooking job. Just as well, since Bree was watching.

Irritation coursed through him. Lark had put Bree in a lot of danger by making her into a mule for who-knew-what. If Lark wasn't dead already, he'd be giving her grief.

At last the page of designs came loose, and he set it aside. Beneath was smoother paper with a faint gray hue. The angular writing looked masculine. Most of it wasn't letters, though, but a long string of formulas.

"Do you know what that is?" Bree asked.

Mark frowned. "Not at first glance."

In fact, it looked like chemists gone wild. Or maybe alchemists. There were symbols there he hadn't seen since, oh, about the time men still wore tights. And codpieces. That was one fashion statement he wouldn't miss.

"I need to take the book apart," he said. "You can keep Lark's drawings if you want them."

"That book isn't yours," she said sharply. "Whatever is in there, Jessica gave it to me."

That wasn't logical. He waved at the page of symbols. "You can't understand this."

"Nor can you." She made a move to pull the book out of his hand. "You just said so."

There was no way he was letting her have it back. Not only did it have information Lark had kept hidden, but it was soaked in fey magic—magic he'd now disturbed and would need time to dissipate. Who knew what the wretched thing might do? He might look up to discover she'd been turned into a potted plant. "I need to study it."

She grabbed the edge of the book, giving it a sharp tug. He brushed her hands away. He wasn't rough, but he was a vampire, and strong. She stumbled away, eyes resentful.

"You're a thief," she announced. "And a strange one."

Mark studied her, wondering how much she'd put together. There were some things about himself that were hard to hide. The sunburn. His lack of appetite. His strength. Still, people saw what they expected, and that was rarely vampires.

"I know what I'm doing," he countered evenly. "I'll get you to Los Angeles. I'll get your son medical help. If there's any monetary value to this book or its contents, it's yours—but I need to understand these symbols."

"That's not the point. Jessica entrusted it to me for safekeeping. You can't keep it."

"It's safe with me."

Her look turned to icy contempt. "She didn't give it to you. What part of that don't you get?"

He was getting a headache. It would have been easy to give way to anger, but he had to swallow his pride and endure her glare. To be fair, she didn't have all the facts. "Listen. The signatures—the bundles of paper sewn together to make up the book—look like they've been re-assembled. Whoever disguised the book must have cut the original apart to do this. Whatever is hidden beneath the sketches is what Lark really wanted to hide. Don't you want to know what that is?"

For a moment, she continued to rake him with her gaze, as if that alone could strip the skin from his flesh. Finally, she turned away to sit beside her sleeping son. She put a hand on Jonathan's dark hair. "You have to admit it's clever," she said more calmly. "Whoever is looking for a valuable secret wouldn't think of looking inside an object that other thieves would want for a totally different reason. It's really good camouflage."

"Other thieves?" Mark asked, confused. Did she mean him?

Her look said he was an idiot. "Industrial espionage.

Rivals were always trying to swipe Jessica's collections. That's why she had a safe on-site."

"Oh." That still didn't answer what the fey woman was hiding. He flipped to the front of the book and peeled away another page, hoping for some sort of introduction that would explain the rest. If he was hoping for something easy, he was disappointed. "Well, the first part of this is written in Latin."

"Who writes in Latin?" Bree said in an annoyed tone.

"It used to be the universal language of educated discourse." He sounded defensive and he knew it. Vampires gave new meaning to the phrase "old school." At least that sounded better than "geek for languages as dead as he was."

"Can you read it?"

He silently read through the first passage. Whoever had written it had excellent grammar. Mark's tutors would have been gratified if he'd ever done half so well.

This is the culmination of my work, the third of three trials I have made. This shall correct the shortcomings of the first two experiments and set the crown on my life's attainments. I have labored alone for many years to understand the workings of a terrible disease, for men are made in the image of the divine and it is our sworn duty to protect them. What is this infection that turns such favored creatures into demons doomed to feast on the blood of their brothers? Indeed, it is only in this century that we have the ability to investigate. Genetics and virology can now combine with the forgotten teachings of unnatural philosophy to crack, and indeed re-create, the foul plague of vampirism. A necessary project, for how can the vampire be stopped except by a foe of equal strength and ferocity? One without the demonic evil transmitted through a vampire's bite?

Mark nearly dropped the book. *Damnation!* Someone had written—or tried to write—a how-to book for making vampires! With alchemy, Latin, genetics and a virus. It was the oddest mix of ancient and modern theory he'd ever seen.

The implications made his head spin. Almost dizzy, Mark sat down on the other bed, facing Bree. *What could this mean?* Making more of his kind wasn't a simple process. No one knew why or how it worked. Magic? It seemed that way, but who knew? If there was a way to understand what made them immortal, or how to control the blood thirst…

"What does it say?" Bree demanded, but Mark barely heard her.

So why do the Knights of Vidon want this? The answer to that question turned his stomach to lead. *For how can the vampire be stopped except by a foe of equal strength and ferocity?*

They wanted to make their own vampires. *By the nine fiery hells!* It was laughable, offensive and terrifying all at once.

He looked up at Bree, wishing he could talk to her. Now was one of those moments he could use a good listener—but she was just a human. A pretty, brave woman with a little boy who needed his help—who was at the moment sleeping off a dose of Mark's own vampire blood.

Some interesting doublethink you have going on, my friend. If the book's recipe for vampires was bad news, how was Mark's home remedy any better? Too many doses of vamp blood had been known to produce interesting side effects, like sensitivity to the sun. He had to get to L.A. fast before his quick and dirty prescriptions caught up with his patient.

Something nagged at the back of Mark's mind, but it wouldn't emerge from the maelstrom of his thoughts. There was too much to think about at once, including the fact that Lark had entrusted the book to a woman with a baby. Irresponsible. Insane. Erratic. Which all spelled fey. Bree was too valuable for such careless treatment.

Valuable? His inner voice was mocking. *In the grand scheme of things, she's nothing but a snack for the road. You're an operative. An assassin with a perverse urge to heal. What could she ever be but a sentimental keepsake?*

How he hated that voice.

"What does the book say?" Bree repeated.

"It's a recipe for a biological weapon." His outer voice was hard and flat.

"What?" She recoiled as if the germs themselves were on the book.

"Who knows you have this book?"

She turned pasty at his words. "Jessica. Me. You."

That wasn't so bad. He relaxed a degree. "We should be all right as long as we stay off the radar. No phone calls. No contact of any kind with anyone."

She blinked suddenly. "I called home. My father's private cell."

He tensed again. "When?"

"Tonight. No one picked up and I didn't leave a message."

He felt his face freeze. Whatever Bree saw there made her anxious. "I called on the room phone. It wasn't the cell phone, so no one would necessarily know it was me."

Mark gripped the book so hard he felt the cover boards dimple. "Ferrel knows who you are. What if your father's phone was bugged?"

From Bree's expression, it was obvious she hadn't thought of that. She acted streetwise, and had survived her share of knocks and scares, but it was obvious part of her was still innocent as snow. He didn't have the heart to ask if her father might be one of the bad guys. He was a famous director, surrounded by throngs of actors, staff, fans… Any one of them could be with the Knights.

"We're leaving now," he growled, and snapped the book shut.

Chapter 14

Memories of pain filled Bree, red and raw. Pain ripping her from end to end. She forgot the agony of childbirth when she was awake. Somewhere she'd read that the brain did that for the good of the human race—otherwise, no woman would ever have a second child. And yet she had dreamed of it often since Jonathan fell ill, as if birthing him again would make him whole.

Her eyelids flickered, letting in a hint of daylight before the noise of wheels on the road lulled her back to sleep.

This time, she was back in New York, working late into the night after everyone but Jessica had gone home. The studio was on the sixth floor of one of those old brick Manhattan buildings, the streets a constantly moving river of lights and cars outside the windows. Bree was drawing the design that was to go onto Princess Amelie's wedding dress. It was going to be couched gold cord picked out in pearls and—though she wasn't sure she believed this part—diamonds. There would have to be a fortune in diamonds to cover the whole bodice, but that's what they'd said. Whatever. Bree had a heap of books on the table beside her with color plates of needlework. This kind of goldwork had to be done by hand, and there were only a handful of professional embroiderers who could do it. Royal weddings didn't fall into a designer's lap every day—especially one as junior as she was—and Bree was thrilled Jessica had invited her to come up with some ideas.

Which was why Bree was there that night. She'd had cramps since that morning, off and on, but they'd been so mild she had blown them off and kept working.

All of a sudden, she felt a change inside, the first hint of it so subtle it might have been just her imagination. She looked up, seeing her face reflected faintly against the glass, her features vague in the halo of lamplight. The lights moved behind the reflection, as if she were connected to the sea of movement yet floating above it, her wide eyes shimmering and insubstantial.

The next moment her water broke, unexpectedly warm. The birth would come hard and fast and sooner than anyone expected.

Bree yelped before she could stifle the sound. The sound brought Jessica out of her office at a run. She threw a layer of muslin down—the cheap stuff they used for making up patterns. It shone like a pale island against the dark wood planks. Then she grabbed Bree's hand, helping her to the floor. "Sail through the pain. Just leave it behind. It can't touch you."

Bree wanted to scream at her, to call her an idiot, but she managed to hold on to some shred of dignity. "It hurts."

"Then I'll tell you a story. Keep your mind off it till the ambulance comes."

Or the baby. It was going to be a race to see which arrived first. Bree cried out again, convinced she was going to rupture like the guy in *Alien,* a horrible space monster clawing its way out of her belly. She was going to die.

"Help me!" she wailed.

"Do you want me to call your mother?" Jessica asked.

"No." What would her mother do, anyway? Bree couldn't imagine. Write a contract? Deliver a brief?

Jessica made a face. "It'll be all right."

"I have to finish the dress."

"The dress can wait. Royal weddings don't happen overnight. Your child will be toddling before Amelie walks down the aisle."

Another wave of pain came, blanking Bree's vision to white. Jessica gripped her hand tight. "I'm going to tell you a story my mother told me when I was just a little girl."

There had to be something in the soft, even tone of the woman's words. Her voice was something to cling to, and Bree clung to it like a drowning woman. "Okay."

Jessica smiled, her expression soft. "My mother used to tell it like this. Long ago strange creatures walked the land—the fair folk and the demons and the beast men. They came at the call of kings who offered them shelter from the fire and sword of human warriors, and for a gift of blood or gold would do the bidding of their mortal lords."

A bright lance of pain forced a cry from Bree's lips. She crushed Jessica's hand, but the woman didn't cry out. She was stronger than she looked.

"Hush, little one, it will soon be over." She stroked Bree's hair. "Listen to my words."

Bree had hardly heard her words right then, but she'd always dreamed them the same way afterward.

"Three princes lived by the sea, mighty knights in the time of the Crusades," Jessica went on. "The eldest was a warrior, the second a sorcerer and the third left to seek his fortune in the Holy Land. In time the third brother returned with a fortune in gemstones from the East."

Bree was lying limp on the floor, dripping with sweat. She was dizzy, the room dark and close, her only anchors the hard floor beneath her shoulder blades and the lifeline of Jessica's hand. She licked suddenly dry lips. "I know this tale. The older brothers killed him for the gems. And then they went to war, one against the other. Kyle told me. It's the story of Vidon and Marcari. He's descended from the warrior king of Vidon."

"So he is." Jessica kept stroking her hair as another contraction passed. "The two brothers split their father's lands between them and made two kingdoms, side by side."

"Why did you say the king of Marcari was a sorcerer?" Bree asked, trying to stay with the story instead of the huge, sucking hole of pain.

"Old legends say that both kings recruited an army of half-demon warriors to fight for them. Vampires and wolf-men, and the fey lords on their winged steeds of shining white. These strangers were mighty and mysterious, loyal but fierce beyond the ways of men. The slaughter was terrible.

"The King of Vidon blamed the strangers for killing so many humans, and sought to murder his unearthly warriors. In contrast, the King of Marcari, knowing he had given the order to fight, blamed himself. He offered protection to the warriors against retribution, and they swore fealty to his throne and called themselves *La Compagnie des Morts*."

The Company of the Dead. Kyle had said the stories of the mythical Company were fairy tales meant to frighten naughty little princes. And yet, he would never give her details. She had the impression they still gave him nightmares.

Jessica went on. "Outraged, the King of Vidon made his human knights swear to purge all magic from the world. The words of their oath still say that, to this very day."

This seemed a bizarre story to tell a woman in labor, and Bree had started to grow afraid. Helpless and in pain, she'd prayed for the ambulance to come.

And then dream-Jessica said something new. Bree didn't remember this part. She was adding things, her brain mashing together reality and fantasy.

The woman leaned close, her eyes sparkling from within. "The real truth is that the Knights of Vidon want to stop the wedding. If Amelie marries Kyle, then the war will finally be over, and they won't have an excuse to fight the Company."

"Why are you telling me this now?" Bree asked in her dream.

Jessica smiled down at her, holding Bree's hand in both of hers. "I've given you the most important pieces of the puzzle. Think about what you see right under your nose, Bree."

Bree jerked awake just as the sign to Eureka, California, flashed by, bright in the morning sun. She blinked, disoriented by the dream—and especially to that bit at the end. That was new.

What you see right under your nose. Puzzle pieces?

There were so many: Mark, Jessica's murder, the long flight to keep Jonathan safe. None of them fit together.

"Are you awake?" Mark began a few moments later.

"Yes."

"I know you don't want to talk about this, but…" His words trailed off, dying a slow death.

"But?" Bree prompted, rubbing her eyes. *Weird dream.* She studied Mark, thinking again how he reminded her of Jessica. They had something in common, but she couldn't put her finger on it. Her subconscious groped for an answer, but came up with nothing but fairy tales.

He slid his sunglasses on. "To do a proper diagnosis, I should know the medical history of Jonathan's parents." His tone was careful. "Congenital diseases, that sort of thing. You never gave me that information at the hospital."

Weary, Bree closed her eyes. Jonathan was wide-awake now, playing bulldozer with his dinosaur and driving her slowly insane with roars and screeches. Insane, but delighted because he was full of energy like a four-year-old was supposed to be. Whatever Mark had given the boy had knocked him into a sleep so deep it had frightened her half to death, but now he seemed almost normal. She'd forgotten how active he could be.

Mark didn't give up. "Some conditions run in families, like hemophilia. Some members of the royal family of Russia weren't able to stop bleeding if they were injured."

Royal family? Was he working up to the Prince-Kyle-as-baby-daddy discussion again? She could hear it in the careful neutrality of his tone. "Kyle isn't the father," she snapped. "I told you that."

He gripped the steering wheel as if he meant to crush it. "This is important."

She glared at him. "I know that. I'm telling the truth."

He was silent for a long moment. "Do you know the medical history of Jonathan's father?"

"Some. He had asthma."

He gave her a surprised look. At least, he looked surprised around the edges of his dark glasses. Maybe it was because she was overtired, but her temper snapped. "What? Did you expect me to say I don't know which one of my thousand lovers got me pregnant?"

Mark shook his head. "No, of course not."

"Are you sure about that?"

"Don't assume what I may or may not think."

She knew she was being unreasonable, but couldn't stop herself. "Why not? When the paparazzi palooza hit, I called everyone I knew in the media to set the record straight—and, hey, I'm a film mogul's daughter. I know them all. No one, *no one,* wanted to believe I was anything but Kyle's mistress. It's hard to plead chastity with a baby in your arms."

"I'm sorry." He sounded more angry than sorry.

"The truth is that Kyle and I were just good friends and neither one of us wanted to wreck that by falling into bed. We. Never. Did. It."

Mark's jaw bunched, as if he were clenching his teeth. "I suppose it was easier for the media to believe you were after fame and money."

"Fame is a nuisance and my parents are already scary rich. And Kyle would have given me whatever I needed, whether Jonathan was his boy or not. What I wanted was to be left alone to be a normal mother."

He turned to her with a frown. "Surely there were people who could have stepped in when things went bad. Why didn't you go to Kyle for help?"

"Jessica was dead and, from what I could tell, I was next. I wasn't going to lead the killers to Kyle's doorstep or take them home so they could murder my folks. My family makes my head explode sometimes, but there are limits to what I'll do to them."

Her attempt at humor seemed to sail over his head. "What about Jonathan's dad?" he demanded.

She didn't want to talk about Adam. It made her too sad. "He died before Jonathan was born, and he had no family to speak of. It would have been easier if there had been loving grandparents somewhere in the wings, but there weren't."

"Not your mom and dad?"

Bree wanted to laugh but remembered wishing she could see them last night. A fleeting impulse. A bad idea. "My father lives in the fantasy world of his movies, and my mother's idea of kid-friendly is an illustrated edition of *Tortious and the Hare: Ten Lessons for Little Lawyers of the Future*."

"They raised you. You turned out okay."

She turned her face to the car window. "Barely."

She didn't want to talk about the details, like the time she hid in the bedroom closet, her hand over her mouth to muffle the sound of her crying. Not all of her nannies had been Mary Poppins. And then later, she'd hidden in the same closet because of the men. She'd had a relationship with that closet.

The only person who'd known about that was Adam. *Poor Adam.* She'd only been his girlfriend a few months. They'd been friends forever. She'd already known it wasn't going to work when he'd headed off to the beach that last day and never come home again. Music and surfing. That was his life, ended at twenty-three.

"When I found out I was pregnant," she went on, "I made up my mind to put my baby first. I wasn't going to raise him like one of those purse-sized Chihuahuas, an accessory that's in one season, gone the next."

"Okay."

"I didn't know how to do it. I'd never lived like a regular person. Not really. So I put some distance between myself and everything I'd known and concentrated on building a life I could control. Something stable and small, a little bit at a time. A job. An apartment. Groceries. Normal people things." She looked out the car window at the bright morning. "That worked really well, as you can see."

He let out a long breath. "You tried to do a good thing."

The words were simple, but they meant more than flowery promises. She'd had enough of those in the past, and they hadn't amounted to much. "I'm just so afraid of disappointing Jonathan. I don't want him to grow up feeling the way I did, that the person in charge just isn't up to the job. It would be better not to have Jonathan think of me at all."

I screw up more often than not. I never learned how to keep people close. Not my parents, not Adam, not Jessica. Bree thought of the man sitting next to her—angry, bossy and an incredibly good kisser. He was doing so much for her, and she wanted to do so much for him. Wipe that scowl off his face, for starters. But it was no good. *I'm trying so hard to live up to the needs of one small boy, there's just no room for anyone else. I'd just make a mess of it.*

Mark was quiet for a long time. They were in the suburbs of Eureka, traffic noises a steady accompaniment to the dinosaur rampaging in the backseat.

"Time for breakfast," he said.

Surprise made her turn away from the window. This was the first time she hadn't had to remind him about food. He never seemed to eat more than a few bites, although he hardly looked starving. She wondered how he maintained an athlete's build on nothing but black coffee.

He pulled into a diner and switched off the engine. "Jonathan will never think you didn't try your best for him. Neither will I."

Bree struggled with his bluntness, not sure how to reply. "I don't know if I can give him what he needs."

"You will. I'll do everything I can to help."

"You've kept us out of harm's way."

"Yes." A tiny thread of satisfaction crept into the word. "That much I can do."

The conversation left her confused, as if she were still half stuck in her dream. *These strangers were mighty and mysterious, loyal but fierce beyond the ways of men.* The words from Jessica's story fit him all too well. *Think about what you see.*

So she did. Mark was a doctor, but he was also an operative chased by armed men. He lived in the remote woods and treated cougars as if they were naughty kittens. He'd kissed her as though she was rare and precious, but had no trouble taking Jessica's book without batting an eye. Mighty and mysterious was a good description for Mark Winspear.

He gave her a sly smile, as if he could read her thoughts. She suddenly understood what it meant to be fascinated, in the most primitive sense of the word. Bree swallowed, irritated, grateful, afraid and wanting him all at the same time. Heat crept through her belly, making a mess of whatever coherent thoughts she had left.

He's one of the puzzle pieces. And try as she might, she still wasn't seeing the pattern.

Chapter 15

"Waffles?" Mark suggested as they sat down in a vinyl-covered booth. "I think those were promised before your breakfast plans were rudely interrupted by gunfire."

Bree reached for her coffee. She had that horrible, groggy feeling that came from sleeping in fits and snatches, but the hot liquid rolled over her tongue like a blessing. The diner was everything it should be: cheerful, homey and redolent with the scent of baking and bacon. A real family place, with high chairs and a kid's menu.

"Can we afford to stop that long?" Bree had to ask, even if her stomach growled at the thought of hot food.

"Everyone needs a rest." Mark pulled off his sunglasses and raised an eyebrow. "And I'm sure the T. rex is very fond of hunting blueberries."

"Rowr!" Jonathan replied, walking the toy up Mark's arm. He suffered it patiently.

Bree remembered that Mark had children somewhere

in his past. Two sons. Would they look like him, with clean, handsome features and olive skin? Where were they? Who was their mother? The questions threatened to choke her, but the last time she'd asked, he'd given her a look that nearly stopped her heart with its cold refusal.

She watched the muscles in his lean forearms as he helped Jonathan with the menu, then with his orange juice. She wanted to leap in and do it herself, but there was absolutely no need. They even looked a bit like father and son, both with dark hair and dark eyes. Did Mark see his own boys when he looked at her son? The thought of it made her catch her breath.

"How far will we get today?" she asked, hoping to distract her unruly thoughts.

Mark looked around, so she did, too. All the nearby booths were empty. She should have checked before she asked the question. Just like she should have checked before calling her dad. *I'm okay as long as I'm on my own. When other people start getting involved, I get emotional and stupid.*

Mark removed the dinosaur from where it had strayed atop the sugar packets and returned it to its master. "It's about an hour and forty minutes to Leggett. The road we're on turns into the Pacific Coast Highway and will take us down to San Francisco. That's about six hours straight through."

Somewhere along the line, he'd stopped being so grumpy. It had happened so gradually, she hadn't noticed. Maybe he hadn't, either. "Let me take some of the driving," she said. "You've gone all night."

He looked amused but nodded. The waitress came and took their order. Waffles for Bree and Jonathan, a bloody-rare breakfast steak for Mark.

"Where are you headed then? Out for a family holiday?" the woman asked cheerfully.

"Sure," said Bree when Mark looked vaguely panicked. "The weather's great for it."

"Oh, yeah, look at all that sun. Time to work on your tan." She pocketed her pen and hurried off.

Mark shifted in his seat, muttering to himself. "Tan. Family holiday. Great fiery hells."

"What?" Bree demanded, pretending she hadn't heard.

He looked guilty but was saved from having to answer. The waitress returned with a cartoon of a magic castle to color and a handful of crayons. Jonathan picked up a brown one and got busy coloring in the stone towers.

"He has amazing focus," Mark commented in his doctor voice.

"He always has."

"Good motor coordination. Well above average for his age. Have you had his hearing and eyesight tested?"

Her stomach tightened. "Not recently. Why? Is there something wrong?"

"No." He picked up a green crayon and twirled it in his fingers. "I suspect they are advanced, as well."

"Explain."

His brow furrowed. "I can't. Not yet. But it's almost as if when he stopped speaking, other parts of his brain, like small motor coordination, developed beyond his chronological age."

Bree felt cold. "I thought you said this was a blood disease."

"I didn't say it wasn't." His finely sculpted mouth turned down at the corners. "But it's got an unusual symptomology."

A sick feeling washed through her, and she shifted in her seat. She didn't want to admit it, but Mark was right. Now Jonathan was coloring madly, the pink tip of his tongue clamped between his teeth. He was filling the sky with blue, his hand moving at lightning speed. Yet the crayon never strayed beyond the cartoon's border, leaving even, smooth strokes. Bree doubted she could do as good a job.

Nothing she did could erase the paleness of his skin, or the dark circles under his eyes. He was too thin, his little arms reminding her of the hollow bones of birds. *How did this happen? What did I miss? When was it that my attention wavered, and this disease swept in and took my baby?*

"Hey." Mark reached across the table, catching her hand. His skin was cool as he squeezed her fingers. "We're working on this, remember? I said I would make a diagnosis, and I will. We're going to solve this."

"I hope so." His touch broke through her defenses, and her eyes prickled. She closed them before tears could fall. He didn't need to see her pain. That pushed people away, or else made them want to rescue you. She was attracted to him, but didn't want to be his project. That would diminish her. She pulled her hand free, keeping her gaze on the table.

Why don't you give in and let him take charge? her inner voice coaxed. *Are you just too proud?*

Probably that was true. She'd fought to stand on her own two feet instead of taking handouts from her parents, and wasn't about to backslide. But it was more than that. She wasn't going to relax until Jonathan was safe and well. Until then, she wasn't taking any risks, physical or emotional.

Breakfast arrived. This time it was Mark who cut up the food on Jonathan's plate, patiently redirecting the boy's attention to the meal whenever his interest strayed to the crayons, or the dinosaur, or the other people now filling up the diner. The boy's appetite came and went these days, and with it his ability to sit still while everyone else ate. Mark watched over him without complaint.

"There are still berries and whipped cream there," Mark said. "You had better eat a tunnel through them, or your dinosaur will get lost. And maybe you'd better clear a path through that waffle, too. Those are deep craters for a T. rex to walk through."

Bree watched, picking at her own food. She admired Mark's firm, calm patience, fascinated by the way her son responded so naturally to his authority. At the same time, she felt oddly displaced. She had been everything to the boy. Now, however briefly, she was merely part of a team. It was good for Jonathan, but she was finding it hard to let go.

"What a well-behaved little man. He's so quiet," the waitress said when she came around with the coffeepot. "He sure looks like his father."

Mark's expression was that of a man stranded on the other side of an abyss. "He's a good boy." He put a hand on Jonathan's shoulder, the touch infinitely gentle.

Bree bit her lip, but said nothing. She didn't know Mark well enough to understand his every emotion, but she could tell he was growing attached to Jonathan. That made her trust him a little bit more.

Mark picked up a yellow crayon and started filling in the stars on Jonathan's blueberry-spattered drawing.

Puzzle piece, she thought.

They were just finishing up when a motion outside caught Mark's attention. A big white pickup drove in, the driver slamming the door as he swaggered in for a coffee to go.

"C'mon, Susie girl, give it to me hot and give it to me quick," he bellowed. The words were friendly enough, but the tone was pushy.

Jonathan started to whimper and Bree went quiet as a she-wolf on the prowl. It was time to go. Mark shoved his sunglasses back on and went to pay the bill while Bree made a bathroom run with the boy.

Mark got to the counter seconds before the loud man. The waitress took Mark's money.

"Come on, Susie," said the loudmouth. "Move your fat backside. I'm not getting any younger!"

"Wait your turn," Mark said evenly, accepting his change. He stuffed a healthy tip in the jar.

Loudmouth pulled up his pants. "Who the blazes are you, Daddy Knows Best?"

Mark took off his sunglasses, letting the idiot see the predator behind the human mask. Loudmouth fell instantly silent.

In that second, Mark caught a glimpse of his thoughts: *Who is this guy? I wish he'd get out of my face. I need to hit the road. Ticktock.* Then Mark got an image of a puppy in a box, and that box in a lonely ditch. It hadn't happened yet, but it was on the man's agenda. *Nuisance. Problem solved. Then off to the auction to see a man about that second car.*

Mark wanted to wash his brain out with soap and water. Yet, at the same time, an idea was taking shape, something he'd read in a medical journal a few months ago about animal-assisted therapy helping children who had fallen behind with speech. He was beginning to think that Jonathan had forgotten how to talk while his brain was busy doing other things—what, Mark still had to figure out, but that was a question for later. What Jonathan needed right now was motivation to relearn language—and an opportunity had just fallen into their laps.

He took Loudmouth's arm, firmly and gently. "Take me to your truck."

Bree took Jonathan to the little boy's room. When they got back, Mark was waiting by the door. The pickup was pulling out of the lot.

"I half expected that guy to start a fight," she said.

"He changed his mind." Mark led the way back to the car, a spring in his step. He wiped his mouth with a paper napkin, dropping it in the trash can on the sidewalk.

She wanted, and didn't want, an explanation, but Jonathan suddenly started pulling at her hand. "What, sweetheart?" she asked, trotting after him.

In the parking spot next to where the pickup had been was a cardboard box, the flaps on top folded shut. Jonathan was making a direct line for it.

Bree gripped Jonathan's hand more tightly, pulling him close to her side. The boy whined and tried to twist out of her grip. Visions of severed heads or violent explosives filled her mind. "It's an abandoned package. Should we call the fire department or something?"

Mark's lips twitched. "I don't think so."

He lifted the flaps, letting them peer inside.

Bree let curiosity draw her closer, but she didn't let Jonathan get an inch ahead. Even with Mark there, she wasn't taking any chances. But when she leaned forward, her heart melted. It was a doughnut of pale yellow fur.

It was too perfect, and too awful. "A puppy? That horrible man in the pickup truck left a puppy?"

"Almost." Mark reached into the box and picked up the tiny creature. It couldn't have been more than six or seven weeks. It whined, moving from a doughnut shape to a boneless, fuzzy sausage shape draped over his hands. "It looks like a lab cross."

Jonathan lunged, but she held him back. "Is it sick?"

Mark shook his head. "It's just small. It should have stayed with its mother a little longer."

Bree relented and let Jonathan approach it. "Gently!"

How had Jonathan known what was in the box? Kids could be eerily perceptive, but this was almost superhuman. It was another strange, inexplicable thing, like the book, or her dream. Bree felt herself drowning in frustration. Nothing fit together.

Except the boy and the dog. Jonathan folded the tiny puppy into his thin arms and buried his face in the soft fur. Mark gave her a conspiratorial look. "We can't leave it here," he said.

"Can we seriously take it with us?" Bree made a face. "If kids are sticky, puppies are, uh, stinky."

Mark looked pained. "At least we're not driving the Lexus."

"But what if something happens? If the puppy doesn't thrive or we have to keep running and can't keep it…" Jonathan would be hurt. She couldn't have that. "Surely there must be an animal shelter around."

The traitorous puppy started licking Jonathan's face. He giggled, his cheeks turning pink with pleasure. Bree and Mark exchanged a look, two adults experiencing a moment of surrender. But the sound of Jonathan's laughter was so infectious, she laughed, too, making Mark's lips curve into a smile. A sweet warmth blossomed in her chest. It was good to have someone to share this moment with.

And the man had a killer smile, with more than a tinge of melancholy. *He had two sons.* She wanted to weep for him.

Mark ducked his head, hiding that smile away. Bree remembered he hid in his cabin in the woods, or behind a white coat. He was as unused to connecting with people as she was. She put a hand on his arm. "It's too late. I guess we keep the critter, but don't blame me if you end up shampooing the car seats. You had something to do with this puppy just happening to be on the sidewalk."

A glimmer of wicked satisfaction crossed his face so fast, she wasn't sure she'd seen it. The fact that she'd said yes meant something to him.

"We had best find someplace that sells pet supplies," he said mildly. "We've had breakfast, but that little fellow hasn't."

Chapter 16

Now Marco Farnese, vampire assassin, not only had a human woman and her frail child under his care, but a puppy named Custard, too. Interesting to know that the world still had the capacity to surprise him.

It made him uneasy, as if things were sliding out of his control. Perhaps he had let the penitent, doctoring side of himself run the show for a little too long. Or maybe he was upset with himself because he was enjoying this insane road trip despite Ferrel and Lark's book and everything else—and he hadn't actually *enjoyed* anything in centuries. There was a simplicity to his purpose. Protect the innocent. Heal the sick. Be the hero. Very few moments in his long existence had possessed that kind of clarity, free of kings and politics and their endless shades of moral gray. This mission was almost a gift.

They had passed through the stately beauty of the redwoods and were nearly in San Francisco. It was past time to get in touch with Kenyon and find out where one of the Company's choppers could pick them up. Except he didn't want the journey to end. Every hour on the road was one more hour when he belonged to this little family.

The fact that he delayed—well, that was the reason why he didn't deserve a family. He was selfish. That had already been proven once.

Marco Farnese had been a young man about court once upon a time, with a wife and two sons. As he was neither royal nor as rich as his cousins, he had been given as tribute to the rogue vampires secretly terrorizing the noble families of the city. It was an easy bargain, in fact the Commander General of the Knights—the Nicholas Ferrel of old—had brokered it. One son of a noble house sacrificed to the pleasure of the vampires in exchange for a year of vampire-free peace in the city. Mark was a husband and father, but that weighed little. He'd been dragged from his bed one night, and his life was over. The rest was literally history—centuries of it. Mark had spent years as his brutish sire's pet assassin, until finally Mark had killed him, too.

But all that had come later. At first, he had tried to return home, wanting more than anything to be with his mortal family. They needed his protection. He needed their love, some reassurance that he was still Marco.

His selfishness had been their death. Harboring a vampire was, in the eyes of the slayers, a burning offense. Ferrel had carried out the sentence, and that had started Mark's vendetta against the Knights.

And now here was another family he couldn't bring himself to leave. Apparently, he had learned nothing. That craven need for kind words and smiles was stronger than his duty to protect the very people he cared for.

He'd thought that needy part of him had died long ago.

Vampires were supposed to be beyond such desires. Yet somehow Bree and her child had stirred those embers back to life. It was up to him to stomp that fire into the dust. *Do I have the courage?*

A glance at the dashboard clock told him it was close to eight o'clock. He could see the lights of San Francisco straight ahead. Bree had spelled him off for a while, but he'd been driving more or less constantly for two days. He needed a rest, and he needed relief from the constant scent of warm, living humans.

"Let's find someplace to stop," he said.

He felt more than heard Bree's sigh of relief. She wasn't complaining, but he could tell she was restless. She'd read that magazine through three times. He turned into a motel twenty minutes later. The old neon sign flashed Vacancy in brilliant blue.

"Wait here." He parked next to the door.

The clerk registered them without taking his eyes off the TV on the wall. There was a football game on, the sound turned up high enough to bother a vampire's sensitive ears. When Mark asked to use the office phone, he got no more than a grunt. Mark picked up the cordless handset and walked as far away from the TV as he could get.

He paused for a moment before dialing, his brain scrambling to find reasons why he didn't have to contact headquarters. But there were no excuses. If he really cared for Bree and Jonathan and, yes, little Custard—whatever happened to names like Fang and Rover?—he would do the right thing and call for backup.

Still, it was an act of will to punch the numbers and lift the phone to his ear. His stomach went cold as he listened to the familiar ring.

As always, it was answered promptly. "Faran Kenyon."

"It's Mark."

"Where in the fuzzy balls have you been? Your phone went dark."

"I took the battery out. You weren't the only one tracking it. I'm assuming your end of the line isn't bugged."

"If it is, we have bigger problems." Kenyon's voice was tired. "Then again, you never know."

After the vampires' old leader had defected to the Knights—around the same time Jack had died—their safety measures had been severely compromised. The past six months had been a game of security whack-a-mole.

Was that a good enough reason to keep his location secret?

Just get it over with. "I'm calling from a motel just north of San Francisco. We need pickup."

"All we've got nearby is an Mi-17."

"A military transport?"

Kenyon sounded defensive. "Sam and some of the boys had it out in the desert for training. It's not like we keep a vast selection of aircraft for extractions here at home. Most operatives have the wits to get their butts in a sling overseas, not in their own backyard."

"An Mi-17 is a bit conspicuous for a motel parking lot."

"No, really? After dark it could be fun, with the floodlights and everything." The words oozed sarcasm.

Mark played the scene in his head. Vampires were supposed to be secret. Great big choppers were anything but, especially when they touched down in suburbia. Mark hated explaining these things to the local police. "No good. We'll have to get out of town first. In daylight."

"Can you wait that long?"

Mark looked around the office. The clerk was still transfixed by the game. "We've lost our tail for now."

"What's your route?"

"They'll be expecting us to keep going straight down the coast. My plan was to cut east and loop around L.A. Come in from the south."

"Where will you be by morning?"

"Here. We need rest."

"Okay. What are you driving?"

"A Forester." Mark gave him the license plate. "Give me until noon, then start looking on the 46 near Paso Robles."

"You got it."

Mark hung up with a feeling of relief, followed by a surge of hunger and desire. He'd been given an extra night with Bree, all the way until tomorrow afternoon.

He would make the most of it.

Bree had never had a dog, but a few hours with one curled in her lap had convinced her they were necessary for happiness—at least until Custard demonstrated a significant lack of potty training. Fortunately, he was still a small dog.

And Jonathan loved him. Her boy rolled in the grass behind the motel, romping until both boy and dog were exhausted. Jonathan tired easily, but he could keep up with the tiny puppy. In the time it took Bree to finish a shrimp salad, both were snoozing in a pile on the grass.

"They bonded so fast," Bree commented. "They already seem to read each other's minds."

Mark nodded, a frown line between his brows. "I was hoping that being forced to give commands to a dog would encourage Jonathan to speak."

"You did?" She smiled slowly.

"Animal-assisted therapy works wonders with children."

"Clever thinking, but I wonder if he even needs words."

Mark seemed to ponder that. "I'm not sure he does."

Something in his tone made Bree uneasy. "What's on your mind?"

"I'm not sure. There's still much that puzzles me."

She had little to say to that.

They cleaned up the remains of their take-out meal and put boy and dog into one of the two beds. The room was more like a suite, with a living area flanked by bedrooms. Bree closed the door on her sleeping son while Mark pulled out Jessica's journal and finished removing the false pages.

"You say that's all about a biological weapon," Bree said. Her gaze traveled from the book to the stack of loose pages covered in Jessica's sketches. It was hard to believe such beauty hid something so ugly.

Mark raised his head. His eyes seemed to take a moment to refocus, as if his thoughts had been far away. "Yes. A genetic ailment carried by a virus. From what I can tell, it's not meant to be contagious unless introduced directly into the blood."

"You don't think…" Bree trailed off with a look of confusion.

Mark shrugged. "I have some background in this kind of science and I'm convinced this author was mad."

"On the other hand, if it didn't work, why would the Vidonese want it so badly?" She sat down opposite him at the little dining table. "I find it hard to believe these are Kyle's people."

He made a face. "Vidon and its royals have changed with the times, but the Knights have not. I heard that many of the Knights want to leave the service of the king. They adhere to a code from the past, and feel the Throne has grown too modern."

"Code?" Bree asked.

Mark shrugged. "I do not know the whole story. I'm not one of them."

"Thank heavens for that." She reached across the table, sliding her fingers over his. They were cool, the palms calloused as from an ax or spade. Whatever else he did in his man cave in the woods, he worked hard. Her stomach fluttered at the look in his deep brown eyes. She definitely had his attention. It made her bold.

"You don't like thanks," she said. "So I'll give you truth. I haven't forgiven you for taking that book, and I think you stole the car we're driving, but you're a good protector."

"I'm a beast," he said quietly. "You've only seen the best part of me."

"And I'm okay with that. For now."

"And you think there will more than just *for now?* My forevers are very long."

She wasn't sure what he meant by that, but she heard the challenge, and a lot of bitterness. *Baggage.* Fair enough. She had hers, too. "There might be. Or not. We've only just met."

He leaned his chin on his hand, his eyes hooded but far from sleepy. Bree's heart was racing, her breath stolen by just how handsome he was. Tempting, like a delicious morsel she knew she shouldn't eat.

"You have reservations?" His mouth quirked.

"I'm cautious," she admitted. "I think you are, too. We don't know everything there is to know about one another."

"That's true enough."

"Your secrets aren't any of my business. Mine aren't yours."

He gave her a smile. It was close to one of those heart-stopping grins that showed his dimples, but darker. Much, much darker. When he spoke, his voice was husky. "I want to make everything about you my business."

"Oh." She lowered her eyelids, forgetting that she didn't flirt anymore. That she was trying to be adult and reasonable. "And what makes you think I'll agree to that?"

She'd forgotten her hand was over his until his strong fingers slid around to grip her wrist.

"Beasts don't ask permission," he growled.

Bree felt a surge of adrenaline, but it wasn't the terror of gunfire and car chases. This was deeper, more elemental. This fear was tempered by the anticipation of battle, and she wasn't unarmed.

If he was the dragon, she was the sorceress. She was done waiting and watching, wondering what Mark might do next. She leaned across the table to whisper in his ear.

"I think we're ready for some grown-up time, don't you?"

Chapter 17

Bree tilted her head back and he slowly raised his hand to her hair, pushing it away from her face. It swished across her neck and cheek as he stroked her, his fingers slipping through the thick, tawny waves. She leaned into his hand, ready to purr like a cat, and then leaned closer to kiss him again.

The contact of their lips shocked Bree. She had kissed him before, but now it was *more*. He was more. Intent. Intense. She couldn't name the change, but he tasted like a man who had made up his mind to sin. The notion made her shiver, caught between anticipation and the unknown.

The tiny table was between them, and now Bree pulled away from Mark long enough to circle around so they could stand without a barrier in the way. She approached him tentatively, suddenly feeling naked though she had not shed one stitch of clothing. Her pulse felt loud and full, as if her veins were too small to hold the pounding surf of her blood. Heat crept up her skin, prickling under her arms and aching at the tips of her breasts. When she stopped he was only a few inches away. Those few inches felt charged, as if static could arc between them in a sparkle of light.

He ran one hand down her arm, his fingers tracing the flesh with a feather's lightness until he found her hand. Then his fingers laced with hers.

"Mark," she said softly.

"Hush." He put one finger across her lips, stopping any more words. His voice was low, almost inaudible.

She caught the finger between her teeth, nipping it lightly. He curled his finger back into his palm, a flash of amusement in his eyes. Then the humor stilled, the pupils of his eyes drowning in the dark brown of his gaze. Bree's stomach fluttered with impatience, but she made herself savor the moment. It had been a long time since she had the luxury of wanting a man and having that desire granted.

And he was a dream. The light that hung over the table was bright, hiding nothing. The sculpture of his face was at once rugged and beautiful, like something hewn from stone by an old master. There was art, with all its careful attention to geometry and balance, but the material was hard and strong.

She wound her fingers into the front of his shirt and stepped backward toward the other bedroom, tugging him along.

His eyes glittered hungrily, but there was caution there, too. "Are you sure?"

No, she wanted to say. She had too much history to do this lightly. There were risks and considerations, dangers and consequences. But there was also life. For once, she wanted a bit of it for herself. "Yes."

Then his hands were on her shoulders, fingers tensed as if he were not sure if he was pulling her close or pushing her away. Her fingers were still wrapped around a fistful of his shirt. The tension between them was nearly audible, throbbing like the deep note of a cello.

And then her arms were around his neck, his beard grazing her cheek. He lifted her easily, his hands under her as she wrapped her legs around his hips. Their lips met again, his kiss devouring her mouth. It went on and on, their tongues meeting, fencing, exploring with all the curiosity bottled up during those long hours in the car. Bree felt herself melting inside, a long ache winding through her core like the spring of a clock turned tighter and tighter. She wanted Mark. She craved release.

They moved, Mark backing her up to a wall, letting her feet touch the floor again. He did it all without breaking that kiss, but the change in angle allowed her to press different parts of her against new parts of him. His arousal was obvious, bringing a fresh urgency to the embrace. Mark's hands were on her, too, caressing the span of her ribs to cup her breasts. Feeling wanton, she arched into his touch.

Finally, he let her come up for air. With her hands threaded through his thick, dark hair, she stared into his eyes. They seemed to glitter, the ferocious hunger in them pulling at that spring in her belly. Her nipples grew harder, so sensitive she both wanted and did not want the pressure of his questing fingers.

"Oh, Doctor," she murmured.

"Not the bad doctor jokes."

"I'm having a medical emergency."

"We haven't even started."

She let her hands trail down the thick muscles that flared between neck and shoulder, then down the curve of his chest. It was like stroking marble, but he flinched when she got to the lower part of his flat belly. When her fingers found the button of his jeans, he was walking her backward through the bedroom door.

"Do you have protection?"

He chuckled. "Of course I do. Men are eternally optimistic."

He closed the door quietly behind them. Gently, she pulled down the tab of his zipper and nearly started as he sprang free of the confining denim. She let out a huff of breath. "Oh, yeah."

Mark chuckled, a guttural, male sound that resonated low in her spine. He herded her toward the bed, the edge of the mattress catching her behind the knees so that she automatically sat down. But he kept coming, forcing her to scramble farther until she was on her back. Then he was on top, straddling her. Somewhere in the rush he had taken her shoes and kicked off his, but she wasn't sure when. Her insides squeezed with anxiety, suddenly sure he was much more experienced at this than she was. She had sown her wild oats, but he… Her brain let the metaphor wander.

He bent, running his hands under the edge of her sweater, pushing it up inch by inch. His cool fingers seemed greedy for her warmth, caressing as they went, honoring, stroking, exposing her midriff to the soft light of the bedside table. As the gentle glow touched her skin, so did his mouth. Bree closed her eyes, swamped in sensation as he nipped at the vulnerable flesh of her belly. His teeth were surprisingly sharp, leaving gooseflesh in their wake.

"You even taste like sunshine," he murmured.

"You're allergic to it," she protested.

"It dazzles me."

He slipped the sweater over her head, then pulled off his own. Bree's stomach flipped, her focus lost for a moment to the lean, hard muscle of his body. He was equally fixed on her, one finger running along the ivory lace of her bra, pausing to linger at the peak of her nipple. Holding his gaze, she reached up, unclasping the front of the garment. She felt it give way, the heaviness of her breasts falling free. His breath caught, and then she felt his mouth close around her to suck. An exquisite sensation pulsed through Bree, making her squirm.

This felt so good, so right. It had been so long. Her brain floundered, able to grasp only thoughts like *good* and *yes*. Deep down, somewhere below the layers of sensation, she was aware that she trusted Mark enough to let go of her thoughts, to be Bree again, and not only the defender of her child. When had that happened?

And then his jeans were off and they were skin to skin, the soft velvet of his manhood brushing her as he moved to slip on a condom. The rest of her clothes were gone, too, leaving her vulnerable, her skin pale against the dark flowered quilt of the bed. Vulnerable and very wet.

She reached up to him, her hands skimming the strong muscles of his shoulders. She could see the tension in his neck, in the bunching muscles of his forearms. She stroked down the length of his arms, pulling him to her. Even that mild pressure made him shudder as if in pain. Curious, her gaze found his face.

What she saw there robbed her of breath. His features were carefully neutral, as if wiped clean of anything that might scare her off. But he could not hide his eyes. There she witnessed raw hunger, as feral as anything from her darkest nightmares. She could only guess that all that tension was Mark's effort to keep himself in check.

A sane response would be to flee, to put solid walls between her flesh and so much devouring need. Instead, the desire pooling in her belly spilled into her blood, warming her like hot brandy. Bree's heart pounded harder, as if readying her for a race. Mark's eyes flared, impossibly dark, impossibly intense. He leaned forward, planting his hands on either side of her, bringing his face kissing-close.

Bree reached up and wrapped her hands around his wrists. "How do you want this?"

"Don't talk," he whispered. "I can't talk."

Then he kissed her, as if to stop any more words. His thumb ran along the arc of her collarbone, sliding along the curve of her breast. He sighed, the sound ragged as it heaved out of his chest. The sound told her exactly how much he wanted to let himself go, to take instead of tease, but it also said he intended to savor every moment. His lips traced the line where his touch had been, sometimes in light butterfly kisses, sometimes in sharp nips that sent arrows of pleasure to unexpected places. A tiny moan escaped her, bringing a slight smile to his lips before he bent once more to his task. It was as if he were mapping her as systematically as any explorer planting his flag.

When she tried to reciprocate, he held her down, his eyes unfocused and wild. "No. It's better if we do it this way."

Bree slid her knee up his side, giving him the soft skin of her thigh. He pushed her leg back down, his hand firm but gentle.

She wanted to scream, every fiber of her being on fire. "I can't lie still. I have to move."

"No."

She put her hand to his face. He replaced it on the mattress. "No. Don't you dare."

"But—"

He put his lips to her ear, barely making a sound. "Let me do this my way. I'm not completely safe."

The words sent a chill through her, but that got mixed up with her oversensitive nerves and just inflamed her more. He resumed his work then, tonguing her nipple until the sensation bolted all the way through to her toes. Not safe? No. Not at all. He was torturing her, but not in any way that would put him in jail. "Mark…"

"Shh."

Lying still left her no option but to feel every touch, every lick, every time he blew across her damp skin, leaving a thrill of sensation that raised the fine down of her body. He had reached her midriff by the time the first orgasm took her. By the time he reached the cleft of her thighs, she was cursing him. But by then he had her again, and the sweet, pulsing pain of her desire swamped any thought of rebellion.

He was good at this, this…torture. Damn him, he was good. But she wasn't doing this his way all night. She caught the hard, full length of him and stroked. She heard that ragged intake of breath again as she guided him exactly where he needed to fit. She was more than ready, but the fullness of him made her moan.

"No," he muttered. "No."

What was with this guy? "Yes." And she moved her hips.

He didn't protest again, his body giving an answering thrust. He made a harsh sound in his throat, half snarl, half cry of pleasure

This was more like it. She arched to meet him, feeling sensation spiraling through her as delectable pressure began to build once more. Yes, this is what she wanted. Bree closed her eyes, losing herself in Mark's strength, the sheer power of his body working against hers. He was magnificent.

And that tightness in him was beginning to give way. She could feel it with every thrust, as if he were a bow-string unraveling, stretching, ready to snap at any moment. It fed into her excitement as the speed and urgency of their lovemaking increased. Her face was wet with tears—of gratitude, of release, of the surrender of her own crazy, overburdened soul—she wasn't sure and it didn't matter. It was all perfect and she let go one more time. There was nothing gentle in it, desire ripping through her like a blade. With a final thrust, Mark squeezed his eyes shut, throwing his head back with a rough cry.

Bree clung to him, conscious of his convulsion at the same instant as hers. Time dropped away for a breathless pause, a perfect, inexplicable sum of them both. And then it slowly spiraled away, taking her strength with it.

Only then did he lie down beside her, holding her close. Bree curled next to him, her head under his chin, her body satisfied beyond any encounter she had ever known.

But it felt wrong.

She arched her neck, looking into Mark's face. His eyes were guarded. He had finished, no question there, but he had held part of himself back. The bowstring might have frayed, but it had not given way beneath the onslaught of their passion. The wild, dangerous creature that had stared out of his eyes was still safely on its leash.

Logic said she should have been grateful, but her heart felt heavy. She might have trusted him, but he wasn't ready to share everything with her. *He's not completely safe.*

Or at least he didn't think so. What the blazes was

that all about? The guns and spy stuff? Or something more personal?

He noticed her looking at him. "Thank you," he said softly.

"Likewise," she replied, touching his rough cheek with her fingertip. *What's wrong?* She wanted to ask, but she didn't. Instinct said he'd shared as much as he dared for one night. Pushing would spoil it. Nevertheless, it left her with one corner of her soul hollow, as if what they had done hadn't happened and she was still sleeping alone.

Mark pulled the blanket over them, cuddling her close. But within his embrace, she could feel the subtle tension of his body.

Chapter 18

They had turned east just south of Paso Robles. On Mark's instructions, Bree was watching for a helicopter in the clear blue sky overhead.

She was confused and tense after last night, wondering if she were inventing trouble where it didn't exist. They'd had sex—great sex. Then they'd had a nice breakfast. So what was wrong with that? Was she expecting vows of eternal adoration? A marriage proposal?

Bree wanted to slap herself. She was trying to give her romp with Mark more importance, to see his desire as more than a healthy libido. She'd done it before and here she was doing it again. Her fantasies of a happy family seduced her into making mistakes. *Enjoy the sex and move on. That's what he's going to do. You've been down this road time and again. Expecting more is what hurts in the end.*

Mark suddenly swore and stepped on the gas. Her

stomach lurched, still mired in her swamp of self-examination. The roar of the engine snapped her back to the here and now. Bree's instincts to flee or fight ramped to full throttle.

"What is it?" she demanded, gripping the door handle in one hand and Custard in the other. The puppy had been asleep in her lap until that second. Now he yipped in protest.

"The Escalade. They've found us."

"How? Did they listen in when you called for the chopper?"

"Maybe." His voice was controlled, but he smacked the steering wheel hard, making the car swerve. "It's not impossible that they've got a tap on home base. One of our own defected months ago. Who knows what information he gave them."

Hurt fury lurked beneath his clipped words. More emotion he didn't want to share. Well, fine. This wasn't the moment for it anyway. Bree turned her mind to the practical. "How do we lose them?"

They were nowhere near a town and the promised chopper was nowhere in sight. Then she spotted something arching above a stand of trees. "Wait, is that a Ferris wheel? If there's a crowd, lots of people…"

Mark gave a single, approving nod. "There's a road sign up ahead."

It wasn't exactly a road sign. It was a large piece of cardboard pinned to the stump of a lightning-blasted pine. It read County Fair, Fri–Sun Only in hand-lettered paint. An arrow pointed north. In unspoken agreement, they turned north.

Mark pulled the car into a rutted field, parking it next to a muddy pickup. There had to be hundreds of cars in ragged rows. The nearby town might have been small, but the fair obviously drew folks from all the farms and hamlets around.

"Good thinking," he said, quickly killing the motor. "We'll lose them easily enough in here."

They wouldn't be able to use the same car again. Bree gathered their things in record time, stuffing them in her backpack. She squashed an almost-full bag of puppy kibble in with her dirty clothes and Jessica's book—which he'd finally returned to her custody. Mark picked up Custard, who tried to cover his sunglasses in slobbery licks.

They had to leave the car seat. It made Bree uneasy, but carting it around would attract attention, and it was too big to run with. As it was, they probably had only a few minutes to disappear into the crowd before Nicholas Ferrel caught up. They'd have to become invisible fast.

They hurried along the chain-link fence to the gate. Jonathan trotted at Bree's side, pointing at the brightly painted rides as they swooped and dipped against the perfect, blue sky.

This should have been a time for cotton candy and merry-go-rounds. Her son's happy smile brought an ache to her chest. Her parents at least had managed to avoid subjecting their daughter to actual gunfire.

Mark paid the clown selling tickets and they went in.

"What's the plan?" she asked, looking around.

The place looked so typical her father might have used it as a set for one of his movies. Straight ahead was a large sign listing the attractions. Besides the midway, there was a craft show in the barn, an exhibition hall for flowers and vegetables, the local 4-H Club, a ring for dressage, country music in the band shell and food. Bree could smell popcorn and barbecue on the breeze.

Mark absently rubbed Custard's ears as he studied a map pinned to the side of the ticket booth. "According to this, there's another parking lot at the far gate. If we go through the fair and out that side, I'm sure we could find suitable transportation."

He meant steal another car. Shame and anger heated her cheeks. "You make it sound so easy."

"We'll make it right," Mark said quietly. "But we have to get away first."

Nodding, she pulled Jonathan closer. It really was a matter of life-and-death. That didn't make her like it any better. She'd done a lot of stupid things in her life but up until now she hadn't broken the law. Much. But it was her son at stake. She'd steal the Golden Gate Bridge if it got her any closer to a cure.

Still cradling Custard, Mark led the way into the throng of fairgoers, clearing a path with his tall form. Bree gripped Jonathan's hand tightly in hers. She could feel the boy lagging behind as one thing after another caught his attention. A llama. A juggler. An old man playing the accordion. She picked up her son, hurrying to keep up with Mark's brisk strides. She knew what would happen after a few minutes; the noise and confusion of the crowd would overexcite Jonathan and he'd be in tears. Not the best option if they were trying to sneak away unnoticed.

The path seemed to wind on and on between rows of vegetable stalls and the modern equivalent of medicine shows. Even growing up on the West Coast she had no idea there were so many remedies for fatty livers and achy chakras.

Nothing for single mothers with a bad case of morning-after jitters.

Someone was selling wind socks. She looked up, her eye caught by a bright orange koi. It was then she saw Ferrel. He was standing a dozen yards away with his back to her, but she knew the set of his head and shoulders. A jolt of dread hit her like an electric shock.

"Mark!" She caught his sleeve, dropping her voice to a whisper. "Over to the right."

"They saw where we were going and got ahead of us. Clever," he muttered. With a gentle hand at the small of her back, he turned her toward the nearest barn. Custard began squirming, wanting to see what was going on.

The sign on the side of the barn said it was a livestock exhibit. Even from yards away, it smelled like straw and animals, the sound of bleating sheep and excited children echoing from the dark interior. A man in coveralls and a scruffy beard was sitting on an overturned barrel, watching the door. He held up a hand as they neared. "Can't go in there, sir, not with a dog."

Bree swore silently, barely resisting the urge to turn around and see if Ferrel was following them yet. Her back itched, just waiting for a hand to fall on her shoulder and a gun to press into her back.

Meanwhile, Mark pulled off his sunglasses, smiling affably. "No dogs?"

"Nope."

"Not even one so small as this?"

Bree could see the man waver, obviously falling under Mark's charm. *How does he do that?* Bree wondered. Mark had missed a career in sales.

"Look." Mark waggled one of Custard's paws. "He's so short, his legs aren't even touching the ground."

The man stepped aside. "Okay, but keep hold of him. He's smaller than some of the chickens."

No sooner had they ducked inside than Jonathan squealed with delight. The huge barn was a maze of enclosures. Closest were goats, sheep and miniature horses.

Shafts of sun fell through the windows, spilling across the straw-covered floor. Dust motes danced in the light.

Mark started for the exit on the opposite end of the structure, but Jonathan lunged toward the Shetland ponies. Bree hauled him back, wishing Mark would slow down a moment. The boy's little arms reached for the pint-size steeds, whimpering as though his heart would break in two. Bree took a firmer grip of his hand, feeling like the meanest mother on earth.

A cluster of goats watched them critically. A blue rosette announced they were first-place champions. *Bully for you,* Bree thought crossly. *Smug doesn't cut it when there's someone after your bacon. Just ask the pigs.*

The moment of distraction was exactly enough time for Jonathan to wriggle away. Bree snatched at the air where he'd been a moment before, but it was too late. "Jonathan!"

Horror shot through her. She dodged toward the ponies, thinking that's where he would go, but instead he scampered for a pen of sheep. His path went right by Mark, who reached down to pluck the boy from his headlong rush. Instead, Custard bounded out of Mark's arms, making him lose both boy and dog.

"Jonathan!" Bree's stomach lurched as the world narrowed to the sight of her boy clambering through the bars of the pen.

Not to be outdone, Custard zoomed across the straw in a kind of darting waddle. On instinct, Bree dove for the trailing leash, but it slipped between her fingers as the puppy ran right under the rail of the pen. An enormous black sheep with curling horns gave a startled bleat and tried to butt Custard, who gave an affronted yap.

The sheep were stamping and shuffling backward into the corner of their pen. Bree fumbled with the gate of the pen, light-headed with panic. There was only a rope loop holding the gate closed, but her fingers were clumsy, numb and tingling with fear. She had no idea if sheep would attack. She didn't think so, but she was leaving nothing to chance—and all they needed was an animal stampede to blow their escape. Talk about the worst fugitives ever.

The rope loop finally slipped over the post, allowing the gate to swing free. She heard Custard yip when a hand grabbed her arm. "You can't go in there, ma'am."

Bree whirled, ready to smack anyone in her way. It was the man in coveralls from the door, his round, flushed face in a stony frown. Fury and frustration made her voice shrill. "My son! He's in there. He'll be hurt."

"Your son?" The frown deepened. "Where?"

Bree whirled around. All the sheep were in a clump in the back corner of the pen, looking worried, but there was no boy and no dog. "Where is he? Where did Jonathan go?" And where was Mark?

"I think you'd better leave the barn, ma'am."

Her mouth went dry, bewilderment overtaking her. Barely a second had passed. *Jonathan was there. He was right there.* But there wasn't a trace of him now. She was completely alone.

"No!" She tried to pull away. If only she could get into the pen, have a better look around. "My son was in there with the sheep. He's little—he's not quite four!"

"I can see the whole pen, ma'am, there are no boys in there." The man gripped her so hard she would surely have bruises. "Come on, let's go outside. Is there someone we can call for you?"

She saw Ferrel standing in the doorway to the barn, the sun glinting on his fair hair. *No!* She stumbled, her feet trying to carry her anywhere but straight toward the enemy. Her guard hauled her upright and shoved her into Ferrel's waiting hands. She started to twist away, but he clamped iron fingers around her wrist.

"I'm very sorry," he said apologetically, giving a sad smile to the attendant. "We lost our son a year ago. I'm afraid she's not quite over it."

He delivered his lines with just a hint of tragedy. It was far more convincing than if he had buttered the lie with too much grief.

Mr. Coveralls looked sympathetic. "I'm sorry to hear that, sir."

"It's a lie!" Bree shot back, but neither man paid the least attention. "He's kidnapping me!"

"Let's go for a walk," Ferrel said pleasantly, and he marched Bree back into the sunlight.

"Where's Jonathan?" she demanded.

Ferrel answered through gritted teeth. "Safe. And he'll stay safe if you cooperate."

She studied his profile: the sharply ridged brow, the straight nose, the clean angle of his chin. Handsome, in his way, but boiling over with anger. Just like her. Her rage burned like whiskey on her tongue. "It was you in the airport, wasn't it? Months ago. You drugged us."

"Yes." He'd pulled her around the corner of the barn, into the shadows, and forced her back against the wooden siding. Bree took a breath to scream, but he pressed closer.

"Don't even think about it." He lowered his head until his face was only inches from hers.

Bree pulled her chin back, trying to see around Ferrel. Panic bubbled inside her, but she forced it down with an act of will. She had to use her head, not just react. What were her options? Did she even have any?

They were off the main footpath here, away from the

crowds. To passersby, they'd look just like any couple on the brink of a kiss. It was all she could do not to shrink away.

Where was Mark? She had to believe he was looking for Jonathan. If anyone could get her son back, it was Mark.

Ferrel's eyes were gray and narrowed with temper. He held up his cell phone. "You make one wrong move and I'll give the order to kill your brat."

A stab of terror shot through her, but she swallowed hard, forcing herself to stay calm. "I doubt that. You've gone to a lot of trouble to get him."

"You want to test that theory?"

Bree curled her lip, almost beyond caring what he did to her, if she could only get him to leave her son alone. "What do you want?"

"I want you to stop and think about what you're doing."

The sincerity of his tone surprised her. It almost sounded real. "What are you talking about?"

"Marco Farnese."

"Mark? Dr. Winspear?"

Ferrel's nostrils flared, as if the name smelled bad. "Call him what you like. He's a monster."

"He's not the one threatening me. He's not the one who killed my boss." She pulled her wrist out of his hand.

He let her. "I'm sorry for that, but we want what Lark gave you. It's imperative that we have it."

The journal. "Why do you want it so badly?"

"What did you do with it?"

"I don't have it," she lied. The book was in the pack hanging from her shoulders, beneath a bag of puppy chow and mere inches from Ferrel's furious face. She pressed her lips into a hard line so that they would not tremble. She was terrified, but her mind felt razor-sharp. The longer she kept him talking, the more time Mark would have to find Jonathan.

"You didn't have the journal the last time we met, either."

That was true. Quite by chance, the book had been in Bree's carry-on. She'd stashed the bag in an airport locker just before they'd grabbed and drugged her. Weeks later, she'd retrieved it from the airport's lost and found.

"No, I didn't have it then, and I don't have it now. I sense a pattern," she shot back.

"I repeat, what did you do with it?"

She tilted her head, beyond frightened now. "You know, you dress well enough, but you don't strike me as all that fashion forward. Why the interest in Jessica's sketches?"

His look grew suspicious. Bree guessed he knew very well what was beneath the drawings. "Where is it?"

"Gone. We were on the run. I loved Jessica like a big sister, but I lightened my load. The book is in a landfill someplace."

"You lie."

"Think what you like." An abyss of weariness began to suck away her anger. A year of running and hiding took its toll. Bree fought to stay furious. Fury helped her fight.

She wondered what came next. More threats? Torture? He would probably kill them no matter what she said.

That thought made her stomach churn. She twitched involuntarily. Ferrel pushed her back, raising the cell phone like a weapon. Bree barely stopped herself from spitting in his face.

Ferrel was playing a life-and-death game, but she didn't understand the rules or the prize—and he wasn't the type to give the game away just because she asked. If she wanted information, she'd have to play it just right.

She lifted her chin, her whole body turning cold at the thought her gambit might go wrong. "There's no point in taking my son hostage. I can't give you what I don't have."

Ferrel shifted his weight, bringing his face that much closer. She could smell his breath. He'd been drinking coffee not long ago. "The book isn't all we want. If it were, you'd be dead."

Bree shook her head in confusion. "What are you saying?"

"Those needles weren't just for sedatives."

Her mind groped, trying to make sense of his words, but the pieces were already falling into place. Jonathan's illness had started after that. "What did you do to my son?"

She frantically wished Mark were there, but he was nowhere in sight.

Ferrel gave a slight laugh. "You have no idea what I'm talking about, do you? I must sound like a complete babbling lunatic to you. Let's just say the fact you'd fallen off the grid made everything perfect. An adult and a child nobody would miss and ideal for our needs. Poor Brianna, you're just too innocent for words."

Chapter 19

It was the wrong thing to say. Anger turned Bree's vision red. She stomped on his foot. It wasn't enough to do more than make him grunt in pain, but it bought her a precious second. Bree slammed the heel of her hand into his nose. It was at just the right angle, and she heard a sickening crunch of cartilage. Ferrel reeled back, and Bree slid out from between him and the wall of the barn. "Sorry, but you didn't want me to scream."

Blood gushed freely from his nose. He turned to grab for her, but Bree drove her heel into the side of his knee. Ferrel was a big man, but he toppled with a yelp of pain, dropping his cell phone. She smashed it with her heel.

Bree sprinted for the confusion of the midway. Ferrel's cry had attracted attention, and bystanders were running to see what was the matter. She dove into the crowd, her shoulder throbbing from the blow. It was the same arm Mark had grabbed when she'd started to slip from the floatplane's pontoon, and it was done with action-adventure.

She shoved the pain aside, thinking fast. They had her boy. She had to stay free in order to get Jonathan back. She couldn't let anyone detain her—and if the man in the livestock barn was any indication, Ferrel knew how to use the fairground workers against her. Asking for help would likely backfire. Besides everything else, the police were still looking for the lunatics at the Gleeford Ferry—which included both her and Mark.

She had to find Mark.

Ferrel's blood had splattered onto the fuzzy pink jacket the doctor had bought her in Redwood. She stripped it off and stuffed it into a trash can as she ran past.

Dodging between the milling people hid her from sight, but it also made her blind. It was chaos, with banging, popping and squealing arcade games all around. Tinny speakers played what passed for music. A traditional calliope accompanied what must have been an antique carousel.

The noise confused her, but Bree didn't dare stop moving. *Where am I going? Where did Mark go?* No doubt he'd gone after whoever took Jonathan, but how would she find them and get the blazes out of there?

After that she'd figure out what the hell Ferrel had been talking about—but she needed to focus on survival right now.

She frowned, looking around. High above, the roller coaster swooshed by, happy screams trailing in the air like pennants. Bree shivered despite the warm air. The bright colors and vibrant energy of the fair felt like mockery. *What would Mark do? What would he expect me to do?*

He always had a plan. He'd do something logical. Before everything went wrong they'd been heading for the parking lot on the far side of the fairgrounds. There was a good chance he'd look for her there. Bree craned her neck, trying to figure out where the path she was on would take her.

And there were the men she'd nearly run over at the Gleeford Ferry—all three of them with somber jackets and mirror shades. Bree swore out loud. They looked oddly interchangeable, as if they'd come out of a box. Bad Guy Model 36A—men in black special edition. They slid like sharks through the throng, moving with the same liquid grace she'd seen in Mark. One of them pointed. They'd seen her.

Her stomach plunged, freezing her like a doe in the lights of an oncoming truck. Then instinct took over. She dove into the beer garden, pushing past the guy checking IDs at the gate. The tables were topped with umbrellas that obscured the view enough to give her a little cover. She dashed between the chairs, or tried to. There wasn't much room and she had to turn sideways, and in some cases that was not quite enough to give her clear passage. She knocked at least one chair hard enough to spill somebody's beer. Loud curses followed and once a piece of pretzel bounced off her head.

The commotion made her easy to follow. A quick glance over her shoulder said her pursuers were gaining on her, and this time she didn't have a Lexus to whisk her away from trouble.

There was an empty table right at the back of the beer garden. She used one of the chairs as a step to clear the fence, then sprinted toward the entertainment stage, her backpack bouncing against her shoulder. Her lungs were starting to protest against so much running. She was in good shape, but this was a far cry from a relaxed jog around the park.

The stage was a sturdy raised platform surrounded by a sea of crates, cables and stagehands wearing county fair T-shirts. Towers of speakers sat on the corners of the platform, blasting out enthusiastic bluegrass. Bree couldn't see the performers from her vantage point, but she wasn't there for the tunes. She dashed under the platform before the sound crew could stop her. The noise pounded through her bones and teeth, and she covered her ears as she moved. Halfway along, she risked a look back.

To her astonishment, Ferrel's henchmen had stopped cold, hunching over with a look of physical pain on their faces. They were holding their hands over their ears, too. *They can't take the volume.* Like so much, it made no sense, but she wasn't going to complain. She saw them take off again, running in a different direction. They'd probably circle around the blast zone from the amps and try to cut her off at the other side. She had to take this opportunity to drop out of sight.

Bree bolted forward, out from under the stage and back into the press of booths and tents. This part of the fairgrounds seemed pure carnival, with old-fashioned signs and barkers in top hats. She could smell animals and heard what she thought was the trumpet of an elephant. About halfway down the row of tents, she heard a cry of protest behind her. Her stomach jumped in fright. *They're catching up!* She swerved left and dove into the first tent she came to, letting the flap fall shut as she stepped over the threshold. Gloom descended as the triangle of sunlight disappeared.

Only a candle lantern hung from the pole above. Otherwise, the tent was dark, draped in red silks and scented with heavy incense. A table sat in the center of the space, covered with a fringed cloth that reached the Turkish carpet. Bree caught a glimpse of a woman sitting there, cards spread on the table before her. *Fortune-teller.*

"Help!" Bree said, her voice faint and hoarse.

The woman looked up, large dark eyes wide with astonishment. Her ruby-red lips parted as if to answer.

That was all Bree had time to see before a furious shout sounded just outside the tent. With a jolt of terror, Bree scrambled under the long, fringed tablecloth. There was barely enough room to hide, but she squashed herself into the tightest ball she could manage, pulling her backpack close and wrapping her arms around her knees. For a long moment all she was aware of was the cramped space, her fear and the sequined toes of the fortune-teller's slippers.

Then a swath of sunlight leaked under the fringe of the tablecloth. Bree sucked in a shaking breath and held it.

"We are looking for a woman with long, fair hair."

The voice was deep, more bass than baritone. The timbre was curious, less human than elemental, like the sound of rocks grinding as a tomb door slammed shut. Trapped, unable to move, Bree started to tremble.

"Do you see any fair-haired women? Get out." The fortune-teller stood, wooden chair scraping back against the carpet. Her voice was low and clear, as carefully modulated as any actor's. "I charge thee by the Seven Wards of the Summer Isles to leave this place."

A soft laugh rippled, picked up by more deep voices. "Your curses do not work on us, witch."

"Do not try me." The reply was thick with warning. "I have curses enough for the living as well as the awakened dead. You of anyone know better than to count my threats as mere superstition."

"We are servants of the Holy Knights of Vidon."

"You are abominations. Get out of my tent."

A long pause followed. Bree squeezed her eyes shut and pressed her face into her knees. She was trying to breathe silently, but it was all she could do not to pant with terror. *Please, please, please go away!*

They finally did. The daylight vanished, leaving the tent once more in gloom. The corner of the tablecloth lifted, the fortune-teller's face appearing sideways in the gap. She was in her forties, with waving dark hair silvered at the temples. A tiny ruby glittered in the side of her nose.

"Hello?" the woman asked.

Cautiously, Bree crawled out from under the table. Apprehension crept down her spine. "Are they really gone?"

"For now. They do not have the power to defy me here, but they will keep looking for you."

Her words filled Bree with dread. She sank onto her heels, her limbs too rubbery with spent adrenaline to stand. She would have liked nothing better than to lie down. "Thank you for saving me. For now, anyway."

"My name is Mirella." The woman cupped Bree's chin in one ringed hand. She turned Bree's face toward the light as Mark had done. "It was my duty. You have been blessed."

"Blessed?"

"I see you are under the protection of the fair ones. Someone in your past, someone who gave you a task to perform, was fey."

"As in fairy?" Bree raised her eyebrows. *A task? Does she mean the book?* "Who are you talking about?"

"I don't know whose paths you've crossed. But if you think hard, you will know."

Jessica? She was the only person who had ever trusted her enough to ask her to do anything. Fey? Jessica was special and wonderful, but even if Bree believed in miracles and unicorns—which she didn't—weren't fairies powerful beings? They wouldn't be murdered by thugs.

"I imagine there is a great deal in your life that does not make sense." Mirella's red mouth turned down at the corners. "It is too bad that we do not have time for explanations. For now, accept this one fact—you are dealing with powers beyond ordinary experience. Assume nothing."

Bree nodded. She hadn't assumed anything in a long time. "Those men chasing me…"

"Are still just men. But barely, I think. The Knights of Vidon are playing with the same hellfire they swear to fight."

Bree's gut turned cold. "What do you mean? What sort of crazies are they? They have my little boy."

Mirella's hand touched hers. "I'm sorry."

Bree slowly stood. "How do I fight them?"

She expected Mirella to say she couldn't, or that it would take a knight in shining armor or maybe a giant. "I need practical advice. I need to walk out of here with a plan."

"Then ask yourself why they want your son," Mirella said in a reasonable tone.

"I don't know. I don't understand any of this. Do you?"

"I am no wolf or fey or demon. I am merely a human who can tell fortunes and spin a few spells." Mirella gave a slight shrug. "Do you have help?"

"Mark. He was with me until they stole my son. I think he went after them."

"Good. A strong man is good. You should not be alone in this." Mirella took Bree's hand, holding it between hers. She studied Bree's face intently. "I see a crown in your past and a blade in your future. Death stands behind and before you."

Bree's mouth was dry as ashes. She wanted to dismiss what the woman was telling her, but at the same time Mirella's soft voice held her spellbound. "How is that supposed to help me?"

"To save your boy, you must find what you have lost. Blood will be sacrificed before this is done."

"Sacrifice. That can't be good."

"It can." Mirella gave a sad smile. "But we seldom understand it at the time. Aren't you going to ask about your lover?"

Despite herself, a flush crept up Bree's cheeks. "I have to go."

Bree hitched her backpack over her shoulder. *My lover.* She remembered her elation, and then her confusion the night before. "He does not love me, anyway."

"Maybe he does not dare."

"That's crazy."

Mirella's smile turned sly. "Then you had best tell him there is room for hope. Even the bravest sometimes need an encouraging smile."

Chapter 20

Mark liked dogs, as a rule. Some of his best friends were werewolves. However, Custard was pushing his doggy luck the moment he jumped out of Mark's arms and scampered after Jonathan.

Custard had made a rush at the black ram, yapping with glee. Mark had a vision of squashed dog and howling child. Since Bree was closing in on her son, Mark tried to scoop up the pup. Vampires were fast, but puppies wiggled. When Mark had finally got hold of the little wretch, saving him from woolly death, everything had gone wrong.

Disaster had only taken seconds.

Help!

He heard it as clear as a voice in his ear, but knew it wasn't ordinary speech. *Telepathy.*

Mark looked up to see Ferrel's henchman vanishing

through the door, Jonathan in his arms. *The kid spoke with his mind!*

But that wasn't nearly as immediate as the fact he was being kidnapped. Mark's heart turned cold, his fangs descending, sharp and lethal. As if sensing the change in him, Custard went perfectly still.

The ticket-taker from the door chose that moment to start hassling Bree.

In a microsecond, Mark made the necessary decisions. Getting Jonathan back was the priority. Bree was there to run interference with the idiot.

Mark slipped out the back. Once he was on the path leading away from the barn, spotting his quarry was easy. The henchman, in his black suit and shades, was the one with the Vandyke beard and mustache. He'd wrapped Jonathan in a yellow windbreaker, pulling up the hood to hide the boy's hair.

Fresh uneasiness clutched at Mark's gut. Jonathan looked limp, as if he were asleep. He remembered Bree's story about being drugged in an airport. Had they shot Jonathan with something to keep him quiet? The boy wasn't strong enough to handle more than a tiny dose of sedatives.

Uneasiness turned to fury. Mark doubled his pace, holding Custard tight. Aside from a tiny whine, the puppy stayed utterly still and quiet. Mark projected his mental voice. *If you can hear me, Jonathan, know that I am coming for you. I will be there to protect you. You are not alone.*

Before Mark could catch up, Vandyke met two other men. Mark swore, slowing down while he adjusted his plans. Frustration clawed at his nerves. Taking three men down in a crowded fair was bad enough, but to do it without Jonathan getting hurt would take some thought.

They paused outside a pavilion set up for a country radio station. Despite the fact the volume wasn't at full blast, Mark couldn't hear their words. He hung back, pretending interest in a display of fly-fishing gear while he watched the three men closely.

There was something wrong about these guys. The way they stood—a little too aggressive, a little too fluid in their movements. The way they smelled. Not human, but not quite *not* human, either. Jessica Lark's journal was all about genetic manipulation. Were these the faux vampires the author of that book meant to create?

A ripple of disgust passed through him. Being a vampire was bad enough. He couldn't imagine walking the planet as someone's science experiment.

Of more immediate relevance—there was no telling how good these Frankenvamps might be in a fight. There were three of them, one of him. Even if he was a cold-blooded assassin, centuries-old and as lethal as they came—he had a kid and a puppy to worry about. It was like fighting with both hands tied.

Mark fumed a moment, but there was nothing to do but suck it up. He crouched, taking advantage of the pause to tuck Custard into his backpack, on top of the nest of his clothes. Not the ideal arrangement, but it left him with two free hands. As he handled the soft, wriggling fur, his irritation congealed into worry.

You're going soft. There was a reason he kept to his cabin in the woods. Mark didn't do soft any more than he did kids or dogs or vulnerable women—but he was doing all that plus some. He'd made love to Bree. *Stupid.*

At least he'd managed to keep his vampire side in check. Only old vampires—older even than he was—ever had that much control, but he had done it. He'd wanted her that much—and she'd been worth every moment. But what a risk. If he'd slipped, he would have revealed himself. Forget that, he could have killed her. Even the memory of her scent made him weak with hunger and desire.

I took her. I wanted her. Marco Farnese was old, entitled, powerful and deadly. He scoffed at worldly convention.

Sadly, he was also Mark and had to look at himself in the mirror every morning. He might have had a brain capable of complex genetic research in addition to knowing fifty ways to kill with a common table napkin, but shreds of everyday human remained in his soul. When he met someone like Bree, they flared up like a rash. *I cannot, must not be with her. There are rules. Vampires hide.*

Not that he couldn't love and be loved. He'd had a family once. But vampires mated forever. Was he getting a second chance?

No. The thought froze him, nearly made him dizzy. *No.* He was the one who lived alone in the woods. The family man in him had died, burned at the stake centuries ago. *No.*

He looked up, and the place where the men had been was empty. Frantic, Mark jumped to his feet, slipping his arms through the backpack. Two of the men were striding toward the barn where Mark had left Bree. The man with the Vandyke beard was going in the opposite direction, Jonathan still in his arms. He was already several dozen yards away.

Still reeling from his earlier thought, Mark felt an instant of confusion. Bree was alone. He wanted to go to her, but if anything happened to Jonathan, she would be crushed.

He hated having to choose, but went after Vandyke. Now Mark's quarry seemed to be hurrying. That meant there was probably a rendezvous ahead. Reflexively,

Mark touched the small of his back, where his gun was hidden beneath his coat. If they got out of the crowd, he would feel a lot better about drawing it.

Instead, he took out his cell phone and battery. Why not? Ferrel had found them anyway. He pushed the battery back in and speed-dialed Kenyon.

"Ah, there you are," Kenyon said as he answered. "Back on the grid at last."

Mark could barely hear him over the din of the rides and music. The midway was right behind them, the clang and rumble of the roller coaster only a stone's throw away. He raised his voice as much as he dared. "We're at a fairground. Forget discretion. We need help."

"I'll get a lock on your phone. We'll get there as soon as we can."

"Speed would be good." Mark hung up.

They were running out of time. The gate to the second parking lot was straight ahead. Vandyke had his cell phone out, too, probably alerting whoever was going to pick him up. Trying to keep the knapsack—and puppy—as steady as possible, Mark broke into a smooth lope, closing the distance to his foe. There were fewer people here, and only one opponent. He would have to make his move now.

He shouted for the man to stop, but his words were lost in the sounds of the midway.

Vandyke was almost at the gate, Jonathan hoisted in one arm like a sack of groceries. It was then that Bree rose up from behind a bin of plastic umbrellas—the ones fairgoers could rent for fifty cents on a rainy day—and used one as a spear, shoving its long metal tip into his ribs. It would have barely tickled such a big man, except Bree made it count, snarling as she put her weight behind it.

"Get your hands off my boy!" she roared.

Mark decided he was officially in awe—but all her bravery was for nothing. Vandyke turned, almost in slow motion. The movement pulled the umbrella from Bree's hands, letting it fall to the ground with a bounce. Clearly, the point hadn't stuck, though it had broken the skin. He could see a patch of blood glistening on the dark fabric of the man's jacket.

It all happened in a matter of seconds, barely enough for Mark's brain to catch up with the icy panic inside. He put on speed, ignoring the fact he was supposed to be human. He was needed there, at Bree's side. Her opponent still had Jonathan, and the man was swinging his free arm around to take Bree down.

Mark caught Vandyke's wrist with all his fury, prepared to crush bone and flesh to a pulp. It didn't work— the man had a vampire's strength. Mark slammed his other fist into Vandyke's jaw, but his aim was off. Jonathan was in the way.

Still, Vandyke's center of balance faltered when Bree slammed a foot into his back. Mark grabbed the boy at the same time their opponent went to his knees, then finished Vandyke with a boot to the head. As Jonathan's warm weight sagged against Mark's chest, a powerful wave of protectiveness surged through him.

But the fight wasn't done. When Bree reached for her son, Mark passed him over as quickly as he could, then shrugged out of the backpack and handed that over. Her eyes widened as she saw Custard's black nose peeking out the gap Mark had left in the zipper. Nevertheless, she slung the strap over her shoulder without comment, adding it to the weight of her own pack, and backed out of the way.

His hands finally free, Mark drew his weapon, keeping it close to his body. There weren't many people in this part of the fairground, but waving a gun around would still attract attention. The fight with Vandyke had been so fast, no one seemed to have seen it, but he couldn't count on luck anymore.

In fact, it seemed to have run out. The silver Escalade pulled into view just outside the exit, kicking up dust from the gravel road. The doors opened to let Ferrel and two others jump out. Mark's stomach tensed as he put himself between the oncoming men and Bree. Even if the nearest chopper was close, it would take time to arrive—ten, twenty minutes maybe. This battle was up to him.

"Stay behind me," he said to Bree, keeping the gun close to his side. "We're working our way slowly toward the gate."

"Got it."

There was no ticket-seller in the booth, just a sign that read Back in Fifteen. The Knights of Vidon strolled in without interference. The only thing that lifted Mark's spirits was the sight of Ferrel's face, swollen and bruised. Bree's work? It was a good start that he meant to improve on.

The henchman with the Vandyke beard was back on his feet. His sunglasses were broken, revealing odd, yellow eyes like those of a lizard. Revulsion prickled Mark's skin, and he heard Bree's gasp.

Then the man rushed, his mouth dropping open as long, ivory fangs descended from his upper jaw. They were grotesquely huge, twice as big as any vampire's. Mark experienced a moment of fascinated horror, and then he aimed and pulled the trigger. The noise of the shot barely registered against the fairground din, but he saw Vandyke flinch.

Unfortunately, that was all he did. Mark thrust the

gun into Bree's hand. At least it would keep Ferrel at bay. The others would require something more old-school. They were circling now, joining their friend to form a snarling pack.

Mark's own beast stirred, and he let it rise. The intoxicating thrill of the hunt swamped him, ripping a feral growl from his throat. He crouched, hands raised to rend and tear. This was nothing Bree or her boy should ever see, but it was the only way. He had to defend his own, even if doing that meant showing his dark side.

One of the faux-vampires made a lunge for Bree.

Reason snapped. Mark's fangs slipped down and he sprang. Vandyke tried to block him, but Mark slid under his guard, landing a sharp jab to the man's windpipe. Vandyke reeled back, choking. Apparently these fake vamps still breathed like ordinary humans. Mark would remember that.

They probably needed their heads, too. Mark moved to slide around behind him, but Vandyke made a knife appear from his sleeve. It was a smooth move, and the silver blade sliced into Mark's ribs, probing upward for the heart. The metal burned, but Mark choked back the cry of pain. Instead, he twisted away, grabbing Vandyke's head from behind. A quick, fierce wrench, and the neck snapped with the sound of a breaking twig.

Mark stumbled back as the body dropped. Vandyke had missed his heart, but he'd done damage. Mark wrenched the knife from his side, betting a sharp blade would work on these monsters whether or not they had a vampire's sensitivity to silver. Mark wheeled to grab his next opponent.

That death wasn't nearly so clean.

Chapter 21

The sound of the chopper grew louder, dust billowing up as it landed on the swath of grass and dirt beyond the parked cars. Bree was curled up behind the wooden ticket booth, Jonathan wide-eyed and silent on her lap. She bent over him, shielding him from the sudden wind. She heard car doors slamming, then saw the Escalade barrel toward the road, Ferrel at the wheel, his one surviving sidekick riding shotgun. *Fled to fight another day.*

Cold, heavy dread rooted her to the patch of dirt where she sat, as if it were the last safe place in the world. The horror she'd just seen had crushed the last of her strength. There was no hope of making sense of any of it—fangs, claws, men who were suddenly ravening beasts tearing flesh and bone. Hallucination? Hysteria? Or reality? It didn't matter. She couldn't stay there. There were fanged killers, right over there, and she had a child to protect.

If only she could stop shaking and act. She'd survived

so long on bravado, but that pig-headed refusal to lie down and die felt perilously brittle right now. *Dig deep. Run. Keep your boy safe from the monsters.* It was the only thing a mother could do.

Slowly, she leaned far enough to see around the edge of the booth. Automatically, she looked for Mark first. He was poised by the gate, snarling at the disappearing cloud of dust where Ferrel's car had been. His muscles strained, as if he was about to hurtle after the Escalade and tear it to pieces. Yellow eyes glinted—no, *glowed*— with savage hatred. His lips were drawn back, exposing sharp, white fangs. Unlike the other creatures, everything about him looked in balance, natural, lethal as a panther ready to spring. Almost beautiful—except Mark's face, clothes, hands, everything were covered in blood. He'd torn the second man—*thing*—limb from limb. Ferrel's creatures had claws and fangs. But so had Mark.

A stab of anger pierced her, a sense of profound betrayal. *I trusted you, Mark Winspear.* All the time she had trusted him, he was really this *thing* and she had put her life, her body and her baby in his hands. The man she'd come to know was a lie.

What else about him was false? Had he been preparing a trap for her all this time? Had he been luring her and Jonathan—with the book he'd so wanted—into that mysterious medical facility? What kind of place was it, anyway?

Bree pulled her head back around the corner, panting quickly, on her way to a panic attack. *What are those guys? What is Mark?*

Bree's face went numb as the shock of understanding washed through her. Fangs. Claws. Glowing eyes. *Vampires? Is that it?* She'd grown up around Hollywood. She knew the legends—Dracula and the rest. Mark even had the trace of an accent. He barely ate. He hated sun. He was insanely strong and fast and mysterious. *Please let me be wrong, this is just too weird.* But she didn't have a better theory.

It figured. People she trusted disappeared or died or turned out to have feet of clay. Every time that happened, she had been plunged into disaster. Her parents, boyfriend after boyfriend, Jonathan's father, Jessica. Somehow, whether they loved her or not, they'd all found a way of leaving her with a mess. But she'd never had one *literally* turn into a monster before. This was definitely a first.

I trusted him. I slept with him. And it had been the best sex she'd ever had. But wasn't that just part of the myth, too? Vampires were the best seducers out there? And dead? Oh, good grief. *Crazy. This is crazy. Bree, get out of here!*

By the time she had finished the thought, she was standing with Jonathan on her hip and Custard's puppy nest slung over her shoulder. She had no money and no car, but flight had always been her go-to answer. She'd always figured it out.

She ran for her life, just as frightened as when she'd run through the hail of bullets to the floatplane. Dead ahead was a low fence that separated the grassy walkway from the back of the rides. If she could climb over that, she could take cover in the noisy commotion of the midway.

Or so she thought. Maybe a few gunshots could be hidden under the noise of the roller coaster, but the combination of a helicopter, gunfire and dismemberment drew a crowd. Fairgoers were leaning against the fence, cell phones out, blocking her escape.

"Hey, isn't that the girl Prince Kyle was dating?" someone shouted to their friend.

"Nah, she was hotter. And what would she be doing here, anyway?"

Good question. Almost to the fence, Bree risked a look behind her.

The chopper had landed. Men clad from head to foot in black uniforms—even their faces were heavily shaded—were waving back the handful of bystanders who had climbed over the fence. Others were packing up the bodies.

"Cut!" a man in a black uniform was yelling. "Cut, that's a wrap!"

Confused, Bree looked around for cameras, booms or any of the personnel that made a film shoot run. There was someone with a video camera, but it was a tiny, handheld thing.

"Beautiful!" the man in black yelled. "Marvelous. Such verismo."

Realism? She nearly laughed—or gagged. And then she got it. People shot films, big and small, all the time, but few in the crowd would actually know how it was done. As long as the public *thought* these guys were making a movie, it would buy the cleanup crew enough time to get away. As the old saying went, people saw what they expected to see.

The audacity of it staggered her, but she wasn't surprised. Her surprise-o-meter had exploded when the fangs came out. She turned back to find a way over the fence, and nearly walked into Mark. A wild need to scream and thrash came over her, to get away from the monster at all costs.

"You're needed back at the set," he said in a careful voice, catching her arm.

She had just enough brain left to form rational words. "I can't go with you. Not after that."

"Bree." It was the only word he said, but it made her slow down.

She should have looked at the blood and gore, but it was his expression that stole her breath. After tearing his enemy to pieces, she would have expected triumph, or rage, or even icy superiority. Instead, sad weariness dragged at his features, as if he'd finally seen too much.

"Mark?" she said softly, not expecting—and maybe not wanting—a reply.

But of course he heard her. "I'm sorry."

"You protected us. I get it. But—"

"I didn't want you to see that."

She didn't know how to answer. *He didn't want me to see him.* To see him for what he was. This was what he'd been holding back last night.

Tears ached, hot behind her eyes. He had defended them once again, but this time it had cost him more than money or cleverness or courage. He had sacrificed something deeper, something she had no right to ask of him. And now this was the consequence—blood and alienation.

"You didn't have to," she said weakly.

"Didn't I?" His gaze was almost hostile.

Bree's throat closed, choked with unshed tears. Beneath this new fear of him was a thick layer of guilt.

He'd killed for her. Twice. He'd torn another man apart with nothing but hands and teeth.

And she'd seen him stabbed, but he was standing there as though nothing happened. Why wasn't he dead or bleeding? It wasn't natural.

Mark was a brutal, bloody killer and by rights she should be terrified of him. And she was. Except she owed him everything.

Bree closed her eyes, scraping her fragmented wits together. *Whatever he is, he protected my child.* And Mark had promised to cure her son. At the end of the day, that was all that mattered to her.

Except he's a monster, the voice in her head argued back. By every logical rule, she should get her child away from him.

She didn't know what to think. Bree sank to the grass, rocking her sick, silent child, too exhausted and bewildered to stand anymore. "I don't know what to do."

Mark crouched beside her, keeping his voice quiet. They were near the crowd, too easily overheard for this kind of conversation. "Trust me."

"I can't." *I don't trust anybody. Every time I do, it destroys me.*

"Why not? What do you think I'm going to do?"

"You tore those men apart. What do you expect me to think?"

He pulled back as if she'd bitten him. "That I prevented them from killing you and stealing your child."

"How do I know you're not going to do that to me?"

"I'm not a rabid beast." The words were ice-sharp.

Swearing under her breath, Bree clenched her teeth, doing her best not to cry. She'd hurt him. He hated her. But then what did she expect? What did he expect? This was too far outside her world.

Bree realized she'd squeezed her eyes shut when she felt someone between her and the sun. She looked up to see the man in black who'd been playing director.

"This is Brianna Meadows," Mark said, his expression closed down, as if he had locked up his thoughts. At some point, he'd wiped some of the blood off his face and hands. She was grateful for that much, though the sight and smell of it on his clothes still made her queasy.

Feeling too vulnerable on the ground, Bree got to her

feet to confront the other man. He was the tall, dark and handsome type that made her think of cowboy movies, or something involving flying aces and daring escapes—but he had that same *otherness* as Jessica and Mark. Fairies? Vampires? What secrets did this one have?

"Hello," she said, hearing the caution in her voice.

The man gave a professional smile, with just a dash of down-home charm. "My name is Sam Ralston. We're taking you and your boy to our facility. It's secure, and we have a great hospital there."

"Please say you still want to go," Mark said softly.

She heard the rest of the sentence: *even after you've seen what I really am.* He was hiding behind that blank, closed mask. Cautious of her opinion.

It was too much. Bree's vision blurred, tears finally finding release. She thought of his words back at the cabin: *Knights were overrated, if you ask me. If you want to protect a treasure, ask a dragon.* And what a dragon he was. "You said you'd get us to safety. You did it."

He gave her a long look, the mask slipping as a thousand emotions chased through his eyes. "Of course I did. I never say what I don't mean."

Chapter 22

What would have happened if she'd said she wouldn't go? It was a good question. Bree had never been a gambler—at least not the type that went to Vegas—but she suspected that conversation would not have gone well. The men from the Company wasted no time getting her into their big black chopper.

Bree barely remembered the helicopter ride to the Varney Center, just that it seemed to take years. Jonathan was in her lap. He had fallen asleep, his breath coming in light, quick pants. She didn't notice her hometown slipping past below them, or the black-clad men crowded into the other seats. She was aware of their presence, outwardly friendly but shimmering with potential danger. They didn't matter. Only her son was relevant. Her son, and Mark.

He approached only twice, both times to check Jonathan's vitals. He didn't try to meet her eyes.

"He's getting worse, isn't he?" she asked softly.

She was trying to see the doctor before her and not the monster that had torn a living body to pieces before her eyes. But memory kept trying to superimpose the nightmare over Mark's handsome features, and no amount of willpower could make it go away. She was grateful he'd slipped a jacket over the bloody shirt, but his jeans were still spattered. The sight of it sent a prickle of sickly sweat over her skin.

She prayed she'd keep it together as Mark felt Jonathan's temperature, then bent to put an ear to the boy's chest. "His core temperature is starting to drop."

"What does that mean?"

Jonathan stirred in his sleep, whimpering.

Mark looked up, worry in his dark eyes. He put a hand over hers for the briefest second before he pulled away, as if aware his touch might not be welcome. "I'm going to radio ahead so we don't waste any time."

He moved away, leaving Bree even more anxious.

While Mark was at the front, Sam Ralston nudged Mark's backpack with his foot. "What's he got in there? I think it's alive."

With a guilty start, Bree realized she'd forgotten all about the dog. "Jonathan's puppy. Is he all right?"

Sam bent down, pulling open the zipper. A smile lit up his face, making him look genuinely friendly. "Hey, there, little fella. Oh, he looks fine."

Custard's head popped out, eyes bright with curiosity, and he gave a tiny yap, and Sam grinned. Apparently even special ops vampires liked cute baby animals. Every head in the chopper swiveled to look.

Including Jonathan's. His eyes blinked open sleepily. "Custard?" he asked.

He spoke! The word was slurred and rough, but Bree understood it perfectly. Her heart lurched in her chest, giddy and aching and broken all at once. "Yes," she said shakily. "Custard's here."

She looked up, wishing Mark had been there to hear. For once, her wish was granted. He was paused halfway back to his seat, eyes wide with surprise. *Good. He'd heard it, too.* That meant she hadn't imagined it. Bree caught his gaze.

Triumph flashed between them. Mark had been right about the puppy, because now Jonathan was holding out his arms, asking for the thing he wanted most in the world. "Custard!"

Mark didn't smile or act as if anything was different, but she could see his happiness in the buoyancy of his movements. Wordlessly, he picked up the puppy and held him so Jonathan could pat the soft fur. Custard wiggled happily. Bree felt Jonathan relax against her.

Sam's eyebrows shot up. "Isn't this a bit movie-of-the-week for you, Winspear?"

"Shut up," said Mark in flat tones, handing the dog to Sam.

Jonathan was too relaxed. Not moving. "Mark?" Bree whispered. Panic gnawed at her, making everything sharp and bright. "What's wrong?"

"Get him on the floor!" Mark snapped. "I need to do CPR."

Minutes later, they landed on a roof. Mark raced out first, Jonathan in his arms. Bree was right behind him, aware of someone yelling at her to keep her head down and away from the rotor blades. She could feel the heat of the rooftop through her shoes, even though much of the roof had a sunshade. It was a lot warmer here than it had been up north.

Beneath the protective cover, there were more men in black uniforms, as well as a bunch in white coats. Two men and a woman in scrubs rushed toward them with a gurney. Mark put the boy down, and instantly the others converged, one with a breathing mask. They started to push the gurney away.

"Wait for me!" Bree cried, running now. There were glass doors ahead, sheltering a pair of rooftop elevators from the wind. The gurney was sliding into an elevator. "Wait!"

But there were men in her way, big men in black. "Please stay here, ma'am."

"No, I have to get to my son!" She shoved at somebody, trying to get past, but it was like pushing against a mountain.

"I'm sorry, ma'am. Protocol."

In a matter of seconds, Mark and Jonathan were gone.

Panic ate at her insides. Bree stood alone in the mass of milling men, Custard in her arms. Beyond the roof, L.A. stretched in a blanket of haze, at once familiar and too alien for words.

Sam touched her arm and leaned close to make himself heard over the din of voices and rotors. "If anyone can do something for your son, it's Winspear. You know that, don't you?"

Bree nodded, because that at least made sense. "Are you all vampires?"

He winced at her blunt statement, but then shrugged it off. "No, not all of us. There are some humans here, too. My fiancée, for one."

Bree's jaw dropped.

"And don't forget your token minority werewolf," said another voice. Bree turned to see a tall man with fair hair and Nordic features. He grinned. "My name is Faran Kenyon, and I'll be your guide through Castle Dracula."

Custard started barking excitedly, his stub of a tail

waggling like mad. "Hello, little brother." Kenyon bent down to scratch Custard's ears.

Bree closed her eyes. She was in a madhouse, dealing with men who thought they were dogs. All she wanted was to be at Jonathan's bedside, but he was with the doctors. She had to be patient. If she played their game right, she could figure out where they'd taken him. She blinked Sam and Kenyon back into focus. "Werewolf?"

"It's not contagious," Kenyon said automatically. "Don't need the moon to change. Don't nom on people unless they ask for it. Don't even mind cats. Much."

"Good to know." Bree wasn't sure what else to say.

"I'll leave you, then," said Sam, giving a slight bow. It looked very old-fashioned. "If you need anything at all, just ask for me. I'm at your service."

"What's this I hear about specimens?" Kenyon asked Sam.

"Nicholas Ferrel's men weren't altogether human," Sam replied. "We brought back bodies."

"Oh, goody. I love takeout." Kenyon sounded disgusted. "Well, run along to the lab, then."

Sam took a playful swipe at the other's head. Kenyon ducked with inhuman speed, then turned to Bree. "Let me take you somewhere quieter."

"When can I see my son?" she asked.

"I don't know, but we'll find that out first thing." Kenyon gave her a sympathetic smile and led the way through the glass doors. He seemed younger than the others, more easygoing. "That was quite the road trip you had. I can't imagine being locked in a car with Winspear that long."

"He was great." She sounded defensive.

Kenyon locked his bright blue gaze on her. "Really? He never lets me play with the radio."

Despite herself, Bree felt her lips twitch. "It took him a while to warm up." *But when he did...*

Heat crept up her face. Kenyon hummed, taking a great interest in the ceiling.

When the elevator doors finally opened, he ushered her in, swiped his card again and pressed four. Bree noticed there were buttons for twenty floors above ground, and five below.

"I don't know how much Mark told you, but the Varney Center is a secure facility. We do a lot of different things here—mostly research, but also training, administration and operational deployment. I'll give you a card so you can get around the main areas, but the underground is off-limits, as are floors eight through twenty. Most of the people around here are, uh, employees."

"And not human," Bree said.

He shrugged. "We have some human specialists who work here, mostly in research."

"I know the story about the two kings and the diamonds. You're the *Compagnie des Morts.* You're spies or something, fighting the Knights of Vidon."

He looked surprised. "Did Mark tell you that?"

"No. Prince Kyle did. And Jessica Lark told me some."

Kenyon's face went serious. It made him look a lot older and not so laid-back. "We do security work with a lot of international clients. That's not automatically espionage."

Not automatically sounded like a fudge to her. "Whatever it is, it sounds dangerous."

"It is." Kenyon turned to the left. "The Horsemen take the jobs no one else can do."

"Horsemen?"

He shrugged, falling back into boy-next-door. "All the good operatives have code names. It's a guy thing."

"Do tell."

He shot her a half smile. "Mark is Plague. Sam is War. I'm Famine."

He meant the Four Horsemen of the Apocalypse, then, but that was only three. "Who is Death?"

His face fell. "He was killed. He died around the same time as your boss."

She took a guess. "Jack Anderson?"

"Yeah. He was the best."

The elevator doors opened and they got out. The hallway had no windows, but in every other way it looked like a top-notch hotel, with thick burgundy carpets and brass light fixtures. Custard sniffed the air curiously.

"Mark said you found Jack's killers."

Kenyon gave a short laugh. "Yes, but never the whole story. He was working with Jessica at the time, and her death was connected. You're our first break on that case."

They stopped at a door marked 50 in brass numerals. Kenyon swiped a key card through a reader and opened the door. "This is where you'll be staying. You're on the same floor as the medical wing, so you won't have to go far to visit your boy."

Bree stepped inside. It was a suite of rooms decorated in dark reds and creams. It would have done any Hilton proud. "This is lovely."

She set Custard down. The puppy bounced in a circle and then ran to sniff Kenyon's shoes.

"Get cleaned up and have a rest," he said, trying to chase the puppy away from his shoelaces. "There's clothes—nothing much, but they're fresh. I'll have some food sent up."

"What about Jonathan?"

Kenyon gave another sort-of smile. "I promise to let you know as soon as there's any information."

Bree paced nervously. "One question. How come no one knows about this fabulous medical facility?"

Kenyon looked up, a slight edge of warning in his expression. "Like I said, we're a secure facility. If you found out about it, it was because our best agent told you. Mark's never done that before. He must have his reasons."

Already uneasy, that made Bree fold her arms protectively over her stomach. "Will I have to sign a confidentiality contract when it's time to leave?"

Kenyon looked away. "Let's worry about that when the time comes. Mark is the one who takes care of that sort of thing anyhow."

Bree's stomach went cold. *What does that mean?*

"Let me go check with the hospital and see how things are going," Kenyon said quickly. "Make yourself comfortable in the meantime."

"Okay."

Kenyon exchanged a glance with Custard, who then trotted to Bree and sat down on her foot. His warm weight was unexpectedly comforting. Kenyon was gone and the door closed before she looked up again. *Werewolves can move fast if they want to.* Something to remember.

Lost, she looked around the room. She could shower and change—undoubtedly should—but she was hungry for information. She pulled out her cell, popping the battery back in. No bars. There was probably a signal blocker in the building.

There was a TV on the wall, but no computer. No other phone. She dislodged Custard from her foot and checked the bedroom. It was cool and dark, but there was no phone by the bed, either.

A sick panic began crawling up her throat. She'd been keeping it together, pushing aside the memory of Ferrel's sidekicks with the fangs and yellow eyes, of Mark turning monster, of the gore and horror of the fight. She'd clung to the fact that Mark had stood by her and Jonathan, made her head rule her instincts to scream and flee.

But the moment of crisis had passed, and she didn't need to be so strong anymore. Bree fell onto the pretty white quilt of the bed, letting the soft mattress take her weight. The very luxury of the place seemed sinister. She felt far more secure when the world was showing its ugly side.

Slowly, she curled into a little ball. She was in a building full of monsters with no way to call out, and they had taken her child. Custard scrabbled at the side of the bed, trying to get up to her.

This is crazy. Nobody had done anything bad—at least not to her. They'd done nothing but help her. There was no reason to be afraid.

She bounced off the bed again, hurrying back into the sitting room. *Everything's going to be okay.* Yet she was so nervous she couldn't swallow, just like the old saying about having her heart in her mouth. Why was she so scared? Was it instinct? Premonition? Or just the fear of a mother hoping against hope that all would be well?

She couldn't wait for Kenyon to come back. She needed answers now, and then she would be able to calm down.

Bree tried the door. *Locked.*

Prisoner.

Chapter 23

Mark turned to Sam. They were in the autopsy suite, peering into the bodies of Mark's erstwhile opponents. "I think this tells us more than we wanted to know."

"Science-speak aside, they're mutants." Sam shifted uncomfortably. Like many strong men, he was more comfortable killing than studying the remains. "What does that tell us?"

"That everything is starting to make sense, although I wish it weren't. Let's get out of here."

Mark slammed out of the autopsy suite, Sam on his heels.

"How is everything making sense? I don't see it," Sam said. "And where are you going?"

Mark didn't answer, his mind already racing ahead. Jonathan was in a private room with so many tubes and drips that he seemed more machine than child. Mark's stomach had hurt to look at him. It was one thing to treat strangers, but he'd spent time with the boy. He'd watched Jonathan's delight while playing with the toy dinosaur, the dog and even just a handful of crayons. He'd cheered him on while he figured out how to put together a puzzle from one of those candy eggs. Kids made everything new.

Mark had even caught himself planning to take the boy into the woods to teach him about the plants and animals there. As if Jonathan was one of his own sons, lost so long ago. For a moment, he'd had a family again. He'd thought he was falling in love. But that was madness. Nothing would ever happen—especially now that Bree had found out the truth.

Her eyes had said it all. *Get away from me and don't come back.* Bitterness soured his mood, so sharp he imagined an actual taste in his mouth.

Mark stormed down the hall, Sam still following. They made a sharp turn into a tiny room with a sink and coffeemaker. One of the lab techs was reading a magazine at the table. She took one look at Mark's face and left.

He flung himself into a chair. "They're all connected. Ferrel. The boy. That book. Lark's murder. Now that I've seen the science it's starting to tell a story."

"How? You just got here." Sam sat down opposite him.

"I had a theory. It didn't take that long to check a couple of facts. I've more to do, but I'll be surprised if I'm wrong."

Sam waved a hand. "So tell me. Where's the beginning of all this? I can't figure it out."

"Not a surprise if you haven't read the journal." Mark sighed. He should have seen it before. "It starts with a crazy vampire. Remember Thoristand?"

"With the castle and the grubby robes? Seriously?"

Ralston Samuel Hill—once a lieutenant colonel in the

American Civil War—had picked up some of his mortal partner's slang.

Mark wasn't sure if he was annoyed or amused. "Very seriously. Thoristand wasn't always behind the times. When I met him, he had developed an interest in natural philosophy, or science as they call it now. He had already studied anatomy and alchemy, astronomy and magnetism. He was a fascinating man, but he was encroaching into areas I dared not tread."

"Such as?"

He shrugged. "You are familiar with the story of Dr. Frankenstein's monster?"

"Yes."

"Then you will understand when I say Thoristand's pride as a scientist outweighed his judgment as a man. The more I read of the book hidden beneath Lark's sketches, the more I believe it to be his work."

Sam made an impatient gesture. "So he was a mad scientist, and that book is his work. Where does that get us?"

"Is there anything here to drink?" Mark jammed his hands into his hair.

Sam got up and looked under the sink. There was a bottle of Scotch. He set that on the table, and then found a couple of plastic cups.

Mark poured them each a shot. "According to the book, Thoristand believed science would provide the answer to what he saw as the vampire problem. You know the song—too many predators making more predators and not enough humans to eat. True, he was a vampire himself, but he wasn't in favor of adding to the undead population."

"So?" Sam asked.

"In that book, he's attempting to replicate the genetic changes that take place when a human turns into a vampire, and introduce them through a virus. Not just mad science, but extremely risky mad science."

Sam raised his eyebrows. "But doesn't the virus just make more vampires?"

"He's creating a hybrid. Mutants. Humans strong enough to fight us."

"Oh, brilliant. I'm not liking this story."

"That was merely groundwork. Now the tale gets more interesting. A splinter group of the Knights of Vidon killed Thoristand five years ago."

Sam tasted his Scotch and made a face. "So? They kill vampires on principle."

"My guess is they wanted his research. Eventually they found out Lark had it, and they killed her to get his journal."

"Why did she have it?"

"Not sure." Mark sipped the drink. It was cheap and rough, but he was too weary to care. "I suspect the fey found it. Or stole it. That's more their style. So would be keeping an object like that for a future bargaining chip. Lark worked with us, but she made sure to cover her own needs, as well."

"Let's say that was true," Sam conceded. "Why did this splinter group of Knights want Thoristand's research? They're nothing if not anti-monster, anti-magic, anti-everything that's not purely human."

"When we had our altercation with the leaders of the Knights last spring, none of them could say why Lark was murdered. They were probably telling the truth. I think what we're dealing with now is Nicholas Ferrel's core faction."

"The splinter group."

"Exactly," Mark agreed. "A small number of extremists, if you like, willing to throw the Knights' code out the window and out-monster the monsters. They created the mutants."

"Which brings us to the bodies in the morgue. But there's a problem."

"Which is?"

Sam waved a hand. "Ferrel doesn't have the book yet. No book, no recipe, so where did those mutants come from?"

This was the part of the story Mark didn't want to tell. He sat quietly for a moment, listening to the hum of the lights, the sounds of the building around him. Machines. People. The beep of the monitors around one little boy's bed. Or maybe it was his imagination that he could pick out that single sound among so many.

Mark cleared his throat. "According to what was in the book, there were three versions of the formula. The one Thoristand wrote there is the last. It was supposed to have worked out the bugs of the first two trials."

"Bugs?"

"You saw the damage when we opened up those bodies."

"I'm not a doctor." Sam made a face. "I just saw bloody flesh."

"It was obvious those creatures wouldn't have lived long. Tinkering with genetics is risky. The Knights probably used the first viable version of the formula to make them. Maybe they found it when they killed Thoristand. But they need the final formula before their warriors will live longer than a few months."

Eyes narrowed, Sam leaned forward across the table. "Then do they know the mutants are going to keel over a few months after they change? Are they sacrificing their own people just to match us in hand-to-hand combat?"

"Ferrel's crew are fanatics."

At that, Sam poured himself another drink. "Do we know what's in the formula? Or what the difference is between the first version and the third?"

"We do." Mark frowned. "I had Kenyon do a scan of our records. Thoristand sent his early research to the Company executive—everything up to his second version of the formula. There's every possibility Carter gave a copy of it to the Knights when he was playing double agent and sold us out."

Sam curled his lip. "Carter. That figures."

"He hated us."

Scowling, Sam set down his glass. "So let me recap. Version one they got from Mr. Crazy Vampire when they offed him. Version three is in the book the fey got somehow and Jessica Lark hid. Version two was in our own files but may be been leaked to the Knights by a traitor?"

"Exactly." Mark noticed Sam skipped over the fact that Carter had been his maker, and that Sam had killed him for betraying the Company only months ago. That wound ran bone-deep.

They sat in silence for a long moment. Sam was still brooding when Mark's pager buzzed.

Mark rose, glad he'd barely touched the Scotch. "I have to go."

Sam just nodded, lost in his angry memories.

The page was about Jonathan. When Mark burst through the door, there was a nurse on either side of the bed, checking everything there was to check. One of the junior doctors was scanning the chart.

"What happened?" Mark demanded. He was already reviewing the vitals, but he could hear Jonathan's labored breathing. Panic lanced through him. *No, no, no. This can't be happening!* He was a whisker away from diagnosis, but until that was confirmed, he couldn't come up with a treatment.

"Respiratory distress," said the junior doctor. "Cardiogenic pulmonary edema would be my guess."

"Don't guess," Mark snapped, letting his fear drive his temper. "Get films."

One of the nurses leaped to the phone to call for the X-ray technician.

"Vasodilators?" the doctor suggested. "Morphine? Or maybe a diuretic?"

"Have you checked his kidney functions? This is a child, not a guessing game. Or do you regularly prescribe by closing your eyes and picking a drug off the shelf?"

"Oh," said the young idiot, turning pale. "Kidneys not doing so well."

"Then perhaps think harder." Mark wanted to strangle him. Sadly, that didn't work so well on the undead. "This child is on the edge. Any mistake could be fatal."

Jonathan's body temperature had been dropping before, but now he had spiked a fever. Still, his skin was more gray than pink, his dark hair looking even darker against his pale brow. Mark suspected Ferrel's men had given him a second dose of whatever drug they'd received in the airport, and it was shutting down his organs one by one. Some of the effects were textbook, others made about as much sense as vampires, werewolves and fairies. Medicine never quite kept up with the paranormal.

And Mark was sure now that's what he was dealing with. Jonathan's verbal abilities were coming back online, but they had manifested first via telepathy. Mark had heard that cry for help by the sheep pen, he was sure of it. And there were those fantastic reflexes when Jonathan caught his milk at the ferry, and his hand-eye

coordination when he was coloring in the restaurant…
Something was happening to the boy that wasn't covered
in standard diagnostic texts.

Suddenly, Jonathan choked, his raspy breathing going
into a long, painful rattle. His limbs began to shake violently.

"He's seizing!" said Mark.

"What should we give him?" the junior doctor asked,
this time smart enough not to guess.

It was a febrile seizure, simple enough to treat but
Jonathan was weak. There were medicines the fey used
that worked better on children than those designed for
human adults. "Start a drip with Tincture of Rosebeam."

Mark ordered a low dosage to start and willed the
fever to drop, wishing that even the smallest part of his
vampire strength could flow into the child. He wanted,
needed Jonathan to fight.

The drug didn't help. Mark increased the dose. That
didn't help, either.

Come on, come on. He wasn't sure who he was urging anymore—it might have been himself. He had to
solve this.

"What else can we try?" he asked.

Another doctor had come to assist. The team began
making suggestions. The X-ray technician showed up
just to add to the commotion.

Mark didn't hear any advice he liked. Meanwhile, he
could feel Jonathan's breathing slow. With a sense of
mounting horror, he realized he was losing.

He'd tried the sensible. Now he'd go with his gut. He
bit his wrist, and then let the blood wet Jonathan's lips.

"That's against protocol!" the junior doctor exclaimed.

Jonathan took a deep breath like a swimmer emerging from the depths. Pink flushed into his cheeks like a

tide, and the machines above his head resumed a steady rhythm.

The steel band around Mark's chest let go, but he wasn't happy.

"Protocol says—"

"I can suggest a thousand anatomically inventive uses for your protocol," Mark snarled. "Where's Schiller? I want a report."

"Right away, doctor," said one of the nurses, who ran from the room.

Mark swore long and viciously. He was not letting Jonathan slip away. Nevertheless, the junior doctor was right, which only made things worse.

Schiller marched into the room, white coat flying behind him like a sail. He was a short, stocky werewolf in his early sixties, bald with a fringe of grizzled hair and thick black-rimmed glasses. He was the best blood specialist Mark knew.

"I want to start a drip of OV-negative," Mark announced. "Point-five solution."

"Vampire blood?" Schiller said with surprise.

"Small amounts worked before, when we were on the road. It's palliative at best, but—"

"You gave it orally?" Schiller interrupted.

"Yes."

"Be careful of the concentration!" the werewolf admonished. "He's only a child."

Frustration made Mark's fingers curl into fists. "I know that." And he knew the terrible consequences of Turning a child. Spending eternity in a child's body was a cruelty few could endure with their sanity intact. "That's why I'm giving him a low dose. Have you made any progress with the blood samples?"

"It's as you suspected," Schiller said sadly. "There is genetic damage."

"Can we fix it?" *Can we save him? Can I at least give that much to Bree?*

Schiller frowned. "I'll have to examine the mother, but I have more work to do first. Bring her to me in the morning."

"But can we fix it?"

Schiller folded his arms. "You should know the answer to that, Doctor. You're a vampire. Everything depends on the blood."

Chapter 24

Hours later, Bree was still pacing the room, looking for a way out. Pushing aside the curtains had revealed a blank wall where the window should have been. Opening the door required a keypad. There weren't any hidden panels, bookcases that disguised secret passages or trapdoors under the carpets. An employee had shown up to take Custard for a walk. On his return, he had dropped off her backpack, but a search of the contents revealed that the book was gone. Only Jessica's sketches of the wedding clothes remained.

He'd also brought pasta with scallops in herbed cream sauce, a light California white wine, crusty bread, French roast coffee and crème brûlée for her, and a full kit of puppy necessities for Custard. Until she smelled the food, Bree hadn't realized how hungry she was. Anxious though she was, she forced herself to eat for strength.

The food was excellent. She doubted the vampires had done the cooking.

Stuffed to capacity, Custard had abandoned her to curl up on the bed. Bree, on the other hand, started her search of the rooms all over again. There were no windows and she was getting claustrophobic. Nothing in the place let in light or air, and she was suffocating.

Waiting for news of her son was slowly turning her to ice. When the door finally opened, it was Mark. After one look at his grim expression, Bree's heart all but stopped in her chest.

"It's Jonathan, isn't it?" she said. "Tell me."

Mark gave a slow nod. "He's stable. I thought you'd want to know right away."

Her vision blurred and she ground the heels of her hands into her eyes, as if she could physically push back the tears. She sank down into one of the chairs, suddenly too tired to stand. "Thanks."

He knelt in front of her, taking her hands. "Bree."

Her breath was coming in short, jagged gasps. *I don't want to cry.* She felt vulnerable enough.

"Listen to me," he said. "I know you've had a lot to take in."

Ya think? But the voice in her head was more plaintive than snarky. "I'm a prisoner!"

His voice was gentle. "We have to go through a clearance procedure before we can let people walk around the facility. Kenyon's doing that right now."

It sounded reasonable, but she didn't know what to believe. There was something he wasn't telling her. She could see it lurking right beneath his reasonable, compassionate, professional mask—the one that was as much a part of him as the stethoscope and white coat. *And where do the fangs fit in?* If only those were the product of a massive hallucination!

He was wearing that long white doctor's coat right now, but she could still see the edge of that bloody shirt above the collar. He'd been so focused on helping her son, he hadn't taken time to change. She remembered the knife going into his side.

"Take off your coat," she said.

"What?" His brow contracted.

"Take it off."

He stood and did as he was told, tossing the lab coat onto the sofa. Bree's gaze wanted to be anywhere but on the ruin of the shirt, but she forced herself to take in every detail. *This is reality. Take a good long look so you know it's the truth.* "Now the shirt."

Clearly puzzled, he complied. This time, though, it wasn't a quick job. The shirt was plastered to his skin in places where it had dried wet. He made a faint sound as though it hurt to peel it off.

The sight of his lithe, muscular chest rekindled memories of their lovemaking. Bree swallowed, a confused mix of emotions colliding inside her. He was every bit as amazing to look at as he had been last night, but now she knew what that perfect body hid.

Mark dropped the shirt into the garbage. When he turned back to her, she could see the angry red scar where the knife had been. It wept tiny beads of blood where the shirt had pulled away.

An ache throbbed in her throat. It wasn't pity for his wound, though she felt that, as well. Everything she understood about the world had just crumbled. She rose from the chair, taking a step toward him.

"So it's true. The whole vampire thing is real." Her

fingers touched the white flesh next to the scar. "You should have died from this."

According to legend, he should have been cold as a corpse. He wasn't. He was cool, but not out of the range of what she'd consider normal. *Of course not, we made love. I would have felt it.* Then again, she'd wanted him so badly nothing short of bat wings would have slowed her down.

When he spoke, his voice was flat, revealing nothing. "I won't die. Not for a long, long time."

"Aren't you dead already?" *Surely I'm not having this conversation.*

"Not medically speaking."

Her fingers slid over his ribs. No, nothing this vital could be dead. She forced her gaze upward from his admittedly fascinating chest. She thought again of the cougar, also beautiful, wild and deadly. No wonder Mark hadn't seemed afraid of it back there in the forest. They were peers. Her mouth went dry, but was it fear or desire?

Her fingers still lingered on his skin, feeling the play of muscles as he shifted. "Not medically, but..."

"I died to the world of humans long ago." He said the words as if he had spoken them a thousand times before, perhaps to the bathroom mirror. "I'm not one of you anymore."

"You're a doctor."

"I'm also a killer."

"You must be very confused." She placed her palm flat against him, letting herself stroke his skin.

He blinked. "Yes."

The single word held just a touch of sarcasm. That was the Mark she recognized. "Explain this to me," she whispered. "How is this possible?"

He caught her hand, folding it in his own. "That's what I need to talk to you about right now."

"Okay."

He picked up the coat, shrugged it on, and the moment of intimacy was gone. His features settled into the lines she recognized as his doctor face. Like one of her father's pet actors, Mark wore a series of masks. They weren't necessarily lies, but those clever faces made digging down to the person underneath all that much harder.

"Sit," he said, gesturing to the sofa.

They sat, a few inches short of a polite distance between them.

"This all has to do with Jonathan's illness, and Jessica and the book," he began, almost crisply. "It all fits together like a puzzle. I'll try to make it as clear as possible."

The words alone made her heart pound with anticipation. A flicker of interest crossed his face, as if he sensed it. The predator. That was part of him, too—another mask, or maybe the absence of one.

"You've figured it out?" she asked, thinking as much about him as this ridiculous, terrible situation.

"Maybe a piece of it." His lips twitched, but the smile died before it reached his eyes. "There was no way you could have solved it without knowing about us."

"You mean vampires?"

"Yes. One thing you have to realize is that not all vampires work for the Company. I didn't until relatively recently. There are others out there, good and bad."

"What made you join the Company?" she asked, interrupting his flow.

Mark seemed to consider the answer. "There were a lot of reasons. Perhaps the main one is that I needed to belong to something. After a while, vampires retreat from the world. Eventually, the isolation catches up. I needed to reach out."

Bree thought of Mark's cabin in the woods. That was a retreat if she ever saw one. "Why withdraw like that?"

His face went perfectly blank. "The human mind wasn't made to live so long. Eventually you lose too many people. Everyday things cease to mean much."

"That sounds like depression," she supplied.

He sighed, but it was half a laugh. "Perhaps. Or just madness."

She wasn't touching that one. "How old are you?"

He looked away. "Not relevant. And not what I need to talk about."

"The puzzle," she said, realizing that she'd been stalling. Part of her didn't want to hear this. She wasn't sure she could take bad news.

"This is the first piece. For centuries a vampire named Thoristand lived in the remote areas of Marcari. He was very old, born before the Crusades."

Over a thousand years old. That life span was hard to grasp. Surely that was older than Mark? How old *was* Mark?

But then Bree's attention was firmly fixed on his tale about Jessica's book and three versions of a secret formula. She heard the pain in his voice when he spoke about Jonathan. It was the one time his professional mask slipped.

Without thinking, she took his hand. He flinched in surprise and his words trailed off. He was looking at her hand on his, clearly perplexed.

"Go on," she urged. She hadn't meant to reach out like that, but now that she had, she wasn't pulling back. Her gut said it was the right thing.

He licked his lips, the first sign of nervousness he'd

let slip. "The contents of that book are just the logical conclusion of Thoristand's experiments."

"I thought you said it was a biological weapon?"

He gave her hand a squeeze, as if thanking her for not screaming and running from the room. "It is, sort of. Thoristand was concerned that vampires were making too many of their own kind. If that kept happening, eventually there would be too few humans to support the vampire population. So he decided to take matters into his own hands and engineer a solution. He was already deep into live trials before anyone found out what he was up to."

"What was he doing?" Bree asked, although she wasn't sure she wanted to know.

"He was trying to create hybrids capable of beating vampires on the field of battle. Half vampires if you like. Human, but with the physical advantages of our kind."

"It didn't work. You beat them."

He shook his head, watching her face carefully. "I'm a trained assassin. If I had been an ordinary vampire, that trio of them could have killed me. Vampires are still the top of the food chain, but not by much."

A trained assassin? It made sense, but how could that *not* make her stomach flip over? A wave of queasiness passed through her. Now she pulled back her hand. He made no effort to stop her.

She folded her arms across her chest. "You said this had to do with Jonathan's illness."

Mark closed his eyes. "He tested positive for the virus."

Shock brought her to her feet. "That's impossible! They stuck me with a needle, too! Neither of us grew fangs!"

Mark smiled sadly, as if he'd anticipated her response.

"The first formula was lethal to the people who took it. This formula is far more subtle—mild enough that an adult with a healthy immune system could throw off the virus. To you, it was no more than a case of flu. In a child, the effect was more profound."

"But surely..." Bree panicked, words sticking in her throat.

He met her gaze squarely, fully the medical doctor now. "You must have noticed Jonathan's eye-hand co-ordination is above normal. He has reflexes far beyond the norm. Probably better sight and hearing, as well."

"He stopped talking." Her voice faded to almost nothing.

"Probably his brain was busy adjusting to the other changes. There would have been new pathways to map, more information to process. Learning language could wait until all this other input was sorted out. By itself, the loss of speech wasn't an indication of illness. It was a developmental hiccup."

"But he *is* sick."

His steady, almost ruthless gaze wavered. For a moment she saw only a man who cared. "Yes. Very. We're calling in every specialist we know to work on it."

Suddenly weak, she nearly fell back into the chair. A black hole opened inside her—a vast nothing, and at the bottom of it, implacable anger. The rage started to boil up. "Why do this? Why do it to a child? Why not use more of their soldiers?"

Mark put his hand on her shoulder. When she didn't resist, he pulled her under his arm. "I'm so sorry."

"Why?" she demanded. "Why did they do it? He's only a little boy!"

Mark's voice softened, deepened. An anger as deep as her own flared beneath his clipped words. "An adult and a child were the perfect pair of test subjects. No one would notice if you vanished, because you already had. When they injected the virus, you were already captive and they had every intention of killing you, so why waste their own people?"

"Dear God," Bree breathed. She was stunned. "That's what Ferrel meant. We were guinea pigs."

"And then you messed everything up and escaped. Not only was the book with the third formula missing, but their experiment was on the run."

"Good for us."

"Best of all, you lived." He gave her a bitter smile. "Chances are, they didn't hold out much hope for formula number two, but the longer you two lived, the more important you became. There was every chance you might be viable specimens. They had to get you back and study the results. So they chased you from one side of the continent to the other."

"But what about the police who lied to me back in New York? The paparazzi? The lies about Prince Kyle being Jonathan's father?"

"Don't ever underestimate the Knights or their resources. They want the final version of the formula in the book. Failing that, they wanted proof the second version worked. They stopped at nothing to achieve their ends, be it lies, corruption or murder."

"But now we're here," she said quietly. *A prisoner, not sure if I can trust the Company any more than I can the Knights.* She remembered the fortune-teller's words: *death stands behind and before you.*

They fell silent for a long time. Mark waited, still as stone.

"Will Jonathan live?" she finally asked.

A look of pain shot through his eyes. "I don't know. I will do everything in my power to save him."

She heard the confession in his voice. *Mark loves him.* The realization brought tears to her eyes. On some level, it was the signal she had been waiting for. Here was the one reason she could trust Mark, at least where Jonathan was concerned.

It didn't make everything better—her reality had imploded, she'd slept with a vampire and she was stuck in a building full of monsters—but her dragon was guarding her child.

The dragon looked stricken. "Please believe we are doing our best."

She tried to get her mouth to smile, to take away some of his hurt. It wobbled. "If Jonathan or I die, will we turn into vampires, too?"

He tried to smile back, just about as successfully. "I doubt it. I should test your blood, though, just to be safe."

She gave a shaky sigh, wondering if she would ever feel safe again.

He wiped away a tear that escaped down her cheek. "Trust me, whatever happens, I'll look after you."

Chapter 25

She was hurting. He could see it in those changeable eyes that were now the gray-green of a stormy sea. But there was nothing he could do or say to stop the tears. Bree had fallen into his world of nightmare, and there was no way to undo it. Human or horror, they shared the same shadows now.

He wiped away another tear, feeling the heat of her body in that single drop. Her skin was satin under his fingers, smelling of fairground and dust and sun and that peach-sweet perfume that was her own.

"Bree," he murmured.

Somehow he was lucky enough to be holding her again, despite everything she'd seen him do. It might have been the white coat. People trusted doctors—rightly so in most cases, but he was a vampire, an assassin trying to wipe clean a few of his sins. Only his conscience kept the predator from his patients. A conscience was a flimsy thing that was easily cast aside. Did the fact that he clung to it count? Did it make him less of a monster?

What did Bree see when she looked at him?

And that thought made him afraid in a way he hadn't felt for centuries. When she raised her face to his, a tiny frown line between her brows, every muscle in his body tensed.

"What?" she asked softly.

"Are you afraid of me?"

He felt foolish the moment he said it. He let go of her, stepping back. She let out a little huff of breath, as if the question had physically struck her.

"How could I not be?" She lifted her hands apologetically. "I saw what you did."

"Do you want me to go?"

Her lips parted, that soft wide mouth that tasted like life itself. He didn't want to know what she was going to say. If he was afraid before, this terrified him.

He caught her arms and pulled her close, roughly stopping her with a kiss before she could answer. He didn't want to hear that lovely mouth tell him to leave. It might have undone him.

Her fingers found his sleeves and slid upward to his shoulders. The gesture was tentative, as if she wasn't sure if she wanted to hang on or push him away. The same confusion sounded in her heartbeat, quick and light as a bird's. It reminded him of wild things that left the safety of the woods, creeping closer and closer to take food from his hand, wondering if they dared trust.

Her fear hit his blood like whiskey, urging him on.

Insistent, he parted her lips, plundering with his tongue, drinking down her hot breath. This time he could not hide his fangs as they descended, responding to his rising lust. He heard the gasp as she found them, felt their sharpness. It turned him on. *You're mine. I will protect you, defend you and yours, but make no mistake. You belong to me.*

They were primitive thoughts, straight from the beast-side of his brain. His doctor-side might wrap them up in a more civilized bow, but the burning need to have her wouldn't change. Bree was in his bloodstream as surely as a fever, and he would not rest until he knew she felt the same.

It was against all logic. The Company all but forbade unions between humans and vampires, but Mark played by the rules if and when it suited him. He had been an independent operator too long. The Company would want him to use his hypnotic talents to erase Bree's memories before he let her go. She would remember nothing of this, not one kiss.

He'd be damned if he was letting that happen. He was Marco Farnese, nobleman, swordsman, vampire—and she would never forget his touch.

He slid one hand beneath her shirt, feeling the hot velvet of her skin. He traced the delicate bones of her ribs, exploring until he found the softness of her breasts. Bree made a whimpering noise in her throat that made him go stiff. He caught the scent of her desire, smoky and dark. Her body knew him and responded, her back arching to push the peak of her breast into his hand.

"Mark," she got out, confusion filling the single syllable. "I'm—"

"We'll go slowly."

Taking it slow was demanding all the control he had. His teeth had scraped her lip, letting a single drop of blood touch his tongue. His mouth exploded with the taste—salty, but bright as berries. Mark inhaled a shuddering breath, almost a prayer as he surrendered to the sensation. He was lost.

He needed more.

He wanted Bree's blood—hers and hers alone—as an addict craved his next fix. She was the one woman, the only woman who mattered.

It was rare that a vampire felt this. It had never happened to him before—no, not even with his wife, Anna, so long ago. He had loved her first as a man, before he had been Turned. Of course he had loved her after. But this thing he felt now was supernaturally intense, with the bone-crushing power of all his centuries in its spell.

When vampires truly loved, they loved once only. This was it.

He rose, pulling Bree up with him. Her face was flushed, her mouth plump and rosy from his kisses. She looked so intensely alive. So delicious. "Come," he commanded.

Blinking, she seemed to bring him into focus. "Mark," she said softly. "I don't know."

She wanted him. He could hear it in her heartbeat. It was pulsing, thick and strong and a little too fast. His body ached in response.

But she doubted him. He refused to let that continue. Mark took her face in his hands, leaving a light kiss on her forehead. "You're safe with me. Let me prove it."

Her eyes were lost. "I don't know how to love someone like you."

Like a fanged, slaughtering beast. He couldn't find words to answer.

She dug her fingers into the fabric of his coat. "It was one thing when we were on the road. Everything seemed so simple. But now— I don't have a good track record.

I don't make good decisions. Everyone always ends up leaving me, or dying, or—"

There was one promise he could keep. "I won't leave you."

With that, he caught her in his arms again, lifting until her feet left the ground and wrapped around his body. He would hear no more arguments. She was his.

Bree struggled a moment, pushing away like a cat that doesn't want to be picked up. Mark refused to budge, remaining adamant. "Bree, stop."

It was as if something inside her cracked, and she gave in. With a frustrated moan, she crushed her mouth to his, kissing as though she was terrified that he would disappear in a plume of smoke. Mark met her onslaught fiercely, reveling in her greed.

And so he took her to the bedroom, evicting a sleepy Custard and shutting the door. They fell onto the bed, tearing off their own clothes and each others' in their desperate haste to find buttons and zippers, a condom and bare, smooth skin. He was hard and full, aching to the point of madness.

"Now," she begged. "Now, please. Don't wait."

He eased himself inside her, slowly. Bree threw her head back on the pillow, moaning in her impatience.

It was all the invitation he needed.

His mouth found the willowy smoothness of her neck and bit. She cried out in surprise, but the sound melted into a sigh. Bree writhed, shivering as the venom from his fangs reached her blood. Rich in erotic stimulants, it sharpened pleasure to an almost painful pitch. Her nipples grew hard against his chest, her body began to pulse around him as her fingers dug into his flesh, scoring his back.

Salty blood welled from the bite, filling his mouth

with life. The predator in him roared its triumph, owning her blood and her pleasure. The vampire's bite could tear and rend, but it could also seduce. Healing agents would seal the wound within hours, hiding it from sight, but the mark it left on her desire would be indelible. He would make this so unforgettable, she would never think of another lover.

Her blood flowed through him, electrifying each cell as it warmed his body. Mark began to thrust, drawing a cry from her with every motion. She rose to meet him, each time more roughly than the last as control gave way to lust. He swallowed another mouthful of hot life, nearly losing himself too soon in the bliss of it. He pulled himself back, stroking, pushing, drawing out the pleasure until he thought he would go mad.

And when he had her at the brink, he slowed, letting the moment hang. "No," she complained. "No, I need more."

"Patience."

She writhed in protest, weaving her fingers through his hair, raking his scalp with her nails. The added sensation of it made him shiver as he lapped the last drops of blood from her skin, closing the wound he had made with his tongue. And then he bent to suckle at her breast.

With a sharp cry, Bree went over the edge, the pulsing of her body teasing him, milking him. He held on long enough for one last, hard thrust, spilling himself as his mind flattened to a white haze.

He had never come so hard before. The moment went on and on, all his preternatural strength sustaining it until he thought his sanity would shatter. When it finally released him, spent and dizzy, he was lost.

Mark rolled to the side, throwing a protective arm over Bree. Her life swirled inside him, effervescent, fleeting.

He combed the masses of her tawny hair through his fingers, wondering at the acute intimacy of feeling her within and without. He was too old to need much fresh blood for pleasure—a few ounces at most—and yet it warmed him like a campfire. A woman held everything. Love. Light. The very sustenance of life. How could a man not guard her with every fiber of his being?

She turned to face him. He tried to read her expression, but her eyes were closed, private. Her fingers searched out his face, tracing the line of his cheekbone. Her feathery touch was oddly erotic.

"How did this happen to you?" she whispered.

He never told this story. Ever. "It doesn't matter."

He caught her palm and kissed it. He didn't want to say more. Not about the cruelty of his maker, or the horror of waking up to find himself changed, or the blinding thirst they had cursed him with. There was nothing good in those memories.

Instead, he wrapped her in his arms, holding her. She burrowed into his shoulder, never looking him in the face. Never seeing him. She'd seen enough that afternoon, he guessed, when he'd shown the monster inside.

He was the one with the strength, but she had the power.

Mark closed his eyes then, wishing he could believe she would ever love him back.

Chapter 26

Bree sat at Jonathan's bedside, unsure of how long she had sat there. She was stiff and cold, as if her blood had congealed from sitting still too long.

Hours, or days, or years ago she had awakened to find herself alone, a key card resting on the bedside table. She'd showered and dressed and then found a breakfast tray waiting for her. The clock had told her it was the next morning. A curiously formal note from Mark had told her how to find her son. This wasn't the morning after she had dreamed of, but it was the one she'd needed. Somehow Mark had known she had no room to be anything but Jonathan's mother right then.

Bree reached over, pushing back a stray lock of her son's hair. He had grown fragile, as if he were one of those leaves she sometimes saw in the fall, with nothing left but a translucent web of connective tissue. This virus that was tearing away at his organs, at the very building blocks of his body, was leaving no more than a shell.

It seemed unfair that he had finally spoken, only to relapse utterly. For a moment she thought she'd had him back again, truly Jonathan and not this tired, silent child. He'd been such a happy, loving toddler—but this was all that remained to her. A bed, a chair and a mass of tubes and machines. The boy was barely there at all.

Fear for her son hummed inside her, but somewhere she'd lost the ability to cry it out. There was no simple relief anymore. The past few days had been too much for both of them.

Mark had been the best and the worst of it. She owed him everything. He'd saved her, he'd killed for her, he'd made love to her—yet she had no idea how to handle what he was. Sleeping with him was—well, it was mind-blowing, but calling that sex was a bit like comparing Custard to Cujo. Mark was bigger, fiercer, just *more* than any male she'd ever met, and far out of her league. He was *deadly*. And he frightened her out of her wits.

And he'd bitten her! There wasn't even a bruise, but she remembered the pain and—Holy Christmas—the orgasm. That had to be some vampire survival thing that kept blood donors coming back for more. She was mad at him for having done it. She was even angrier that he'd been holding out on her. How many times between Seattle and L.A. could they have experienced that mind-exploding sex?

What am I doing with him?

She'd slept with him. While her son lay dying. And she'd lost herself in it.

Guilt nauseated her, making her even more thankful that Mark had not stayed the night. She knew that logically a woman could have a lover and a child, that perhaps she needed both right now, but she wasn't ready to be reasonable.

She touched Jonathan's damp forehead, noticing how frail his features looked, his eyes too big for his little face. *I would give my life for you.*

If only saving him were that easy. She'd slit her wrists in a moment.

"Hey," a voice said.

She looked up to see Kenyon's tall form. She felt a slight lift inside. Unexpectedly, she was glad to see him—even if he had locked her in her room. "Hello."

"I took Custard for some quality time in the park. I hope you don't mind."

"No, not at all, thank you."

Kenyon pulled up a stool and sat down. His bright blue eyes were serious. "How is the kiddo doing?"

Bree shook her head, not trusting herself to speak. She leaned forward, putting her head in her hands. *I will not break down. I'm stronger than that.*

Kenyon put a hand on her back, rubbing it lightly, the way a mother would comfort a child. It should have been intrusive, coming from a virtual stranger, but it helped.

"Listen," he said. "I'm not going to say that everything is going to be all right, because I don't know. I'm not a doctor. But some science guys from Europe have flown in to take a look. If there's an answer to find, they'll get it."

Bree raised her head, horrified at the thought of the medical bill. "That's a lot of expense."

Now Kenyon grinned. "Hey, don't you worry. The Company has deep pockets, and this is as personal to us as it is to you. We insist on organic vampires."

"I'll still be in debt to the Company forever. I could never have done this on my own."

"But this is why we're here. We solve problems that

are too big for ordinary mortals." He said it with a sly, tongue-in-cheek pride. "Someday I'll tell you about the time Mark saved the world with nothing but a pocket wrench and a package of orange drink crystals. They could make a TV series about something like that."

Despite herself, Bree smiled. "How old is Mark, anyway?"

Kenyon instantly grew cautious. "I'm not sure. He doesn't talk about the past. Most of the vamps don't."

That was disappointing. "Why not?"

"I don't think the whole undead trip is bunnies and roses, if you know what I mean. There's baggage."

"But we've all got that."

"Yeah. And that's the secret to dealing with them." Kenyon gave her a searching look. "Let me give you a piece of unsolicited advice. Your baggage is just as valid as theirs. You and I might not have lived as long, and maybe we haven't been locked up in dungeons or cursed by naiads or whatever undead drama is going that week, but we matter, too."

Bree didn't get what he was saying. It must have shown on her face.

Kenyon shrugged. "Vampires aren't human. They're part beast, and those beasts are all alphas. They're great at taking care of others, but they respect people who know their own worth. Insist on being heard. Don't let them run over you. Act with integrity. Keep your word with them. Once you've won their trust, they'll be loyal to the death."

She frowned, still trying to grasp what he was driving at. "Loyal in what way?"

"Every way. Vampires mate for life. You just have to see Sam and Chloe together to understand that."

"The Sam I met? Sam with the human girlfriend?"

"Yup. It's like every girl movie you ever saw rolled into one big mushy script. Kind of revolting, actually."

"Aren't werewolves romantic?" She was sorry the moment she said it, remembering that she didn't actually know Kenyon at all. He was just so easy to talk to.

He flushed, easy to see beneath his fair skin. "I, uh— No. I got a D-minus in the Valentine category."

She grinned. "That's a shame."

"Well, this kind of national treasure—" he swept his hands from head to foot "—should not be monopolized by one person. It's only fair that I keep myself available."

She stayed at Jonathan's bedside until the medical staff chased her away. It was well into the afternoon when she walked down the long hallway that ran through the medical facility and toward her suite. Doors stood open here and there. Drowning in other problems, Bree paid little attention. She nearly walked past an occupied room before the features of the patient clicked in her memory. Backing up three steps, she took a second look.

It was Larson, the pilot. She'd forgotten he'd been moved to Los Angeles.

He was alone. She slipped into the room.

"What are you doing here?" he asked, pushing himself up on his pillows.

"Just making sure I didn't kill you back there on the plane." She squeezed his hand.

"Not quite." He managed a smile. It looked as if it cost him. Although she couldn't see beneath the covers, it looked as if one leg was immobilized. The bullet to his thigh must have done more damage than she had known.

"I'm glad you made it okay," he said.

She felt a flash of anger. He'd betrayed them. True,

he'd fought on their side in the end, but he'd put them all at risk. "What happened back there?"

He winced, looking away. "Aw, miss. I got caught between the devil and the deep blue sea."

"I heard there were threats against your family."

"Yes."

"Are they all right?"

"Yes. The Company's keeping an eye on them. Keeping a lookout for the Knights." He sagged back against the pillows. His complexion was naturally ruddy, sunburned from long hours outdoors, but he turned gray at the mention of Ferrel's men. "I'm so sorry."

"You helped us in the end."

"I should never have doubted Winspear. I should have gone to him straightaway, but I couldn't leave anything to chance."

She agreed, but that was easy for her to say. From what Mark said, Larson had grandchildren. Would she have done anything different?

She decided to be forgiving. "If it had been Jonathan, I might have done the same thing."

He took her hand, pressing it. "Thank you. All I know is that when my granddaughter looks at me, she sees a giant. Foolish or not, I couldn't trust her safety to anyone else."

Bree left him after that, meandering slowly back to her room. Larson had left her unsettled, thinking about families. It was true, a lot of how a person felt about themselves came from family—they became the clown or the darling, the smart one or the hopeless case. Who could blame a man for wanting to be the avenging giant?

The discussion made an interesting counterpart to Kenyon's observation about vampires. They responded to people who stood their ground—hard to do without a positive self-image. Her history left her on shaky ground there. She hadn't even wanted to come near her old hometown.

Bree unlocked the door to her suite and stepped inside. Custard lay on the floor in a tired heap of creamy fur. Kenyon must have worn him out. The dog turned big brown eyes on her, ears lifting. Suddenly, she was hugely grateful that he was there.

She knelt, tickling the soft, warm belly. He wriggled, his tail moving most of his back end as it wagged. Suddenly exhausted herself, she lay down on the floor, mock-wrestling with Custard and letting him lick her face. It felt good to make somebody happy, even if they only came up to her shin.

She held the dog inches from her nose. Here was the one person she could talk to, the one who would never judge her. Bree ached to unburden herself, and the words spilled out in a burst of heartfelt frustration. "What do I do about Mark?"

Custard drooled. She couldn't have said it better herself.

"I've never believed in love at first sight," she began. "Never."

Not even with Mark. The first time she'd met him, she'd pointed a gun. Protecting a child and running from the Knights robbed her of any luxury she might have for instant romance.

Custard whined, and she set him down on her stomach. He curled up, snuggling under her chin. *Okay, maybe there's love at first sight for dogs. I'm just not such a pushover for guys.*

But then had come those long hours she'd spent with Mark in the car. They had given her the time she needed to unwind and take a closer look. It had felt like months of dating telescoped into a few days—fast, but thorough. Mark had proven himself, over and over.

He wasn't perfect. He was set in his ways, a bit pushy and a little too prone to spoiling Jonathan. But how many guys would—or could—have gotten them safely to L.A.? How many would have remembered pancakes and dinosaurs and condoms and even rescued a puppy?

And biting aside… Her stomach knotted, her entire body nearly jittering in confusion. The whole supernatural element was a lot to deal with.

"Who believes in vampires, anyway?" she muttered. "I lived in L.A. and New York. You'd think I'd have seen it all."

Custard snuffled a reply.

"But believing isn't the biggest problem. I mean, I saw the knife wound almost healed. I saw the fangs. He's the whole deal. Old. Powerful. Deadly."

Custard lifted his head. From this angle, with him sitting on her chest, it made his black button nose look enormous.

"So tell me, little guy, what does he want with me? I'm just a single mom."

And that was the crux of the matter. What had happened on the road had been like a hothouse flower, protected from the cold wind of reality. It was like summer camp, or a cruise, or Las Vegas—a time-out. Once Jonathan was better and the crisis was over—well, any man prone to rescuing others would be off finding his next project, right? Why the blazes did she think she could hold Mark's interest?

She had to know because, against her better judgment, she was falling in love with him.

Chapter 27

It was always the cold Mark remembered first, back in those bad old days. People born in the time of central heating had no idea how cold stone buildings could be. It was especially frigid below ground, with a trickle of water creeping over the lintel and dripping down the stairs to pool inches from his feet. He recalled shaking, hands clasped around his knees. Someone had taken his cloak and doublet. All he had was his fine silk shirt, useless for keeping warm.

The iron fetters on his wrists clanked as he gripped his legs more tightly. He needed blood. He hadn't had any in days.

Somewhere in the back of his mind he grasped the fact that this was a dream more than a memory. Most of the details were right, though—he didn't need fantasy to make a nightmare. He had looked down at his hands, noticing just how pale they were. The gentry prided themselves on their white skin, untouched by the sun. He'd started to laugh at the ridiculousness of it. He'd finally attained the height of fashion by the simple fact of being dead.

"You laugh," said a voice. It was funny how Mark forgot that voice when he was awake, but it always came back in a dream. He hated it with all the fury of an avenging ghost—except no one had shown enough courtesy to kill him. Instead, they'd turned him into this *thing*.

"You laugh," the voice repeated. "What do you find so amusing?"

Mark was crouched by the wall, his head bent. A pair of boots appeared in his field of vision, soft and fitted like a glove. Buffed to a shine, one toe twitching impatiently. With a Herculean effort, Mark lifted his head.

Nicholas Ferrel. The first one. Commander General of the Knights of Vidon.

"You slight me, Marco Farnese," said Ferrel. Like all his Ferrel breed, he was fair-haired and handsome, but had the morals of a serpent.

"You murdered my wife and children." Mark didn't bother to raise his voice. Bluster was a sign of weakness. "I will kill you for that."

"Do you really think so?" Ferrel gave a bark of laughter. "You are weak, barely turned and wasting away with hunger. What makes you think you could so much as scratch me?"

"It was your soldiers who dragged me from my bed and took me to the devils. You know what they made me."

"The town has an agreement with Agremont."

Agremont was master of the marauding nest of vampires. He was the one who had drained Mark's life.

"Yes, you were the price for the city's safety!" Ferrel snapped. "A noble child to buy a year of peace! But you returned. The bargain was that you would stay willingly and be their chore boy. The notion of one of the illustrious Farnese scrubbing their floors amused them."

A sacrifice so that many could live. The ghastly bargain had been Ferrel's idea—not that anyone knew that now. That was the thing about history. It got rewritten as time went on. Ferrel was remembered as a hero, Marco Farnese as the monster.

"He wants me to be his assassin." Mark slowly rose to his feet, sliding his back up the wall. The chains clanked, dragging at his wrists. He was so weak from thirst. "I didn't want that. I was a good man. I had a family."

"And now you don't. That's your fault."

"I never touched them."

"Impossible. They say loved ones taste the sweetest."

"I never bit them." It had been hard, so hard. Newly made as he was, their blood had sung to him, but he had never, ever wavered. Vampires five hundred times his age could not have done it, but Mark had never lacked for will.

"I don't believe you," Ferrel spat. "They consorted with a demon."

With me. Mark trembled, but it was no longer the cold and lack of blood that troubled him. This time he shook with rage. Ferrel had sold him, sacrificed him, and then murdered his beloved and their sons. "You call me a demon?"

"I call you hell-spawn," Ferrel's eyes mocked him. "Do you think your Anna opened the door because she loved you? Think again. It was fear. It was your *seduction*." He hissed the word.

Mark's jaw clenched, but he forced out a reply. "No."

"Once you were done, the only means to save their

eternal soul was to burn them on a pyre of flame. It was your pollution that made it necessary."

Fury ripped through Mark, opening a chasm where his reason had been moments before. He snarled, lunging and snapping fangs inches from Ferrel's face. The man jerked away.

"I rest my case," said the commander general. "Demon."

"Then kill me."

"Perhaps." Ferrel was holding a pair of gloves as soft and finely made as the boots. He slapped the gloves across his palm, making a sharp noise. "Or, since you so loathe your new master, perhaps I have more interesting uses for you. Even a rabid dog might have its purpose. If you won't kill for Agremont, perhaps you shall kill for me. Sooner or later you'll be hungry enough to bite anybody."

Mark wrenched against the chains that were bolted into the stone with huge, iron staples.

"Don't bother. Only an ancient could break those bonds."

An avalanche of helplessness slammed down on Mark, driving him to his knees. Ferrel's truth bit deep. He wasn't the human he had been. There was mad thirst and madder instincts to stalk and kill.

And he had seen the look in his wife's eyes when she thought he wasn't looking. She loved the man he had been, not the creature he was now—yet he had refused to notice. Maybe her affection had been a lie, but he had desperately needed it. Needed some anchor before what remained of his humanity slipped away.

But now his family was dead. Burned at the stake. There was no humanity left.

He wrapped the chains around his wrists, gripping

them with cold, desperate fingers. He pulled, straining every muscle but hearing only the futile scrape of metal against stone.

Ferrel watched his efforts, a laugh bubbling up from somewhere deep in his gut. The laugh became a guffaw.

Something inside Mark snapped.

In the seconds that followed, he proved even a young vampire could break the chains. He hadn't taken a life before then, but what happened next changed everything.

Agremont had trained him to become an assassin, but it was Nicholas Ferrel who'd truly made him a monster.

"Winspear!"

Mark jerked awake. Sam was poking him. "What?"

"Nightmare?" Sam asked.

"Yeah."

Mark scrubbed his eyes, slowly coming back to the present. He was at the break room table, head down on his arms. It was the twenty-first century, and he was a doctor now. Thank the stars for that much. Anyone who wanted to live in the time of doublets and sword fights— and mud and pox and public executions—was an idiot.

Sitting up slowly, he scowled at Sam. "What time is it?"

"Four o'clock."

Mark tried to figure out how long he'd been asleep. He didn't need much downtime, but he'd been awake since— had it been his cabin? Surely he must have grabbed at least a few hours since then? But he never slept in hotels—not when he was guarding someone. They just weren't safe enough.

Safe. Bree. His body tightened, remembering their encounter. *I bit her.* A wave of shame and pride and a fierce need to dominate flooded through him. In a building full of vampires, the instinct to put his brand on her had been too strong to resist. The taste of her blood still lingered faintly, like nothing he'd ever encountered before.

He wanted more. On a deep and slightly terrified level, he knew he would never want anyone else. Bree was everything he needed, the happiness he had lost and all the hopes he had ever dreamed of. His mate.

But once she was back among her own people, would she want him? His soul had been twisted by Agremont and Ferrel and centuries of darkness. His vampire DNA held the beast—surely, as a doctor, he should know what that meant: predator. How could she love that?

Mark swore under his breath. *Impossible.* No sane woman wanted a guy who sucked her blood. Okay, Sam's wife-to-be did, but she was— Well, Chloe worked in the service industry. She put up with a lot from people.

Sam poured himself a coffee, the sound homey and familiar. He poured another for Mark and held it out. "That looked like some nightmare."

"Maybe it was someone I ate," he quipped, accepting the mug. The joke made him uncomfortable. His nightmare, and all those sharp feelings of shame and defeat, was too close to the surface.

Sam sipped the coffee experimentally. "Schiller wants to talk to you. He's in his office. He says he has an idea how to cure your young patient."

Mark's mug barely hit the table, sloshing coffee, before he was out the door.

Bree managed to stay away from Jonathan's bedside an entire two hours. Another minute would have made her go mad.

She stepped into the quiet hospital room, and then froze, alarm surging through her. There was a strange woman standing over Jonathan's bed. She wasn't wearing scrubs, but a linen dress Bree recognized as one of Jessica's designs. The cut, the drape, the very essence of it evoked sharp memories of her time at the atelier. The sting of that lost happiness brought an ache to her throat. Bree held her breath for a moment, forcing the sadness down. The dress was nothing. She needed to know what this woman wanted with her son.

The look on the woman's face was puzzled, as if staring at Jonathan would make her understand a difficult equation. As curiosity hardened into protectiveness, Bree detached herself from the door and marched forward. "May I help you?"

The stranger started at Bree's tone. "Pardon me. Are you the boy's mother?"

Bree's lips parted in astonishment as she studied the woman's face. She'd seen a thousand pictures of those large, thick-lashed violet eyes and those perfect cheekbones. The woman's hair was thick and dark, touched with mahogany lights. *Princess Amelie.*

"Your Highness," Bree stammered. "I'm sorry. I didn't realize…"

Her words dribbled to a stop. She'd hoped she might meet Amelie one day, but maybe when she was accepting the princess's praise for her beautiful wedding clothes, not when Bree was tossing her out of her son's hospital room.

"It is I who intrude. Forgive me." The words were tinged with a charming accent, but it was the smile that caught Bree's attention. It was brittle, sad and lost.

"What can I do for you?" Bree said again, but this time she meant it.

Amelie cast a glance at Jonathan. "When I heard he

was here, I wanted to see him. I wanted to know if he truly was—"

She wants to know if Kyle is the father.

"No." Bree knew she probably shouldn't interrupt royalty, but she couldn't stand the hurt on Amelie's face. "No, he isn't. Don't listen to the gossip. A man named Adam Swift was Jonathan's father. Kyle was—is—my friend, but we were never lovers. Not once. I am sure the doctors here could provide a paternity test to prove what I say."

Amelie visibly relaxed. "I am so sorry, but I had to know. There was so much talk."

"I know." Bree had to smile. "Don't get me wrong, Prince Kyle appreciates a pretty woman and he likes the attention but—no. When I knew him, he already had you in his sights."

Amelie lowered her eyes. Bree got the impression that behind the public mask, she was actually shy.

"You have a beautiful child," said the princess. "I am sorry he is not well."

"I'm sorry all those rumors caused you distress. I tried to put a stop to them."

Amelie tilted her head in a gesture Bree recognized from newsreels. "So did Kyle. I shouldn't have doubted him but—it is not easy being so public a figure. Trust becomes difficult."

With a cautious look in her violet eyes, the princess sat down on one of the hospital chairs. She looked like a little girl afraid to be sent to bed early. "I understand you have had quite an adventure getting to Los Angeles. Please, sit and tell me all."

Bree didn't answer right away, but first looked down at Jonathan. A surge of love and sadness shot through her, making her breath catch in her chest. She wanted to give all her focus to him and ignore this interruption, but she sensed Amelie still needed something from her.

How to respond? Bree had grown so isolated, either hiding or running, she'd almost forgotten how to carry on a conversation with another adult.

Except Mark. Somehow he was always the exception.

She touched her son's dark hair, wondering what to say to the woman. "Yes, it has been an adventure. May I ask, how is Prince Kyle?"

Amelie gave a tiny, elegant shrug. "He is very well. Very busy. He is—how do you say it? Getting up to speed with affairs of state. His father, the king, wishes to hand off more responsibility to his heir."

Bree smiled. "Kyle will enjoy it and hate it at the same time."

"Exactly." Amelie gave a quick smile, but still looked uncertain. "I am going to ask something entirely impertinent."

Bree met the princess's eyes, wondering what was behind the question. There was nothing in Amelie's face but guileless curiosity. Maybe she really was the gentle, slightly naive girl that Kyle had claimed. "What is it?"

"Who was Adam Swift?"

Bree's mouth opened, shocked more than angry. That was nobody's business.

"Don't be cross!" Amelie held up her hand. "There is no reason to tell me if you do not wish to."

But how do you refuse a princess? "Adam was my best friend from when we were children. He was a musician, a good one. He died in a surfing accident."

To Bree's surprise, saying it felt good. She sat down in the other visitor's chair, suddenly too tired to stand. "We were very, very close."

"I am sad for you," Amelie said gently.

Tears burned Bree's eyes. Adam's death was so senseless, it hurt to the core to even talk about it. That's why she never did.

She had cried herself out long ago, but she was so tired, there were no defenses left. "I don't think we would have stayed romantic partners over the long-term. He wanted a life in the music business, traveling all the time, and I didn't. But he never lived long enough for us to figure it out. We, uh, didn't intend to have a child together but I would never undo it. He gave me an incredible gift."

Amelie's expression was soft and sad. "How unfortunate that he will not see his son grow into a man."

"He would have been a loving father." Adam was the one who saw her through all the breakups and breakdowns of growing up. He was the rock she'd leaned on. Losing him was like her foundation splitting in two. "It bothers me that Jonathan will never have that connection to where he came from."

"He has your family."

"Not quite the same. I'm not close to my parents."

Amelie shook her head. "Ah, but that is so different from my situation. My family, its very royalty, is who I am. It defines me. It sometimes suffocates me. That is why the notion of marriage is so terribly important to Kyle and me. We are more than a man and woman saying our vows. Our houses will unite."

"That sounds so daunting."

Amelie grew serious. "I must make sure my marriage is a good one, because I am gambling with the happiness of a nation as well as my own. So thank you for being so frank with me. I needed to know the truth about your son."

And why this gentle-looking woman flew all the way to California to make sure Kyle didn't have any lovers or

children she didn't know about. He's got his hands full.
And yet—she couldn't help liking the woman. There was
a grace about her that went far beyond mere beauty. Still,
it was time to change the subject.

"I used to work with Jessica Lark, you know. I worked
on your wedding trousseau."

Amelie's face puckered in distress. "I have the dress,
but the rest was lost. But of course you know that. Poor
Jessica!"

"I still have the sketches for the rest of the clothes."

Amelie's eyes grew wide. "Then you must finish
them!"

"Me?" Bree automatically looked toward Jonathan.
"I'm so sorry, but I can't."

"Why not? Are you not able?"

"I could do the work, I know how, but—"

"Then think about it, at least."

Bree wished she could. A princess's patronage was the
gift of a lifetime. Everything she'd ever wanted. But she
was a mother first, and Jonathan needed her attention.

Amelie put a hand on hers. "I understand you have
other concerns. Don't decide now. Everything will unfold as it should."

Bree's throat was tight. "But your wedding is in February. Getting it all done now—even if I could—would
be a huge job. Maybe someone else could do it?"

The princess sat back in her chair, thoughtful. "No.
You were Jessica's chosen. When it is time, you will
begin."

But Bree'd had her fortune told, and it didn't sound
anywhere near that hopeful. *Too bad Amelie and Mirella
didn't compare notes.*

Both women started when Mark knocked on the open
door.

Chapter 28

Mark. Bree flushed, a tingling flooding over her body as she remembered what they'd done the night before. She couldn't help letting her gaze linger on the line of his shoulders. She swallowed, mouth suddenly dust-dry.

Mark's expression was thoughtful, cautious at first. Then he met Bree's eyes and gave her a look that made her blush deepen. It was like staring into a fire of banked coals, knowing that flame could burst back to life at any moment. Time seemed to hang suspended until, finally, he gave her a polite nod and turned to the princess.

"A thousand pardons, Your Highness," Mark said, making a graceful bow that said he was a man from another time. "Forgive my intrusion."

"You are never an intrusion, Dr. Winspear." The princess held out a hand, palm down.

Mark bowed over it. "I need to speak with Bree about the treatment of her son."

Bree sat forward, her heart speeding. Was it good news? Bad news? She wanted to blurt her questions, but Amelie was already talking, and a warning look from Mark made Bree hold her tongue.

"Then you must do so at once. I, meantime, have a security detail with strict instructions to whisk me home to Marcari for another session of organizing cakes and place settings." The princess rolled her eyes. "I had no idea our new wedding planner would be such a task mistress, nor that she had all the vampires in the Western Hemisphere under her thumb."

Mark smiled. "Chloe has Sam as her husband-to-be. If she can manage him, well, as the moderns say, they shall be a power couple to be reckoned with."

So Sam's human fiancée was the royal couple's wedding planner. An interesting detail, but Bree fidgeted. *What about Jonathan's cure?*

Amelie was still addressing Mark. "I want the Horsemen back at the palace as soon as possible."

"You have trusted members of the Company as your guard, Your Highness. They are loyal to Marcari and always have been."

"I want the Horsemen. Nothing else will do. I know you are training new recruits, but as soon as that is done, my father requests that you return to the palace."

Mark nodded gravely. "As you wish, Your Highness. I will come as soon as I can."

"I know you, Doctor. You will come when you are good and ready." Her tone was scolding, but also affectionate. Amelie rose and kissed his cheek. "I tolerate your insubordination because your reasons are always from the heart."

The smile he gave her was indulgent, like an uncle humoring a willful niece. "Always, my lady."

Amelie turned to Bree. "You must forgive me for intruding on you. If there is anything at all my family, or my kingdom, can do for your son you have but to name it. I am certain Kyle feels the same."

The look on her face said she meant it. She had come to get answers, but now she was willing to help. Bree looked at her son, wishing a cure was as easy as asking a favor of a princess in a pretty dress. "Thank you, ma'am. I truly appreciate your kindness."

Amelie gave that small, shy smile. "Then farewell to you both for today, and good luck."

She swept out of the room in a swirl of designer skirts. Bree got to her feet, for a moment distracted by what she'd heard. "She wants you in Marcari?"

Impatient though she was, Bree felt strangely bereft.

Mark gave a slight shrug. "For the wedding. Security will be paramount."

Bree looked after the slender, dark-haired princess, a hollow feeling growing inside her. Amelie had put everything on the line for this union. It was no mystery why she wanted her trusted guards—but if Mark was leaving, where did Bree fit into the picture? Or did she?

She forced the thought away. *Jonathan.* She cleared her throat, struggling to keep her voice steady. "You have news about a treatment?"

"Yes. As you can understand, we're dealing in highly theoretical science here. However, testing confirms Ferrel injected you and Jonathan with the second version of Thoristand's virus. In a way, that's good news. We know what we're dealing with now."

Bree's pulse hammered in her ears. Mark's words were meant to be reassuring, but they stirred up her deepest fears. "You said he wasn't likely to…to change." Her mouth could barely form the words.

Mark touched her hand. "He's not. This version of Thoristand's genetic cocktail is essentially a failure. It was meant to be more subtle, but as a result it is not powerful enough to complete the transformation. All that it's doing is damaging his organs. We need to introduce an antibody that will reset his genetics to their proper pattern."

"How?" Bree grasped at the idea, but was afraid to hope. "Is that even possible?"

Mark's tone was businesslike, but she could hear excitement just below the surface. "Fortunately, we have been able to access some of the best geneticists around. We need a significant sample of living DNA."

"DNA? Jonathan's father and his paternal grandparents are dead!"

"Easy." He took her hand in his now, pressing it. "We can work with your family, because what we're actually looking for is mitochondrial DNA. That's inherited from the mother. We'll need blood and tissue samples."

She exhaled a grateful breath. "I'm all yours."

Mark winced. "I'm sorry, that won't work. You were injected. We need clean samples. It will have to be your mother."

Light-headed with disbelief, she fell back a step. Her back hit the wall, and she braced herself against it. She might have fallen otherwise. "You mean my blood isn't fit to save my own child?"

Mark said nothing, just shook his head slightly.

Of all the things Nicholas Ferrel had taken from Bree—her safety, her career, her sense of safety—this was the worst. He had stolen her ability to nurture her child when Jonathan's very life depended on it. There weren't words enough to describe the depth of this violation.

Bree pressed her face into her hands. Shame and anger wrestled inside her, bringing a hot flush to her cheeks. "I hate him. Ferrel—"

"I know. We'll deal with the Knights, don't you worry. But right now we need to think of Jonathan. Is your mother in town?"

Bree jammed her fingers into her hair. "I think so? But, um…" She trailed off weakly. "I haven't seen her in years. I don't know if she'll help."

"Why wouldn't she help? It's for her grandchild."

How could she answer that? That was exactly what she'd been thinking when she phoned her father just the other night—and got his answering machine. "It's complicated."

Where had her mother been during all those years? When she'd needed guidance for those first few dates? When she'd needed someone to intervene when the drinking got too much for a girl of seventeen?

"Complicated how?"

"She was never there. She never flew out to New York to see Jonathan. She was always too busy."

Mark took Bree's arms, holding her gently. "Will you try? For Jonathan? He doesn't have long."

She knew that. She could see it written in his hollow cheeks, the dark circles that sat like bruises under his eyes. Bree hung her head, fear, reluctance and a traitorous hope fluttering in her belly. Once more she cursed Nicholas Ferrel for driving her to desperation. "Of course."

Going home was going to hurt. Not just swallowing her pride and asking for help, but the fear that her parents would turn their backs on her one more time. She would have thought the wound would hurt less after being rebuffed time and again, but it never did. Mothers could kiss life's injuries and make them better, but they could also cause overwhelming pain.

Mark kissed her on the top of the head. "Then let's go. We have no time to waste."

The house Bree had grown up in was really a mansion, although they never called it that. At eight bedrooms—plus a pool house and separate servants' quarters—it wasn't the largest place around, but the hilly property it sat on gave it more privacy and a better view than most. A large, arched gate sat across the entrance to the winding driveway. From there, all anyone could see was the corner of the red peaked roof jutting above the rocks and trees.

Bree chewed a nail, trying to sort out her feelings. She'd picked up the phone to call, but hadn't been able to push the numbers. Instead, she'd checked her mother's webpage. The schedule on her blog put her in the city that week, taking personal time at home.

That meant she was probably in the house. Seeing the place brought a nostalgic ache to Bree's heart, and yet there was an ocean of anger, too. She had vowed never to come back even once.

Five bucks says the folks won't last ten minutes without sending a press release all about how they saved their grandkid. They'd never know the supernatural details, of course. Bree figured they could fill in the blanks with whatever their publicist suggested.

"Is all this silence because you're nervous?" Mark asked.

"Maybe."

"Everyone wants their family's approval. We're just wired that way."

"I never thought I'd be the prodigal daughter, coming

home with cap in hand. I always thought I'd walk away and be free of all this."

Mark didn't answer. He just patted her knee and pulled up to the gate, bringing the Mercedes to a full stop. He looked cool and calm in the air-conditioned shade of the tinted windows. In an Italian-cut sports jacket and hand-sewn loafers, he looked the part of a high-priced medical man, handsome, successful and full of authority. He'd be the first man she brought home that her mother would relate to.

"Does this look right to you?" Mark asked quietly, pointing ahead.

On a normal day, the gate was locked and operated through an intercom. Today, it was ajar about a foot. Bree shrugged. "Sometimes Dad leaves it open if he's expecting a lot of company."

"Not smart."

"He was never a big fan of the Fort Knox look. He said he needed to believe in humanity's better nature." Despite herself, Bree smiled. "He didn't say he *did* believe in it, just that he needed to. I understand that more now than I did as a kid."

Mark gave her a sideways look. "You're still very young."

"But wise in experience, O ancient one."

She hopped out of the car and pushed a button on the stone gatepost that powered the mechanism the rest of the way open. They'd put it there because her dad kept losing the remote. The feel of her thumb on the sun-warmed metal was familiar enough to remind her she was truly home and this wasn't a dream. She got back in the car feeling as though she was retreating to safety.

The car crawled up the winding drive. It was a beautiful house, with white walls and a red-tiled roof, arched doorways and wrought-iron detailing. The architect who had designed it had used a light hand with the Spanish styling. It was more than a mere imitation of the real mission houses, but something unique. That, Bree knew, had been her mother's influence. Everyone assumed Bree got her artistic sense from her dad, but Althea Meadows had an eye for design, too.

The thought filled her with an unexpected hope. Maybe, just maybe they did have something in common after all. When Mark stopped the car, she touched his arm. "Let me go in first."

"Are you sure?" He turned off the motor, swiveling in the seat to look at her better.

"Yeah." Bree fidgeted. "Give me about twenty minutes to talk to them before you bring in the doctor's bag. There are some things we need to get through in private."

Mark looked around, scanning the grounds for any signs of life. Bree did the same. The place did look quiet, but it wasn't like there were always gardeners and pool boys around.

"Do you have your cell phone?" he asked.

Bree patted her pocket. "Check."

Mark held out his hand. She gave him the phone and he thumbed the buttons. "I'm putting my cell phone number in it. If you need me before fifteen minutes are up, just call."

"Twenty. I'll need at least that much." She gave him a slight smile. "Don't worry. These are my parents. They're scary in their own way, but they're not psycho killers."

"Good." He bent and kissed her, a mix of gentleness and desire. "Knife-wielding lunatics are so last year."

Her lips throbbed with the pressure of his touch, but being at her old home stirred up too much doubt to relax into the kiss. The princess and, in his own way, Larson had been right. Family did in part define who she was, and she had to rewrite that definition.

She needed to be Mark's equal, not his rescue mission. Not the party girl or the celebutante or a faceless woman on the run. She was Bree. This was her chance to change the programming her childhood had given her as surely as her parents had bequeathed their DNA. And, most important, she had to get what she needed to save Jonathan's life.

Bree dreaded letting her past into the present. She would do what she had to, but there was no way she would enjoy it.

She put her hand on the door handle, grateful for its coolness. "Wish me luck."

Chapter 29

Growing up, Bree had always gone in the side door by the kitchen, but today that felt too casual. She had slammed the big oak door that opened onto the flagstone courtyard when she left. It only felt right to go back in the same way and ask for peace.

Like the gate, it was unlocked. Bree opened it slowly, catching the familiar scents of home: flowers, furniture polish, but most of all, an indefinable *something* that said it was a large place, full of rooms the maids kept clean but few people actually lived in. As a teenager, Bree had called it a *vibe*. Maybe that was still the best word.

She stepped into the cavernous front hall and listened. The silence was eerie. If her dad had been home, there would have been the constant chatter of his people—some staff, some just hangers-on. Her mom didn't have a retinue, but usually more of the household staff were around when she showed up. Today, the house was utterly silent. Shadows flittered against the white walls. A fountain on the porch trickled water. There were no sounds of human habitation—and yet the gate and door had both been unlocked. Uneasiness eddied through her.

"Hello?" she called.

Silence.

Bree ventured in a little farther, leaving the door open behind her just in case she needed to make a quick retreat. She'd refined her paranoia since she'd stood there last.

"Hello?" She turned left and went swiftly through the front room—nobody ever used it—and into the smaller sitting room beyond. This was as close to a family gathering place as they'd had, with soft, squishy furniture and a long oak coffee table strewn with movie magazines. There was a dirty wineglass on the coffee table, another on the mantelpiece. That in itself was unusual. Their housekeeper ruled with an iron hand.

Her gaze fell on the glass-fronted liquor cabinet, her new best friend in those first few years after she'd come home from school. She felt a sudden urge to smash it in, to tell it once and for all who was boss. She hadn't tasted alcohol since Adam had forced her into rehab, and since leaving for New York, she'd had to be 100 percent focused, too focused to mess around. Her life had changed utterly, and she'd had to get stronger.

She stalked past the cabinet, giving it a smack as she passed. The bottles inside rattled like loose teeth.

The strange silence persisted. Bree thought about calling Mark, but summoning a trained vampire assassin because she'd found dirty wineglasses and a lack of noise sounded—well, kind of airheaded. Not the sort of thing that commanded respect.

Instead, she decided to try upstairs, mounting the curved white staircase. Sunlight fell through a row of tiny arched windows, dappling the carpet. The layout upstairs was simple, just a series of doors leading to bedrooms and bathrooms, the occasional closet full of linens. Bree shivered, memories flooding back. Sometimes bedrooms weren't just bedrooms. Sometimes they were where she'd hidden to stay ahead of visiting men and their grasping hands. Once, that was where she'd been caught.

Bree forced herself to turn the knob and open the door. She forced herself to look long and hard at the furniture in the room, especially the bed. Could she call what had happened a crime? Yes. She was too young, only fourteen. She'd been drinking. She'd said no.

But she'd spent years too ashamed to say a word about it. That took trust in someone with enough power to make things right. Her parents had power, but…well, the trust part said everything, didn't it?

The man had been some talent scout in his late twenties, handsome enough but reeking the desperate stink that comes from living on the edge. Bree wasn't even sure she knew his name, or maybe she'd blocked it out. But he'd done what he'd done, and she'd blamed herself for it. She'd made bad choices for years afterward and still felt the echo of that emptiness he'd left behind like a stain.

She looked at the bed, and thought of herself back then. Thought of herself now, with a sick child, a vampire lover and Nicholas Ferrel to worry about. She'd faced it all and hadn't crumbled. *I've survived an awful lot. I'm anything but weak, and I'm not invisible. In fact, I'm bloody impressive.*

Then she thought about what's-his-name who got his rocks off raping little girls. *Screw you.* She shut the door. *If I ever find out who the hell you are, you're going to pay.*

There was nobody upstairs. She took the servants' stairs back down to the main floor. There was one place in this house she'd ever been happy, and that was the kitchen. The women who worked there had been the ones who'd bandaged her knees and baked her cookies.

She wanted to get there so badly, to replace the bad memories with something pleasant, that she forgot to be careful. Bree pushed open the door and burst into the room, at first blinded by the bright sun glinting off the pots that hung from the ceiling rack. It was just the same as she remembered it, with a red tile floor, herbs on the wide windowsill and a huge farm table surrounded by chairs—and there were people in those chairs. Her mom *and* her dad—she hadn't expected to see him.

Her first thought was: *here's where everyone is!*

The second was: *my parents are tied up and everyone else has guns.*

Mark had gotten out of the car and now stood in a shady spot between a boulder and a tangle of thirsty-looking juniper bushes. The rocky hill rose steeply to the right of the house, climbing up another thirty feet before it hit the scrub-covered peak. High above, an eagle wheeled against the blank blue sky.

From here he could see the side of the house as well as the front. Most important, he could hear. There was the hum of traffic—that never really went away anywhere near the city—and the occasional chirp of birds, but they weren't loud enough to block sounds coming from the house.

Sun blared down with an almost audible splash. Even in the shade, he felt as if he was slowly grilling. He looked at his watch. Bree's twenty minutes were up. He'd expected something by now—cries of joy or at least shouting, but he'd heard nothing. From what she'd said about her folks, maybe they'd made her wait for an appointment. Maybe he should go in and make them pay attention to their beautiful, amazing daughter.

He slipped from the shade and sprinted across the blazing courtyard to the shadows beside the porch. Listened. Still heard nothing. Something was definitely strange.

He began gliding along the side of the house, staying close to the wall so no one glancing out a window would spot him. He was close to the back of the building when he finally heard something. Heartbeats. Too many to easily count. The air here smelled like food, so they were near the kitchen. *Isn't that where all the good parties end up?*

There were heartbeats, some speeding, but no words. *Frightened people, all gathered together.*

Hostages.

A trap.

Mark's stomach dropped when he heard footsteps. *Bree!* His hand went to his gun, but his sixth sense made him wheel at the last moment. He caught the briefest glimpse of a shape on the hill. *Sniper!*

A bullet slammed into his side, throwing him against the house.

Bree looked from one face to the next, her mind skidding as if it had hit a patch of ice. Random details stuck: her mother's wide eyes above a strip of duct tape, the sugar bowl still on the table, her father suddenly struggling and one of the armed men slapping him so hard he nearly fell from the chair. There were five bad guys.

She recognized one of the faux vampires from the fairground. The others might have been human, but she wasn't sure. *I can't take any chances.* The only plus was that Nicholas Ferrel wasn't there.

The villains were staring at her like so many cats around the last mouse in the world. And their weapons weren't the discreet handguns she'd seen up until now. They were automatic rifles, sleek and black and deadly. She took a step back. Not out of fear—she had gone far beyond that to some other place where colors were far too sharp and her blood sounded loud in her ears. She needed to think, and movement bought her time.

But her brain wasn't working properly. *Thank God Jonathan isn't here. He's safe for once, with Kenyon and Sam and the rest.* But he wouldn't be safe long if she couldn't rescue her parents.

"We knew you'd come sooner or later." It was the faux vamp who spoke. He was wearing shades. Maybe he had those creepy lizard eyes, too. "You'd have to in order to save your brat."

"So? You want a gold star for guessing the obvious?" Apparently terror made her snarky.

"Where is the book? And the boy?"

"At vampire central," Bree shot back. She took another step toward the door. "Only the cool monsters get to go there."

"And you. You're going to call someone and convince them to bring what we want, or you and your parents are going to die."

"My dad's worst hacks write better dialogue."

He pulled the trigger, shooting out the globe in the overhead light. *Rat-tat-tat!* A series of flashes blossomed, and the glass exploded, shards spewing over the whole kitchen.

Shock blazed through her. Bree wheeled and bolted back up the stairs, instincts reverting to old patterns. She knew where in the house to hide. She'd done it dozens of times before.

The stairs looked endless, as though they'd multiplied by three when she'd turned her back. Chairs scraped and pottery shattered behind her. The men were shoving through the kitchen to catch up. Adrenaline pumped through Bree so fast and hard her limbs felt weak, as if she were trying to speed faster than her muscles could respond. *Go, go, go!*

And then she was in the hall, her feet muffled on the thick carpet. She had to get to the door she wanted before the first pursuer hit the top of the stairs and saw where she went. Her hand hit the glass knob, turned it and skidded inside the last bedroom in the row.

"Where'd she go?"

The shout came in the midst of a lot of loud footfalls. She pushed the door shut soundlessly, knowing just how to press right *there* so it wouldn't click. Then she went for the closet. It looked like the usual type with mirrored bifold doors. Bree pulled one open and breathed a sigh of relief when she saw it was still stuffed with her mother's off-season clothes. She pushed past them, wriggling through to find the best secret any closet ever had. There was a jog in the design, a hidden alcove right at the back. Someone searching the place could shove the clothes around looking for fugitives and miss it entirely.

Bree had spent whole nights in that tiny refuge. Of course, she'd been smaller back then. Wedging herself into it was not as easy as she remembered, but she did it. She even remembered to take her cell phone out of her pocket before she was too cramped to move.

With the closet door closed, the cell was the only light. Its bright, neon colors had never looked so beautiful. Not a full set of bars, but enough that the call should go through. She pushed Mark's speed dial. *What I would have given for someone like him all those years ago.*

The place smelled just as she remembered it, ripe with the stink of her own fear and the scent of her mother's perfumed garments, gone stale from being shut up in an airless closet.

The phone purred in her ear, ringing somewhere outside. Indoors, she could hear the clump and bang of the men searching through the bedrooms. Looking for her.

Ring. Ring.

Her stomach was turning cold. Sure, Mark would come, but if they found her, would he be quick enough? Were there too many for him to fight?

Ring. Ring.

They were in the next bedroom now. She was invisible, but could one of those pseudo vampires smell her? She hadn't thought about that. What if they could hear her breathing? "Help! Help!" she whispered into the phone, even though Mark still hadn't picked up.

The bedroom door opened. *Please answer. I need help now. I need to know you're going to come for me now.*

It went to voice mail.

Chapter 30

Mark opened his eyes, realizing that he'd lost consciousness. He sat up too quickly, forgetting the wound in his first confusion. He thought he'd heard a phone, but maybe that was just the ringing in his head. Pain speared through his side, making him cry out, as much with surprise as hurt. That was followed by a surge of dizziness. *A poisoned bullet?* There were very few substances that could kill a vampire, but more that could make him useless for a few hours.

The agony resolved itself into two separate pains, one in his back. *Through and through.* That was lucky. The Knights used silver. At least it wasn't stuck in his system.

Rage mixed with fear for Bree, and the emotion seemed to make the dizziness worse. Mark bent his head between his knees, sucking in air and trying to calm himself. He was too angry. He'd underestimated Ferrel, and now Bree was paying the price.

Mark had known it was possible the Knights might have watched Bree's parents, but he'd not anticipated a direct assault on them. It made sense, in a twisted way. They knew all about the virus, and undoubtedly had their own experts on staff. They must have guessed Bree would come here looking for a cure. So what if Mark had beaten them on the road? All Ferrel had to do was sit back and wait.

Mark swore violently, scrambling to get his feet under him. He rose slowly, using the wall as support. Ribs crunched as he moved. Some must have broken. That was going to hurt for a while. He leaned his back against the house, letting nausea wash past. Standing was better. He felt more in control.

At least until he touched the sticky mass of blood on his shirt. His hand came away red. He swore again. No wonder he felt so weak. With enough blood loss, even a vampire went into hypovolemic shock.

"Feeling woozy?" Ferrel's voice sounded to Mark's right.

Mark turned only his head, letting his body rest a moment longer. The man was in the shade, hard to see at this angle, but there was no doubt it was him, and that he was holding a rifle with a scope. "You did this?"

"Did I pull the trigger? That would be a yes, and before you ask, the bullet was coated in a poison. Did I set this trap? Yes again. Did I set this whole scheme in motion—well, I have to share the credit there. The Knights of Vidon is hardly a one-man organization."

Mark stalled, gathering his dwindling strength. "Did you kill Jessica Lark?"

"Personally, and with pleasure. I strangled her with her own monogrammed scarf, and then I dropped a match on her studio."

The cold sneer in his voice brought an answering flood of hate in Mark. In that moment, all Ferrel needed were the boots and gloves, and Mark might have taken young Nicholas for his ancestor. "Why kill her?"

"She wouldn't tell us what she'd done with Thoristand's book."

"What did it matter? He was a madman. His formulas are lethal." Mark slipped his hand toward his gun, ignoring the spikes of pain from his side.

"They need work, but someday they might make us equal to you."

"You think we're evil, so why do you want to be like us?" Ferrel was indeed like his forefather. They both had a disposition for gloating when they should be paying closer attention to their supposedly vanquished foe.

"You're stronger, faster and deadlier. We need to fight back."

Like this? Mark raised his Browning and shot. He'd moved vampire-quick, too fast for Ferrel to see, much less react. The man crumpled with a scream of pain, clutching his leg. Mark raised the weapon again. A bad leg didn't mean Ferrel couldn't shoot.

Slowly, making sure he didn't fall over his own numbed feet, Mark inched along the wall toward Ferrel. When he got close enough, he kicked the man's rifle out of range. Ferrel stared up with fierce, angry eyes, his fingers running red as he clutched his wound.

"So kill me."

"I tried," Mark said with bitter amusement. "Whatever the blazes you shot me with skewed my aim."

Ferrel's face remained a sneer. No fear or regret flickered in his eyes.

Another wave of dizziness swirled through Mark as his anger surged. "But perhaps I should try again. You infected Bree and her son. You killed Jessica. Your people killed Jack Anderson, the best friend I had. When will you stop?"

Ferrel's eyes were growing glassy. Mark had missed any arteries, but the wound was still bleeding badly. "We will stop when every last vampire is dead. That has always been the mission. Tripping you up was just a personal pleasure."

It would have been so easy to shoot right then. Easier by far than tearing chains from a dungeon floor and shredding Ferrel's forefather into gobbets of bleeding flesh. Just one quick bullet to the head, so clean it barely qualified as the act of a monster.

But Ferrel was down and unarmed. Anything Mark did now would be self-indulgence. "If I kill you, there will be some brother or nephew or best friend who'll pick up where you left off. I'm bored with it."

Ferrel showed his teeth in a snarl. "Kill me or don't kill me. I've done my work. The Knights are already on the move. Your actions are too little and too late."

Mark gripped the Browning hard enough he felt the metal strain.

"I don't want to play your games anymore. Your bait doesn't tempt me. I'm going to tell the crown prince what you've done to an innocent woman and her little boy and let him figure it out. That's why he gets the shiny gold hat."

"You would leave vengeance up to a princeling? A mere boy?" Ferrel sneered.

"I've killed far better men than you. You're hardly worth the effort."

There was no reply. Ferrel had passed out. Frustration and foreboding surged through Mark, sending a tremor through his poison-racked body. *What did he mean by too late?*

Whatever it was, Mark had to prove Ferrel wrong. He clenched his hands, forcing them to stop shaking. He was an assassin and a doctor. Pressure situations were his natural habitat. But Bree was involved, and that changed everything.

With an act of will, Mark forced himself into cool, calm detachment. He tore a strip off Ferrel's shirt and tied it tight enough to stop the bleeding. He didn't do more than that. There was no time, and the smell of fresh, warm blood was tempting—but with so many strange serums in use, there was no way he was drinking any Knight's blood.

First, he picked up Ferrel's rifle and picked his pockets for extra ammunition. Then Mark pulled out his cell phone and dialed Kenyon to ask for backup and an ambulance. Finally, he noticed the missed-call icon.

It was Bree. The message was brief.

"Help me!"

It was time-stamped five minutes ago.

Damn it to the nine fiery hells! Panic surged up in Mark, smacking him like a kick to the guts. *Too little and too late.* Bree had been in trouble the whole time he was wasting his breath on Ferrel! Another wave of sick dizziness sent a trickle of sweat down his spine.

He slid back along the wall to the window. First, he listened. Hearing nothing, he stretched up to peer inside.

Two figures bound and gagged at the table—not Bree, probably her parents. Two armed men guarding them. These two looked human. The respiration, blink rate and heartbeat all seemed normal. *Good.*

He'd heard more heartbeats before. There had to be more of Ferrel's men around, probably hunting for Bree.

He didn't have time to peer through every window looking for them, so he'd go for a simple plan. He'd make a noise and flush the others out.

While vampires couldn't actually fly like a bird or a bat, they could levitate. With a roar, he smashed feetfirst through the kitchen window.

The two guards swiveled, spattering the wall with bullets. Mark had expected as much. He dove beneath the spray of fire, rolling to come up behind them. These two he took out with two neat shots before they had a chance to turn around. If someone was actively shooting at him, he had no qualms about paying them back in kind. They fell with the sound of falling laundry bags.

The house was suddenly silent again, as if everyone in it was straining to listen. One of the men rattled his last breath into that awful quiet.

The upstairs contingent would be joining them any moment. Mark grabbed kitchen shears from the utility jar on the counter and wasted no time in slicing through the prisoners' zip ties.

"Are you Bree's parents?" he demanded, ripping the duct tape from the man's mouth.

"Y-yes," he stammered.

"There's help on the way. Get your wife outside to the car you see there and get inside and lock the doors."

The man nodded slowly. The woman, who had Bree's features, peeled off her own gag. "Bree went upstairs. They're after her."

Her voice was filled with worry, but it was steady. *She has backbone like her daughter.*

"I'll look after her," Mark said.

"Good." Bree's mother stood up stiffly. "Let's go, Hank. Hurry."

Still no sign of the people upstairs. Were they setting

a trap? He considered the staircase outside the kitchen door and decided there had to be another. This one was too small and narrow to impress. He ghosted through the house and found a second, grander affair and started up that way. Hopefully, his assailants wouldn't expect him to look past the obvious route into their snare.

He reached the top of the stairs, his head feeling clearer. The poison on the bullet—what little of it had remained as the shot tore right through him—was working through his system. Unfortunately, now there was absolutely nothing to dampen the pain in his ribs.

He took a few steps forward, keeping Ferrel's rifle ready. He'd holstered the Browning to give himself a free hand. He could hear heartbeats. The trick was to pinpoint which room they were in.

Far end of the hall, to the left.

They assumed they were going to ambush him. *Nice try. I can he-e-ear you.*

Mark got another five yards before a figure wheeled out of a doorway to his right, planting a gun at Mark's right temple.

It was one of the faux vampires—this one without a heartbeat. Silent. *Curse it to the darkest hells!*

The creature gave an ugly smile, showing fang. "I bet you'd die if I blew your head off."

Chapter 31

Bree held her breath as the closet door opened. She couldn't see which thug pushed the clothes to one side, then the other. All she could see was a patch of sunlight flutter on the floor as the hems of her mother's winter wardrobe swished back and forth.

He must have been human because he didn't smell her and didn't hear her heart pounding. That didn't mean he couldn't kill her—or worse.

She hadn't tried to dial the phone again, but she held it like a talisman, slippery in her sweating fingers. *Please come, please come, please come.*

But inside, deep inside in the place where her younger self still dwelled, she knew it wasn't going to happen. Nobody ever came. In the end, nobody picked up the phone. The names and reasons might change, but not the outcome.

Tears of fright slid silently down Bree's face. She'd heard the crash downstairs, and then gunfire—it felt like ages ago. That had sent everyone running. Bree had wanted to dash out, too, to see what had become of her parents and Mark and...

She pressed her face into her knees. *I'm just too scared to move.* Yes, she'd survived a lot—but enduring wasn't the same as taking a risk. She was good at running, but this? She had no gun, no superstrength and nothing but bad memories.

The hangers slid on the closet rail with a sound like raking claws. *Skrick. Skrick.*

Whoever parted the clothes had come back after the gunfire to finish searching the bedroom, and he was being thorough about it. A hand reached in, fumbling around the periphery of the closet, looking for her. She had the impression that hand was big and hairy, tipped in claws, but she couldn't really see in the dark. It was just her mind painting in the awfulness.

The hand was getting closer, groping inches from her face. Bree clapped her fingers over her mouth, forcing back a whimper of fright, just like she had as a child. History repeating itself: Bree weeping, paralyzed and terrified, in this closet.

The hand withdrew, and whoever it was muttered and swore but didn't bother to shut the door. Bree leaned forward an inch, trying to see out through the gap between two skirts. She saw only the edge of somebody's shoulder, but she could hear better now. There were two speakers. There had been three distinct voices a few minutes ago. Where had number three gone?

One of the men spoke. "Ha! Brown's got him, the vampire bastard."

Bree's heart jolted. *Got Mark? Got Mark how?*

Then she heard it from down the hall, faint but clear. "I bet you'd die if I blew your head off."

Her breath froze, terror morphing into something dark and monstrous. Her hands knotted around the phone as that feeling bubbled and popped like an overheated potion, boiling until the pressure of her rage was unbearable. It took about three seconds.

Oh, no, you don't! Mark's head looked just fine where it was. She quietly slid out of the narrow space before she realized what she was doing. Her brain skittered for a moment, shrieking with dismay at what her body was up to.

Whoa! That's far enough. She crouched in the bottom of the closet among the shoes and tried to quiet her frantic breath. She slipped her phone into her pocket, wanting both hands free. The next thing she heard was an angry exchange of voices, but the words were lost under her panic.

I can't just rush out there and start breaking heads! But she did have the element of surprise. All she needed to do was to distract Mark's opponent long enough that Mark could break free. Put like that, it didn't seem such a horrendous task.

She picked up one of her mother's shoes. It was really an ankle boot with spike heels cased in metal. Four inches of steely death and uppers of hand-stitched suede. *Weapon? Check.* But she still didn't move. Her knees were starting to shake. Closet equaled safety. Outside the closet were the bogeymen. But there were her parents, and Jonathan, and Mark at stake.

She heard a hammer click as a gun readied to fire— not a good sign for Mark. She bolted forward with a shriek worthy of a ghoul.

Holy Christmas! She was out of the closet, and she wasn't going back. Bree threw all her heart into the attack. The two thugs were crowded into the bedroom doorway. Right in her path, a balding head just started to turn her way. Bree swung the boot overhand like an upmarket hammer of death.

The shoe-weapon hit the bad guy's head, the sharp metal heel slicing open the flesh with the ease of a knife. He screamed as his face was flayed in a bloody ruin. His companion swung around, eyes widening. Reflexively, the nose of his automatic rifle came up, but Bree was moving again, swinging the boot and diving between the two men. A hail of bullets chased her, but she was already in the hall, scrambling to get out of the way. *Rat-tat-tat-tat.* Poofs of fluff spewed from the bed where the loser talent scout had terrorized Bree long ago.

Then came the sound of the Browning going off, bits of skull and brain flying down the hall. Bree dropped, cowering against the baseboards, her hands over her head. The sound came twice more. *Blam. Blam.* And then silence. The only sound she heard was the ticking of a clock downstairs.

Then footsteps. Metal sliding along the floor. Someone securing the guns so no one could come back from the dead and start shooting again.

Bree raised her head a fraction. A body was halfway down the hall, head smashed like a Halloween pumpkin. The last of the faux vamps. Her first reaction was a surreal sense of confusion. Wasn't he the one with a gun to Mark's head? Did that mean her desperate gamble had worked?

"Bree."

And then he was there, a few feet away. She slowly straightened, her gaze traveling up his tall, strong form. The sports jacket was a ruin, soaked in blood, and he was standing awkwardly, as if something inside him was broken.

"You're hurt."

"Ferrel got his last licks in before I took him down." His face was grim, his dark eyes searching hers. "He won't be bothering you anymore. Once the Company is through questioning him, he will have to answer to Prince Kyle for what he's done to you and Jonathan. What Ferrel did is an embarrassment to Vidon. I wouldn't be surprised if they give him to Kenyon for a chew toy."

A sudden, nervous laugh escaped her. It sounded close to hysteria. *That can't be good.* She stood up shakily, using the wall for support. He jumped forward to steady her, putting a hand at her waist. Suddenly, they were very close. "Thank you," she breathed.

"Bree, if you hadn't shown up, this would have ended very differently." He looked as if he wasn't quite sure whether to scold her or kiss her. "But that was very brave and very risky."

"You make me do crazy things."

"I'm sorry."

"You're worth it." She rested her forehead on a relatively clean patch of his shoulder. "I love you, Dr. Winspear."

She felt him stiffen. "Bree, you know what I am."

"Yeah, and you know what I am."

He stroked her hair, his fingers slow. "I think I loved you from the moment you pulled my own gun on me. You're a fierce woman, Brianna Meadows. I don't think you see that."

"I hid in a closet," she mumbled.

"A ninja shoe closet." He lifted up her face, and kissed her thoroughly. "You do battle when it counts with whatever you've got at the time. That's a real warrior."

The crisis was over. The cavalry arrived only moments later.

* * *

"Remind me to take you to the next holiday sale at Armand's," her mother said in her usual dry tone. "I could use a point guard."

Bree sat on the front porch, utterly numb. Her brain had been in retreat from the moment they left the carnage upstairs to go outside. Someone had shoved a bottle of water into her hand. It might have been Faran Kenyon. The place was crawling with people from the Varney Center taking care of business. "Where's Mark?"

He'd been there a moment ago. She couldn't remember him leaving.

"He's gone to get that nasty wound of his checked, remember?"

She didn't remember. Images flickered across her brain, jerky as an old celluloid film that had broken and been reassembled all wrong. Fragments of memories, nothing more. It was a relief. Some of those images would be hard enough to live with as it was. *I'm so very tired.*

"Where's Mark?" she asked again. He'd really been there, right?

"Bree, honey?"

Bree blinked, trying to focus on the woman in front of her. She was sure it was her mother, but everything felt oddly distant, as if she were watching a movie.

"Mom?"

Althea slid onto the step beside her. Bree felt her arm around her shoulders, though that, too, felt oddly distant. "That nice young man over there explained why you came here."

Bree saw Kenyon giving orders to a bunch of the cleanup crew. The significance of what her mother was saying slid away like a darting fish. *Why had she come here again?* "And?"

"Of course I'll give you whatever you need. He's my grandson, and you're my daughter. A little blood is hardly a sacrifice, for heaven's sake!"

Mirella's words came back to Bree. *I see a crown in your past and a blade in your future. Death stands behind and before you. To save your boy, you must find what you have lost. Blood will be sacrificed before this is done.*

The crown had to be Kyle. The death in the past—that could be Jessica or Adam. The Company of the Dead had been in her future. She'd lost her parents, and now her mother sat beside her, opening a vein. But the blade? She still wasn't sure about that.

"Okay," she said, not quite remembering the question, but thinking that answer would do.

"Who is that man?" her mother asked.

Nicholas Ferrel lay on a stretcher being loaded into one of the Varney Center's ambulances. Unlike the others, he was still alive. She guessed he'd regret that soon enough.

Bree pulled herself together enough to answer. "He's the one responsible for a lot of this."

"Why?" Althea squinted at her. Their features were similar, but her mom's eyes were brown and, at the moment, they were filling with concern. "Bree, are you hurt? You look strange."

She gulped, feeling her chin start to tremble. "I needed you. I needed you so many times."

Her mom put her hand over Bree's, squeezing. "I think you're in shock."

Bree snatched her hand back. "I've been in shock since I was fourteen!"

Her mother went utterly still.

"I know." Her voice had that ultra-reasonable tone her mother used with skittish witnesses. "You're not the only one who's been through some changes. I'm getting older,

Bree, and I have come to understand that I've made a lot of very serious mistakes. I'm trying to fix— No, I'm trying to *lessen the damage* I've done. I know I can't fix it. Not entirely."

Bree nodded, mute with roiling emotions. A moment ago, she'd felt nothing. Now she was choking on a log-jam of unsaid words.

Her mother went on. "I began with my relationship with your father. That's why we were alone today, just the two of us. No one else. We needed to talk. In a strange way, it was a piece of good luck, because none of the staff were caught in this terrible mess."

"Yes," Bree managed to say, letting the curtain of her hair hide her face, just like she had as an adolescent. "That was good luck."

Her mother tucked Bree's hair behind her ear, a maternal gesture Bree had forgotten. It had been too long. "Bree, darling, I started with your father because he was easy. We've let things slide, and that needs to be put right, but we understand one another. We're both ambitious. We're both willing to overlook a lot in the name of our careers. That's why we're still together. Now, you— you're a different story."

Bree looked up, her eyes hot and prickling. "I have a lot to say to you."

Her mother gave a crooked smile. "Good. I want to hear it all, no matter how much it hurts. You and Hank are the most important people in my life."

Without knowing who started it or exactly when, the two women embraced. Bree felt her mother draw a long, shaking breath that sounded like tears of relief. An answering ache squeezed her heart.

It was only a beginning, but as long as they could talk and hug, there was hope.

Chapter 32

Ten weeks later

Mark stood in the doorway of the house they'd rented just blocks away from the Varney Center. He'd broken every rule in the book by living with a human woman, but he was Plague, the feared assassin, the medical genius who'd cracked the code of Thoristand's virus and the guy who took down the Commander General of the Knights of Vidon and all his nasty minions. If he wanted suburbia, no one was going to argue.

The place wasn't overly big or small, but it was nice enough for the short-term and there was a yard. Despite the centuries, some things didn't change: kids and dogs and the need for young things to burn energy before their elders collapsed with exhaustion.

And in-laws. They were still a special experience.

Bree's dad was getting out of the Jaguar parked at the curb, a big smile on his face. This was his default setting.

Every day for Hank was a new story to tell, a wonder unfolding before his lens. He was hard not to like, really, and Jonathan adored him. After all, in many, many ways, they were both kids excited to be alive.

"Grandpa!" Jonathan squealed, zooming out of the house at top speed, Custard galloping in his wake. Mark was sure socks and paws barely hit the sidewalk.

Mark narrowed his eyes, watching. Obviously, the boy was much better. He'd designed the treatment himself, along with Schiller and the brain trust the Company had assembled. Recovery had been swift and steady. It was nearly Christmas, and Jonathan was talking, running and playing like a healthy boy.

His physical reflexes were still above average. In fact, he's lost none of the advantages Ferrel's virus had given him, with the exception of telepathy. Mark had never seen evidence of it again. Only time would tell, but in his professional opinion, he'd have to say Jonathan was cured.

Hank knelt to hug his grandson and ended up embracing Custard, too, as the dog barged in for a major face-licking. The multimillionaire movie king laughed with delight. Boy, dog and granddad collapsed in a tangle on the lawn.

As Bree had put it, Hank was a delightful grandparent though he didn't exactly qualify as a responsible adult. But, at least she was getting along with her folks, more or less, and that was a big step.

Mark felt Bree come up behind him and slip her arms around his waist. "Watching the show?"

"Best ticket in town." He shifted so that she could stand beside him. "Are you okay with going to Marcari so soon after getting back together with your parents?"

She shrugged. "It's only for a while, and they'll be

over there for the wedding anyway. It's the pinnacle of this year's social calendar. My mom won't miss that."

They walked down the porch steps, still arm in arm. Hank was disentangling himself from his giggling grandson and getting to his feet. "Reporting for babysitting duty!"

It would be the first time Jonathan had been away from Bree overnight. Mark intended to make use of every moment.

"You have all our numbers, right?" Bree asked.

"Programmed into my phone."

"Not too much sugar, or he won't sleep."

"Got it."

"Don't let him watch anything scary."

Mark squeezed Bree closer. "Have a good time, Hank."

"I've got something for you," Hank said, handing them a disk. "It's a first cut of the new film."

Mark took it. "We're honored."

It was a costumed extravaganza of *War and Peace* to be released in two long films. It was a brilliant book, if you liked long, dark and complex, but this was a whole night of precious grown-up time. He wanted short and mindless.

Hank winked as he got child and dog into the Jaguar. "Good date-night movie."

Mark remembered Napoleon's march through the Russian snows, all the starvation and the corpses cold and stiff with frost, and wondered about the man's idea of fun. "Women do like uniforms."

Bree clung tightly to his hand as her father whisked away their boy, honking as the car turned the corner and left their sight. She chewed her lip, but didn't say a word.

"Can we watch a comedy?" Mark asked as soon as they got inside. The living room was big, but the Christmas tree was enormous, occupying one end of the room like a miniature forest. They'd had to push the other furniture forward, making the TV viewing area half its usual size.

Bree already had popcorn and sodas on the coffee table. "We'll watch ten minutes just to say we did, and then we do whatever you like."

Mark sat, trying to be gracious as the opening credits rolled, but was soon distracted by a stack of papers behind the popcorn. "What's this?"

He picked up the top folder and opened it. The letterhead inside read MeadowLark Designs. He understood the reference at once: Brianna Meadows and Jessica Lark.

She blushed. "Princess Amelie wants her wedding clothes. I thought I'd take the designs from the book and make them a reality. It'll be Jessica's work and mine, so we'll both take some of the credit. What do you think?"

"I think it's great!" He closed the folder. "It's time you got back in the game."

She turned off the TV, silencing the dolorous sound track. "We're going to Marcari anyway. I can make sure everything is done right. I contacted some of Jessica's old employees and they were happy to work on the collection. With their help, it seems doable."

She sounded cautious, but Mark knew why. "If you're not comfortable with how much time it takes away from Jonathan, speak up and we'll figure something out."

She nodded. "You don't think I'm taking on too much?"

"I'm behind you 100 percent. We'll adjust however much it takes to find the balance you need."

She kissed him. And that was the simple beauty of their relationship. All she wanted was someone in her corner, someone to watch her back and let her catch her breath now and then. He could do that, and he loved her like mad.

What she gave back—well, it was enough sunshine and rainbows to melt a thousand Russian winters. Take that, Tolstoy.

He deepened the kiss, drinking in her sweetness and feeling it go straight to his zipper. Then his hands were exploring the hem of her T-shirt, seeking the hot, smooth skin beneath. A ball of pleasure and hope burned in his chest, so intense it hurt.

"Marry me," he whispered, and then nearly gulped. Nine hells, he hadn't meant to say that. It might be too soon. She'd seen him at his worst. He had to get her past that, let her see most days he didn't leave a lake of carnage in his path. He was a doctor, after all, and maybe even a nice guy. Sometimes, anyway.

She caught her breath, moving her lips so that they tickled his ear. "Okay."

He pulled away, a little shocked. "Okay?"

Bree furrowed her brow. "Was I supposed to say no?"

"No. Yes is good. Yes is very good."

"You're surprised." Then she laughed and pushed him back on the couch, straddling him as best she could on the narrow cushions. "A gypsy fortune-teller foretold your coming."

"Tall, dark and handsome?"

"She called you a blade. You're kind of like a sword, but you're a surgeon's scalpel, too. She said you were my future."

A blade. He supposed that was better than a blunt object. "I like being your future."

"Always."

And they kissed again, letting lust burn away doubt and worry and the shadows of the past. It would burn through them, clearing the path for more tender feelings to grow. That was how it healed. At least, it had Mark's medical approval. "Movie time is over."

"Did it ever start?" Bree was pulling down his zipper one tooth at a time, making him wait. She was leaning forward, her long, tawny mane sweeping across his chest.

He pulled off his shirt to take advantage of her hair's silky feel. She bent and nipped his flesh, leaving dainty teeth marks in her path. It was oddly arousing, especially as she worked her way south. Or maybe it was the scent of her desire, that musk of peaches, that had his beast flat on its back and purring.

She took his arousal between her teeth, gently biting and sucking. *Nine hells of Abydia.*

"I want all of you," she murmured.

She had it, however she liked it, but all he could do was groan. He was hard and throbbing and she had far too many clothes on. He resolved the issue of her T-shirt with a ripping sound. She wasn't wearing a bra. *Oh, yeah.* Her breasts were free, round and peaked, and ready.

His mouth found them, his fangs descending with his arousal. He had to be careful.

Bree writhed against him as he slid his tongue over a nipple. He shifted so that they were sitting up, the remote falling to the pine floor with a clatter. Then she was in his arms, half-naked, and then they were on the soft sheepskin rug in front of the Christmas tree. Santa could keep the other presents clustered under the branches. His was right there before him, and he unwrapped her the rest of the way.

He began his assault at her anklebone, licking along the gentle curve of her heel and calf. Bree had the strong legs of a runner, the muscles long and defined. The act of possession, of marking each inch of her, took time. It was well worth it. He had discovered many sensitive spots only dedicated lovers added to their repertoire. Mark didn't miss one. He used his fangs to tease and his breath to tickle, lighting on every sensitive point inside the knee, up the insides of her thighs. By the time he reached their apex, Bree was completely his.

"Now," she murmured.

A gentleman never kept a lady waiting. The welcoming heat of her electrified every nerve. The hunger rose in Mark, the need for this one woman who was his mate.

He was her future. She was his. They were one.

He thrust, feeling her clench around him. He worked the sensation, making her rise to meet him, to cry out his name. He kissed her breasts, and her collarbone, and the long arc of her neck. And then her blood was in his mouth. The double-edged sword of his venom swamped them both, predator and prey, driving them both to the shattering pleasure of their release. Mark growled with the triumph of his possession.

She was his. His woman. His family. Everything in his world.

Later, much later, Bree lay beside him, naked on the sheepskin like some pagan goddess. The glow from the Christmas lights painted her flesh with soft licks of red and green and yellow. Mark ran a finger down the side of her breast, over the dip in her waist, up the flare of her hip. *So beautiful.* He felt himself getting hard again, but she looked too lovely to disturb, languid and rosy from loving.

She had other ideas. Bree rolled close enough that she was half on top of him, one knee thrust between his legs. "So, Santa, have I been a good girl?"

Mark laughed, a soft fire of happiness in his chest. He held her gaze, feeling the strength of the connection between them. They saw each other clearly and liked the view.

His hand strayed to her hip, caressing the silky skin. "I have a whole sleighful of toys for you. No assembly required and the batteries never die."

"I'm counting on it." Her grin was wicked, but it was more than that.

It was for him, her husband.

* * * * *

SPECIAL EXCERPT FROM

 HARLEQUIN®

NOCTURNE™

A tormented werewolf enslaved to demons
turns to the only one who can free her—the
sexy and handsome navy SEAL she tortured
and left for dead.

Read on for a sneak preview of

DEMON WOLF
by Bonnie Vanak

The moon hung like a silver nickel in the sky.

Hovering in the woods, Keira waited for lieutenant commander Dale Curtis to arrive home.

Other houses on the street showed signs of life. Lights flicked on. Children ran in the backyard and then ran inside as their mothers called them in for supper.

Or their mothers threatened to zap them inside. It was a paranormal neighborhood, after all.

Hiding in the shadows, she felt a pinch of deep melancholy. She'd adjusted to loneliness during the infrequent intervals when the demons gave her brief freedom so she could find new men for them to torture. Keira had beaten the demons by refusing to associate with anyone, refusing to give them new victims.

They'd found one, anyway. This last session had sliced off a piece of her heart. Dale Curtis had taken her spirit and turned it inside out. She'd almost killed him. And then, a miracle had happened.

The commander's friend had arrived in the house where Curtis was being held prisoner and chanted a cleansing spell to vanquish evil. The spell had sent the demons temporarily to the netherworld and freed her. But in a few weeks, as they always did, the Centurions would use their bolt hole to this world and break free.

Then the real fun would start. They'd find her, find Curtis and force her to torture the SEAL once more, maybe until he died. The demons would steal all his strength and courage and become solid entities, tasting the pleasures of the flesh once more.

Keira touched the valise containing the silver armband, which enslaved her to the Centurions. When the demons had vanished unexpectedly, the bracelet had unlocked, freeing her from their spell. Only by enslaving herself to another could she escape them.

And lieutenant commander Dale Curtis was the only living person with enough power and courage to destroy the Centurions.

Crouching down, Keira watched the commander's house. Beneath the light of the nearly full moon, she waited and hoped, and wondered if this brave man would be the one to kill her captors and finally set her free.

Don't miss the exciting conclusion to DEMON WOLF by Bonnie Vanak, available only from Harlequin® Nocturne™ in June 2014.

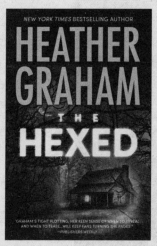

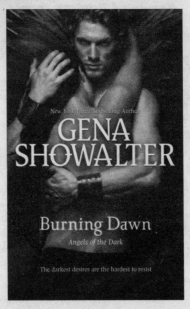